Nev's first book **Gods of the Green Moon** is still available on Amazon in either print or eBook format.

Some nice folk have described it as:

A rip-roaring tale of magic and good versus evil

An engaging and magical tale

Unputdownable

and

Pacey, absorbing, thought-provoking with a fair sprinkling of dry wit.

Thank you everyone!

Neville Pitty-Rose's

The Goodness Within

Pub Dog Press

Copyright © 2016 Neville Pitty-Rose

All rights reserved. No part of this publication may be reproduced, in full or in part, stored in a retrieval system, transmitted or disseminated in any form or by any means, without the prior written permission of the author, nor otherwise circulated in any form of binding or cover other than that in which it is published and without a similar condition being imposed on the purchaser.

www.nevpittyrose.com
facebook.com/goodnesswithin

Cover by Dan Anderson
www.dan-anderson.com

ISBN-13 978-1519156785
ISBN-10 1519156782

A truth told with bad intent
beats all the lies you can invent

William Blake

PROLOGUE

MIKE

Mike Hennessy was buzzed. Really buzzed. More than tipsy and only a drink or two away from properly drunk. He tipped his head back and poured another small bottle of whisky down his throat, the first alcohol he had consumed for over ten years.

The booze trickled into his system with an intimately familiar and satisfying warm glow, his muscles twitching in pleasure as his very soul welcomed the triumphant return of an old friend. Four empty bottles rolled around the floor at his feet.

Mike figured he would probably have enjoyed his fall from sobriety slightly more were he not currently strapped inside a plummeting aircraft moments away from an impact that would probably kill him and everyone else on board.

MARION

Marion Crandall gripped the armrests as hard as she could, her knuckles white and her eyes screwed tightly shut. She was waiting for her life to flash before her, but wasn't sure if her eyes needed to be open or if keeping them closed was OK. She was fairly certain it would be incredibly boring to anyone but her, but even so she was hoping certain parts could be skipped, or at least fast-forwarded.

Marion tried to stop over-thinking. Over-thinking things had ruled every element of her life so far, right up to getting on this stupid plane. She decided to keep her eyes shut as it made it easier to ignore the screaming noise of everyone around her. She didn't want to miss anything.

ROYCE

The stewardess had one long leg up on the rim of the stainless-steel toilet bowl and her short skirt was hitched up around her waist. Royce Brims pounded into her from behind like his life depended on it, as if he could keep the plane in the air by the sheer force of his orgasm.

Her leg slipped off its precarious perch and her foot splashed down into the chemical blue water in the bowl. His penis was pulled out of her and he came over the back of her starched red uniform, a chafing, joyless spasm. A disappointing final effort from one of the biggest rap stars on the planet.

He tucked himself away and helped her take her wet, blue foot from the bowl. The whole plane was juddering and vibrating and the air pressure kept dropping and making his ears pop.

I finished too early, Royce thought. *This crash is taking too long.* He reluctantly cuddled the stewardess, the two of them pressed uncomfortably together in the cramped beige cubicle.

LUKE

Until the announcement instructing all passengers to assume emergency positions, Luke McDonald had spent the entire flight eyeing up a very pretty girl sitting two rows in front and across the aisle from him. She was currently hugging an older man in the seat next to her, who Luke presumed was her father. Her head rested on his shoulder, his face in her hair. Their eyes were closed and they looked very peaceful, as if they were already dead.

Luke had been in the process of memorising her face for possible future reference when the aircraft lurched alarmingly and they all heard the explosion. He looked around with detached fascination at the chaos.

Aside from the girl, he was the only young person on board, at least in first class. None of the adults appeared to have assumed the emergency position, the stewardesses had vanished, both toilet cubicles were locked and there was general panic all around him; screaming, sobbing, desperate declarations of love or confessions of betrayal. The aircraft stank of sweat and urine and shit but Luke didn't really think he was going to die. Besides, if the crash didn't kill him, the force of his stepmother's hug probably would.

JENNIFER

Jennifer held the boy tightly, even though Luke had always been distant and cold with her. They hadn't even been that close before his father, her second husband, had died. To be honest, it hadn't ever really bothered her that much. They both had their own grief and issues to deal with, and by unspoken agreement she and Luke had both taken them somewhere else.

Still, she desperately wished she had someone who really loved her to hold her in the final few moments as the aircraft went down. She had only been a teenager the first time she married, and in her mid-twenties the second time. Now she was thirty six and single and, if you believed everything Grazia had to say, nearly out of options. She believed she had been unlucky in love and definitely had more to give, then immediately felt a twinge of guilt as her hug was returned by the boy. Maybe if by some miracle they survived this she would try to connect more with him.

In probably her final moments, she tried to feel grateful that she wasn't going to die completely alone.

PART ONE

DANDRIDGE

Richard Dandridge had dozed off, and it was only his feet slipping from the edge of the cluttered desk and jerking him awake that stopped him from missing the precise moment the world changed forever. Dandridge had been dozing in his high-backed leather orthopaedic chair, luxuriating in the ergonomic benefits of additional lumbar and posture support, vital to someone who spent a lot of time fully-reclined.

He was sat in a small red brick hut surrounded by electronic machinery of indeterminate purpose and origin. One of them had started to make a soft, slightly fuzzy beep, like a smoke alarm needing new batteries. The small, squat, red-brick hut formed one quarter of a grid of four identical huts that sat unobtrusively at the outer reaches of Royal Air Force base Wenham in Gloucestershire, England. They were nudged right up against the fourteen foot high perimeter fence and almost in the trees. Weeds and wild tomato plants grew up between them. In the summer they smelt of overripe tomatoes and weedkiller and the winters were so cold that Dandridge kept coats and blankets in a box for his occasional visitors.

The base was mainly used as a flight training school with three runways, an air traffic control tower and a couple of elegant stone and red brick operation buildings. As the base had grown in prominence, an array of grey prefabricated, semi-permanent aluminium structures had been erected alongside the more traditional buildings. A squadron of Hawk T2 aircraft were housed in two corrugated hangars for a regular rotation of young officer trainees intent on a future of flying at unimaginable speeds encased in thin metal and plastic.

Wenham was also used as a depot for onward deployment of personnel, logistics, aircraft resupply and storage for the Royal Air Force and wider military.

Dandridge's huts were not quite off-the-books or off-the-record but digging too deep would reveal only a blurry overall picture, like peeping through net curtains, form and shape clearly visible but specific details tantalisingly out of reach. All four huts were filled to all four corners with metal racks completely filled with an array of hardware, an intricate electronic jigsaw puzzle with no reference picture or end point, slotted together so organically that the huts might have grown up around them like protective brick shells.

The buildings were crowned with various satellite receivers and antennae, pulling in transmissions and communication traffic from around the world. These were logged, noted and stored as a series of numbers on a constantly updating algorithm deep inside one of four mainframes. Each gave a slightly different little chirrup or belch every now and again when a key word or phrase was detected, or if comms from a significant place, person or frequency was sent or received.

None of it was new or state of the art and yet all of it

fitted together for a common purpose; monitoring, recording and deciphering global radio and satellite audio traffic. An ear on the world, and Dandridge's hearing was pin-sharp.

Dandridge was wearing a set of old aviator headphones with matted sheepskin cushions and a leather and magnesium headband worn shiny from use. They were plugged into a rusty silver receiver under his desk and he was listening to a live feed of a Leningrad Cowboys gig when he nodded off and his brown brogues hit the concrete floor. He snapped awake and noticed the blinking green LED light that wasn't usually blinking, and the persistent accompanying fuzzy beep.

The beep was emitting from a small device sitting to one side and behind all the clutter. It was a small CUBEsat, a build-it-yourself-receiver designed for the keen amateur audiographer to listen to satellite communications, one of his more modern machines. Dandridge had ordered it from Amazon, built and wired it into his main uplink channels to increase its limited range and used it to listen to mission control chatter from the launch of a new Indian GSLV satellite.

The small square device started to chatter and buzz. In the depths of one of his mainframes the algorithm hiccuped, recording unusual variances that raised a small green hazard icon on a large CRT computer monitor that had an old black screen burned in with ghostly images of past hazard icons.

He turned off the music and tuned in to the signal. At first he thought it was just white noise, although he did detect an occasional repeated pitch variance that indicated a broadcast not entirely random. He checked other transceivers but the signal only seemed to be coming in on the CUBEsat, which didn't make any sense given he had set them to scan the same frequencies.

His first thought was that he was probably missing

something really obvious and spent most of that day tearing his hair out trying to locate the signal on anything other than the cheap homemade device.

When that yielded nothing but regular and infuriating static, he spent hours modulating the signal from the CUBEsat, filtering out background noise and hiss, fine-tuning it to its best possible clarity. He checked in with the boards and forums of all the ham radio organisations and discovered that it wasn't just his CUBEsat that had picked up the strange transmission, it was all of them. The boards at AMSAT, IARU, EURA and SETI had all lit up with confusion and chatter. He posted a few messages and questions to see what he could dig up and determined that everyone could hear the same thing but no-one could figure out what it was. Not only were his own Milcom antennas and transceivers remaining stubbornly silent or annoyingly static, but the really big guns like the massive, billion dollar US SATCOMS in Mexico also seemed blissfully unaware.

At some point on the second day Dandridge figured he had probably reduced the sound down to the most basic elements. He recorded a section on his Olympus DS-5000 ProDictaphone and took his headphones off. He had not removed them for over sixteen hours and his earlobes were bright red and throbbing slightly.

His car was parked in its usual spot outside the huts. The immaculate 1979 MGB caught on the first turn of the key, not always a given. Despite his impatience he let it idle for a minute to warm the little 1500cc engine, then gunned it along the perimeter track towards the main administration building.

Group Captain Frank James was tucking into his dinner of baked potato and four-cheese coleslaw when the door to his office opened and his secretary announced Dandridge's arrival. He put his knife and fork down. Dandridge and the other chap who worked in the huts generally kept themselves to themselves, by necessity staying under the radar. The amount of critical data filtering through their headphones and machines every second of the day had the potential to cause multiple and simultaneous international incidents.

On the last occasion Dandridge had emerged from his freezing building was to report a coded communiqué passed in morse code over an obscure channel between four Ultra-Large Crude Oil Tankers spread out across the globe and holding more than 500,000 tonnes of crude oil between them. The coded message Dandridge had intercepted was strange enough for Group Captain James to raise an alert and in a joint operation between the US Navy SEALs and the British Special Boat Service, all four ULCOTs had been boarded and the crews arrested, revealing members of a known terrorist organisation among their number. Thousands of pounds of explosives were rigged along the hull of all four vessels.

If they had gone up, hundreds of thousands of barrels of crude oil would have spilled into the sea with catastrophic economic and environmental consequences. The operation was completely classified. Nobody but the participants were aware it had ever happened, and it had all started because Dandridge had noticed an unusual hiccup on one of his ancient machines and reported it back. Not even Dandridge knew the full results of his report.

The Group Captain was sitting behind an ancient, pitted wooden desk and wore an immaculately pressed Air Force blue shirt and dark navy tie with tie-clip. Dandridge entered his office wearing a t-shirt with an image of a yellow Ford Capri and the slogan 'My other ride...is your sister'. His ears still glowed red and caused James to double take.

'Am I interrupting, sir?' Dandridge asked.

'Yes, I'm having my tea,' James answered, indicating the steaming potato in front of him.

'I can come back if you'd prefer, sir.' The food made Dandridge realise he hadn't eaten anything for even longer than he'd been wearing his headphones.

'You're here now. Tell me. What have you found?'

Dandridge placed his dictaphone on the desk between them. He pressed play and the recording of the transmission, isolated to maximum clarity, filled the Group Captain's office.

'What exactly are we listening to, Richard?'

'I don't really know, sir. It came in yesterday morning and this is as clear as I can get it.'

'And why are you playing it to me?'

'Well, this seems to be a continuous looped signal repeated over and over. It's bypassed all conventional communication channels and somehow aimed at very specific receivers. I can't trace the source of the transmission at all, which indicates an extremely strong signal beyond the power of my equipment or a constantly shifting source, which is unlikely given it's strength-' Dandridge stopped, suddenly realising that he wasn't entirely sure he could vocalise his next sentence. He wasn't even sure he wasn't going completely crazy.

'What? Spit it out, man.'

'Well, obviously I'm not sure of anything yet or really how to explain it properly, but I think that there's every chance that it might be-' This was definitely a lot harder than he had thought, even to someone he trusted like Frank James.

'For Christ's sake, Richard. My sodding potato's going cold.'

'I think it might be extra-terrestrial.' The sentence came out in a rush and hung awkwardly in the air between the two men.

'You're fucking with me, right?' The Group Captain said eventually.

'I don't think I am, no.'

'I was hoping you were going to say yes. So what exactly should I do with this information?'

'I don't know, sir,' and he genuinely didn't, he just knew he had to report it to someone and Frank James was the closest person he knew with any authority.

'Well, your hunch isn't enough. Bring me something back, something more conclusive. Some more recordings, some more evidence, anything. At the moment, I have no idea what to do with this.'

'Me either.'

'Well, you recorded it from a radio right?'

'Yes.'

'Radio is generally a two-way form of communication. Try replying.'

'Well, there's something else, sir. I'm not the only one to have heard this. It appears that most amateur audiographers have intercepted it too. They're all replying to it, although there's been no response so far.'

'You're smarter than all of them Richard, that's why the MoD keeps you on the payroll. Go and figure something out. Until we get more than this recording, fascinating as I'm sure it is, there's nothing we can do. And Richard?'

'Sir?'

'Please change your shirt to something more appropriate. Better yet, perhaps a collar?'

Dandridge returned to the driver's seat of the MG and started the engine to run the heater, feeling the warm draught swirling weakly around his knees. He couldn't shake the feeling that he was onto something really big, but had found himself an unwilling participant in a race with the rest of the world.

MIKE

Mike sat in the boardroom between two colleagues whose names he couldn't quite remember. The table was as long as a cricket pitch and every evenly spaced chair was occupied by a person in a dark business suit. The man speaking at the head of the table looked slightly glossier than anyone else, his dark suit slightly more expensive, better cut, a deeper navy blue, the matching tie a band of purest shimmering silk emphasising his deep tan and perfect golden highlights.

Mike was struggling to concentrate. His hands shook slightly as he poured himself another glass of sparkling water, noticing in a slight panic that he had nearly emptied the bottle.

'Are you OK, Mike?' the man at the head of the table asked suddenly, his smile bright, teeth glistening whiter and straighter than a Disney princess. Everyone swivelled around to look at Mike.

'I'm fine,' he mumbled in reply, 'maybe a touch of 'flu. Please, carry on.'

The glossy man turned back to the presentation on the screen behind him and continued to reel off facts, flow charts and financial statistics, clicking a trigger to progress through the slides. The board members listened attentively, some making notes on the blank yellow pads in front of them using company branded pencils.

Mike excused himself and went to the executive toilet. Locked safely inside a cubicle he took out a small bottle of Absolut Vodka from his pocket, raised it reverently to his lips and downed it in two gulps. His head cleared, his body calmed down and the shakes loosened their grip on his muscles.

It had worked perfectly for so long, the alcohol carrying him successfully through the most important period of his career. It had given him exactly the confidence he needed to argue coherently in court, to win case after case, bring in clients, network within the company and industry, to be indispensable to the firm. He was proud to be only the second person in his company to make it to the board by thirty, although the first, Glen O'Herlihy, had committed suicide two years ago so didn't really count. Living without that bottle of confidence was inconceivable, but he was still just self-aware enough to recognise that his drinking was becoming more of a problem than a solution.

He let himself out of the cubicle and stared at himself in the mirror. He took out a small travel toothbrush and rubbed the rough bristles over his teeth and gums and pulled cold water through his hair. He buttoned up the middle button of his dark grey suit and stepped back into the board meeting with a smile and full of apologies.

'Sorry, Barnard. Must have been last nights Madras. Do not go in there,' he jerked his thumb backwards and the men at the table all laughed, big manly guffaws. The two women present looked at each other and smiled thinly. Mike took his seat and picked up a pencil and a pad, redirecting his interest towards the pie chart in front of him.

The meeting seemed to go on longer than he ever could have thought possible. It appeared that Barnard was going for some kind of world record number of slides with colourful infographics to try and interpret. Barnard loved infographics. Mike was desperate for another drink long before it was all over, his heart leaping for joy when the slide marked 'Thank You' finally - *finally* - came up on the projector screen at just after two in the afternoon. He knew he could squeeze in a few pints at the pub around the corner in relative solitude as the meeting had ended outside the usual midday to two o'clock timeframe of the average City of London lunch break.

He ended up having four pints and retired back to his own office with a tuna baguette from Pret A Manger that tasted like dust wrapped in a hessian sack. He reviewed case files and dozed, eventually emerging at half seven. The office was quiet, although there were a few screens still on and people working or on Facebook, hurriedly minimising the distinctive blue page when he walked past, smiling and nodding sociably at him as he went.

He pushed his way through the revolving glass doors at the reception area of his building, a glass and chrome edifice of the type that had sprung up in the City during the last few years. They all had receptions the size of football pitches filled with waterfalls and botanical atriums and were manned by overly made-up receptionists and thuggish security guards with yellow nametags, buildings that had given the whole square mile an air of false modernity, an elegant old city gent dressed in hipster clothing.

Mike weaved between the people dawdling along the narrow pavement and within five minutes reached his destination, a traditional old boozer with opaque windows, sticky red paisley carpets and a permanent underlying aroma of bleach and urinals. It hadn't changed in over two hundred years, save for the two giant new crystalline office buildings either side of it.

There was nobody in the pub Mike recognised, which suited him just fine. He found a spare barstool and moved it so he had a view of the TV, then ordered a pint.

From the moment he ordered that first pint of the evening his memory became a slow, hazy blur filled with random imagery and white noise; some laughter, some cheering, some vomiting, snippets of random conversations that he would never again be able to fully recollect. His next conscious memory was the following morning, swinging his legs over the side of the spare bed, a pulsing throb of pain behind his right eye as his feet hit the dark wood floorboards. He rode out a wave of nausea and staggered downstairs to the kitchen, vaguely noting that he was still fully dressed.

'Have you seen the papers this morning?' Joy Hennessy asked her husband.

'Of course I haven't seen the fucking papers this morning,' Mike replied, opening a cupboard and taking down a box of paracetamol and a box of ibuprofen. He pressed two out from the foil packaging of each and swallowed the four pills down with a glass of water, wiping his mouth with the greying sleeve of his once-white work shirt.

'Did you sleep in that?' Joy asked.

'Not all night.'

'Mike-'

'I'm OK. It was a leaving do, so I had a few. Sorry if I woke you up when I got in.'

'You didn't. You passed out on the sofa, mid-wank.'

Joy held up her mobile phone. On the screen was a picture of Mike, unconscious but still in his suit jacket, shirt and tie, his blue trousers and pale blue boxer shorts bunched up around his black socks and shoes. Mike stared at the picture, taking a couple of seconds to recognise himself.

'Oh god, I'm so sorry Joy. I was really drunk.'

'When you drink you always seem to want to cheat on me, with yourself.'

'Is that strictly classed as cheating?'

'Only if you actually finish. I'm emailing this to your mother.'

On his commuter train to work that morning, Mike noticed an unusual buzz in the carriage, a strange atmosphere, nobody quite willing to break the commuter code of silence, but somehow excited. *Perhaps Kate is pregnant again* he wondered as he closed his eyes and fell asleep, his aching head resting on the filthy but blessedly cool window.

He walked back in through the glass double doors of his building and past the burly security and the receptionists, smiling and nodding at them as he always did. They were huddled together, nattering like schoolchildren. Mike ignored them back, but the strange, buzzing atmosphere persisted as he stepped out of the lift and made his way through the cubicles towards his office.

'Caroline, what the fuck is going on today?' he asked as he passed the desk of a PA to one of the senior partners, 'Is it weird out here or is it my hangover?'

'You haven't heard? It's all they could talk about on breakfast news this morning, and look at the Metro,' Caroline replied breathlessly, her cheeks flushed. She showed him the front cover. There was a single word headline - 'CONTACT?'

'And what does that mean?' Mike asked.

'Aliens,' the PA whispered and blushed, almost as embarrassed to say the word out loud as Dandridge had when he had first tried to report it to Frank James.

Mike laughed loudly. 'The fuck it is,' he said and went into his office and closed the door.

JENNIFER

The funeral had been meticulously planned, right down to an exact allocation of sausage rolls per mourner. Right on schedule, at three thirty in the afternoon precisely, Jennifer Jones was sat in the living room on a giant paisley sofa, receiving visitors. It was one of those sofas that had wooden arms and trim and a high back that made it almost impossible to obtain a comfortable or relaxed sitting position. Jennifer was fairly sure her mother-in-law had chosen it for that very reason.

Like all the people shuffling awkwardly past her or murmuring quietly in the chintzy living room, she was wearing black. Black dress, black hat, black shoes. On this day of all days she had never felt more uncomfortable, this day when she wanted to feel true to herself but forced to eschew her usual loose flowery frocks, hair ribbons and fake Birkenstocks.

Their friends - she wasn't nearly ready to call them just 'her' friends yet - had already exhausted their allotted number of sausage rolls and were clustered together in the kitchen drinking Becks from the bottle and starting in on the Hula Hoops and Twiglets. She wanted to join them, but at the same time didn't really know what to say. She knew that even though they meant no disrespect, their conversation was entirely about the unidentified radio signals that had been front page news that day.

She had seen the story on Breakfast News of course. She and Stephen always watched Breakfast News on the BBC, and even today when her mind and body were operating on the most basic autopilot she had switched it on as part of her routine as automatically as she would brush her teeth or have a wee. Her interest level had flickered for a few seconds as she listened to Bill Turnbull droning on about it, but then she remembered what day it was and her stomach flopped again and her heart broke a little more. Stephen would have loved this story. He always loved the stupid stories.

Stephen's parents sat either side of her on the ghastly sofa, a sofa she had endured many times before but had never in a million years thought she would have to sit on at her husband's wake. Her mother-in-law, for all her fussiness, over-organising, questionable decor choices and constant disparaging of Stephen, Stephen's father and men in general, was holding her hand and refusing to let it go. Jennifer could tell she was only barely holding on, although she was not entirely certain if it was her actual emotional state threatening to come out or the fact she had already run out of sausage rolls.

Stephen would have picked up the bowl and ignored her protests as he stuffed every single one of them in his mouth right in front of her, crumbs and half chewed processed sausage spewing out until they both broke down in laughter, but Stephen was not here. Stephen was gone.

Occasionally someone would shuffle past them and be forced to bend down in order to be heard at the acceptable, hushed level of funeral conversation.

'I'm so sorry,' they would say, 'Stephen was .... ' Insert superlative here. He was many superlatives, and each one was true.

'Thank you. And thanks so much for coming. There's plenty to eat and drink,' Stephen's father would reply and everyone would attempt a smile. Jennifer suspected that most funerals began with the intention of celebrating a life well lived, but tradition and grief inevitably intervened to turn the whole event into a massive downer. It's hard to celebrate a life when it's cut so short, so unexpectedly.

Jennifer squeezed her mother-in-law's hand and stood up. She went and stood in front of their old JVC stereo system. It had a tape deck, but the tray was jammed shut with the original cast recording of Les Miserables stuck inside. Not wanting to depress her guests any more than necessary she selected a vinyl record from the shelf. It was an old Kate and Anna McGarrigle folk album. Stephen's parents loved folk music. As 'Schooldays' filled the oppressive quiet, the guitars and mellifluous vocals lifted the mourners and the small group of people began to gather and congregate towards the music. Jennifer stood in front of the turntable, her eyes closed, swaying slightly to the tune.

She felt an arm around her slim waist, and her hand being held. She didn't need to open her eyes as her father-in-law danced her around the living room.

ROYCE

Generations of schoolchildren have taken advantage of the glorious few minutes of unsupervised freedom before the arrival of a slightly late teacher in the classroom. Royce Brims and his friends were no exception, unknowingly following in the footsteps of their fathers and grandfathers, yelling, throwing stationery and paper aeroplanes at each other, standing on desks to see who could wipe most bogies on the ceiling tiles and throwing compasses like darts at that day's selected unpopular kid. The difference between Brims' friends and their forebears was the addition of shouted rap sing-offs where each kid whipped up a lyrical masterpiece about a close member of someone's family in bizarre and unlikely sexual situations, usually paired with an animal. For that unique twist on bad classroom behaviour, they could perhaps be lauded.

The harassed looking teacher walked in and slammed down his stack of marked exercise books on the desk, the sharp noise catching the attention of his unruly class. The mayhem subsided slowly, with some snickering and subdued laughter.

'Seats, quickly. Quickly please. Right, let's take the register. Victoria Baxter?'

'Here.'

'Adam Beadle?'

'Here.'

'Royce Brims? Royce Brims? Brims, I know you're here, I can see you.'

'Then why are you asking?' Royce was slouched backwards as much as his uncomfortably upright school chair would allow, his elbow perched on the seat back, the heady rush of bad behaviour still coursing through his veins.

'I'm taking the register, as usual. This is not a new occurrence, Brims.'

'But you already know I'm here, Mr. Penetti,' he said, to sniggers from his friends at his comeback.

'That's not the point of the register, Brims. Please answer when I call your name in future. Dennis?'

'What *is* the point then?' Royce cut in, encouraged by the reaction of his friends.

'You really want me to tell you, Brims?'

'Yes.'

'It's a legal document required by law that proves, in front of twenty three of your classmates and peers, that you were actually here when I called out your name and that I didn't just write down that you were present when in fact you have been abducted by aliens and subjected to a battery of horrible tests.'

'Like what?'

'What, 'like what?'

'Like what horrible tests?'

'Royce, I'm not an expert on alien torture methods, although frankly I could give them some pointers. Now shut up and let me continue.'

Penetti finished the register and opened a book.

'Today, we are going to learn about Oliver Cromwell and the Roundheads versus the Cavaliers.'

There was a groan around the classroom of twenty-four twelve year olds.

'I think I'd rather be tortured by aliens.'

'Brims, I think I'd rather you were tortured by aliens too, but I can assure you that our history is crucial to us as a species. It may well be that we are moving forward into a fascinating and unknown new age for this planet, but if we do not learn from our history then we are doomed to repeat it, as they say. And if there really are aliens out there, don't you think we will want them to think we are intelligent beings who have actually learned from our mistakes and evolved into a civilised society? What Cromwell achieved was one small part of that step towards the civilisation we know today, albeit with a considerable amount of violence and religious persecution.'

'None of that really matters sir, because I'm going to be a famous rapper and so I don't really need to know about Cromwell or his religious prosecution.'

'*Persecution*, Royce, and if you want to be a famous rapper, you had better learn what it means.'

'*The systematic mistreatment of an individual or group by another person or group.*'

The teacher held his hand out.

'Sir, not again, please,'

'The phone, Royce. You know the rules.'

Royce reluctantly slipped out from behind his desk and walked to the front of the class. He handed over his phone to Pennetti who took it and placed it in his desk drawer.

'You'll get this back at the end of the day. Now everybody settle down and let's learn about Oliver Cromwell. Turn to page 42 in your texts.'

There was a second collective groan and a shuffling of paper as books were opened and Royce sat back at this desk. He opened the text book to the correct page with no intention of any further participation in the lesson. No point at all as he was, definitely and without any doubt in his mind, going to be a famous rapper. He wedged his chin under his palm, his pencil, already chewed beyond repair, between his lips. He fixed his eyes on the view out of the window, mentally linking rhymes and rhythms in his head, over and over again.

DANDRIDGE

Two weeks later and having managed to decipher not a single element of the sound or locate precisely where it originated, he began to feel he was dead last. The transmission was still ongoing, never changing. Nothing had changed, and it seemed that nobody else was having any luck either.

On the fourteenth consecutive day of fruitlessly fiddling with frequencies and attempting to trace what should have been an immutable originating point but wasn't, Dandridge decided to go home and clean his car instead, which always calmed him down and cleared his head. The MG was a unique shade of duck-egg blue. According to the old German chap he bought it from it had been painted using exactly the same paint as the underside of a Messerschmidt BF-109. Dandridge doubted the veracity of this claim, but it certainly had been very resistant to rust or chips and more resilient than the engine which had needed two total rebuilds in eight years.

He navigated the narrow country lanes towards his house, listening to the engine with a satisfied reverence as he double-declutched and revved out of the corners.

He turned the old car onto a long wooded driveway and as the chunky new Pirelli tyres crunched onto the gravel he saw a large black SUV parked in his space outside the house.

His house was not nearly so well kept as his car; a run down, once-white-now-greyish cottage with peeling window frames, missing roof tiles and an abundance of weeds growing unchecked around the border.

He pulled up next to the SUV and killed the MG's engine. Beside the Cadillac Escalade his car looked like a child's toy. He climbed out and saw a man dressed in a black suit leaning against the driver's door. The man bleeped his key fob and the SUV's hazard lights winked twice. Dandridge inserted his key into the driver's door of his own car and twisted it. He felt the old locking mechanism thunk into place.

He let himself in to the house and the stranger wordlessly followed him along the dark hallway to the kitchen. Dandridge filled the kettle and switched it on before facing the plain looking man across the breakfast bar.

'Coffee or tea?'

'Coffee. Please.'

Dandridge set two mugs on the stained surface. One said 'I Heart.fm', the other was orange and had a Crunchie logo emblazoned across the side.

'So what can I do for you?'

The man extended his hand. 'Mr. Dandridge, my name is Ernest C. Adler.'

Dandridge shook the proffered hand.

'What does the 'C' stand for?' he asked.

'It can stand for many things. Christian, Community, Charisma. But mainly, it just stands for 'Christopher.'

'Fair enough, Ernest C. Adler. So how long is it going to be until you show me your Home Office identification?'

Adler reached inside his suit jacket and held up a black leather wallet, open at the clear plastic window. He held it up in Dandridge's face for a few seconds before snapping it shut. The kettle began to boil and Dandridge turned back to the two chipped mugs.

'Is instant OK?'

'I suppose.'

'You've got to give me a good reason to get out the Fairtrade Ground Arabica, Mr. Adler,' said Dandridge, spooning some Nescafe Gold Blend into the mugs.

'Would the security of the entire planet in your hands be enough, Mr Dandridge?'

'Just Dandridge. And no. Wouldn't be the first time. I am assuming this is about the transmission?'

'Indeed.'

'And why would the security of the planet be down to me, exactly? I only heard it first, with about a billion other people.' Dandridge poured the boiled water into the mugs of instant coffee, added milk, and handed one to Adler, who sniffed at it slightly disdainfully before taking a sip.

'When the transmission was detected and hit the news, the Prime Minister tasked me to ensure that it is deciphered and responded to from within the United Kingdom.'

'I can't decipher it. Not my thing.'

'This is a big, popular story. It's barely been off the front pages for two weeks. Usually a story like this is reported and drops away within hours. If we are successful in deciphering this signal the Prime Minister believes that confidence in the UK's ability to lead the world in scientific realms can be restored, the credit can be claimed by the government and could draw the country together in ways not seen since the Second World War.'

Dandridge snorted for the second time.

'So this is just a diversion to mask his fading popularity.'

'Perhaps, but I don't care. His reasons are his own. I have a job to do, and you're the guy who can help me.'

'Great. But I already told you, I can't decipher it. I'm not your man.'

'OK. Here's a story for you. About twenty two years ago, a Navy Radio Officer serving on frigate HMS Harkaway intercepted a signal exactly like the one we began hearing a couple of weeks ago. He didn't know what it was, and figuring it might be a coded signal of some sort he felt it was worth recording and reporting it.'

'Seriously?'

'No. I've driven all the way out here to make up stories.'

'I am so glad I didn't waste my good coffee, Adler.'

'The recording was quite short, about a minute and ten seconds in total and seems to cut in halfway through. Presumably it took the Radio Officer a few seconds to identify it as unusual and record it. Then it faded and he couldn't get it back.'

The two of them moved through to the living room and Dandridge had to move two stacks of magazines and books from the sofa before they could both sit down, Adler twisting around uncomfortably to face Dandridge. It was the only seating in the room.

'You could hoover once in a while,' Adler observed.

'Get on with it, Adler.'

'Well, the recording was listened to by a few higher-ups, but nobody could figure it out or thought it was worth anything. And then, and here's where it gets really funny-'

'Can't wait.'

'About three years ago, a young Lieutenant serving on a Naval base in Clyde stumbled on an archive of old radio comms traffic dating back from about 1950 or so, all stored on different tape formats and logged in huge bound volumes. All gathering dust. To cut a long story short, out of curiosity he listened to a few and by sheer chance heard the weird noise recorded from the Harkaway that everyone had forgotten about. He thought it was interesting and copied it on his mobile telephone, setting it as his ringtone. Can you believe it?'

'Not yet.'

'It turns out that his girlfriend at the time was an Assistant Professor of Ancient Linguistics at the British Museum. An expert in aeons old hieroglyphs, Sanskrit texts, Arkadian, Sumerian, Mayan, all that shit. Anyway, she heard the ringtone and became obsessed with it. Recorded it and studied it for months and months, convinced it wasn't random sounds but a code of some sort. The ironic thing is, it was the ringtone he set to her contact in his phone, so she only heard it when she dialled him by accident.'

'Amazing. So did she translate it?'

'She has theories.'

'Theories? Welcome to the party, pal.'

There was a pause as Adler sipped his coffee.

'Are you going to keep me in suspense much longer here, Adler? I've got loads of things to do.'

'Like what? Spring clean? So this girl, she identified specific sounds, picked them apart, placed them in various orders, loudest to softest, softest to loudest, distinct beats, other noises. I don't really know, I'm not the expert. But it turns out that the sound is virtually identical to our new transmission.'

'From what I can tell, the signal is a fairly continuous sound with occurring peaks and troughs, irregularly repeated. If it is the same as the new one, and she didn't have the full recording she wouldn't have been able to determine beginnings and ends, line breaks.'

'I know. But you haven't met her. She's smart. Really smart.'

'So what does she think it means?'

'I don't know.'

'What? You came all the way to my house to feed me some bullshit story and you can't even give me the punchline? Fuck you, Adler. I'm not going anywhere, even if - *especially* if - the Prime Minister is suffering from an excessive case of hubris.'

'You misunderstand. I didn't just come here to feed you some bullshit story, Dandridge. I came because I am easily worth the good coffee and because I didn't want to send my colleagues to come and just pick you up without any explanation at all.'

'Colleagues?'

'We're going. Now. Pack a bag.'

MARION

As soon as he walked in the door she knew she utterly hated the radio guy. She estimated he was in his mid thirties at least, which was way too old to look like a student. Dressed in a musty-smelling t-shirt with a slightly offensive slogan on the front and a stretched neckline that indicated he might have slept in it, Dandridge spoke with a complete disregard for rank, experience or feelings. It was plain to her that he thought she was a complete fraud.

'Are you the Professor?' he said as he walked in to her office in the British Museum.

'*Assistant* Professor. Marion Crandall.' She held her hand out. He took it and they shook. Then he sat down in her seat and stared at her as she tried to surreptitiously wipe her hand on the back of her skirt.

Marion worked hard to maintain an appearance of efficiency and focus to bely the image most people had of stuffy, distracted academics working in windowless basements translating Aztec runes at the British Museum. She was 26 years old with strawberry blonde hair tied sternly back, her face covered by large black-rimmed spectacles. She wore a smart, tailored white blouse under a buttoned-up pink cardigan paired with a black pencil skirt and heels, but somehow Dandridge seemed to see straight through her smart, angular appearance to the dishevelled academic underneath.

'So, you've got a recording from your boyfriend's mobile phone that you reckon matches the new one. Let's hear it.'

'Ex-boyfriend, actually.' Marion pressed play on her Dictaphone, an Olympus DS-5000 the same as his. Dandridge nodded in approval as the noise of the first transmission intercepted years ago by an efficient and curious Navy radio officer filled the room. Adler stood silently behind them. The recording lasted just under a minute.

'OK,' said Dandridge, 'so what do you think it means?'

She opened a plain notebook almost completely filled with scrawled, illegible handwritten notes and began to talk, walking Dandridge and Adler through her reasoning, referring back to ancient dialects that used tonally similar rhythms and patterns to communicate.

Two hours later, Dandridge sat back.

'Adler's right, you are smart,' he said, 'but this could all be speculative bullshit.'

'Oh yes. But I don't think so. It's simply not random enough, and when I heard the new transmission I knew it was the same. I couldn't have got so far with the original sound without the new one.'

Dandridge sighed, 'OK, so now we have to run the new recording through your process, see if we can isolate more identifiers and link the connections.'

'Not tonight,' cut in Adler. 'It's past ten, we'll come back in the morning. Dandridge, I'll take you to your hotel.'

'Which is?'

'The Zetter, across in Clerkenwell.'

Dandridge looked at Marion. 'Going our way?' he asked her.

The Zetter was a smart boutique hotel on the border of Central London and Shoreditch. Dandridge checked himself into his room, where he and Marion proceeded to have fast and unsatisfying sex, all awkward elbows and knees, the kissing too wet.

Afterwards, and to Marion's relief, Dandridge went into the en-suite and took a shower, returning clean to the bed and lying naked on the covers next to her. Five storeys beneath their window East London traffic whooshed continuously past them, the occasional siren cutting through the muffled quiet of the double glazed windows. The curtains were drawn against the evening but the London street lighting seeped past the edges into the room, bathing them in an unreal soft orange glow.

'You do know that there is no way we can definitively decipher those sounds?' Dandridge murmured, almost asleep.

'You've said that about forty times. You can't seriously think I'm not on to something?'

There was a pause, and Marion thought he had fallen asleep. Then he spoke again. 'You're definitely onto something. But maybe it doesn't need to make sense. Maybe it's not supposed to. Maybe we only need to prove that we're intelligent enough to try.'

'Maybe. But prove to who?'

They lay in silence for a while before she asked, 'So what do you do for the MoD, exactly?'

'I'm a radio guy,' Dandridge mumbled, 'that's all. An audiographer. And librarian. A library of sound. Basically, I run a depository of intercepted communications. Shit, what do I actually do?'

'Fucking hell, Dandridge,' Marion knelt on her elbow, facing him, shaking him to wake him up from his half-doze, 'you mean, you spy on people? Like the NSA?'

'No, not like the NSA. Open, international channels and networks only, non-encrypted comms. Well, some. But only very occasionally.'

'That's what they say too,'

'For a start, the NSA are American. If I was anything like them I would probably be MI5 or GCHQ. Government funded, multi-billion dollar operations that allegedly monitor every citizen under the guise of the Terrorism Act and who engage in mass data analysis, phones, text, emails, online search habits, everything. I, on the other hand, operate out of four sheds, one of which used to be a lavatory. So no, it's not me. I'm not saying it doesn't happen, but it's not by me. I'm just a last line of defence is all. Goddamn it, now you've woken me up.'

'Who monitors when you're not there?'

'All the common transmission channels and base

frequencies are monitored automatically on a trigger-word alert system, but I have an assistant too. Poor chap, I suppose I should call him.'

Marion rolled on top of Dandridge and kissed him. 'You can call him later,' she whispered in his ear. This time, the sex was slightly better.

JOSH

Josh got a text from Dandridge late on the first day of his disappearance. His texts were always written in a mixture of text-speak, needless detail and gibberish. '*Honey, bn abducted by Ministry Of D, guy called Charisma. Cover 4 me. Will b n touch*'.

He hated when Dandridge called him 'Honey'. Just because everyone called him by his surname he automatically assumed everyone wanted to be referred to in the same way, and Josh Honeyball had never been particularly fond of his. Even as an adult it was way too open to playground interpretation and he had spent his entire life having to slowly spell it out two or three times over the phone, as if the person on the other end of the line couldn't quite believe it.

However, since that first text message three days ago Dandridge hadn't been in touch at all and his car hadn't budged from the driveway. As long as Josh had known him Dandridge was a creature of habit and if he didn't polish the stupid thing every other day he was a wreck. He was also not answering any texts, Facebook pokes or emailed links to bizarre and mildly inappropriate Nordic pop videos on YouTube for which he was usually a sucker.

Josh Honeyball was 25 years old, six foot four, blonde, blue eyed and a first class honours graduate in Electrical Engineering from Imperial College in London. The morning after his graduation Dandridge had turned up at his parent's house in Ilford at nine o'clock in the morning. Josh was suffering from a hangover that would have felled a rhino and had only been home and asleep for about an hour and a half. He could barely speak, reluctantly responding to his mother's shout to come and meet the stranger, eventually shuffling in to the living room in only his pyjamas.

Dandridge spent half an hour chatting and laughing with Josh's mother and barely said a word to Josh. This was a huge relief given he was in no state to answer any question with any degree of coherence.

Then and there, Dandridge had offered him a job. He vaguely remembered asking the important questions such as what the job would entail, what the salary was, where they would be based, gym membership, pension, prospects, etc. Dandridge had offered absolutely no useful or concrete information or assurances whatsoever, in fact what he described was elusive, vague and poorly described at best. Josh's mother however was completely sold and utterly delighted, accepting on her son's behalf and offering their guest another slice of victoria sponge to celebrate.

So Josh put aside his half-planned trip to India and a week later arrived as directed at the airfield with two suitcases containing the entirety of his possessions. He was detained at security because Dandridge had neglected to fill out the appropriate requisition and personnel documents. After a day of administration in which he was made to fill out his own reference forms and a stationery requisition for an extra chair that would take a fortnight to be delivered, he was finally shown where he was going to be stationed. He walked out in horror. Dandridge caught up to him and started showing him the equipment and somehow two years later he was still there. Huts 2 and 3 were now filled with the smartest, most capable monitoring equipment in the world, albeit made from parts bought from Maplin and eBay.

In the first few months Josh had stayed with Dandridge in his slightly grubby, unkempt house, although given he had just left a student flat shared with seven blokes, he considered it relative luxury.

Josh had never had a preferred type and generally copped off with any man he felt an affinity with or slight attraction to, and even those were nebulous standards at best, but even by Josh's reckoning his employer was not the sort of man he would ever have thought he could go for.

Initially, he found Dandridge slightly annoying, too intense and a bit lacklustre when it came to personal hygiene, even before considering he was at least ten years older. Josh rarely went with anybody over twenty five, but to his delight and relief he discovered that Dandridge was every bit as energetic as a man half his age and possessed an infectious enthusiasm and a sharp humour, always engaged and interested in everything, determined to push himself and his little world within the huts forward. He seemed to do no actual physical exercise, except for polishing his car, but he was lean and wiry, one of those irritating people who could go without sleep for days at a time with no ill effects, unlike Josh for whom eight hours was an absolute minimum prerequisite.

They engaged in an intensely energetic and physical relationship for some months, keeping each other warm in the winter, in the house and in the huts. It was Josh's longest relationship to date and certainly the best and most consistent sex he had ever experienced.

The living arrangements had suited them both perfectly for a while, mentally and physically, but Josh came to understand that he was only Dandridge's latest thing, someone he was happy to love and spend all his energy on until the next distraction, whatever or whomever it might be. Josh resented the thought for a while before inevitably succumbing to his body's more base urges, the satisfaction of which Dandridge was extremely adept. The more he lived and worked with him, the more he came to understand and accept the man's thought processes and energies. His resentments eventually dropped away to be replaced with an unbreakable, but often stretched, affection.

After nearly four months of being together practically every day and night Josh instinctively decided it was time to find his own place. He found a small, clean one-bedroom flat in nearby Cirencester and moved in within a week, although rarely spent much time there. It wasn't easy for a gay engineer from Ilford living in Gloucestershire but he did occasionally manage to escape the base.

When his phone buzzed during the third day of Dandridge's unexplained absence, Josh was sitting with his headphones on listening to a conversation in Russian between commanding officers of two submarines engaged in training manoeuvres in the Adriatic. As the name flashed up on the smart phone screen he felt another tinge of annoyance, realising he had succumbed to surname syndrome. 'Dandridge' it read. He pulled the headphones around his neck and hit the green button.

'Where have you been?'

'Is the CUBEsat still receiving?'

'Of course. Where are you?'

'Trying to decipher the transmission.'

'You can't decipher noise, Dandridge.'

'Apparently, you can. Well, you can try. Sort of. Anyway, I'm coming back. I'll see you in about-'

Dandridge walked in to Hut 4.

'Fucking hell, boss. Where have you been?' Josh leapt to his feet and the two embraced warmly.

'Make me some tea.'

Josh ran across into Hut 3 and put the kettle on. When he got back, a woman was standing behind him.

'Honeyball, this is Crandall.'

Marion Crandall stood behind him awkwardly in the cramped hut, looking around her as if this was the opposite to what she had been expecting, which of course it was. It always was.

Josh extended his hand. 'It's Josh, actually,'

Marion smiled. 'Marion. Nice to meet you, Josh,' The two shook hands.

'We've been working on the transmission,' Dandridge said from underneath the console where he was fiddling with some wiring.

'I figured, but you could have let me know you were

OK. I've not been worried sick in any way though.'

'Good to know. Right, we're here for a little experiment,' as he popped back up, his face flushed.

Josh heard somebody clear his throat. A man dressed in a black suit stood in the doorway to Hut 4.

'Oh sorry, this is Ernest C. Adler. My handler.'

'What does the 'C' stand for?' Josh asked.

'Are you sure that the transmission has not stopped, been interrupted or changed since it was first detected?' Adler asked, ignoring the question.

'Yes. Identical frequency and sound, no variances or interruptions so far. It has been repeated-' Josh checked a small black screen, 'just under seventy five thousand times. Seventy four thousand, eight hundred and-'

'Whatever,' Dandridge interrupted. 'Josh, get a whole sequence up on ProTools would you please?'

Josh booted up the audio mixing software and loaded up a single recording of the entirety of the transmission. The soundwave appeared on the timeline across the 30 seconds as sharp peaks and troughs.

'Now copy this onto it,' Adler handed him a USB stick. He stuck it into the side of the massive PC tower and dragged and dropped the .wav sound file onto the desktop, before then importing it into ProTools. The two sequences now lined up on two timelines, one above the other, Crandall's recording slightly shorter than the original. Josh stood up to let her sit down. She put on Josh's headphones and expanded the timeline so she could see every microsecond variance close-up, a visual representation of sound. She waved her hand at them dismissively.

'OK, I guess we should let her do her thing for a bit,' said Dandridge. 'Where's that tea?'

JENNIFER

The news was still full of the transmission, which had so far resisted every attempt to decipher or interfere with it. Occasionally, the story was displaced by something fresher and more newsworthy, but it would always seem to circle around to hit the top spot or front page again.

Jennifer remained stubbornly disinterested in the story, knowing that Stephen would have loved and followed it avidly. He would have scoured the internet for news and would probably have bought one of those CUBEsat things to listen to it himself. His enthusiasm would have infected her and carried her along laughing, but without him she was unable to generate so much as a flicker of interest. Her emotions and engagement had dipped and dulled considerably since his funeral and she was only vaguely aware of life happening around her, like she was listening through a pair of woolly earmuffs or staring through particularly dense net curtains.

Fortunately work kept her busy and she threw herself into it. She was working at a small creative advertising agency designing product packaging for a new air freshener range. She was a freelance designer, but her willingness to take on any and every less than exciting project that came up had made her extremely popular within the small agency.

She was frowning at the glowing screen of her Mac, carefully manoeuvring a stock image of an apple onto the expanded outline of the air freshener packaging when a strident male voice cut through her concentration.

'You having fun?'

The voice cut through her autopilot and she jumped, causing her stylus to jerk fractionally, which for the apple on screen represented a huge leap from one side of the screen to the other, dumping it in the grey netherworld of the background. She pulled off her headphones and looked up, blushing. 'I'm sorry?'

'Are you having fun?' The man standing at her shoulder and staring intently at her screen had short black hair with grey flecks at the sideburns and stubble that she suspected he kept trimmed to remain at the same rugged length. Unlike most of the staff at the agency for whom dressing smartly was only something people in other industries bothered to do, he was dressed in a new-looking blue checked shirt and plain tie under a dark grey jacket, trousers and shiny brown brogues.

'Yes, sorry. Of course,' she flustered, 'I'm nearly done here. I'll send it up for review by three, though the brief says it's not due until end of day tomorrow.'

She was still blushing.

'That's great,' he said. 'It's probably really important.'

Jennifer smiled. 'It's the new Winter range. I'm told it's extremely important.'

'Oh yes. Of course.'

There was a pause. The man looked at her screen and Jennifer looked at the man, by now realising that her blush wasn't in any danger of fading.

'Can I help you at all?' she asked.

'I think the apple needs to be closer to the cinnamon. To emphasize the perfect union between the two fragrances.'

'Oh, right. OK.'

Jennifer felt slightly disappointed at his response and at the same time surprised at herself for this reaction. He was still leaning over her with one hand on the side of her desk. He smelled good. Really good. She felt herself blushing even redder. Her husband, the man she had been with since their second year of University, the only man she had ever slept with, who she still loved with all her heart and who had only been in the ground a month almost to the day and here she was getting a hot flush from an older guy.

She felt ashamed of herself and put her headphones back on, clicking on the apple to rescue it from the outer reaches of her desktop and placing it back into position, zooming in so she could nestle it a few pixels closer to its cinnamon brethren, arranging them to appear as if they had always belonged together in this formation, a confluence of identities creating an atmosphere of perfect olfactory zen.

He watched her carefully. 'Beautiful,' he said, then moved away from her desk. She breathed a sigh of relief.

The days passed but now there was now a small wrinkle in her velour armour. The older guy began visiting her desk every day and it was disturbing her carefully scheduled routine. She wasn't ready to move on. Not nearly ready. Stephen was everywhere, in photos on the walls, his smell on clothes in their shared wardrobe, a box of his University research papers behind the sofa, still with multi-coloured Post-It note bookmarks sticking out. She still cried herself to sleep most nights, the last time she had seen his face burned into her mind, his ruddy cheeks redder than his post-box red coat, orange tinted goggles perched on his forehead, skis under one arm.

But each day, the guy persisted on coming to her desk to see what she was working on, making a tiny change here or adjustment there. She had discovered his name was James McDonald, a senior partner at the agency. He always spoke to her professionally, on one occasion completely rejecting all the work she had done for two days and taking the brief back to the creative team for an overhaul.

He didn't visit either of the two other designers or review anything but her output, but she was sure it wasn't just because he didn't like it. In fact, given the number of new briefs that she was being chosen to design she was certain that she was the preferred freelance designer in the firm.

On one day when he didn't show up, she was mortified to realise that she had started to look forward to his visits, which could occur at any point in the day. She caught herself daydreaming about him, her attention drifting from the design on the screen in front of her and imagining him leaning over her desk, inhaling his luxurious, expensive scent. He always wore the same aftershave, despite his stubble. She would jerk back to reality with a blush, and glance across to her colleagues hoping nobody had noticed.

And then he began to visit her in the evenings too. Sometimes she would wake up in the middle of the night, flushed and panting from a dream she didn't want to remember but could, in 4K HD, 60 frames per second clarity. She could never get back to sleep afterwards.

At the beginning of the second month of the transmissions she was handed a new brief to create a label for a new hazelnut scented furniture polish.

She stared at the specified dimensions and trim lines, visualising how she was going to place all the company logos, stock images of hazelnuts, ingredients and warning text about the dangers of drinking hazelnut scented furniture polish.

She was concentrating on the brief so hard that she only noticed James McDonald was present when she smelt his expensive aftershave.

'You do know they give you all the rubbish briefs,' he said.

Jennifer flushed, cursing her body for giving itself away yet again. 'Yes, I know. Actually, I told the team to pass them to me. I don't mind.'

They looked at the brief together for a few seconds.

'Not very sexy,' he said, finally.

'What?'

'The product.'

'Oh, I see. No, it's not. But it is essential, if you want your furniture to smell of hazelnut, anyway.'

'Do what you can with it, we can review it tomorrow with the client. I'm off to a board meeting now.'

'Have fun.'

'Actually Jenny, after the board meeting there's going to

be company drinks and maybe a canapé or two at the Ship and Shovel over the road. I'd like you to come along.'

'It's Jennifer. And thank you James, but I can't make it tonight.'

'That's a shame. If your plans change please do come, you know where we'll be.' He wandered away.

The other two designers in the open plan space unplugged themselves from their glistening white headphones and started firing questions at her, laughing and joking about the senior partner of the agency blatantly asking her out - *yes he did, it was so obvious, you must go, he's loaded, no we haven't been invited, not directly anyway, but I sucked off Phil in the account team and I might tag along with him before heading on somewhere else, and oh my god, are you blushing?* and so on.

It was the first time that Jennifer felt no part of their conversation had underlying sympathy and consideration. She smiled and chatted back, feigning complete ignorance and telling them how she had always blushed really easily.

She started on an anecdote about the time she had stayed at Stephen's parents house and his younger brother had walked in on her sitting on the toilet and how, to this day, she simply couldn't not blush whenever she saw him.

At the mention of Stephen's name they smiled but fell silent and the moment was over. The three of them turned back to their respective briefs for the day. Jennifer stared at the screen, elated. She had experienced a tiny chink of normality in her broken life, and it warmed her.

JOSH

Hut 3 was warmer than Hut 4 because of the heat generated by the equipment stacked up along the walls. When the weather was cold Josh spent as much time tinkering in Hut 3 as he could.

It did not surprise him in any way that Dandridge had returned from his London trip apparently in some kind of relationship with Marion Crandall. It seemed to Josh from just a couple of days that Dandridge really liked her. She was smart and funny, and Josh had always suspected that Dandridge would bat for any side that would have him.

A couple of nights ago, in the early hours as he had slept in his chair in Hut 3, he had been woken up by the sound of Dandridge's little car being started, idling for a minute and then driving away. He had dozed off again and in the morning Adler had gone too, taking his huge black SUV, practically the size of one of the huts, with him. Since then, Josh had monitored things alone, a condition he didn't like much but was fast getting used to. Dandridge and Crandall had not reappeared.

As Crandall's new soundfile played out on a loop, Josh kept to his own routine, eating his meals in the NAAFI with the base personnel where it was warm before showering and changing in the basic gym facilities and taking a long stroll back to the huts where he would stay until the following breakfast. On the evening of the third full day, he pulled on his jacket for a walk around the base, fantasising about a large slab of lasagne and chips with a token green salad, when out of habit he twisted the volume knob on the CUBESat to check the transmission. It was still there, and so was Crandall's version on the same frequency, one incoming, one outgoing.

As he was about to turn it down he shook his head once and paused. He had probably imagined it and went to turn it down again, but something made him pause until the whole original sequence had played out. And there it was, towards the very end of the sequence, a slight, almost infinitesimal variance. He slid his mobile phone out from his jeans pocket and dialled.

'What?' was the reply after a couple of rings.

'It's me,'

'I know it's you, your name comes up on the caller ID. 'Honeyball' it says here.'

'What are you up to?'

'Crandall and I are watching Grand Designs. Do you know she has never seen it?'

'Crazy. Good to know you're filling your hours with something worthwhile. Can you get over here, I might have something.'

An hour later, Dandridge sat in his beloved spine-preserving chair with Crandall standing next to him, listening intently to the signal. She had noticed it immediately, eyes closed, her head cocked to one side exactly after hearing the variance.

'Do you think this affects your response, Crandall?' Dandridge asked. Josh sighed inwardly. Two solid days of fucking and he was still calling the woman by her surname.

'No idea. I'll need some time to see if I can find any transcribed instances of that particular sound from our existing references and if it relates to my response sequence in any meaningful way. It probably doesn't, but I think we need to try. Josh, could you call Adler and let him know, please?'

'I already did.'

She and Dandridge swapped seats and she waved her hand abstractedly, dismissing them. They left her to it, stepping outside into the freezing air, stamping their feet and blowing warm air into cupped hands.

'Want to go to the NAAFI?' asked Josh. 'I was on my way there. The coffee is fine, if you don't mind instant. Clive cleans the proper machine at six. There'll probably be a few chaps around, nobody's in the air at the moment.'

'I guess so. It's too cold to wait out here.'

They climbed into his car and drove to the main building. Josh knew that the air base pilots and personnel were professional around Dandridge but didn't really know what to make of him. Their work in the huts was classified, and nobody except the Group Captain or his immediate staff were allowed to approach them, so there was naturally an element of scrutiny and interest whenever either of them ventured into the more populated parts of the base.

Dandridge parked in his usual space, which wasn't really a space at all, merely the area nearest to the main doors, and they made their way to the canteen. There were a few groups of uniformed personnel sitting around talking. It was the end of an unusually busy afternoon shift and so Clive had kept the proper coffee machine going. Dandridge would probably have preferred the instant but in deference to his companion ordered a cappuccino, while Josh didn't have to say a word to be presented with an extra hot soya vanilla latte.

'Even your coffee's gay,' remarked Dandridge as they sat down at a vacant corner table. Josh flipped him the bird and they sat in the warmth in companionable silence. A group of pilots dressed in green overalls sat at a table across from them, their legs stretched out into the aisle.

'Do you only call people by their surnames because of your time as a pilot?' asked Josh, noticing the last-name only name tags on the overalls. 'The Air Force does seem to be a surname-only kind of place.'

'I suppose,' Dandridge responded. 'Although there is another reason I prefer just my surname.'

'What?'

'I suppose now is as good a time as any. When I was a kid I always wanted to be an astronaut. Always. I lived it, breathed it. I spent my whole life working towards it. I was insufferable, from age - god, I don't know, four maybe, till I was a teenager. Rockets and spaceships, that's all I ever cared about. I was obsessed. To me, flying into space was the greatest thing a person could ever achieve. My dad was a cartoonist for a newspaper, a good one. Satirical, political stuff. Well, one afternoon when I was about six he created a daily strip for a national newspaper called-'

'Oh my god. Not really. You are fucking kidding me. *You* are *Little Dickie Dandridge?*' Josh burst out laughing and the pilots looked across at them. 'Of course! Little Dickie Dandridge, the boy who wanted to be a spaceman! I can't believe you never told me this before! I can't believe I never put this together!' He started laughing again.

'Sshh. Not so loud. I have spent a considerable amount of time trying to shake off the label, especially when I was a pilot. I didn't mind so much at the time, but now I would prefer to just be 'Dandridge', and not an excitable little cartoon boy running around his sitting room with a broken model rocket being chased around by a scruffy cartoon dog and breaking things every day.'

Josh couldn't hide his delight. He kept sniggering into his latte while Dandridge sat back looking resigned, but wearing a half-smile.

'So what happened? Why *did* you quit flying?' asked Josh.

'I didn't quit really. I did my tours in various sandy Middle East resorts then retired from active duty. I didn't really have the temperament to instruct. I developed something of a short fuse, so it was suggested that I fuck off and do something else.'

'PTSD?'

'Maybe, but I doubt it. I'm just too impatient. I'm better now I'm grounded for damn sure. I had my time, lived my dream. Now I have the huts.'

'Not exactly an F-15 though.'

'That's the US Air Force,' a man in green overalls said, standing by their table.

'Can we help you, Lieutenant Perron?' asked Dandridge as the tall man stood awkwardly for a moment. He had short black tussled hair that probably looked neater just after he had got out of bed and before he custom-tussled it, deep brown eyes and skin that indicated some kind of South American heritage, Brazil maybe. The airman was shuffling and looking at his feet.

'Yes. Excuse me for asking sir, but I wondered if everything was OK out there, in the huts. I figured you were involved, in some way. With the transmission, I mean.'

He spoke to Dandridge, but his eyes were on Josh. Dandridge stood up, scraping his chair back against the laminate wood floor with his knees.

'Everything is absolutely fine thank you Lt. Perron. Under control. Honeyball here knows all the details and can fill you in on the parts he is permitted to tell. Josh, I'm heading back. When you're ready.'

Dandridge pitched his empty coffee cup into the waste bin as he left. Perron stood for a few moments more until Josh motioned for him to sit, feeling slightly confused.

DANDRIDGE

Dandridge walked from the NAAFI out to the car. He unlocked the MG and climbed into the black leather driver's seat, feeling the usual pleasant buzz of anticipation before he turned the ignition key. The engine caught and he revved it gently. He twisted the heater dial to 'on' and the car began a vain attempt to demist the windscreen. There was no chance of it succeeding. He drove slowly back to the huts, squinting through the foggy glass, pulling up outside Hut 4. No sign of Adler or his ridiculous SUV.

He walked in as Marion was taking off the headphones.

'Did you get me a coffee?' she asked.

'No. You didn't ask for one.'

'I didn't know you were going. You didn't tell me.'

'So how do you know that's where we went?'

'Josh just texted me. He's getting me an Americano. You can be a selfish prick sometimes, you know that?'

'I can?'

'Yes. Anyway, how do you broadcast this? I have incorporated the new sound, but I'm not sure it's worth it.'

Dandridge hit 'shift' and the spacebar. Crandall's new sequence began to play out on a loop.

'I'm going back to London. I'm still only three pages into a twelve page Achumari manuscript.'

'OK.'

'OK. That's it? OK?'

'What do you want me to-'

'Oh I don't know, Dandridge, you work it out. I know we're not married or anything but maybe 'I'll drive you to the station in my tiny car' might be nice, after what we've been through.'

'I was going to offer-'

'Of course you were. Never mind, I'll get a taxi.'

'If you don't want me to drive you I can organise a car from the base.'

'I want you to insist on driving me because you'll, ooh I don't know, miss me a bit, maybe-?'

Before their conversation could escalate into an argument, they heard an engine approaching fast, and a car pulled up in an abrupt skid outside the door. Adler slammed the door open and pointed at Dandridge.

'You,' he said. 'come with me.'

ADLER

Ernest C. Adler's official Foreign Office job title was 'project manager', which as a cover story worked wonders in switching off people's interest on his rare social appearances. In reality, it only scratched the surface of the tasks he was engaged to perform. If a thing needed to get done, a decision made or result achieved, it was Adler that ensured it happened, using meticulous research and planning, talking to the right people and setting up pieces like dominoes before choosing the exact time to knock them all down.

He had prevented wars, rigged elections, passed laws, resolved disputes and brought down multi-million dollar industries and all from the shadows, always in the background, the proverbial ghost in the machine. Usually the individuals or parties concerned were not even aware they had been carefully stage-managed, manipulated and part of a wider strategy. His mind was constantly working out angles and solutions, searching out the facts and people to achieve his goal, however abstract or morally ambiguous.

When he received his latest brief from the Home Secretary he had done his research as usual. He had spent days investigating every possible avenue, becoming known on the blogs and talkbacks of all the amateur radio monitoring websites, following leads around the world in a Home Office Learjet 85, interviewing professional and amateur telecommunication experts and frequency managers at every level, from military and governmental right down to an old white-bearded Englishman called Albert Pepperfield listening to pulsed radar signals out of an RV in the Mojave desert. Eventually, a trail of breadcrumbs and a number of obscure online forums on extra-terrestrials lead him to Marion Crandall and her obsession with the strange recording that her ex-boyfriend had stumbled across.

Adler had tracked her down to her small office in the basement of the British Museum and had known immediately that she was the one to help him, although at the time he had no idea that her original recording and the new transmission appeared to be from the same source. When he introduced himself, she had spent hundreds of hours surrounded by scrolls and parchments and papers scrawled with hieroglyphs, symbols and letters, entirely consumed with working out what the transmission meant. Once he had found her, he needed to pair her with someone who understood patterns and frequencies and sound, preferably from the military to give the UK an official cache when and if they were successful.

He had initially contacted five RAF airbases, including RAF Wenham, and spoken with each of the commanding officers with regard to the best personnel to approach. Group Captain Frank James from Wenham had responded immediately and without hesitation, lifting the classified status from Dandridge's operation and furnishing Adler with the info he needed.

Now, three weeks later and after an urgent call with Captain James, Adler slammed open the door to Hut 3 and practically dragged Dandridge into the SUV.

'What the hell are you doing?' he protested.

'We found something,'

Adler steered the huge car directly over the runways and fields of the airbase towards the control tower, taking the most direct route between two rows of parked civilian freight aircraft and bouncing across Runway Two with a squeal of tyres in front of a Royal Air Force C-130 transport aircraft loudly taxiing and readying for take-off.

'Jesus, Adler, you can't do that!' yelled Dandridge, holding on for dear life as the vehicle forced it's way across the airfield, testing the manufacturer's claimed 4x4 ability for the very first time in its short life. But Adler ignored him and raced on until he slammed on the brakes and slid to a halt in the gravel underneath the control tower. They both ran up the stairs two at a time where the two ATC's on duty were staring at a green radar monitor, with Group Captain James standing between them.

'Dandridge,' said James, not looking up.

'Sir?'

'I want you to tell me what the fuck *that* is,' James pointed at something on the radar. It was extremely large, and moving towards them. The C-130 roared away over their heads, buzzing the tower far too close in protest at the black vehicle with which it had so very nearly collided. Adler ducked instinctively.

'I couldn't possibly say, sir. Looks big though.'

'I know it's big. Have you heard anything?'

'Not really, sir. The transmission did recently change, a minor variance in the signal, but only minutely.'

'Are you sure?'

'Yes, sir,' Dandridge looked insulted. 'We replied, but only about ten minutes ago.' He addressed the Air Traffic Controller in charge. 'How big is it, Captain?'

'As big as this base, more or less.'

'And it's heading here?'

'If it maintains trajectory.'

'How long?'

'Twenty minutes at current velocity, holding steady, which indicates-'

'It's powered,' Dandridge finished.

There was a roar as four combat F-35 Lightnings took off and sped away.

'Whatever it is, keep a safe distance and do not engage,' murmured James, an instruction relayed by the ATC to the pilots. While the five of them stood and watched the shape blip closer to the centre of the black screen, and now joined by four new blips representing the fighter jets, the base was placed on full alert.

Adler and Dandridge could only watch as the huge

shape crept closer and closer. Both men had been willing to do their best with the strange transmission, obeying orders and instinctively happy to follow the trail to its logical conclusion but neither of them had actually and truly believed it was extra-terrestrial. The thought was too out-there, too fantastic to fully comprehend.

The radio reports from the four pilots were garbled and incomprehensible, mainly static. The ATC kept asking them to repeat.

Group Captain James had binoculars pressed to his eyes, staring upwards at the sky which was now full dark under almost complete cloud cover.

'I see something,' he announced, 'relay caution.'

'What do you see?' asked Adler, as the APC relayed a caution to the four Lightning pilots.

'A light. It's white. Bright white, I can just see it through the clouds, getting bigger. It looks like a... a... spider. A circle of white, with legs coming out from the body, trailing outwards from it. Maybe... ten legs. It's getting closer now.'

Dandridge and Adler stared upwards. There was definitely a light in the sky, a blurry white blob shining through the cloud cover. After a few more seconds they could see the blurry white tendrils emanating from the main body of the light. There was no noise or heat, but the air began to shimmer and vibrate around them, making it hard to look at. The airfield was illuminated in an eerie, ethereal, shimmering glow that got brighter and brighter as the object got closer and closer and the white spider filled their vision.

Then finally the low clouds burst open and all at once, without giving them any pause to gather their thoughts, and completely filling the sky, there it was.

JOSH

There appeared to be a giant glowing spider heading straight towards them. Josh and Marion were utterly rooted to the spot, unable to tear themselves away from the sight. Josh had dropped Marion's Americano and the hot coffee soaked through his shoe. He didn't notice.

As the shape got closer they could make out the white legs. Josh's heart began to pound in fear and he was sweating profusely through the cold. Then it burst through the clouds and stopped, hovering almost directly over them. Josh could see that the white spider was actually some kind of propulsion unit, a huge white not-quite circular glow with thousands of white threading tendrils emanating outwards along the underside of a much larger black structure. The glow from the strange spider-engine on the underside illuminated the entire airfield.

Above it loomed a tower at least as tall as a skyscraper, probably higher. Josh realised with a shock that it was at least as wide as the airfield. There seemed to be some kind of pointed section of the hull sticking out only a few feet away from the huts, outside which he and Marion were standing, awestruck. He began to wheeze and hyperventilate, his brain trying very hard to shut down.

The Lightnings screamed over them, circling the great machine whose descent had scattered the low clouds. Josh and Marion craned their necks up and realised that they couldn't make out where it ended.

'Should we be running away?' Josh whispered, 'Is it going to... you know... like in *War of the Worlds*?'

'I don't think running would do any good,' whispered Marion. 'If Orson Welles was right, then they have been preparing for this for a long time, plotting the invasion.'

'Who's Orson Welles? I was talking about the Tom Cruise film,' whispered Josh, not taking his eyes from the glowing blackness hanging over them.

The ship was hovering a hundred feet off the ground, rotating slightly but not looking all that steady in the mid-air. There was a low, constant rumble and the air seemed to vibrate around them. There was no heat but the whole thing gave off a strange mirage-like shimmer.

His eyes were slowly getting used to the black shape, adjusting slowly to the variances in darkness. Then he saw something appear on the side, something bright white, standing out clearly against the unbroken darkness. It had a distinct shape, humanoid. A creature. An alien. Josh's mind once again slammed to a halt.

Then the low rumble became louder, and the visible shimmer emanating from the ship became almost unbearable to look at. Both he and Marion distinctly heard a noise, possibly an explosion, somewhere in the bowels of the ship, and the black shape lurched downwards as if it was on strings and one side had been cut. The whole thing slid sideways through the air, the lowest point pulling up and stopping slightly just a few feet from the ground, above one of the runways. The figure on the edge of the machine toppled. It seemed to fall, stumbling and sliding uncontrollably towards the edge, before somehow finding its feet and running upwards towards its original position against the side of the ship. The figure was far too high up for Josh to make it out clearly or to see what it was doing.

MARION

If she was being honest, her eyesight wasn't that great. She wore glasses to drive and to lecture but was too vain to wear them all the time. She had left them in Dandridge's MG, but she couldn't bring herself to stop looking at the impossible black shape in front of her to fetch them. She was squinting to see the figure that Josh was claiming he could see, but it was no use.

Then there was a second explosion, much louder than the first and followed by a sudden rush of intense heat, the shimmering mirage surrounding the ship making her head swim. Josh pulled her to the ground and threw himself on top of her, *whumphing* the air from her lungs.

She squinted out from underneath him and saw flames. The fire lit up a section of the side of the great ship, which even she could now see clearly enough.

Then it seemed to just collapse out of the air, its final strings cut, and she felt the ground shake as it fell the last few feet and hit the base.

The whole world around them vanished as the huge ship impacted with the earth and sunk hundreds of feet into the ground like a gigantic fencepost. A vast, dense cloud of earth and gravel and dirt was kicked up by the weight of it, and Marion hid her face underneath Josh as they were both enveloped by the cloud. She couldn't open her eyes and there was too much dirt in the air to be able to breathe. She felt herself being pulled to her feet, and Josh propelled her into Hut 3 and slammed the door. There was air, thick with dust. The back of Josh's shirt was torn open, his back covered with blood. Marion stared at him in horror.

'Josh! You're hurt!' was the only cliché she found to say.

'I'm OK. I think a shard or fragment or something from the explosion cut me.'

'It looks deep. Do you have a first aid kit, a sheet, or a blanket or something we could use to stop the bleeding?'

'No. Only my coat, but it's GoreTex. It repels liquid.'

'Great. There's a blanket in the car we can use. Lie down, stay here.'

Before Josh could protest she flung the door open. The dust and dirt was thick and impenetrable and the air still shimmering, but she ran outside to Dandridge's parking spot with the crook of her elbow protectively covering her mouth and nose.

The car was in flames, a large chunk of alien spacecraft sticking straight out of it like a dagger.

Her heart sank. 'Shit. He is not going to like this.'

She ran back to Josh and checked her phone. No signal.

'How do you feel, Josh?'

'A bit woozy.'

The remains of Josh's shirt was soaked with blood. She sighed. 'Oh crap.'

She took off her own shirt and pressed it against Josh's back. She wasn't wearing a bra, and Josh laughed.

'Hey.'

'Oh god, no, I wasn't laughing at you, you have absolutely lovely breasts. I was laughing at the fact you might be meeting a new alien species today, without a shirt on.'

'Aliens I can cope with. Men, that's something else.'

She pressed the thin material over the laceration across Josh's back.

She checked her phone. Still no signal. At least a mile away, between her and Josh and any kind of medical help sat a vast alien spacecraft. She wasn't quite sure what to do.

Then one of the receivers in the huts gave out a burst of static, then a gratifyingly familiar voice. *'Everyone still alive over there?'*

ADLER

Adler stood up, blood trickling down his forehead into his eyes. He wiped the blood away. The landing had blown out every pane of glass of the bauble-shaped control tower. They had been thrown to the floor, scrabbling for cover as best they could. By some miracle they all seemed relatively unhurt.

Captain James was the first back on his feet. The others followed suit more slowly and gingerly, brushing broken glass from their clothes and hair until all five men were standing in a row, speechless, trying and failing to process the indisputable fact that they were staring at an alien vessel that looked larger and taller than any human built structure, and sitting right where the airbase used to be. Its landing had been abrupt and there was still dust, smoke and debris billowing up around it from where it had crashed into the earth. The control tower was just above the cloud level, but all the other buildings were invisible, either crushed or obscured.

Then the four Lightnings flashed past them with a scream of engines and a blinking of lights. The pilot's voices started to come through again, clear and static-free. They sounded panicked.

The ATC quickly got back on the radio. 'Valley 1, loud and clear, please report.'

'*Sir, the base. It's gone. All of it. There's nothing left, except you and the main building.*'

Dandridge grabbed a headset mic.

'Perron, what about the huts, can you see the huts?'

'*Affirmative, sir. Huts are intact. Your car might need some work though. Perimeter and outer buildings are still mostly intact. There are no runways operational, repeat, no runways operational.*'

Captain James took the radio. 'Valley 1-2, continue circling the object, repeat, continue circling the object, report any movement, but do not, repeat, do not engage.

Valley 3-4, divert to Kemble, repeat, divert to Kemble. Land immediately and await further.'

An ATC flicked a switch and relayed an instruction to Kemble Civilian Airfield to allow the two aircraft to land.

Dandridge fiddled with the instrument panel, cutting his fingers on the shattered glass.

'Everyone still alive out there?' he said into the mic.

Marion responded. Josh was hurt, badly.

'OK, we need to get someone out to him, but we don't know the full casualty count yet,' Captain James said, 'we can't risk spreading ourselves too thin.'

'The whole base has been spread rather thin, wouldn't you say?' Dandridge said, to a glance from James that could have frozen molten lava.

'I'll go,' said Adler, 'do you have a first aid kit?'

The ATC pointed at a large green plastic briefcase under one of the consoles. Adler grabbed it and took off down the stairs. He burst out from the door at the foot of the control tower and ran to his car, which was parked within six feet of the outermost tip of part of the alien vessel. The earth around the base of the ship had shifted and cracked like an earthquake and the car was half in and half out of a large crack in the ground, feet away from being completely crushed. Adler climbed in awkwardly and put it in reverse, flooring the accelerator. The vehicle spun its wheels in the mud, the engine roaring in protest. It slowly started to draw upwards and backwards before eventually bouncing down onto all four tyres. Adler shifted into 'drive' and put his foot down.

Somewhere underneath the alien ship every single aircraft which had been on the ground were completely gone. All the buildings on the furthest edges of the perimeter were still standing but with severe structural damage and shattered windows. Bouncing over the cracks and debris, Adler steered around the base of the huge craft, circling it till he got to the huts.

Crandall appeared to be topless. He registered no emotion as he helped her to clean, disinfect and dress Josh's wound with the basic first aid kit from the control tower.

'He needs a hospital.'

'I'll take him,' said Marion.

'No. Stay and meet the guests, if there are any and they don't vaporise us all,' said Josh, 'I'll live, at least for an hour or so. Adler, give her your jacket for Christ's sake. Go.'

Adler made sure Josh was as comfortable as possible for a man lying face down on a concrete floor before he and Marion, now buttoned up in Adler's dark jacket, stepped outside and faced the alien ship, the shimmer in the air now evaporated. He walked right up to the dark hull, to what seemed like a huge looming prow or a point of some sort. He reached out and touched it. Nothing happened. It was silent and cold and metallic.

DANDRIDGE

At almost exactly the same time as Adler, Dandridge was ignoring Group Captain James orders and had approached the vessel. He was also approaching a prow of some kind, sticking out towards them. He touched it gingerly but felt the same as Adler, cold and metallic. He stood back.

'So,' he thought out loud, 'what now?'

'What the fuck have you done, Dandridge?' asked Captain James, staring upwards. 'It's highly likely you have just killed us all.'

'Possibly, but I'm rather hoping it's quick so nobody can resent me for too long.'

They heard a metallic, echoe-y clanking sound and an object bounced off the prow in front of them and landed in the dirt at their feet.

They stared, apparently not quite having used up their capacity for being dumbfounded. It was a ladder made of thick, flexible metal wire rope.

'Well,' said James, 'it seems advanced alien technology hasn't yet come up with something that works as reliably as a rope ladder.'

They all looked up and against the black sky they could just make out a white object beginning a long descent down the ladder. It was at least forty stories up.

They could hear helicopters.

'The press are here already,' Dandridge said, 'so whatever that thing is, we need to protect it from too much prying, at least until we are sure of its intentions. Get Perron to keep them as far away as he can. Clear out the main buildings, evacuate them all. We can take it into your office.'

'Take it into my office? And then what, offer it a cup of tea? Dandridge, what about protection, security? It could be here to-'

'Captain, this isn't Independence Day. This ship clearly

just crashed. There is a creature descending from a fucking rope ladder. Chances are, they are helpless.'

The Group Captain sprinted to the main buildings, in front of which a small crowd of on-duty personnel had gathered. He began shouting orders and they scattered, relieved to have something tangible with which to occupy themselves.

The two ATC were back inside the tower and on the radio, issuing warnings and setting up a no-fly zone around the airbase. Dandridge watched as the two remaining Lightnings flew a little way off and buzzed the press helicopters, who seemed to take the direct hint to stay at a distance. Two fully armed combat aircraft controlled by confused and jumpy pilots shouting at them would pretty much ensure complete obedience.

Then he was on his own, staring up at the white creature on the ladder. His heart began to thump. He realised he was absolutely terrified. Not believing in aliens was a lot more difficult when you were staring at one descending a ladder right in front of you. It would appear that he was going to make first contact. He made a mental note to cross it off his bucket list.

It was ten storeys lower down, and getting closer, step by step.

Dandridge could sense movement behind him and knew that Captain James was corralling a small force of some kind, but he couldn't lower his head or take his eyes off the descending figure.

As it got close to the ground, Dandridge stepped back to allow it to descend unimpeded. He found himself in front of a small greeting party comprising Group Captain James and about ten young RAF pilots, armed and gawping in disbelief.

Twenty steps. Ten. Five. Two. One.

It stepped, slightly awkwardly, from the last rung of the ladder and turned to face them. A humanoid creature - two legs, feet, arms, hands and a head. The head was squarish in shape but proportionally much the same dimensions as a human.

It was wearing no clothes or garments. Its skin was textured slightly like leather, but bright gleaming white, except for a series of intricate dark blue markings running from the top of its featureless face and down across it's shoulders to the groin region, smooth like a Ken doll. It stood unmoving, facing the small group, hands at its sides. The head had no features at all - no eyes, ears, nose or mouth. Dandridge wondered how they were going to communicate.

He stepped forward and held out his hand. The alien creature stepped forward and took it. They shook. The hand was dry and warm, the grip firm. Dandridge felt a jolt of joy and wonder.

He stepped back again, and they stood, facing each other again for a few seconds. Then James stepped forward and he also shook the alien hand, smiling broadly in spite of himself. He indicated the main building behind him and the three of them - Dandridge, James and an alien creature, trailed by a dozen airmen carrying small arms, walked across the car park and through the front door.

ADLER

The white alien with dark blue markings stepped off the wire rope ladder in front of Marion and Adler, who for the first time in a very long time, had not a single idea what to do next. In the end, Marion did what Dandridge was doing at almost the same moment on the far side of the ship, and held her hand out. The alien reached out and took it. They shook.

'We need to get to the main building. To the Captain and Dandridge,' said Adler. He pointed at the SUV and the alien turned to face the vehicle. As the head didn't seem to have any eyes or visible external features Adler just presumed it could see, somehow.

'What about Josh?' asked Marion.

'You stay here with him. I'll send a medic back as soon as I get there.'

Adler opened the door, and the white alien with the blue markings climbed in obediently, shifting its backside on the leather seat.

'This is going to be a strange drive,' Adler remarked to Marion as he ran around the front of the car and opened the driver's door.

He turned the key and the large engine burbled into life. Adler noticed the silent alien gripping the seat as the engine started. He aimed a smile towards the blank face, he hoped reassuringly, and started driving back around the alien ship towards the main admin building.

In order to skirt around the crashed ship, he was driving at the very edge of the airbase perimeter. As he rounded yet another point of the ship he skidded to a halt as twelve large SUV's virtually identical to his own but with dashboard mounted sirens and lights were coming towards him the other way. The silent alien instinctively placed his white hands on the dashboard to steady himself. Some men in dark suits, also identical to Adler's own, climbed out, crouching behind the open doors, guns drawn and aimed at them both from between the car and the open door.

The alien sat passively in his passenger seat. Adler got out.

'Guys...'

'Out of the car!' one of them shouted.

'We need to get our visitor to the main building. For his protection.'

'On your knees.'

'Actually son, I think that I need to drive him to the main building. Please lower your gun. I have no idea what this creature's intentions are but it has shown no hostility. We need to take it somewhere safe and-' Adler looked up, to where he could just hear a helicopter, '-away from prying eyes. My name is Ernest C. Adler, I work for the Foreign Office and I have the authority in this situation. I am reaching for my identification,' Adler reached into his pocket and saw the two dozen men tense up. Then he realised that Marion was wearing his coat.

'OK, it appears that my colleague is wearing my jacket,' Adler gritted his teeth in annoyance. 'OK,' he said, 'I have no ID on me. Will one of you gentlemen kindly let me know what the protocol is for contact with an alien species? Anyone? We are in a unique situation here and I need to get this alien to the main building right away. So unless anyone has the slightest idea what you actually intend to do when you have shot me and taken the creature into custody you need to let me past.' There was silence. 'I'm just going to get back into my car now and drive to the main building. Please let me through and follow me, or shoot me now. Up to you.'

Thirty seconds later, Adler was leading a convoy of identical black Cadillac Escalades around the giant crashed ship towards the main buildings, the alien sitting passively next to him. There was a small crowd outside. Group Captain James had evacuated the building and apparently nobody quite knew what to do next. The crowd parted to let the convoy through and they all stared in the tinted window. They parked in a semi-circle around the entrance. Adler hopped out and ran around the side to open the door. He led the alien out, and up the stairs towards the office, followed by three of the dark suited men. The door was open.

'Ah, Adler,' said Dandridge. 'Brought some friends along, I see. Didn't take the goon squad long to turn up. They want to kidnap our new friends and dissect them, I assume?'

The alien sat in a chair in front of the desk, James and Dandridge on either side of it. A cup of tea in an RAF mug sat steaming on the desk. The second alien stepped in and stood next to the other, who stood in greeting. Their sizes, dimensions and whiteness of their skin were identical, but the blue markings running down the bodies looked quite different.

'Did you bring Crandall?'

'No.'

'Why the hell not? She's the only one who might stand a chance of communicating with them. Jeez, Adler.'

'Sorry. I must not be thinking properly. Can't imagine why.'

He turned to one of the suited men. 'Please organise an ambulance to the huts at the rear of this airbase, there is a severely injured man inside one of them. Stay with him at the hospital until relieved. Send the woman, Marion Crandall, back here in your own vehicle as quickly as possible. Do it right now.'

'Did you say severely injured?' Dandridge asked.

'Yes, he got cut across his back. Looks pretty nasty. He was protecting Crandall from the landing.'

'I'll go,' Dandridge said to Adler's man and bounded down the stairs without a backward glance. Adler noticed the two aliens seem to turn towards each other, for a fraction of a second.

'This is not at all what I imagined first contact with an alien species would be like,' he remarked to Group Captain James in the silent office, a silence broken only by the two aircraft still buzzing around the alien vessel.

'Me either.'

DANDRIDGE

Josh lay on his front in the military ambulance with Dandridge sitting alongside him while a paramedic tended his cut. He hissed.

'Don't be such a pussy, Josh.'

'Why are you here, Dandridge?' Josh said irritably, his teeth clenched against the pain. 'Why aren't you with the aliens?'

'They don't need me.'

'What do you mean, they don't need you? You've spent your whole life listening. Listening for something. Everything. Anything interesting, anything unusual. Today is the most incredible, world-changing day in the whole history of the planet. You are right in the middle of it and yet you're here sitting next to me.'

'I just think that my job in the whole thing is finished. Our job. You know?'

'Not really.'

'We were there to monitor things. To listen. We monitored. We listened. We got the job done. The meet and greet, the communication, the politics, decisions. It's out of our hands now. I don't want to be involved any more. Adler's got it now. And Crandall. Plus, I'd rather be here with you.'

'Your attention span is shorter than I thought.'

Dandridge smiled. Travelling in the opposite direction to them, towards the airbase that now lay beneath a crashed alien ship of uncertain intention, thousands of vehicles, some military, most civilian and a lot of press, were lining the road. A lot of headlights travelling against them, a desperate scramble to get as close as they could to the ship. Cars and vans were coming the other way, recklessly overtaking each other in their haste, using both lanes and swerving in and out of the traffic.

The ambulance driver was forced to steer the olive green

Land Rover Ambulance into the ditch to avoid cars speeding the other way. It bounced and jumped across the rough terrain and Josh grit his teeth in pain as he was nearly thrown from the gurney. Dandridge held his hand and steadied him as best he could as the vehicle was forced to manoeuver around trees and debris in the shallow ditch.

A mud-caked red Dacia Duster filled with cheering people was coming the other way, headlights on full, overtaking the queue of traffic driving on the correct side of the road. A white transit van with satellite dishes on its roof and the word "NewsNet' stamped loudly on the side pulled out of the traffic queue to do some overtaking of its own. It pulled out just as the red Dacia was alongside. The driver was forced to evade a collision by swerving into the ditch, right into the path of the green Air Force Ambulance coming the other way. The two vehicles collided with an almighty crash.

MIKE

The world was ending. That was what all the newspapers and the countless experts in various fields of expertise on the television kept saying, over and over and over, as the first dawn broke over a new planet, a new world. A world where the number of species living on earth had actually risen for the first time in about a billion years. All eyes were on a couple of fields in Gloucestershire in England, where the world waited to hear some new detail, any detail, about the visitors.

Mike Hennessy could not give a single shit about contact with aliens. His life had begun to unravel much faster than he would have thought possible. His days were almost entirely spent surviving from one drink to the next. Having his own office helped this enormously and he made sure he always had a supply of Vodka stashed in any number of imaginative hiding places around him. He was more of a scotch man, preferring the deeper, smokier burn when it hit his system, but vodka ultimately had the same effect and didn't leave such a trace on his breath.

As ever, it was the meetings that plagued him. They were hard to avoid. There were the long client meetings where he couldn't easily slip away without offending anyone, or the board meetings where he needed to excuse himself three or four times for the toilet because he could feel the muscles in his left eye twitching and his legs were so restless he had to blame the Underground line running under the office when people started to look at him strangely.

If he had a buzz on, he could fire on nearly all his cylinders. Clients naturally liked his reassuring demeanour and his leadership style; stern, commanding and approachable all at the same time, but always truthful and upfront, no bullshit. The other partners sought his opinion, the junior lawyers relied on his knowledge and guidance.

Even during the slower, coming down headache-y phase he knew he could operate at a relatively normal level. It was after the buzz had gone and the headache transmuted from a low throb to an insistent pinch behind his left eye, when his hands shook and he couldn't find the right words or remember people's names. Then gradually his demeanour would slip, his approachableness would fall away. It felt like the points had been switched in his internal railway. All his power and energy diverted into coming up with ways he could get to the next drink. The points were switching faster each day, the length of time he could cope between drinks getting shorter and shorter.

He had taken to sitting in the filthy shit-stained toilet cubicle on his train to work so he could keep himself topped up right to the last minute, ignoring the irate commuters in desperate need of a morning-after-a-work-do wee banging on the door. He would book lunchtime meetings with clients in bars so he could more easily disguise his drinking.

And then there was Joy, who he still loved but couldn't spend any time with, because she was the sort of person who could open a bottle of red and only have one glass to save the rest for the next day, which was utterly inconceivable to Mike who could easily do two or three bottles in one evening.

They were still together but as with everything else around him he was only vaguely aware of her growing detachment. He had virtually moved in to the spare room and barely saw her in the mornings as he showered and numbly prepared for his commute. When he did see her he was bleary eyed and impatient to be out of the house. He simply didn't notice her spending more and more of her own evenings out of the house, didn't notice on the few occasions she hadn't even come home.

And then the aliens came, and everything changed.

Mike came round slowly in his office in the very early

morning of the first day, Day One, lifting his head groggily from the piece of paper to which he was stuck by a mixture of photocopier ink and drool. The thin blinds across the floor-to-ceiling windows looked nice but were ineffective at actually preventing light from getting in, and it was too bright for him to remain unconscious.

Mike glanced at his watch. Ten past five in the morning. He got to his feet, smelling his own fox breath, and headed to the gym in the basement of the building for a shower, hoping he'd left some clean underwear and toothpaste in his locker. There was nobody around, which was to be expected at this hour, but he was surprised that there was no security at reception, and surprise turned to anger when his security card wouldn't work on the door to the gym. The desk was empty and nobody was around to help him, so he went back to the toilets on his floor and washed up awkwardly, using wet paper towels on his armpits and crotch and brushing his teeth and tongue with his finger.

He went back to his computer and booted it up, idly flicking through his usual websites; the Times Online, the BBC, the Guardian and the MailOnline.

Today however there was only one story on all of them. He flicked from site to site, his eyes bugging out of his head, which was pounding from something other than the booze for a change. He simply couldn't believe the pictures and reports, the sight of the vast black alien ship resting in a field somewhere in Gloucestershire, the chatter, the excitement, the terror, the confusion he was reading. At first he thought it might be a hoax, a joke being played on him, but he realised that to completely take over the internet in this way was unlikely.

A phone rang outside his office, somewhere in the open plan area. It wasn't quite seven o'clock in the morning. The phone rang, then stopped, then rang again, then stopped. Then rang again. Then another phone rang, and another and another. Mike closed the door to his office and kept reading.

By ten o'clock, the office was still absolutely deserted. Not a soul was present and the streets of London outside his window looked deserted too. It was eerie, the lack of noise. The alien arrival had stopped the world absolutely cold. Mike swigged from a bottle of vodka, swilling it round his mouth and swallowing it gratefully as he opened another news website.

The phones on the other side of his office door were still ringing and he realised that he may well be the only one in the office today. He ran down the corridor to the switchboard, unmanned for the first time that he could remember, and forwarded all the incoming lines to the main boardroom. The large room was dominated by a long, teak table upon which sat a single telephone.

One by one the twelve small yellow lights blinked on as calls to the switchboard were diverted to all the incoming lines the boardroom handset could handle.

Mike Hennessy, all thoughts of aliens slipping from his mind, took a large gulp of vodka and closed his hand around the receiver and picked it up.

For three days straight the phones rang off the hook. The twelve little lights on the black plastic handset were rarely dark. Panicked clients, suffering a colossal mental readjustment, trying to come to terms with life on a planet now inhabited by other beings, other lifeforms whose intentions were unclear. The clients of BH&W, together with the rest of the world, had just had their whole existence knocked out of alignment and for a lot of them their first port of call wasn't family or friends or partners - it was their lawyer, an attempt to assert control and normality on a life that they weren't sure was ever going to be the same again, desperately trying to ensure that whatever catastrophe might befall the planet, at least their effects and titles and responsibilities and businesses and relationships and positions were intact, covered, protected, for whatever it might be worth in the new world.

Mike spent the first four days completely alone in the office. He didn't see a single soul, although as the days progressed the activity outside the office window became busier and busier, and not in a good way. He felt too scared to go down to the lobby. There were fires burning in the streets and in a few of the surrounding buildings. Shattered glass seemed to be everywhere. The shock and numbness that had paralysed the country after that first day had turned into something else, something uglier and primal. The internet told him that a lot of the capital and most other major cities and towns were being trashed, looted and burned as the population panicked, stockpiling food as well as stealing anything and everything they could from everywhere that had a smashable frontage, as if the key to surviving an alien invasion was by owning the largest TV possible.

The shouting and screaming crowds beneath his window was unrelenting, but Mike didn't care about any of it. He worked as hard as he ever had in his life, doing what he did best, and he loved every second of it. He was drunk the entire time. After his own vodka supply had dried up, he started in on the company bar, which was conveniently located next to the boardroom. He answered call after call after call, his laptop open in front of him, pulling up files and notes and information, surrounding himself with boxes of case notes, dispensing advice and counsel, calming and expertly guiding and assisting the wealthy, terrified clients of BH&W through the worst upheaval the world had ever known.

He was confident, considered and reassuring. Even though his vision occasionally cut in and out as he switched from the laptop to paper records, he didn't slur and his advice was sound and honest, honed from years of training and practice. He didn't forget a single name, case or history.

As the world spiralled into complete chaos around him

Mike Hennessy barricaded himself in and did his job, the best he had ever done it. He wasn't to know it at the time but he single-handedly ensured the future of BH&W as word spread that they were the only legal firm answering calls.

Very early on the morning of the fourth day since he had first picked up the phone, two senior partners of BH&W risked a lull in the violence that was still afflicting the streets of London and picked their way through the debris to their office. Official warnings had advised travelling in pairs for safety. They walked in past the reception and immediately noticed a rank smell. They followed their noses to the boardroom and found Mike snoring underneath the boardroom table. The room stank of shit and vomit and acrid sweat. He was naked, faeces smeared over his buttocks and down the backs of his legs, piles of reddish mucus-y vomit in the corners of the room. The table was piled high with boxes of legal papers and documents, some spattered and smeared with shit and urine. Twenty or more empty bottles of various spirits were scattered around the room. More papers covered the floor, most in neat piles, but all of them drenched, smeared or covered in a lot more than ink.

As the two men stared in horror at the devastation in front of them, Mike's bladder released in his sleep and he pissed hot, foul-smelling urine over his thighs and onto the floor. He didn't stir.

The partners beat a hasty retreat, returning a day later armed with four members of a private security firm who dragged a barely conscious and unprotesting Mike into a van where he was taken to a police station and dumped into their bulging holding cells. The cells were filled with souls who had lost control of their senses as soon as the aliens had landed, as inconceivable had turned into conceivable, the unimaginable into imaginable and science fiction into cold, unimpeachable fact.

Mike was in the cell for seven hours, his body twisted around itself in agony, retching and shivering and sweating and clenching, desperately craving the one thing it couldn't have. One of the senior partners had given the police a brief statement and they called Joy, who had no idea where her husband had been for the last four days. Alone and terrified, she had barricaded herself into their house as best she could, piling all the furniture they possessed in front of doors and windows as their street was ransacked by desperate people who had lost the logical and orderly centre of their world. The house was set back from the road slightly further than the others and she had escaped the worst of it. Other homes on her street, friends and neighbours with children, had not fared so well.

Joy came and bailed out her husband, who didn't seem to recognise her and couldn't look her in the eyes. She took him home and Mike locked himself in the spare room, downing half a bottle of scotch in one long gulp as she wept on the other side of the locked door.

ROYCE

Royce stared at the boy standing in front of him, sizing him up. Thomas Mabbett was eleven, a year older than Royce. Other differences included: white skin, blue eyes, excessive hairgel, rich parents, bloody nose and split lip. Royce punched him again. Mabbett sat down fast, holding his cheek. He looked like he was about to cry, but there was a crowd surrounding them and he managed to hold it back.

'Fine,' he shouted, 'you win.'

His friends helped him up. They stood facing each other like boxers at a weigh-in, nose to bloody nose, Royce's flat and wide, Mabbett's freckled and upturned. Then they shook hands solemnly. Thomas Mabbett announced to the crowd, 'Royce is alright,' then the group of them walked away and most of the crowd dispersed, pre-adolescent blood-lust now sated. Royce couldn't help thinking that he had won the battle but somehow lost the war.

Royce and his three mates Carl, Kai and Brendan stayed in the park for a while idly swinging on the swings until the mother of a toddler bustled up and demanded they leave so her kid could have a turn.

'Fuck the park,' said Royce, 'it's full of fucking kids. Let's get out of here.'

They wandered out of the safety gate and up the short path to the high street. It was a Tuesday morning, bright and clear and their school was still closed. They emerged onto the high street where nearly all the shops were still shut and boarded up. Some had smashed windows and blackened insides. Some were unburnt but emptied of whatever product they had been selling prior to the madness. The boys turned the corner to find their favourite spot to hangout was still closed, a fried chicken shop whose name optimistically offered 'Ultimate Fried Chicken'.

'This is so *stupid*,' said Royce. 'Fucking aliens. What's so special? I swear, this is the first time Mum's let me out of the house for four days,' and then for effect, 'fucking Thomas fucking Mabbett.'

The four of them ambled along the high street, checking their phones.

'Mum sent me a message,' said Carl, 'school is definitely back on tomorrow.'

'Fucking aliens,' said Brendan.

They walked past WHSmiths, the only shop on the high street magically untouched and still trading, as if the stationery institution was somehow too sacred to ransack. The window displays were covered in offers for two-for-one deals on DVDs of *Independence Day, War of the Worlds, Paul, They Live, The Day the Earth Stood Still, Predator* and other similar films with an alien theme.

There were pictures and posters selling images of alien books, greeting cards, plushies, calendars, stationery. A previously obscure erotic novel that featured explicit human-alien intercourse between a hunky astronaut explorer and a beautiful green-skinned Amazonian-looking alien female with three heads and two vaginas had shot to number one in the bestseller lists. There was a large poster of the two of them rendered in CG with their arms around each other as the hunky astronaut explorer locked lips with one of the alien's three heads while the other two looked on longingly, awaiting their turn. The three boys stopped and stared at the green-skinned, three-headed but still scantily clad and recognisably curvaceous body on the poster.

'Man, that's some sick shit,' said Carl.

They walked on. Royce started to rap.

'Motherfucking aliens, landing on our shit, they think they wanna rule our world, but they ain't got no dicks,'

The others laughed and encouraged, Royce carried on.

'We gonna mess them up they come over my street,
Fuck them up they want to walk on my beat
Don't care if you come in peace,
you gonna be turfed out in pieces, bitch.'

The four of them laughed hysterically as they carried on along the high street towards McDonalds on the corner. Kai picked up from Royce.

'What you mean, you gonna turf them out?
You gonna shit your pants real good
Motherfuckers be about your neighbourhood,'

Royce scowled, his thunder slightly stolen as Carl and Brendan laughed and egged him on for a reply. Harried looking parents ushered their smaller children away from the four boys laughing and shouting their way down the street.

'Ain't no way they getting away with nothing but tongue,
when they come round I gonna get me a gun
and give them a chase
all the way back to motherfuckin' space,
What you gonna do, Kai, lay down and die?'

The others hooted, except for Kai, who looked pissed off.

'Ain't nobody here be doing no dyin' Royce,
We all got a choice,
except your mother,
when she lies right down and lets an alien fuck her.'

Royce fired right back. *'No alien gonna get close to my mother,*
when they all be round your house,
beatin' on ya, just like your father.'

The group fell silent.

'See you guys around,' Kai said and ran off back the way they had come, glancing at the three-headed alien chick as he went.

'What the fuck Royce?' Brendan said at Royce as they reached McDonalds, which was also still open despite most of the windows being smashed and boarded up.

Royce said nothing, just turned the rap over and over in his head.

PART TWO

ADLER

He had done his job and done it well. The call was answered, the transmissions ceased. The UK government was crowing and in a field in England sat a vast alien spacecraft of unknown intent. Their intentions however, short of running for his life if necessary, were not Ernest C. Adler's concern.

Marion Crandall had stepped up as he had known she would. A linguistic Professor's dream he supposed - a completely new language to learn and understand. The government goons that had arrived so shortly after the alien's arrival had taken over from Group Captain James and cordoned off the whole airbase, set up a perimeter, banned the press and restricted the main RAF building to be the sole point of access and contact for any interaction with the visitors. Within a day the entire red brick building was covered in a huge opaque tent and connected via a round opaque tube to a large portable quarantine portacabin which was the middle link in an enclosed chain, connected on the opposite end by another round tube that lead to a new, sealed, ground level opening cut into the side of the alien vessel.

Adler had not even known that portable quarantine buildings even existed, but apparently they did, this one arriving on a giant flatbed truck within four hours, set up and sealed off within five and manned within six.

Once the area was contained and the perimeter set, Adler's job was finished. He slipped away back to his flat on the Brighton seafront and arrived there just in time.

Production and supply chains stopped completely. His flat was always stocked up with long-life and canned food due to his nomadic lifestyle, so he was more prepared than most during the fortnight of catastrophic, panicked rioting and frenzied looting that followed Day One. He barricaded himself in and waited it out, monitoring the world online and on television.

He watched as at least four reported events of mass, organised suicide were revealed, in the UK, America and Japan. The reasons were unclear but thousands of people were dead; poisoned, shot or hanged. One incident happened under the guise of sacrifice to the alien race, a gesture designed to demonstrate complete obedience. Others seemed like desperate last measures before a perceived threat of attack and some claimed in scrawled notes that their minds had been taken over and were being forced to do it by the aliens. This sparked more protests that turned into more riots and violence.

These acts occurring over the course of just a few days triggered an emergency summit in London of all the world's most influential leaders. A day after that, the internet was shut down, suddenly and without warning. Adler was watching a news report and then his laptop screen flickered and was replaced by a blank screen and a flashing cursor. His modem still worked but no data was being received. His television package was reliant on a connection, and it all went dark at the same time. Mobile phones were affected too, but after a day or so texts and calls were reconnected, but mobile networks and wi-fi reliant chat functions and apps remained inoperative.

It seemed to Adler that this act took the wind out of the sails of the more extreme and paranoid activity. He admired the audacity. Citing the 'removal of free speech' the move sparked fresh protest demonstrations in London, which hadn't stopped burning for weeks, and other major cities around the world - but it worked. With the most comprehensive form of communication now denied, the world was shocked into settling down and working to recalibrate, to adjust.

Very shortly after he had begun venturing out into Brighton again, exploring his ransacked, burned town and queuing up with the rest for emergency supplies and rations, he got the call from Whitehall. He had known it was coming.

The world was too damaged. There was work to do.

MARION

It was the numbers that terrified her. She wasn't a numbers person, she was a words person. Numbers were a language that she had always struggled with, and the numbers that she was slowly beginning to understand from the aliens were very large indeed.

She had been virtually abandoned by everyone after Day One. The military assumed control of the site and she found herself working in a giant tent, and she hated camping. Every time she went for a pee, she was accompanied either by a black-suited government goon or an army escort, and every time she needed some air it took nearly three quarters of an hour and a naked disinfectant shower in front of a small crowd of silent goons in blank faceplated hazard suits.

However, it hadn't taken long before she was the defacto showrunner for the whole operation. The General in charge of all personnel on the site began deferring to her in all matters relating to the aliens and running only the quarantine zones. What was left of the RAF facility had relocated to the smaller Kemble Civilian Airbase.

She felt she had no choice but to block out the world burning around her and devote her attention fully to understanding the alien creature who hardly left what used to be Group Captain James' office.

Their form of communication had apparently been nipped, tucked and boiled down to the most basic of sounds, which to her ear were just clicks and abstract noises, some of which human vocal chords were not able to replicate. The first human word the alien seemed to say clearly and which had any meaning was a major breakthrough, and although the word was more like a sound, a hard click followed by a hum - to Marion it sounded like 'Kin', so that's what she named them.

Oblivious to the changes happening around them, they

spent all their days and most nights together, feeling a way past the language barrier. At times it felt like an insurmountable task, but they made progress. Slowly.

After a couple of weeks she had her head down, going over and over basic English phonics when a tap on her shoulder indicated that they had a visitor. She stood up, stretching her back, to face a group of people that included the Prime Minister, the US President and all their staff incongruously crammed into the small office.

The two of them shook hands with the Kin, who stood and spoke, using the few words they had learned. It's voice was low, smooth and inflectionless, emanating from the blank white and mottled blue head like it was coming out of a head-shaped bluetooth speaker. 'Thank you for your help' it said.

The two leaders had a lot of photographs taken and went on a tour of the perimeter of the vessel with Marion and two Kin in a jeep with selected press trailing behind them. They asked questions that the creature did not understand and could not reply. Marion assured them that they were working on communication and the Kin would answer all questions as soon as it was able.

When the whole entourage had returned to London to discuss 'next steps', Marion and the Kin went back to work as if nothing had interrupted them.

Later that day and needing some fresh air, Marion undressed in the quarantine area, ready for her daily hosing down by two men wearing hazard suits. As she took off her shirt, she caught the faint scent of the aftershave the US President had been wearing. She inhaled the smell of the most powerful man in the world for a brief second before the disinfectant hit her skin and utterly destroyed it.

She had tried to ignore it but the diplomatic visit made Marion more aware than ever before what was riding on her shoulders, and hers alone. Although the world had finally begun to calm down, the almost total lack of workable intelligence and information was beginning to create its own issues. Everything hinged on her and the Kin.

But the more the Kin could make itself understood to her the more alarmed she became. They had a breakthrough when the Kin finally understood the human interpretation of numbers. The numbers he gave Marion made her panic. That was the moment she knew she needed help.

She picked up the phone and three hours later, his hair wet from his first ever disinfectant shower, Adler walked in to the office.

'You'll get used to it,' she said to him.

'I hope not.'

The three of them sat down, two human and one humanoid, and she filled him in.

'Why 'Kin'?' he asked.

'It was the first word he said. Plus it sounds cool.'

'Fair enough. It's not every day you get to name an entirely new alien species.'

'Oh my god, I hadn't even thought of that. I just thought it sounded nice. I suppose I need to think of something more scientific.'

"No you don't. It's fine.'

Based on the numbers that had so panicked her, they started to make a list. Adler took a blank piece of white paper from Group Captain James' former printer and together they filled it with everything they thought they would require, under two headings, 'Knowledge' and 'Fulfilment'.

Under 'knowledge' they listed what they knew, which started with the numbers.

As far as they could work out there were four hundred Kin ships in a holding pattern some distance away from the earth, waiting for a signal to approach. Each ship contained about ten thousand Kin, give or take, which meant four million in total including the ones still contained in the vessel sitting outside their window.

They quickly filled four A4 sides with observations and ideas. They listed everything they could think of, no matter how random, oblique or strange. After a while, the paper was covered on both sides. Then they took each item and expounded it in granular detail onto more paper. Within a couple of days they had a thick sheaf of scrawled notes that Marion called a 'manifesto for the new world'. Adler took out his mobile phone, an older model that worked better as a telephone than his old smartphone which was now essentially a shiny paperweight. He dialled the Prime Minister.

An hour later, he and Marion were driving down to London in Adler's SUV, a Police escort blaring blues and twos and carving through the traffic. Marion was amazed at how fast they made it to London when speed limits were only for other people.

'Couldn't you have typed this out, Adler?' the Prime Minister asked as soon as he was handed their notes. He was sat with his back to an ornate fireplace and surrounded by advisors and senior members of the cabinet along the main briefing room table in Westminster. Marion reckoned there must have been thirty people in the room.

'My typing speed is woeful, Prime Minister.'

'I'm going to get this typed up.'

'Now? Shall we wait?'

'Yes.'

The whole manifesto document was handed over to a PA. Ten minutes later it appeared, typed and annotated on the large projector at the far end of the room. Adler hadn't even finished his coffee.

'You employ someone with impressive typing skills, Prime Minister.'

'Take us through this, please.'

So Adler had taken them through it, step by step – his and Marion's plans for the initial phases of an unprecedented, global-scale integration operation. The

Cabinet watched silently, all of them seemingly stunned by the volume of aliens still to arrive.

'How do you know that their intentions are peaceful?' one of them asked, a Northern Irish MP called Nile Cody.

'We don't.'

'I am sure you are aware that every single nuclear capable country have their missiles locked on us – on *you* specifically – for even the slightest twitch of... invasion I suppose, or any kind of evil intent from these creatures. And I mean every single one. Globally,' the PM told them.

'Comforting,' Adler replied, drily.

'There's nothing we can do about it and frankly I don't blame them. However, I have taken the step of-' the Prime Minister looked around at his advisors, all of whom were shaking their heads, '-oh sod it, he has to know. We've taken ours offline. All of them. Trident is gone, history. There's nowhere to point them at but you. And my wife's cousin lives in Gloucestershire. So you see. We need to be sure, Adler.'

'I understand sir. The life of your wife's cousin is at stake. But the signs are good. Marion and the Kin are breaking down the language barrier faster than you might imagine. The Kin has learnt fast. So far, only single words and short sentences. For what it's worth, I think the decision about Trident is the right one. It will send a global message of peace and good intent.'

'Leave the international diplomacy to us please. The numbers are greater than we thought. Four hundred of those massive ships. We're having enough trouble placing our own species around the world without having to find room for four million alien migrants. This is going to be a diplomatic minefield.'

'Of course, sir. From what we understand at this moment they left their own planet for reasons we are not yet entirely sure, and have been homeless for many years, moving through space looking for somewhere to live, sending out that signal for anyone who could find it and answer it. Although time apparently passes slightly differently for them.'

'Where are they from?'

'We don't know yet. A long way, so far that we haven't really got the words to describe the distance. Not yet anyway.'

'Do they reproduce? It's four million now, how many will they be in a year, two years?'

'We don't know,' Marion cut in, grateful to be able to contribute to the meeting, 'it sounds strange, but we haven't been able to make ourselves quite understood in that area, just yet.'

'It's a fairly important thing to know. We can't risk being overrun in a few years if they fuck like rabbits.'

There was a pause. 'OK, Adler,' he said finally.

'OK, sir?'

'Your manifesto is approved. We begin, and we begin today.'

'Are you sure, sir?' Nile Cody's Northern Irish accent cut through the shocked silence, 'you want to allow four million aliens onto this planet? We don't know their motives, their firepower, what they eat. We don't know anything.'

'They have no weapons, no guns. The Kin has no concept of such a device,' Marion said. 'They are obviously advanced, obviously intelligent, and I do believe that they just need our help.'

'They need help. Not necessarily *our* help,' Cody replied. 'They could be an army of some sort. Four million trained killers.'

'You're thinking about this the wrong way,' Marion replied. 'This is not entertainment. We have been conditioned to believe that fictionalised aliens simply want to kill and eat us. But this is real. Their ship crashed, they have stayed inside as requested until we can communicate with them. The other ships have stayed at a distance until contacted. This first Kin seems not to understand hostility in any way. Are we really going to turn down an entire species the chance for a new start simply because we've all watched too many Hollywood movies?'

'Adler?'

'What she said. I trust her. I don't feel any kind of threat within the creature.'

'OK, we move forward with your plan.'

'All of it?'

'Adler, it's the only plan we have. I am sending you back with ten Government staff, even the typist if you want him. You and Crandall choose who else will be most beneficial to you to implement the plan and we'll bring them in immediately. We'll review in a month, back here.'

And that was it. Work on the very first Site for Human and Alien Community had begun the next day. As Marion and the Kin worked tirelessly side by side to understand each other a small city grew up around them. More Kin were allowed outside for brief periods, accompanied by military in black hazmat suits, the blank faceplates making them look weirdly similar to the creatures they were escorting.

They built temporary housing blocks on the site and started a registration process. Human chaperones were brought in and trained.

Adler rolled up his sleeves and undertook the largest agile project management job ever attempted. He instigated a State of International Co-operation, vetting and co-ordinating Kin landing sites around the globe in every country that was remotely willing, capable and with the infrastructure to handle the required physical and financial pressure; England, America, Germany, Canada, France, Italy, Spain, Sweden, Norway, Saudi Arabia, Russia, Croatia, Switzerland. His team worked with Governments and Generals, Presidents, councils, businesses, landowners, lawyers, ensuring that the world was as prepared as it could be for the arrival of 399 alien ships and nearly four million new inhabitants.

There would eventually be four hundred of them, but the world's first Site for Human and Alien Communication and Kinship was completed two years later to the very day that Marion and Adler had received the go-ahead to implement their manifesto, which grew from its initial four page outline into a dense, seventy-two page manual.

Once a busy RAF airbase, the first SHACK became an ultra-modern, four-storey high and four-storey deep glass and chrome building with state of the art technology and research functionality, filled with the finest minds and intelligence Great Britain had to offer and terrific coffee facilities.

While the other Shacks around the world were being constructed, a landing plan was developed for all the ships. It took a further two years to land them all and each was met by leading representatives from each country, as well as Marion and Adler. None of them crashed. Temporary housing to accommodate the occupants of each were already built and in place, an agreed processing procedure for each individual alien, language experts lead by Marion Crandall, medical personnel, security.

English, by necessity, became their common language.

It took a long time, but in an absolutely unprecedented spirit of global collaboration and teamwork, planet Earth welcomed the Kin with open arms.

DANDRIDGE

At the point of collision with the oncoming Dacia he was flung sideways and forwards. At the same moment, the front of the vehicle was being concertina-ed towards him. He connected with the bulkhead between the driver and the passenger compartment which broke his back in two places. The gurney that Josh was strapped onto overturned and his left wrist snapped as he tried to break his fall.

Neither of the two drivers survived.

Thirty-two major traffic incidents were reported during the chaos of Day One within a five mile radius of RAF Wenham. The roads were jammed solid and there was no way an ambulance was going to get to them. Vehicles were still rushing past, desperate to get to the site and look at the alien ship. After five minutes, the surviving passengers from the Dacia flagged down a news van and two locals in a beige Ford Fiesta. They lifted Dandridge into the back of the van. He screamed until he passed out. Josh was loaded into the Fiesta and the passengers of the Dacia stayed with the wreckage and the two bodies, waiting for the police.

The convoy made its way slowly to the overwhelmed hospital, fighting against the flow of traffic.

Dandridge underwent surgery to repair his shattered vertebrae. He was strapped into a full body brace that completely immobilised him and pins were inserted into his back to hold the broken pieces together.

By the end of the first week, as he was slowly feeling his way through the fog of powerful pain medication, Dandridge finally switched on the television. It was wall-to-wall aerial footage of the alien skyscraper, towering into the Gloucestershire sunshine, 24/7 rolling comment, discussion, reflection, analysis. He had nothing to do but watch as the analysis became more frenzied and bizarre.

Rolling news channels had free reign to discuss every possible scenario, development and outcome with the input from members of the public eagerly chipping in from various social media sources. The experts called in to help the discussions became more and more unrelated to the story and even the more outlandish stories began to be reported in the following days newspapers as fact. Without solid evidence from Site One and despite calming statements from the Prime Minister and the US President, the posited scenarios became more and more heightened, more drastic and more serious, given relevance and weight by the news channels.

As the confusion and hysteria rose so did the violence. Society seemed to break apart, exacerbated by the news insistence on showing the worst of the violence, usually witness reports on camera phones, on a constant loop.

Twenty-first century first-world society had been built on fairly thin fabric and it hadn't taken much for fear and insecurity to rip it to shreds. Third-world countries, not beholden to vanity or wealth, but much more vulnerable to ancient cultural religious and gender divides had not coped well either. Every country in the world was suffering, fearful for the future and pushed to tipping point by speculation and wild fantasy, most of which ended in war, invasion and death.

During the third week the Prince of Wales was touring hospitals around the United Kingdom visiting victims of the riots and requested an audience with Dandridge. The Prince was to be accompanied by security, PR people, photographers and press, all of which Dandridge refused point blank. In the event, the Prince arrived as low key as a Prince of the realm could manage, accompanied only by his wife and security.

They watched news footage together on the TV above Dandridge's hospital bed. Aerial footage of Croydon being looted as the rioting carried on unabated. A bomb going off outside Downing Street killing five people. Another mass suicide, one hundred and fifty people in rural America.

'It's appalling,' said the Prince, 'and I don't know what the solution is, except to get rid of these damned aliens.'

'I think they're here to stay, sir,' Dandridge replied, 'and even if they did leave, our eyes have been opened. There's no going back. Aliens exist. It's a fact now. The conspiracy theorists and war-mongering would still be out there.'

'What do they want for heaven's sake?'

'I don't know. But my instinct, for what it's worth, is that they only want sanctuary. The transmission was a call for help. There are good people in there helping to communicate with them. Marion'll get the facts straight.'

'Ah yes, Marion Crandall, the human face of the alien visitors. Very photogenic. I'd like to visit her sometime but currently the security risks are too great.'

'I'll pass on the message. There's post-it notes around here somewhere. Josh could you-'

'I'm pretty sure I'll be able to remember to pass on a message from the Prince without help from a post-it reminder, Dandridge,' Josh replied.

'Are you two involved?' The Prince asked Dandridge.

'Me and Josh? No. We did have a ton of sex for a while, but not any more.'

'Oh right, well then.'

'Sorry, sir,' cut in Josh, 'he forgets himself sometimes.'

'That's OK, my boy,' said the Prince, looking at the TV screen. 'I think we've all forgotten who we are.'

The three of them watched the carnage on the television screen silently.

'You know what the problem is?' Dandridge said suddenly. 'It's the same issue we've had for years now, only before there were so many different things happening in the world that it never really became a problem. But now there's only one single thing happening, and it's destroying us.'

'So what's the problem?'

'It boils down to too much information and not enough

knowledge.'

'I agree, but there's nothing we can do about it.'

'There might be.'

Dandridge outlined his theory to the Prince who outlined it to the Queen, who outlined it to the Prime Minister, who outlined it to the US President and the UN. K8, an emergency summit of all the worlds leaders, was convened at the O2 in London, and after the inexplicably popular Emeli Sande had sung her hit *Read All About It*, they had all clamoured for the centre stage attention that they believed was their due and repeatedly asked questions to which nobody had any answers. But gradually they all agreed to Dandridge's idea. In the end, there wasn't really a choice. Whatever the alien species intentions might be, drastic action had to be taken or there wouldn't be a world left to invade.

So the President gave the order, and within half a day the whole of the world wide web went dark.

Dandridge was oblivious to the effect of his idea as it was put into practice. Reality changed around them again, the removal of the internet seeming almost more foreign and unbelievable to everyone as aliens landing in their backyard. He was released from hospital still unable to walk, his head feeling like a completely separate entity from the rest of him, trapped like a canary in a large metal cage that supported his back.

Josh stayed with him at his small grubby house while they recuperated. He had secondary surgery to remove the large pins and replace them with smaller metal clips to support the weakened and still-healing vertebrae. He underwent physiotherapy to get him back on his feet, re-training the slowly-knitting muscles and spine to respond to the correct inputs. Josh was with him every step of the way.

The process of recovery from a broken back was an extremely long, frustrating road and Dandridge had to take it step by excruciatingly painful step. He worked it out to about 70 percent painful to 30 percent frustrating, although the exact ratio could vary day by day. For a man so incapable of sitting still, despite his now utterly redundant orthopaedic chair, he bore it all with a resoluteness that Josh would not have believed. Dandridge concentrated his entire being on getting back on his feet, treating the accident and recovery as another challenge to overcome, another obsessive hobby to which he could dedicate his whole self.

The breakthrough came when he managed to walk across the whole floor of the physio gym, and he and Josh both wept with joy and relief.

They went home and celebrated with champagne and sex that he optimistically referred to as therapy.

When Josh opened his eyes the next morning, Dandridge had gone.

JENNIFER

London has always been an early morning city; opaque, unreal hours when ancient, rusting gears begin to turn unimaginably vast cogs and flywheels and levers, combobulating dawn into day. On Day One the city struggled to gain traction, the gears failing to make headway for the very first time since settlers arrived on the banks of the Thames thousands of years ago. Shops stayed shut, businesses closed and streets gathered dirt.

Jennifer was fairly oblivious to Day One, Day Two and most of Day Three, because of course she had taken James McDonald up on his offer of drinks that evening, the very evening that the aliens had first appeared, crash landing on top of an airbase in Gloucestershire. The usually painfully loud pub had been virtually silent as everyone present crowded around the single television screen to watch events unfold from the fuzzy footage. An exclusion zone had been enforced and so most of what could be seen through the clamouring press was indistinct, but even from a distance and on the pub TV's slightly smeared screen the alien ship looked huge. Jennifer stared in speechless awe with everyone else. It was not quite the evening she had been expecting.

At closing time the landlord turfed everyone out into the street, the crowd silently joining the stunned throngs moving through London. There was chatter from some people as yet blissfully unaware of the events happening just a couple of hours up the road, but in general the capital was dazed and numb and uncomprehending, as if their whole axis of existence had just been shifted.

Jennifer felt lost. She didn't want to go home, but she didn't want to be in London. For a while she thought she wanted to go to Gloucestershire and stare at the alien ship with her own eyes, a tribute to Stephen who would definitely have made the trip.

Instead, she found herself accepting a lift from James McDonald, who guided her to an older model but immaculate Audi A8 idling in the 'pickup only' space outside the Charing Cross Hotel.

He gave a short instruction to the driver and they drove for eighteen minutes to Bermondsey Road where he showed her in to a small, discreet pied-a-terre where they watched the television news all night, and her lost feeling melted away as they cuddled together for comfort. The impossible night turned into an impossible day and as the light came up Jennifer and James moved from the sofa to the bedroom, ignoring the fires and noise and chaos outside their four walls.

They stayed together for two whole weeks as the world burned, venturing out only to sortie for food, which was becoming scarce. Most shops and pubs had been looted and ransacked. The army guarded a number of supermarkets and food outlets across the city and they queued for hours and hours to get basic supplies, sometimes a loaf of bread, occasionally some bacon and one time a multipack of Walkers Plain Crisps, which soon became virtually impossible to eat.

'Fucking Gary Lineker,' James had observed as he opened a bag for breakfast.

During those first uncertain weeks, they had fallen completely in love, bound together by the new world they were experiencing and discovering together, and of course for the sex, which for Jennifer was a revelation. James was able to bring her to levels of passion and fulfilment that Stephen rarely had.

Every night, sometimes twice, after James had rolled over and her breathing had slowed, she slipped out from under the covers to the bathroom and tried to assuage her burning guilt with silent, uncontrollable sobbing. For Jennifer, Day One would forever remind her of the first time she cheated on Stephen - and how much she had enjoyed it.

The white and blue alien race disembarking from a ship that resembled stacked slices of black metal pizza, now estimated to be twice as wide and three times as high as earth's largest skyscraper, stopped the world in its tracks. Everything changed overnight for the awestruck humans.

The real and true ramifications of an alien species' apparent desire to live on earth had rendered in-fighting among humans virtually meaningless. Wars between nations that had raged for generations ceased completely and overnight as endemic ideas about race, religion, gender and equality were thrown into confusion and disarray. Guns were dropped into dirt, sand and mud.

Survival in the face of a faceless and unexplainable species became priority, and for a while it was every human for himself.

The decision was made to try to stem the free flow of misinformation and organised disharmony that was tearing the world apart. The world wide web was shut down, globally and completely. Channels of communication were severed, gone. Faced with blank screens and cut off from social networks the world was forced back to basics and the continuing talks with the alien species happened with a level of privacy and security unthinkable even just a few days before. However the world was going to shake down, there was no doubt it was going to be a vastly different place.

Jennifer found out pretty early on that James was married and his estranged wife Harriet was pregnant. She lived with her new boyfriend, a banker called Gerry whose name James couldn't say without practically spitting it out, in James' former house in Putney.

After the first crazy few months when simply surviving was a priority, she moved in to James' flat and they rode out the first few years together, Jennifer bursting with happiness and love and desire, feelings that she was unable to prevent as much as her memories of Stephen tried to suppress them.

James' advertising agency was almost dead in the water without the internet. Digital advertising was meaningless, email campaigns, apps and social media connecting brands with consumers was suddenly utterly redundant.

He responded immediately to build up a series of campaigns for his clients within more traditional and real-world experiential forms of advertising, among the first to adapt to the vastly different new rules, and it thrived.

Harriet had their baby, a boy they named Luke. James didn't see as much of the boy as he would have liked, but as the new world grew up around them they were all forced to grow up along with it.

Four years on from Day One and Luke was a quiet, intense child, in that age somewhere between toddler and small boy, who stayed with them most weekends. James' divorce finally came through and they were going to get married, just the two of them with Stephen's parents as witnesses.

They moved to a house in Surrey and Jennifer finally decided to sell her flat, the place that she and Stephen had shared for their two years of marriage and which she had kept, stubbornly refusing to sell, keeping the last tangible evidence of her previous life alive.

Sitting on the pavement outside the building, wearing a summer dress and red sandals and large white Ray-Ban Aviators hiding her eyes, she shed her last tears for her first, late husband, finally crying out the guilt that had plagued her for so long. The sun was shining, reflecting in the tears on her cheeks as she turned her face towards the warm sun, her one remaining battered suitcase beside her. She looked like the cover of one of Stephen's parent's folk albums.

The flat was empty now, the keys posted back through the letterbox. All her belongings were still in boxes in the new home she shared with James McDonald.

As Jennifer sat and waited for James to pick her up, the

sun playing over her face, she watched as a white alien creature walked past her. She allowed herself to breathe, finally feeling empty of guilt for the first time in a long time.

MIKE

Joy's first attempt at intervention was a failure. The town was still overrun, homes had burned, people had run or joined together for safety. In retrospect, it was the worst possible time to try and rescue her husband, but she gave it a shot anyway. When Mike tried to leave the house she blocked the door, citing concern for his well-being in the violent streets, but he elbowed her aside and went out regardless. She didn't see him again for over a week.

Normal life was a distant memory, but when the internet was shut off, the craziness died down and the world eventually began to level out, her research had to be done the old-fashioned way. She went to the library, began visiting support groups and AA meetings and gathering as much information as she could, finding a community for whom the alien madness wasn't even remotely close to the worst situation they had ever been in.

With their help and advice she arranged a party of friends, family and past colleagues and staged a second intervention. When Mike stumbled into the house, eyes red and watery, confused, heavily bearded and smelling of the sweet, rotting smell of alcohol mixed with prescription medication, he simply gazed at them all uncomprehendingly, swaying gently on his feet, unsure why there were so many people in his living room.

His first stay at rehab lasted three days before he vanished for two weeks, turning up back at the house in as worse a state as Joy had ever seen him. The second attempt lasted two days, the third attempt about an hour before he disappeared.

She had met someone else and divided her time between the house and her new boyfriend's flat, but even if she wasn't staying at the house she stopped by every day to check if Mike had come home.

Following his third short-lived visit to the drying-out clinic he went missing for three months, eventually turning up at a hospital badly beaten with a fractured arm and broken hand, the result of a fight over a bottle of cheap wine.

Joy stayed with him for two days and two nights, but when she returned to the hospital after popping home to shower and change he was gone again, leaving a smeared thank you note. He had signed it with a smiley face.

Mike had only been peripherally aware that the world was changing around him. He saw front pages of the papers blowing across the streets - more and more newspapers with names he didn't recognise. He understood, but didn't give a shit, that there was no more internet and that print media had taken up some of the slack. There were hundreds of new newspaper editions on sale every day, each one leaning towards a particular angle, which worked out pretty well for him because the thicker political and conspiracy-lead copies were extremely effective at insulating him when stuffed inside his filthy, torn coat.

He had seen photographs of the aliens, heard interviews and commentary on tiny transistor radios as he lay unnoticed in doorways swigging his preferred brand of cheap sweet wine, but he simply didn't care. His mind was set, all he wanted was to lie in doorways in peace and drink, drink until it was all over. He only felt safe when he was drunk. He didn't need a world with aliens in it however better that cute lady with the pink cardigan on all the interviews was saying it would become.

He had survived on the street during weeks of violence and always managed to stay out of trouble. It had passed, as he had known it would. It was only when the world was starting to feel more like its old self when he was assaulted by three men as he lay passed out in a doorway in North London. They smashed his empty wine bottle across his face, opening up his cheek, a deep laceration that cut all the way through the flesh to his tongue, then kicked and beat him until they were positive he was dead.

His bloodied body was discovered only hours later. Emergency nurses cleaned him up and stitched his cheek, meaning he couldn't speak clearly even if he wanted to. The police questioned him but he had been a good lawyer for too long and was able to read between the lines. He knew they had no intention of trying to catch his attackers and it would have been futile even if they had.

Joy was by his side, as she always had been, and she took him in during his recovery.

A mental switch in his brain was flicked during the painful, silent hours spent recuperating at Joy's new boyfriend Graham's Bethnal Green flat. He realised he didn't want to die a helpless abused object on a pavement. So he started paying attention to things again, and the world slowly began to come back into focus. He quickly realised that he had passed out in one world and woken up in another one entirely.

Joy had sold their house. They had paid off much of the mortgage during Mike's short lived but lucrative career as a lawyer and partner at a large London law firm. So when she delivered him to rehab again and he decided to stay, Mike had enough money to see himself through the worst of it and into a small place of his own. He bought a small, nondescript and inconspicuous flat above a shop on a grimy South East London high street.

It was a daily struggle to ignore the constant itch in his head that he couldn't scratch, the raging thirst and the desire to sink back into the darkness; but he attended AA, recited the prayers and began the slow count of sober days. When he was presented with a small plastic chip to mark his first year sober, Mike felt tears running down his face as the other members cheered and applauded. He had never known that receiving a disk of cheap orange plastic could mean so much. Some of the people around him were crying too, and all looked happy and proud. His previous life at the law firm seemed like a dream that had happened to someone else, the orange disk and what it represented easily his biggest achievement to date, the memory of being made partner at a law firm now feeling hollow and arbitrary. The orange disk in his pocket filled his heart with hope and determination, even as he yearned for a drink to celebrate.

He returned home from the meeting at sunset. It was witching hour for the youths who hung around on the high street beneath his living room window. The shops were closing, the street lights hadn't yet come on and the street was relaxing, relieved of the weight of the day's shoppers. The kids ran around shouting at each other, kicking cans across the pavement and eating fried chicken. Mike drew his curtains across and picked up his phone. He dialled a number from memory and it rang three times.

'Joy, its me. I just wanted to let you know. I made it. One year today. Stop crying. Stop crying. Is Graham there? Good. No, I'm at home now. I might watch EastEnders, if I can get a signal. Joy, I just wanted you to know- No, I do have to say it. I do. And I know you've heard it all before, but I'm so sorry. Sorry for messing it all up. For leaving you on your own when this all happened. And thank you, thank you so much for everything. And thank Graham for me too. OK. See you soon. Bye.'

He hung up and sat on his cheap brown leather sofa, crying silently to himself for a few minutes, hearing the kids shouting beneath his window. Eventually he sat up straighter, sniffed a few times and wiped his eyes, deciding against watching the soaps, an addiction for which he refused to feel guilty or seek help. He went to bed instead.

The following morning just after dawn, one year and one day sober, he went to the shop on the corner and bought four newspapers from the stacks piled up just inside the door.

Now the internet was gone, there were a dizzying

number of papers to choose from, each of them leading on a different aspect or angle on news; international news, politics, entertainment, conspiracies, gossip, sport. He brought his chosen four back to the flat and read them over a coffee and a bacon sandwich. One of the papers, the established Financial Times, was thick with job vacancies in a separate section. There were more and more aliens landing on earth. Maybe he could specialise in alien law? He smiled to himself, rummaging in his cutlery drawer for a biro.

MARION

Marion had a clear view of the alien ship through the glass wall of her office, which was like an aquarium with floor to ceiling glass walls all the way around. It was now just a hulk, a metal shell. None of the Kin lived inside it any more. The vessel's considerable power, the engines, life support and entire internal array had been generated by a specific mineral that apparently did not exist on earth. It had taken over a year to formulate an approximation of the name of the element in any human language and years more for the researchers and physicists and bio-engineers at the Shack to determine that it was simply unobtainable on planet earth. The engineers were still working with the Kin trying to make their ships power-up again, but four years later they were still dead, and beginning to rust. The Kin were advanced and intelligent, but without their natural power supply all the technology was merely a curiosity to be dismantled and examined.

Very few Kin were even still at the Shack. They had been systematically and carefully housed and integration was ongoing. Projected on the large glass wall opposite Marion's desk was a huge satellite image of the earth that seemed to float in mid air like a hologram, which delighted Marion every time she booted it up. It was a long way from the basement at the British Museum. There were four hundred orange marks dotted around it representing each landing site. There were clouds of blue dots spread around the world, most clustered in dense pockets over cities, but a few scattered, more remote ones. As each Kin had disembarked their ship and processed through a Shack they were implanted with a tracker under the left armpit, a condition of their welcome to earth. The tracker had been a part of Marion and Adler's original manifesto, but only she and the other Shack Leaders had access to the tracking information. Four million blue dots.

The language barrier had taken over two years to break down, but they worked out enough during that time to make their plan understood, piece by piece. After four full years she and the first Kin now conversed in English as if he had been born in Gloucestershire, which she supposed he had, in a way.

She picked up a remote from her desk and pressed a button. The image on the wall zoomed into the UK, which was dense with blue markers. She zoomed in even further, to Gloucestershire and the Shack. At this level of magnification, she easily located what she was looking for - a single blue mark identical to all the other blue marks nearby. But she knew this one.

She took the lift to the ground floor and then another lift to the sub-level areas, making her way to the labs.

The original manifesto that the humans had drawn up included complete exploration and study of the alien physiology. The opportunity to examine an alien life form was not only fascinating but vital to understand how the species functioned and how to offer medical attention when required. The clause was the only one completely rejected by the Kin. Any medical issue could be dealt with among themselves, they argued. The point was passed back and forth for weeks but in the end Marion and Adler had relented. The aliens were highly intelligent and the humans wary of breaching moral codes. A compromise was reached in that examinations could take place on deceased specimens only.

They were literally waiting for one of them to die, but so far, none had.

Marion found the first Kin standing in front of a large Perspex containment tank. Inside a thick, clear liquid gel was suspended a dead Kin. Half of its body and face was blackened and burned like a huge roasted marshmallow and what was left of the blue markings had faded to an almost invisible pale blue. The first Kin spoke. They sounded identical, their voices exactly the same soft monotone, but she felt his sadness, his homesickness.

'He saved us all. If he hadn't held the ship together we would have crashed and your planet would have considered us a threat. Billions of us died but four million of us now live, because of him. Promise me his body will never be a part of your research.'

'I promise.'

'I would offer my own body to be experimented upon than allow him to suffer the indignity.'

'I understand. He won't. And you don't have to.'

'You will wait for one of us to die, as agreed.'

'Yes, it was part of the agreement,' Marion confirmed, knowing it was a callous response. 'We are a curious species, you know that. You have told us that you will live longer than us. How? You say you won't decompose in the ground like we do – why? You are a single gender species, but we only have your explanation as to how you procreate and give birth. And why, after four years, have you not done so? In order for us to fully adapt and evolve together, we must know, so we can plan for our future together.'

The Kin turned his blank face towards her. 'You would treat us like animals, to be studied.'

Marion was shocked. 'No, like scientists. Like a species determined to learn, to grow. You have your own homes, a chance to make a living here on earth. We closed our own borders to humankind to accommodate you all. We have offered to construct places for you to worship, welcomed you with open arms. You are fielding a team in the World Cup next year for heaven's sake. I've heard you actually stand a chance. Is that treating you like animals? You know we have done every single thing we can to help you. And in return, you have taught us so much. We are not perfect by any means, but by now I would hope that we can be considered-'

'-colleagues?'

'Yes. And friends. More than just flatmates on this planet, anyway.'

'I misspoke, Marion. My apologies.'

'We're only four years in to this, Kin. It's going to take time, but I promise that we'll make it work. You *are* home.'

ROYCE

'I'm gonna be fucking rich.'

'Royce. Please don't talk like that.'

'Mum, I've just been signed to the biggest hip-hop label in the world. I can say what I want.'

'And I'm your mother and I can still tell you to not speak like that in front of me please. You know what happened to that Jesse Cheever.'

'Mum, please stop going on about Jesse fucking Cheever. He was a stupid reality-show pop star who couldn't sing and drowned in his own swimming pool, to the relief of most of the entire fucking world.'

'He was drunk and high and rich and nobody actually knows how he drowned. I don't want that to happen to you.'

'Mum, are you crying?'

'I'm just so scared. I don't want all this to go to your head and you end up dead.'

'Bloody hell Mum. I won't. I promise.'

Royce Brims, his mother and his new agent Buddy Tucker were all sitting in the executive waiting room of the London office of the hottest record label in the world, *Uzi Bitch Records*.

After bombarding the A&R staff of UBR with dozens of films of his winning rap battle videos and cutting a cheap demo, Royce was about to sign a three-album deal for the label. They were waiting for the Founder, Chairman and President of UBR, the music mogul Henderson Mulcahy himself, to come out and meet them, as was his custom with all new signings to the label.

Royce would never usually swear so much in front of his mother, but he was shaking with nerves.

One whole wall of the waiting area from floor to ceiling was opaque glass. Without warning, it blinked from opaque to completely transparent. Royce and his mum jumped in surprise, although the agent sat in the vast red leather sofa impassively, obviously used to his employer's tricks. The now clear glass wall allowed them to see right inside to a massive office space. A desk larger than a king-size bed was sat in the middle and there was a view right across London. Sat behind the huge empty desk was Henderson Mulcahy, motioning them inside. Sitting at one end of the office on another red leather sofa was a white alien Kin.

Royce pushed open the door and stepped in, followed by his mother and Tucker.

Mulcahy stood up and walked around the desk.

'Mrs Brims.' Ignoring the others, Mulcahy gave Royce's mother a hug, kissing her on both cheeks. 'Thank you so much for coming in,' he said in his unnaturally deep baritone. 'I consider it a necessity for any artist on my label to have a deep connection with their family, especially if their family is as beautiful as you.'

It was a cheesy line but the combination of his voice, his fame, his expensive aroma and his sly grin showing off his gold tooth made Martha Brims giggle and blush like a schoolgirl.

'Mum,' said Royce, 'shut up.'

'Don't speak to your mother like that, son. Mrs Brims, please do take a seat.' Mulcahy indicated the sofa against the far wall where the alien sat, upright and silent. Martha Brims looked at it nervously and went and perched on the opposite end from the Kin, as far away as she could manage. Buddy Tucker, the agent assigned to Royce just a few hours earlier, stood to one side of the desk.

Mulcahy stepped back and appraised the boy.

'How old are you, son?'

'Fifteen, sir.'

'Fifteen. I don't remember being fifteen. I had Facebook and Instagram and YouTube that remembered it for me. Now they're gone and I hardly remember a thing. Maybe it's for the best,' he smiled. Henderson had a peculiar way of emphasising the last syllable of every word. Face-*book*. Remem-*ber*. Although Royce had heard him on the news and TV, he found it slightly hypnotic.

'OK, take your T-shirt off,' Mulcahy clapped twice and all the windows, including the ones overlooking the towering view of London, suddenly went opaque.

'I'm sorry, what?' Royce suddenly snapped back to the present, a present where an extremely wealthy and recognisable rap-artist and music mogul had asked him to take his shirt off.

'Take your shirt off, please.'

He didn't really know what to do. Glancing nervously at his mother, almost more embarrassed to be taking off his shirt in front of her than Henderson, Royce just did as he was told, standing shirtless with his arms folded against his chest.

'Hands by your sides,' Mulcahy demanded, 'turn around. You're skinny, you need to bulk up. I want more muscle on your arms and chest. Your lyrics are edgy, dangerous. Disruptive. You don't look edgy or dangerous to me. And I want a tattoo. Here-' he prodded one of Royce's pecs, 'and on your arms, don't care which, don't care what, unless you choose a Care Bear. Otherwise, you'll do. Put your shirt back on.'

Royce did so, feeling weirded out.

'Welcome to my label, Royce. You and I, we are gonna make ourselves a whole load of beautiful music together. Platinum-level shit. Buddy here-' Tucker stepped forward, '- Buddy is gonna take care of everything. Where you live, what you eat, who you fuck, what you sing in the shower, your training regime - everything. When he speaks, my voice comes out. You do exactly what he says, OK?'

Royce smiled. 'Yes sir.'

'And what you said out there about being rich?'

Royce coloured slightly. 'You heard that?'

'I hear everything. It'll happen Brims, but not without

hard work, and not without my fucking say so. You get me?'

'Yes sir.'

'You ever met a Kin?'

'No, sir. I seen a few, but not up close.'

'Come meet him,' and as if on cue the Kin stood and held its hand out. Royce, shaking slightly, took it. It was dry and warm and not at all what he was expecting. The blue markings on its face looked like two tiger stripes down each side of the face, down the sides and across the torso. The two stripes stopped just above the completely smooth groin area, which reminded Royce of a plastic Iron Man action figure he had played with incessantly a few years back.

'Kin is my muse,' Mulcahy laughed. 'I see you looking. I know what you're thinking. How do they fuck? Right? Excuse my language, Mrs Brims.'

Mrs Brims was staring too. She had never been up close to a Kin before either despite their continuing and gradual integration into society.

The Kin spoke. 'Henderson never swears when we are alone. He plays it up when he has company.' It had no mouth yet the voice came out quite clearly from the smooth facial area. The voice was low and soft, polite. Royce reckoned it sounded posh.

Mulcahy laughed and slapped the Kin on its back. 'That's true, man. That's true! He knows me too well!'

'He refers to me as his muse, but a more accurate description is that I am his assistant. I work for his organisation. It is a salaried position with all accompanying benefits.'

'Kin here is the best assistant I ever had. He never writes anything down and he remembers everything. Remember Google, Mrs Brims?'

'I do. I miss it.'

'Me too, but Kin here – he's like a walking Google.'

'Henderson has a number of assistants working within

his organisation that are my equal or superior. Henderson is a very rich man, the eighth richest man in the world - I suspect that he employs me as a trophy to prove his wealth rather than a genuine asset,' the Kin replied, 'I do have a good memory however, better than that of most humans. It feels good to be useful.'

'And I love his honesty. And I return the honesty.'

Mulcahy placed both his hands on the Kin's shoulders and stared at its blank head. 'Kin, you are right. But you have changed me. You are more of an individual to me, more of a friend, than I ever thought possible. I respect you.'

The Kin cocked its head slightly. Despite the featureless face and inflectionless voice, Royce could somehow tell that it was slightly amused, and did really seem to like Henderson.

'I respect you too, Henderson,' it said, 'but I think we are making our guests feel uncomfortable.'

Royce, his mother and Tucker were indeed feeling slightly awkward at the human/alien display of affection in front of them.

'Not at all,' Tucker protested, 'you are both an inspiration to us.'

'Shut up, Tucker,' said Mulcahy, smiling,' and go make a star of young Royce, here. Make sure he gets some muscle on him.'

'Yes, sir.'

The three of them stood and left the office, the door swishing shut behind them and the glass wall blinking back to opaque.

'He never told us how they fuck-' said Royce, and got a smack around the side of his head from his mother.

JENNIFER

As soon as she moved in to Richard's house, her relationship with Luke started to deteriorate. It wasn't immediate or obvious but the boy slowly began to completely block her out of his life.

Life with James was a whirlwind of nights out, dinners, parties, concerts. Jennifer allowed herself to be swept up in it all and couldn't be happier. She no longer worked for him but he had set her up with her own design firm and he sold her services into other advertising agencies he worked with.

And the sex. Jennifer blushed whenever she thought about it – and she thought about it a lot. She was twenty years younger than James, who was in his late forties. He was the second person she had ever been with, and she had had no idea that sex could be so passionate or satisfying.

But as the months went on her weekends became something else entirely, days to be endured. She began to dread the boy arriving. He was an angelic child to look at, tousled black hair, blue eyes, a cherubic smile. James doted on him and spoiled him every weekend.

Jennifer tried hard to befriend him but he acted like she was invisible all the time, which was a feat of endurance for a small boy that she could almost admire if it didn't make her so uncomfortable and sad. Most small boys would pretend they were superheroes or dinosaurs but Luke wasn't into fanciful stuff and spent all his time pretending his father lived alone, cleaning up after him, standing on a chair to reach the kitchen counter and pretending to cook him meals. James stubbornly refused to see it and they would have blazing rows about him most weeks, James insisting it was a phase and he would grow out of it. Then they would have incredible angry sex and Jennifer would put her feelings to one side until the following week, her heart once again sinking as the sound of the tyres of James' Jaguar crunched on the gravel driveway and Luke's clear, excited voice called to his father from the hallway where he dropped his coat.

On a normal Sunday morning as she was in the kitchen making tea and toast after a run, still in her running kit, she had practically forgotten that the boy was in the house. Luke, now nine, came down from his bedroom in his pyjamas. His hair was mussed and he kept yawning. He took a seat at the breakfast bar.

Jennifer slid him a plate with buttered toast on it. He slid it back. 'Want cereal.'

She ignored him and kept on making toast. He got up and poured himself a bowl of cereal, adding milk from the fridge.

'I met a Kin last week,' he announced.

'Oh really?' Jennifer said, surprised. This was the first proper sentence they had passed between them in weeks.

'Yeah. It was white, with those blue spots on it.'

'Apparently all their markings are unique, like a fingerprint. That's very interesting, Luke. What did it say?'

'It just said that it was thankful they had found a good home with good people.'

'Anything else?'

'Their own home was like earth, once, but it got destroyed.'

'Really? Did it describe their planet?'

'No. They have agreed only to talk about it between themselves. I liked it.'

'You did?' Luke had never told Jennifer about anything he actually liked before. 'Yes. I couldn't see it's eyes or mouth. It was interesting.'

'What else did it say?'

'Not much. I think it was brought in to show us so we could get used to it. I think some of them are moving to the area or something.'

'Yes, that's true. Your father is part of the integration committee.'

'He is?'

'Yes. Ask him and perhaps you could be involved somehow. I know the school has a representative on the committee too.'

'I will. Thanks Jennifer.'

'No problem.'

Jennifer found herself glowing with happiness that she had communicated successfully with Luke.

She went upstairs for a shower. James had gone to his office and would be back at some point later in the morning. She stripped off her running gear and stepped into their en-suite shower. She lathered up, thinking of James, as she often did. As the showerhead washed the suds from her skin she began to rub herself between her legs with the soap, slowly at first, but getting faster as her ardour increased. She placed one palm against the wall of the shower, supporting herself as she sensed her body nearing a climax. The water poured down across the back of her neck and across her shoulders, forming a curtain of water around her breasts.

She bit her lip and rubbed harder, willing it closer. She let out a strangled gasp, abandoning the soap for her fingers and expertly teasing out her pleasure. She turned her face into the powerful jet of water as her hand slowed and stopped.

She switched off the shower and stepped out to find her towel. Luke stood in the doorway of the en-suite, staring at her. To her knowledge, he had never been in to her and James bedroom or bathroom before.

'Jesus, Luke, how long have you been there?' Jennifer said, shocked, and going crimson even through her exercise-and-orgasm-flushed face. She grabbed for the white towel hanging from the rack and held it up in front of her. Luke didn't respond. He stared at her impassively for a few more moments then turned and walked away.

James arrived home as she was blow-drying her hair. She

told him what had happened, blushing again as she said it.

James was silent for a few moments. 'You were what?'

'Don't make me say it again.'

'Christ, Jennifer, don't we have enough sex to satisfy you? We do it every night, pretty much.'

'I know, I know. James, I don't have any problem with the sex at all, quite the opposite, but sometimes I just need a... a carryover.'

'A carryover?'

'Oh come on, don't tell me you don't do it.'

'Of course I do, but generally not in the middle of the day when my son is in the house, that's just dumb, Jen.'

'He's never been in our bathroom! Not once, ever.'

'Well he has now. Please be more careful and close the door at least. He's nine, a really impressionable age.'

'I know, I'm sorry,' Jennifer started to cry. 'He doesn't even like me.'

'Not this again. Of course he does. You're being paranoid.'

'No, I'm not. You just don't see it. It would be nice if you could take my side for once.' She cringed as she trotted out the cliché she had heard her own mother use against her father.

'I'll talk to him, find out what he saw.'

Jennifer wiped her eyes and went to the kitchen to prepare the Sunday lunch. She took a leg of lamb from the fridge and all the vegetables she could find. She spent half an hour peeling and chopping and trying to forget Luke's eyes on her. She made a jug of filter coffee and poured herself a cup as James came downstairs from Luke's bedroom and sat at the breakfast bar.

'Well, he saw everything.'

'Shit.'

'Yup. He didn't really know what you were up to, although he has a vague idea from playground chatter, presumably.'

'Shit.'

'And he doesn't hate you. At all.'

'Bollocks.'

'He said you had a chat about the Kin this morning over breakfast. He had come to the bathroom to tell you something else the Kin had said to the class.'

'That's true, but it was the first conversation we've had for weeks. Forget it, James. I'll never convince you and I'm sick of trying.'

'He's nine. He'll have forgotten about it in a few days. I won't though. Next time you fancy a bit of self-love, you better make sure I'm invited too.'

She smiled as he picked up a knife and they chopped the vegetables together in companionable silence.

JOSH

He dried the dishes with a dishcloth that implored him to 'Keep Kin and Carry On'. Staring out of the kitchen window as he worked, he could see the jagged hulk of the alien ship in the distance, towering into the clear sky. The very top was obscured by clouds.

A lot had changed in the years since the aliens had crashed on the base. It was almost a city out there now, or at the very least one of the best and most futuristic campuses in the world, rising organically around the original RAF buildings and the ship. He saw Marion from time to time and they hugged like old friends, as if they shared some secret, like veterans or old timers.

The huts were still there, clustered almost at the very foot of the ship. Josh now manned them alone. He had repaired the damaged roofs and replaced the broken windows. He upgraded all the satellite dish clusters that now sprouted over and alongside Hut Two like a particularly nasty rash or an outbreak of metal mushrooms. The Huts were warmer and safer as a result. Traditional comms traffic had increased dramatically since the internet went dark, but conversely a lot of the activity was inconsequential and white noise, regular day-to-day comms. The human world had finally relaxed into a relatively conflict-free place, punch drunk and reeling from the extreme violence meted out upon it after the alien arrival. Military communications had settled down to repetitive signals and the familiar beats of diminished, languishing armies.

The morning of Dandridge's disappearance Josh had called his name, padding naked into every room, checking behind every door. But the house suddenly seemed devoid of life, of his presence. Josh had gone back to bed, his muscles still aching and tired from their exertions the previous night, and when he was still alone by the evening he was sure.

He returned to his own small flat in town, but after a few days of lying on his sofa all alone and watching daytime television, the quality of which had not improved despite the absence of the internet, he took the decision to temporarily move into Dandridge's house.

He already had a key, the house was larger than his flat and closer to Site One. Besides, Dandridge had once told him there was no mortgage on it. As long as he paid the bills he would wait there for Dandridge to return.

Nine years on since he had left and the once grey and unkempt house was now as clean and tidy as it had ever been. The walls were whitewashed, the lawn was mowed, the flowerbeds clear of weeds and the front drive freshly gravelled. Josh's green Fiat Punto sat outside in Dandridge's usual spot next to another car, a black Jeep.

He distractedly placed the last plate on the drainer, his eyes still locked on the alien vessel towering into the sky. Flight Lt. Ezra Perron came up behind him and nuzzled his neck. He was dressed in his green flight suit with a jacket over the top. 'You stare at that thing every day,' he said. 'Not bored of looking at it quite yet?'

'Maybe if you did the washing up once in a while you could stare at it for a change,' Josh laughed. Perron took his keys from the hook by the front door.

'You aren't fooling anyone, you know,' he said as he opened the front door. 'Whenever you stare at it, you're wondering where he is.'

Perron closed the door behind him and climbed into the driver's seat of the black Jeep. He blew Josh a kiss as he reversed out of the driveway onto the lane.

It was true. Dandridge had been gone a long time, vanished without a trace. Not a day went by that Josh didn't wonder where he was.

LUKE

He watched his father kiss Jennifer. He may be only nine years old, but he was clever for his age, all his teachers said so. He had never disliked Jennifer as his dad had suggested, it was just that she didn't interest him. He had plenty of things to keep him occupied instead, video games and football and rugby and that half-starved fox he had trapped in the shed. Oh, and cricket. So what interest could Jennifer be to him? She was just a woman that his Dad liked. He knew his real mother didn't like her, but she didn't seem to like anyone very much. She was constantly saying rude things about his teachers too, and he quite liked his teachers, except for Mrs Rosenthal who seemed immune to his well-practiced charm and cheeky smile and who smelled faintly of boiled cabbage.

But now something was different. Something inside him had changed, something indefinable. There was a flicker, the briefest spark of interest in her that hadn't been there before. He didn't know what, couldn't quite put his finger on it. It felt different to the feeling of power he experienced when he tormented the fox in the shed; when he dangled food in front of it before whipping it away and listening to its high-pitched squeals of protest, or when he introduced a jam jar full of bees into the shed to see what happened. Disappointingly, the fox had just eaten them.

After staring at his father kiss Jennifer in the kitchen for a while, he stole quietly back upstairs to his bedroom and lay on his bed, feeling his thoughts drift with the dust-bunnies in the air until his silent reverie was interrupted by the doorbell.

He was summoned downstairs and shook the hands of the two old people who had come in and taken their coats off. Apparently these were the parents of Jennifer's first husband, which was weird. They sat drinking wine for a while before lunch so Luke went back to his bedroom and carried on staring into space.

'Luke!' he heard his father calling up the stairs. He lay there for another two minutes before standing up and going back downstairs. The adults were already sat around the dining room table and Jennifer was spooning out roast potatoes. Luke sat down.

'So, Luke,' the old man said, 'how's school?'

'It's very good thank you. We met a Kin on Friday.'

'Really? That's very exciting. Your father was telling me there are some moving to this area soon. He is part of the integration committee.'

'Yup.'

'What's your favourite subject?'

'Art.'

'Oh really? Jennifer here is an excellent artist. We have one of her paintings hanging on our wall at home.'

'Oh Barry, please, really?' Jennifer blushed, 'I haven't painted for years and years.'

'Well, you should. You were wonderful. And you James, how's the advertising game now? How's business since the Kin?'

'Never been better thank you, Barry. We work to new rules now of course, but its still fun, still exciting. We have to find different, more hands-on ways to engage with our brands and consumers now. We have a clean slate, really. We've managed to compensate for the loss of digital planning and start conversations globally to overcome any remaining brand identity hangovers from before the Kin arrival.'

Barry looked slightly confused. 'OK, well done you. It has been so hard for so many people since the Kin.'

'And you Barry, you're a mechanic? I assume that business didn't change so much? People love their cars, right?'

'Well, as you know, the economy fell through the floor which impacted us a lot of course but yes, we stayed afloat.

Even with so much change going on around us people still want their cars, as you say, although fewer people can afford one now.'

'Cars are an emotional safety net to a lot of people, especially in a time of great change.'

'How did he die?' Luke suddenly said.

There was silence around the table as the adults all turned to look at him.

'Sorry, Luke?' Barry asked.

'How did he die? Your son?'

'Luke. That's an incredibly insensitive thing to say. Apologise and go to your room immediately,' James said, blushing in embarrassment.

'It's alright,' Barry replied. 'He's too young to know how the question sounded. Stephen died in a climbing accident, Luke.'

'Like, a mountain?'

'Yes. He slipped and fell as he was climbing a mountain in the Himalayas.'

'If he hadn't died, then Jennifer would still be with him, right?'

'I don't really know. Probably.'

'Luke. That's enough,' the red of James' face had shifted from embarrassment to anger. 'Not another word out of you.'

Luke watched the reactions of the adults, especially Jennifer, who was staring at her plate.

'What did he do for a living?'

'If you don't stop talking right now, young man, I'm going to lock you in your bedroom for a month.'

'He was training to be an architect,' said Jennifer, lifting her head and looking into Luke's cool blue eyes, which had always contrasted with his jet black hair. His hair used to be curly but had straightened as it grew thicker and longer.

'So do *you* think you would be with my dad if he hadn't died?' he said, staring back at Jennifer.

James stood up and grabbed Luke by the arm, pulling him out of his chair despite the weak protestations of their guests. James shook him, hard.

'How dare you speak like that, you little shit. You've never been shown anything but love, and this is how you act? Say sorry, right fucking now.'

Luke said nothing, but stared at his father as if he were no more interesting than his fox in the shed.

'Apologise, right now.'

Luke turned to Jennifer's in-laws, sitting and staring at their plates. 'I saw her in the shower today,' he said. Both Jennifer and Margaret raised their hands to cover their open, shocked mouths. 'She was rubbing herself between her legs.'

James grabbed him by his upper arm and dragged him upstairs to his room, pushing him in and slamming the door closed. Luke sat down on the side of his bed, staring at his poster of a Sherman tank on the back of the door. He had never seen his father so angry. He stared at the door and played over the events at the table in his mind.

JENNIFER

James stormed into his study and slammed the door.

'I don't know what to say,' she mumbled, 'I'm so sorry. Luke walked in on me having a shower this morning. It must have confused him somehow. He's only nine.'

'We understand, Jennifer. But I think we'd better go. Thank you so much for inviting us over. Thank James for us too. He's so lovely.'

'He is, he is.'

They let themselves out, worrying with their coats and taking an age to determine that they hadn't left anything and were all ready. Jennifer remained by herself at the table as the front door closed behind them. She stared at the cold food wondering how the day had gone so bad so quickly.

Later that day Luke announced that he never wanted to stay with his father or Jennifer again. James was devastated.

Jennifer didn't blame Luke. She blamed herself, and felt the first twinges of guilt.

MIKE

The Kin sat in a wooden chair across a desk from him. Mike had an open legal pad and a fountain pen.

'So what will you be selling?' he asked.

'A number of items,' the low voice said from its featureless face, 'artisan bread, other sundry baked goods. And possibly soap.'

'Right. Is this what you really want to do?'

'That is correct.'

'Soap?'

'Yes.'

'May I ask,' Mike leaned forward in his chair, 'what did you do before? To make a living on your own planet?'

The Kin leaned forward to mimic Mike, its body language indicating some sort of secret about to be imparted. 'It is very difficult to explain, Mr. Hennessy. We did not have specific ascribed roles such as you have here. Work was assigned and remunerated depending on what needed to be accomplished during any given seasonal cycle. We did not work for individual profit, as such, but for a functioning society as a whole.'

'A species with no need for personal gain or greed, interesting. Some human countries have tried that very thing without a lot of success. So what was your favourite thing to... accomplish?'

The Kin sat back and placed its fingertips together to make a pyramid, almost certainly an affectation it had observed from a human. 'We do not like to talk about it with humans, Mr. Hennessy. This is not disrespect, it is just hard to talk about a way of life that does not exist any more. You can obtain a pamphlet from our Shack Representative if you wish.'

'I understand, I didn't mean to pry, my apologies.'

'There is no need for apologies, Mr. Hennessy. If you really want to know - I enjoyed working on the mountains.'

'The mountains?'

'Yes. We would need to gather certain supplements from the higher reaches of our planet when atmospheric conditions were balanced. Minerals, herbs. I liked the solitude, and the view would always 'take my breath away' you would say.'

'And now you want to make soap. Here. In Deptford.'

'And bread. We are adjusting to a new way of life. You would do the same.'

'I understand, and thank you for sharing your story with me, Kin. OK, so to business. You wish to operate out of this building, specifically? You and two other Kin and three humans?'

'Yes sir. We wish to work co-operatively on a de-layered, equal-profit related basis between all six of us.'

'Please, just 'Mike'. I lost the right for people to call me 'sir'. This building is old, pretty decrepit and has a demolition order on it. We can get a surveyor to check it over but if it is structurally unsafe then I am not sure there's much I can do. Plus, you are going to need employment contracts or a work charter at the very least, signed and witnessed by me.'

'Why? We have already shaken all of our hands and agreed the basis upon which we will progress this business venture.'

'Trust me. We'll get it in writing.'

'Do what you think necessary Mr. Hennessy. We like it here very much. There are exactly the correct number of rooms, there are existing facilities and it is located next to the canal, so we will utilise the canal system to ship our items in and out.'

'Deptford is a bit out of the way.'

'This planet is a bit out of the way.'

Mike burst out laughing and so did the Kin. It sounded strange coming from its blank white head with its asymmetrical ink-blue markings.

'OK Kin, I'll look into it and do what I can. The integration manifesto will allow me to negate the demolition order, but only if the surveyors report comes back OK.' They both stood and shook hands.

'Mr. Hennessy, as a part of the legal team on behalf of the Kin, you have been extremely accommodating. Our thanks. But I have one question. Why have you lost the right to be called 'sir'?'

'It's a long story, Kin. I'll be in touch.'

Mike got into his Ford Focus and started the engine, letting the air conditioning blow over him.

He alternated between hot flushes and cold sweats whenever he thought about his past life. His hands still shook uncontrollably and his head ached most days, an ache that paracetamol didn't come close to soothing. He was still too thin and on a cold day the scar on his cheek that ran from his cheekbone to under his jaw was like a livid white trench through his stubble. But he wasn't unhappy, not any more. At AA meetings he described himself as 'room for improvement'.

He took a deep breath and controlled his shakes before driving back to his office in a busy but scruffy part of Greater London. His new business was small but successful, built on the integration manifesto and laws hastily passed about the Kin; how they were to be housed, integrated, employed. Mike had made it his business to learn these laws inside out and exploit them to ensure all the Kin were treated fairly and the incumbent humans were aware of Kin rights and obligations.

He had taken on three employees, junior lawyers who were kept busy with employment rights, property records, land registry documents, all related to re-settling Kin amongst humans.

It was half past seven in the evening when he placed the documents for the New Deptford Bakery Co-Op in a brown folder, sealed them in a brown envelope and addressed it. He stuck a stamp on the outside and switched off the lights in the office, closing and locking the door behind him.

He drove home and let himself into his flat; neat, tidy, quiet and largely empty of anything but basic furniture. He sat down in his familiar armchair next to the window with a view of the elegant old clock tower, lost and ignored on the dirty, busy high street. It was dark outside but Mike's view was lit up like a Christmas tree by bright storefronts; Primark, Boots, WHSmith, TK Maxx, Debenhams, Snappy Snaps, McDonalds.

A gang of young kids were sat at the bus stop passing around a brown, two-litre plastic bottle of something no-doubt awful, taking swigs and laughing hysterically at each other while commuters with white earbuds stuck permanently in their ears waited wearily for buses among the noise. Mike wondered where they were all going.

Bathed in the artificial light of the outside world, Mike curled up in his chair and opened a paperback. He started to read.

ROYCE

'*Jesus*, that really hurts!' Royce shouted as the tattoo artist pressed the needle against his upper arm. This would be his fourth tattoo and he hadn't quite got used to the pain. He had been inked the day after his first meeting with Henderson, and once the pain had subsided he decided he really liked them. He now had a starling on his left pectoral, a rose nesting comfortably in a bed of his pubic hair, a Chinese symbol that translated as 'Brims' on his neck and now he was undergoing the first stage of what would eventually be a full sleeve from shoulder to wrist he had designed himself. Stage one was the head of a panther that would eventually grow the body of a dragon, surrounded by thistles, planets and mystical symbols.

Royce Brims was making it big, just like Henderson had predicted. He had bulked up, adding pounds of muscle to his frame, he had shaved his head and now wore basketball vests of teams he didn't follow. He was about to depart on a tour of the United States to try and convince them once and for all to love his music.

Carl and Kai sat either side of him in the tattoo parlour, laughing and joking. He took a shirtless selfie with them and the tattoo artist. Once the memory card was full Carl would deliver it to the diarist at UBR who would send the photos to all the entertainment and music papers, all the new zines, all the music TV channels. It was hard to gain a following but Royce's stock was high and the photos would be everywhere within a day.

The artist began to trace the outline of the panther's head. Royce swigged from a bottle of Jack Daniels.

'There's no drinking in here,' the artist said.

'What? What about for the pain?'

'Take an ibuprofen.'

'Fucking hell. Carl?'

'I don't carry around ibu-fucking-profen, B. I got some

speed?'

'Nope,' said the artist, 'not in here. You need to keep still.'

'Fucking hell.'

'There's some in the cabinet back there,' the artist nodded over his shoulder. Kai fetched a couple with a cup of water and Royce swigged them down.

'Keep still.'

'Alright. Jesus. You're like my mother.'

'So you're a singer?' the artist asked.

'Rapper. Hip-hop. Royce Brims.'

'OK. Not into rap myself.'

'No, what you into then?'

'Avenged Sevenfold, Black Veil Brides, Kreator, Overkill, Sepultra, a bit of Nuclear Assault. That kind of thing, you know.'

'Not really.'

They lapsed into silence for a while, as the tattooist's needle buzzed and Royce occasionally hissed with pain. Carl's phone rang. He picked up. 'Yo, speak.'

Royce and Kai rolled their eyes.

'Hi Buddy. Yeah, he's here. He can't talk, he's getting a tat. OK. Really? Fantastic! That's awesome, man! OK, what time? Cool, we'll be ready.' Carl hit the red phone receiver icon and cut the call off.

'B, Buddy has got you an interview on US telly, followed by a performance of *White Skin, Black Heart*.'

'Great. Another one. The last two I did they never showed the performance. I was just some random, unknown British black guy before the main guest came on. Last time it was... fuck who was it? Celine Dion?'

'Avril Lavigne.'

'Avril fucking Lavigne.'

'Yeah, but this time it's Late Night with Bill Bolt. He's a big fan, apparently.'

'Really?'

'Yup.'

'We have a flight tomorrow at half seven. Car picks us up at five.'

'Five? In the morning? For fuck sake. This wouldn't happen to Jay-Z.'

'Jay-Z has his own plane. And airport, probably.'

As Carl and Kai ignored the tattoo artist's protestations and swapped the bottle of Jack Daniels back and forth between them, the outline of a panther's head slowly took shape on Royce's arm.

MARION

So far none of the Kin had reproduced and none of them had died. Neither they nor the aliens themselves could work out their life expectancy on Earth and up to this point their numbers remained absolutely even.

There had been accidents along the way involving Kin, car accidents, collisions, bicycle crashes, falls and industrial incidents, but no fatalities. The Kin seemed resilient to outside influences and healed quickly, learning how their physiology reacted to the different atmosphere of earth along with the humans.

So when she got the call from the first Kin late one evening telling her that one of their number had died she struggled to keep the excitement out of her voice.

'Really?' she said down the phone. 'How? Where?'

The first Kin told her. A random accident on a building site in Buenos Aires, hit by a steel girder. Charges were being brought against the crane operator. Another world first, a legal case against a human involving the death of a Kin.

'OK, then I guess we'll go out there,' Marion continued. 'Make sure that the body is stored correctly and I'll round up the medical team from the Shack and sort the flights with Adler.'

She felt guilty for being excited but the thought of the trip to Buenos Aires and the chance for the medical team to actually dissect and study Kin physiology was an exciting opportunity that simply couldn't be passed up. There had been too many unanswered questions for too long.

She had been reading a horror novel in bed in her small rooms at the Shack, but she placed it aside. Her mind was whirring in that way it did when she was excited about something, and it wouldn't let her rest. She would have to be on hand to assist with communication and to document the findings. The Kin should really have a legal representative present as part of the agreement to ensure absolute equality between species. She could sort that out back in her office.

More sleep was impossible so she hopped out of bed and began packing her summer clothes.

PART THREE

MIKE

The screaming, rending, tearing, howling maelstrom of noise and frantic movement of the crash was suddenly replaced by complete and deafening, thudding silence, broken only by the wind whistling around corners and jagged metal edges that hadn't been there a few moments earlier.

Mike was lying on his side, strapped into his seat which was still attached to a small section of the aircraft floor. His right hip pressed awkwardly against the armrest and his head on broken glass.

He lay awake and still for a long time, blinking, unseeing, numb with shock. It took a while, but as his eyes slowly refocused he could tell he was still strapped inside a small section of the fuselage, a torn, jagged metal zero circling a view beyond of a cold white wasteland where the front section of the aircraft should have been. He was too terrified to move, too scared to have to deal with what might come next. He thought he could hear sobbing. His shaking hand reached for the safety belt and after a few fumbles from his rigid, unflexing fingers he unclipped himself. He slid from the seat onto his hands and knees, facing the shattered window pressed into the snow. He could definitely hear sobbing.

He checked himself all over. It took much longer than he would have thought, his brain not even close to thinking clearly. There was a cut on his forehead which seemed to have leaked blood down the side of his face, but otherwise he seemed to be in one piece with no obviously broken bones. He climbed slowly and unsteadily to his feet. In front of him a row of seats were hanging off the bulkhead with their occupants still strapped in. He saw crushed bodies and bloodied arms spilling over the sides of the seats, a pool of blood forming in a lake at his feet. The blood was all over his hands where he had steadied himself. He vomited into the blood and stumbled away, out of the large hole and into the snow. There was wreckage strewn as far as he could see and mangled, burnt, crushed bodies scattered everywhere. All around the crash site the snow was spattered with blood like a giant pink Rorsach test.

He stumbled towards the sobbing sound. A woman was still strapped into her seat which was standing upright in the snow as if it had just been placed there. One arm and half her body was missing, ripped off by a piece of torn metal fuselage lying in the snow a few feet away with the rest of her. Upon seeing Mike stumbling towards her, the woman laughed, blood bubbling out of her mouth.

'Hi!' she gurgled, and her sobbing stopped as she died. Mike retched into the snow again.

Then he remembered his mobile phone and pulled it out of his pocket. The glass screen was smashed and it wouldn't switch on.

'Hey!' a voice rang out as he was desperately fiddling with the ludicrously tiny 'on' button.

'Hey you!'

Mike saw a man he vaguely recognised stumbling towards him. He started towards him and the two embraced in the snow, sobbing in relief at finding each other.

'Is it just us?' Mike asked.

'I don't know man, I don't know, I just woke up. There was a-' he started sobbing again and they hugged tighter, '- there was a stewardess. She's dead. The whole top of her head is-'

'I know,' Mike's voice hitched and hiccupped from his crying, just like it had when he was a boy. 'We need to try and find other survivors.'

'OK. There's another part of the plane over there - but I don't think anyone's alive. Let's go and check together,' he pleaded to Mike, and the two of them made their way to another tubular section of the aircraft. It was lying longways across their path and as they rounded the side Mike could see the long, long trail through the snow as it had rolled and bounced before coming to a stop. The two of them peered cautiously inside.

There were thirty or so seats inside, a few still attached to the aircraft. The whole section had come to rest upside down so they had to look upwards towards the seats, the few human remains still strapped in dripping blood. Most of the seats had been ripped away and were in a jumble on the floor. The hard metal and soft human parts had been churned together like a food processor as the aircraft had rolled and rolled. There wasn't much recognisable left inside.

Mike felt his gag reflex again and turned away, taking deep breaths. The other man was retching into the snow.

They moved a distance away from the horror and sat in the snow.

'We're gonna get rescued, right?'

'Of course,' Mike said.

'I hope it's soon. I'm really cold, and it's getting dark.'

'We need to find shelter.'

'Not in there, man.'

'No, not in there. You got a phone?'

'Yeah,' Royce dug out the phone from his pocket and tapped the glass to activate it. Smartphones had dumbed down after the internet went off, so his was small with only a few visible icons.

'No signal. Nothing at all.'

The two of them stood and made their way back to Mike's section of the plane, when they heard another voice screaming at them. A woman in the distance waved frantically at them. Mike definitely recognised her. His employer. He hadn't actually met her yet formally, he had intended to say 'hi' on the flight.

They hurried over to her. She was standing next to a small piece of fuselage. On one side, two dead bodies lay in a crumpled heap. On the other was an empty aisle seat and the window seat, which held a Kin. A large jagged piece of metal was sticking through its side, and the body was leaking white blood. It looked dead.

'Marion Crandall?' I'm Mike Hennessy, the lawyer the Kin recommended to you.'

'Oh right. Nice to meet you.'

The two shook hands briefly before snatching their hands back, shocked that they could perform such a formal gesture under such circumstances.

'We need to get it out, it's hurt really bad,' she said.

'It looks dead,' said the other man who had not introduced himself.

'I am not dead. Not yet,' the Kin spoke, 'although I am in pain and think I will soon die. If you are able, please make me comfortable so I can prepare for my death.'

Crandall undid the seat harness while Mike and the other man supported the body. They lowered it gently to the floor.

'Thank you. Is this 'irony', Marion?' it asked.

'Yes.' She started to cry.

'What the hell do you mean?' the other man asked.

'I was on my way to an autopsy of the first ever dead Kin in Buenos Aires.'

'And now she has two,' said the Kin.

'We're going to get rescued, you're going to make it.'

'Not fast enough,' the alien said, 'it's nearly dark. The snow hasn't stopped. You need to make a shelter. Regrettably, I am unable to assist you. I would suggest as a temporary measure that this section of the aircraft would suffice.'

'There's two dead people in this section of the aircraft.'

'And about fifty in the other sections we've seen.' Mike said to her. 'The Kin is right.' He turned to the other survivor. 'Come on, give me a hand. What's your name?'

'Royce Brims.'

The three of them gritted their teeth and hauled the two dead people out and found large jagged sections of metal to drag across the two openings at either end. Within half an hour they had a serviceable shelter.

Then the storm hit them.

ROYCE

His star kept rising, just as the panther on his arm kept growing. Much to the hilarity of his entourage that first tattoo had looked more like a large black kitten, but he covered it up and was a big hit on Bill Bolt's late night US chat show. It lead to other appearances on bigger shows; Conan, Fallon, the Daily Show. The kitten eventually became a panther, stalking its way up his arm surrounded by thistles and runes and mystical symbols, to which each one Royce attributed a different, semi-fictional relevance to his life story.

Henderson Mulcahy's faith in Royce Brims was starting to pay off. His single 'White Skin, Black Heart' was the fastest selling single of all time. Since digital downloads were no longer possible, singles were judged by physical, pre-internet style sales figures and were accurate to the nearest single sale.

His debut album, 'Human Resurrection,' went platinum. The swift follow up, 'White, Blue and Black,' consolidated his status. His underwear line became the most worn pant among males between the ages of 14 and 40, outselling previous top sellers Calvin Klein and Bjorn Borg combined. His debut movie 'Siamese Kin' was critically pummelled but made over four hundred million dollars worldwide on a budget of one hundred and fifty million on his name alone, which guaranteed a sequel in which he refused to be a part. He was replaced by Kevin Hart for 'Siamese Kin 2: Kinjoined' which bombed. He was sued by the studio for breach of contract to the tune of more millions of dollars, but the respect he earned from both the public and the music industry for holding his ground and refusing to appear in it sent his stock soaring ever higher.

He was the apparently unwilling participant of a sex tape scandal just before the release of his third album, 'FucKin', which helped it to go platinum on pre-sales alone.

He was forty dates into a sold-out two hundred-date world arena tour. The next few stops on the tour were in South America, via an unscheduled and unwelcome remote mountaintop on which he was now completely stranded.

The temperature dropped to minus 30 degrees on that first night, and although Royce could not know the exact number, he knew it was the coldest he had ever been in his life. Colder than he had known it was physically possible to get. Cold that pummelled his body and overwhelmed every sense he had. There was no part of him that didn't scream for it to stop every single second.

The three of them huddled together, gripping each other tightly, sharing what little body heat they could. They all broke down in helpless sobs at one point or more throughout the long night as the snowstorm whistled and swirled relentlessly around and through their makeshift shelter.

By morning both ends of their small tubular section of aircraft were covered by snow, effectively sealing them in. The temperature had increased by a few degrees without the wind-chill. Royce had even managed to doze off for a few minutes but woke up with a start as the guy called Mike started to clear a path out.

'We're gonna get rescued today, right?' he said. Nobody answered him.

Together they pushed against the temporary barriers they had leaned up against the fuselage. So much snow had built up against them that they could only shift them forwards a few inches at a time, the worlds slowest snow plough. Each time they shifted forwards clumps of snow fell on them and melted in the warmth of exertion.

Soon bright sunshine streamed in and there was a large enough gap to squeeze out. Royce followed Mike outside and immediately lifted his arm to shield his eyes against the glare. He had never known anything so bright.

They were on a plain of snow on a very gradual slope

inside a vast, uneven bowl between mountains that completely surrounded and towered above them.

The larger sections of the stricken aircraft were visible sticking out above about a foot of snow. The smaller sections, human remains and other debris were all buried, pitting and bumping the ground with snowy warts.

'Come on,' Mike said to Royce, 'we need to start searching for anything that might be useful. Anything at all. Check everywhere again and make sure there's nobody else alive. Maybe we can find some food.'

'I ain't going back in there,' Royce pointed to the larger section of the aircraft they had seen the previous day, slightly downhill from them.

'OK, I'll go in. There's more wreckage uphill, over there. Another section from the front I think. Go with Marion. Salvage whatever you can. We need clothes, food, whatever.'

'Mike!' Marion called from inside their refuge.

They gathered inside and the three of them looked down at the Kin. The skin was still white, but the blue markings down its face and body had turned a paler blue, almost invisible.

'Are you sure it's dead and not just sleeping?' he asked.

'I have no idea. It looks fairly dead to me.'

'OK well, this doesn't change the plan. We'll leave it here and see if it wakes up. Let's go.'

Royce and Marion started the walk uphill to the section of the plane that had come to rest further on up the slope. They had to scramble over a scree of rocks and a small ridge to get to it. Royce didn't want to look. His two friends and his agent were somewhere around, and he had not the slightest wish to see their broken dead bodies.

'You go first,' he said to Marion, and turned his back. Marion stared at him in disbelief, before turning and hoisting herself up and into the plane. Royce heard her rooting around, heard her retch and gag. Then she cried out, 'Royce! Get in here!'

Royce hauled himself in and ran over to her, trying not to look left or right at the bloodbath around them. He knelt next to her. Underneath a pile of spilled hand luggage and wedged firmly between two first class seats both with corpses still strapped into them, was a man he recognised.

'Buddy. Oh holy fuck, thank you God, thank you so much.'

'Royce? Oh Jesus fuck, thank fuck. Thank fuck. Royce, get me out of here. I've hurt my arm, I think it's broken.'

'Man, if that's all you got from being in here, you one of the lucky ones,' said Royce, taking hold of one of the seats trapping his agent and yanking hard. It rolled back, landing upright on its buckled runners. The head of the body still strapped into it rolled sickeningly backwards. The neck was broken and the head dangled at an angle a head was never designed to dangle. The lower jaw had been torn off and the tongue lolled out like fat pink bunting.

Royce screamed. He had never actually screamed before, not a truly involuntary, proper, guttural scream of horror. To his own ears it sounded like someone else screaming, someone who sounded like a pussy and who he wanted to stop screaming immediately, but who couldn't or didn't know how to stop. The corpse in the chair was Kai.

MARION

Marion helped Royce out of the plane and he gasped and retched and shook in the snow outside. She went back in and pushed the other seat off Buddy Tucker, helping him out from under the pile of hand luggage, both of them determined not to look at the remains of Royce's friend. Tucker's arm was definitely broken, a splinter of bone sticking through the skin and thin fabric of his shirt like the dorsal fin of a shark breaking the water's surface.

She called to Royce and started throwing the hand luggage towards him and away from the dead bodies. The three of them went through all the bags they could find. Lots of books, newspapers and music players. A couple of thin, decorative scarfs and a trucker's cap was all the extra clothing they could find.

The three of them went back down towards their shelter and sat down, shivering. Mike joined them. He held two large bags stuffed with newspapers and a few caps but no clothes. He threw them down.

'Until we find the luggage we need to keep warm, so stuff your clothes with newspaper, get as much insulation as you can.'

He nodded at Buddy. Both of them wore only shirt sleeves. Royce wore a long sleeve black T-shirt with the logo of his clothing brand, BrimsTone, printed in gold on the front. Marion wore a summer dress and a pink cardigan.

'Mike's right,' she said, 'none of us are dressed for these conditions. We need to find the luggage, and soon. And maybe the kitchen, find some food. We have no idea when we'll be rescued.'

She stuffed her dress with the paper, and the others started doing the same. When it was gone they all stood around looking like Michelin Men.

'Lets split up,' Mike Hennessy said. 'Have we all got

watches? Right, let's meet back here in an hour. Look for anything you think might be useful, then we can all go and fetch it together when we meet back up.'

Marion struck out across the snow in search of the luggage, not feeling any warmer and trying to keep the paper she had stuffed in her dress from falling out.

Twenty minutes later, scrambling among the snowy lumps that occasionally yielded torn metal, dead bodies or hand luggage with nothing but more papers in them, she spotted a large section of fuselage resting in the snow on its curved spine. As she approached she could see that one end was overhanging the edge of what appeared to be a large crack or crevasse in the ice. She approached tentatively, not wanting the edges of the crevasse to crumble away and take her with it. On the section of smile-shaped fuselage, beyond the jagged edges and shattered glass she saw a seat lying on its side, a dead body still strapped into it and another body lying next to it.

One of the dead bodies yelled at her.

'Hey!'

Marion leapt backwards in shock.

'Don't come any closer,' the body continued, 'any movement is going to make this thing slide down there.' The body lying next to the corpse in the seat was talking. It was a teenage boy.

'Any movement I make, it slides further in,' the boy shouted, 'can you get help?'

Marion nodded. 'Yes, yes... hold on, don't move... I'll get help.'

She ran back to the meeting point and waited an excruciating five minutes until Mike and Royce returned. She gabbled her story and they gathered what they could. Mike grabbed some laptop cases and hand luggage with straps they could use for a rope and they ran back to the trapped boy who was sobbing with relief.

'You're not out of this yet, kid,' Mike called out, as he

tried to lash the luggage together to make a rope. It wasn't nearly long enough, ten feet at best he reckoned.

'There's two of us here,' the boy choked. 'My mother too, she's alive. In the seat.'

Marion stared. She had been sure the woman in the seat was dead.

'Is she OK?' Marion called out.

'I don't know. She hasn't said a word since the crash, I think she's in shock, or got hyperthermia or something.'

'OK, here's what we have to do,' Mike said. 'We don't have any rope and this isn't long enough. We can't risk a human chain, the crevasse might collapse and take us all down with it. We need to strip. I'll lash our clothes together, it'll take five minutes. I'll throw it to... what's your name, kid?'

'Luke. And that's Jennifer.'

'We'll throw it to Luke and Jennifer who can then take hold of it and run towards us, hopefully they can make it before it goes over. The whole thing will take less than ten minutes after we strip. If we huddle together we'll be dressed again before we freeze to death.'

There was silence.

'It must be 20 below out here,' Marion said, 'colder when the wind blows.'

'Are you fucking crazy, Hennessy?' Royce shouted. 'Strip? Here?'

'We have to try. Or Luke and Jennifer will almost certainly die. Right here in front of us. You want that?'

There was silence, save for the wind whistling around the slopes.

'OK then. Once we've got everything we can, I'll tie it together and throw it. Luke, Jennifer - you both ready?'

'Yes,' said Luke. 'Quickly, do it.'

Royce stripped first. Mike took his jeans and his BrimsTone T-shirt and lashed them together. Tucker went next, shirt and business trousers. Then Marion, who took off her cardigan, dress and bra. 'You don't have to-' Mike started.

'It's the strongest material here. Use it, quickly.'

Nobody said anything as Mike went last, lashing his suit trousers and shirt together with all the rest. The others huddled close for warmth, Marion's arms crossed over her breasts, Buddy standing behind her against the wind, his useful arm around her protectively, Royce on the other side.

Mike finished constructing the rope. He didn't pause or test its efficacy. It was a one-shot attempt. He just threw it to the two trapped figures. At it's end were the laptop cases he had found with long over the shoulder straps which clanged on the metal. The whole section of the plane slid a few inches closer to the drop.

Marion screamed. '*Come on!*'

Luke grabbed for the rope and took a firm hold, scrambling over the broken surface of the plane as it started to slide, a look of terror and desperation on his face that Mike would never forget as he leapt off the side and landed in the snow just as the whole section tipped up completely and slid downwards into the crevasse.

'*Jennifer!*' Mike shouted. The rope snagged on the jagged, torn edge of the metal as it tipped, pulling Mike towards the edge of the crevasse. He refused to let go. With a screech and a sigh of metal against snow it was gone, a few seconds of silence followed by a crash hundreds of feet beneath them in the blackness of the ice.

JENNIFER

It had all gone so very wrong, very quickly. James simply couldn't accept that Luke had taken against them. After a few months of pleading for Luke to come over, he was forced to visit Harriet and Gerry's London flat at the weekend to visit his son. It worked OK for a couple of years. Jennifer lost most of her weekends with her husband because as long as James was on Luke's turf, he was accepted.

Late one Sunday afternoon as she was catching up on the EastEnders omnibus and waiting for James to get home, she got a call. It was Gerry, who had never called her before. She wasn't even sure how he had her number.

He was drunk and she could tell from the background chatter and the inescapable sound of football on a television screen that he was in a pub. She asked him what he wanted and where James was. Gerry's answer was slurred and she couldn't make out what he was saying. She cut him off and carried on watching the television. It rang again, and when she answered it sounded like he had gone outside to hear her more clearly, although his voice was still slurred and hard to understand.

'Jennifer? You there?'

'Yes. Gerry, what's the matter? Where's James?'

'I just wanted to let you know-'

'Let me know what?'

'I got home early from football. Terrible hayfever, you know how it is at this time of year. Eyes are streaming, can't see a fucking thing.'

'That's nice, Gerry. Is James with you?'

'James... no, no he's not here. He hates football. He's back at the house with Harriet. They've been fucking. I found them. Together. You know - fucking.'

He spoke some more but she didn't hear it. Her heart

had turned to a dead-weight in her chest and the leftover Shepherds Pie she had eaten for her tea was threatening to make a reappearance. She felt flushed, a cold sweat breaking out all over her body.

She was about to hit the red button on her phone and cut Gerry off when she heard him say, *'Don't worry, I gave them both a good hiding.'* She asked him what he meant, but he had gone and she was left saying his name over and over again to complete silence for a few seconds before she realised he had cut the connection. She tried redialling him but got nothing but voicemail. Then she called James. Then Harriet. She called them both thirty times or more before dialling the police.

Her doorbell rang a little under an hour later. Jennifer wordlessly let the Police officer into the house and they sat down next to each other on the sofa. At that exact moment she realised that she hated the sofa; the colour, the fabric, the cushions. She offered the policewoman a cup of tea, for some reason desperate to disassociate herself with the fucking sofa. The policewoman shook her head and slowly and gently explained to her that Harriet and James were both dead, having suffered trauma from repeated blows from a blunt instrument to their heads and bodies. They had been found naked in the master bedroom.

Gerry was taken into custody later that night but was too drunk to speak. He was kept in the cells and interviewed across the following days, during which Jennifer took in Luke, who had been staying at a friends house at the time the pair were murdered.

She and Luke hadn't seen or spoken to each other in nearly two years and although he was much taller, Jennifer didn't see a lot of change in the boy. He was still stick-thin and virtually silent, but given his parents had just been brutally murdered by his step-father Jennifer reckoned he had a pretty good reason to be unresponsive. He moved back in to his old bedroom willingly enough, carrying a suitcase that had been rapidly packed by a police officer in his bedroom across the hall from the room still stained by the blood of his parents.

Gerry denied their murder for about three days after his arrest but when Luke's cricket bat had turned up in a fishpond with Gerry's prints and Harriet's blood and hair all over it he retracted his statement and made a full confession.

If Jennifer had thought that life was as bad as it could get, she was wrong. It got much, much worse. There had been a huge decrease in violent, bloody news stories as the Kin had settled in, and the newspapers and broadcast news desperately latched onto the double-murder like toddlers to ice-cream.

For the weeks before and during Gerry's trial, in which she was obliged to testify, there were photographers, interviews, stalkers, paparazzi camped outside Jennifer's house. She holed up with Luke and waited for everything to calm down, which she knew it would, eventually. All that really mattered to her was that James was gone. Unfortunately Luke seemed fascinated by the coverage and the process and so she watched it with him for moral support.

Then one morning the verdict was finally reached and it was all over. Gerry was handed two life sentences to be served consecutively, and when she cracked open the bedroom curtains and saw no one waiting for her she knew that somewhere in the new world something else had happened and her time in the public eye was over for good.

With the case closed she felt that it was finally appropriate for her to grieve properly for her second dead husband. She sold the house and took her and Luke to live somewhere much smaller on the outskirts of London, a terraced house in an area filled with young families and artisan cafes selling flat white coffee and loose-leaf tea and goats cheese ciabatta sandwiches.

Luke went with her uncomplainingly, his demeanour as ever distant and untouchable. They lived together in the same house but not in the same world. They circled like orbiting satellites, always in sight of each other but unable to get close.

Her design business kept them afloat and the work she did for all of James' old clients kept her busy, and as usual she threw herself into it.

They got along well enough for a few years. Luke grew taller but not much wider, filling out into a teenager but staying exactly as skinny as he had always been. She was living life on autopilot, just as she had been when she had met James, until she received an offer from one of her clients to head up a new creative hub in an emerging centre for design and technology in Buenos Aires.

James had been dead for three years. Her adopted stepson was a stranger to her. It was time. She accepted the offer. She rented the house, put all their stuff into storage and she and Luke boarded a flight to Buenos Aires.

And now she found herself at the very precipice of death, an innocent casualty of fate, a helpless victim once again. She had accepted Luke's comfort as the plane had gone down; was grateful for it, warmed by it, encouraged by the long overdue step forward in their relationship, a welcome feeling of connection and optimism to take with her to her grave.

She had simply watched uncomprehendingly as his comforting hug turned into something completely *else,* as he fumbled around the fly of his jeans and calmly pulled out his erect penis, even as the panicked screaming of the other passengers rang in her ears. He even reclined the first class seat.

What the hell is he doing? She still didn't understand, couldn't understand, until he pulled her underwear aside and forced himself inside her, raping her in her seat as the plane went down. As her eyes and her brain finally clicked into gear and she realised fully what was happening she still didn't struggle, capitulating to the assault completely. She thought and hoped that they would die before he finished.

She waited for the end, biting down on her tongue until it bled, trying to imagine the blackness and permanence of her impending death, much preferable to her current situation. Surely now, surely this was it? Impact. Death. *Come on.* COME ON! Her eyes were squeezed shut, longing for the explosion that would kill them both.

She opened her eyes for a split second and saw the face of her dead husband in the boy looming over her, the same sweat across his forehead, the same look of concentration etched across his face. She felt him coming inside her and she gagged, phlegm burning the back of her throat.

As she grit her teeth and endured his last, empty thrusts, the plane finally - *finally* - hit the ground, the whole side of their section of the plane ripped away, the howling noise of wind, of engines exploding, the screaming of tearing metal and dying people, of tumbling end over end, spinning, rolling, jarring impact over and over again, utter disorientation and blackness.

After an eternity, when it was quiet again, she kept her eyes shut and prayed she was dead.

She wasn't.

In a cruel, cosmic joke they were both left alive and alone on a precarious metal ledge ready to slide at any moment into a crevasse on the side of *a fucking mountain.*

Luke had tried to climb off at first but it kept slipping downwards. In the end, he had a choice; move or die. Through that first interminable night and completely trapped, the two of them both fought with every fibre of their beings towards opposite objectives. Luke was trying to stay alive and Jennifer was trying to die, but despite herself she didn't want him to die too. When morning came she wept with frustration and pain. Her whole body was in agony.

Then the rescuers came with their makeshift rope and desperate plan. Luke's escape shifted the torn fuselage and it started to slide. The weight of it against the lip of the crevasse tilted it up and for a few terrifying seconds she was strapped into her seat and staring directly downwards into the blackness. She could just see the bottom; a very, very long way down, the walls lethal, jagged daggers of ice, glinting blue and silver.

Jennifer had only a couple of seconds to ponder her fate.

The boy was safe, that was the main thing, she supposed. *He was just fourteen, his life in front of him. But he had just raped her. He has to atone for that, somehow. Should he get away with it? He has always been troubled, even more so after his father's death.*

This is the best way, this death. It's OK to die this way. It would save on burial costs for one thing. She would see Stephen and James soon if it wasn't too awkward. They'll get along, right?

But shouldn't somebody be around to stop Luke, to protect him from committing any further acts of violence? Oh right, because she had done such a bang-up job so far. If he gets away with it he's going to do it again, not even sure if she was his first.

How dare he make her feel this way? So confused, so angry, so betrayed, so humiliated. She had done nothing but try to be his friend when his mother was alive and his guardian when she was dead. Could she have done any more?

There's no answer to that. Maybe. But she had to either work harder at it or make him pay for what he's done - probably both. One way or the other, she decided at the last possible instant, *I have to live.*

She was ashamed and humiliated and scared and numb but took hold of the end of the clothes rope with one hand and unclipped the seatbelt buckle with the other. There was a tug, and then she was free and holding on with one hand as the section of the plane with her empty seat still attached to it dropped away beneath her, bouncing down the walls of the crevasse, shattering ice as it went. There was a boom as it hit the bottom and slid away, never to be seen again.

LUKE

He wasn't strapped in when the plane hit the ground. He grabbed one end of his seatbelt and held onto it for dear life as the plane flipped and tore and rolled and burned. At some point the seatbelt had been torn from his grasp and he bounced off the sides a few times, losing consciousness. When he had come round he had been lying on a broken section of fuselage, facing Jennifer. She was conscious, still strapped into her first class seat and staring at him silently. It was snowing, snow flakes so massive he could make out each unique shape. The biting wind drove the snow almost horizontal. There was a thin covering over him. His body ached and his head throbbed where he had been knocked out. He tried to stand up but as soon as he had moved the whole metal section had slid forwards toward the wide black gap in the ice. If he moved, the plane moved. Jennifer just sat silently, her eyes open and glassy, breathing but unresponsive.

They somehow endured the night. The cold was so bad that he thought that they would almost certainly be dead by morning. Cold so inconceivable it was like being stabbed in the heart with an icicle, over and over again. He curled up in a ball and suffered through the winds and driving snow, expecting to slide into the abyss at any second. There was a numbness in his hands and feet and face and he noticed that his fingers were turning grey.

Then the woman and the others had arrived and mounted their naked rescue.

He ignored the screaming pain in his hands and fingers and legs and caught the makeshift rope, scrambling like a monkey across the surface, slippery with broken glass. It started to slide immediately and his heart pounded as he leapt for safety from the moving surface. He landed next to his rescuers, huddled together against the freezing snow and wind. He turned around in time to watch the remains of the fuselage disappearing into the crevasse.

It vanished, tipping over and falling, bouncing and crashing to the bottom of the chasm. His stepmother had gone down with it. He breathed a large sigh of relief. He had won. Not only had he lost his virginity with the woman all his friends and at least one teacher consistently told him they fantasised about when they jerked off, but now she was dead and he wouldn't have to deal with any fallout.

But the man was still holding onto the rope.

'*Help me!*' he shouted, and Luke's brief feeling of elation turned to a plunging dread.

The others broke their huddle and clambered over the snow towards Mike Hennessy. They took hold of him and together pulled Jennifer slowly to the top. As she appeared over the lip of ice and snow some of it crumbled down and she lurched downwards a few feet. Marion screamed and Royce shouted, but Jennifer made no noise, just held grimly on to Marion's bra.

The group pulled her up until she was lying in the snow at the top. They all gathered around her, pulling her to relative safety away from the edge of the crevasse.

Mike untied the clothes and they got dressed in their wet things. He instructed them to run around to warm up, which they did. Luke sat next to Jennifer, silently watching them.

ROYCE

The cold was relentless, exhausting, permeating deep into their bones. It was Terminator-level cold, cold that absolutely would not stop until they were all dead. Royce idly wondered if he was the only person who had ever remembered that film in this desolate place. He reckoned he probably was. Night was falling and their clothes were still damp. It had started to snow again after some respite during the day but the wind still blew icy daggers into their hearts. They had managed to rescue the two people from their crazy death slide, but for what? They were all going to freeze to death out here anyway. Not even so much as a hint of rescue. None of them had any signal on their phones and nearly all of them had stopped working in the cold and wet anyway. They had no luck finding any luggage or food and had no way to make a fire. Only the lawyer vaguely knew how, but everything was damp anyway.

The woman, Jennifer, had not escaped from her night out in the open unscathed. She had frostbite on her hands and her fingers were turning black. It must have hurt a lot, but she said nothing. She didn't say much at all. She also kept as far away from the boy as she could, even as they huddled together for warmth. The boy wasn't looking much better, and he was constantly rubbing his hands together and hissing in pain.

Royce couldn't get the sight of Kai from his head. He could see Kai's dead eyes, broken body and lolling tongue. He had seen his friend's insides and it freaked him out. He kept bursting into tears uncontrollably. What with the screaming and now the crying, he had never felt so raw, so vulnerable. He used to take the piss out of people like him. The tears froze on his cheeks. His face was numb.

The night passed. Then another one.

Hennessy kept telling them to keep moving, keep looking, keep searching. The spent the days scouring the land around the wreckage, picking over what scraps they could find. By the third day they reckoned that at least half the aircraft was missing, probably somewhere behind one of the mountains it had collided with, or maybe vanished into the crevasse that had so nearly claimed Jennifer and Luke.

For food they had nothing but a few scattered bags of peanuts that they had shared among themselves. Hand luggage was plentiful but contained little of any real use, mainly more newspapers and books. No luggage, no galley and no more parts of the aircraft.

After four days, it was all they could do to huddle together, shivering, waiting for rescue or death.

'You're Royce Brims,' the boy, Luke, said to him on the fourth evening, his teeth chattering.

'Yeah. Thanks for noticing.'

'Bet you wish you were on your yacht somewhere right now.'

'I don't have a yacht, but I stayed on Henderson's a couple times.'

'Henderson Mulcahy?'

'Yeah.'

'What's he like?'

'We only met a few times. He's OK. Weird, sometimes.'

'How?'

'It's hard to say. He's been rich a long time. Sometimes he forgets what it's like to not be-' Royce paused.

'What?'

'I don't know. To not be the centre of attention maybe.'

'I bet you like to be centre of attention too.'

'Hell yeah. You're pretty smart. How old are you?'

'Fourteen.'

'Fourteen. I remember being fourteen. It was the year my mum let me go out with my mates, hang out. It was the year I started to rap in public.'

At the mention of his mother, Royce started to cry again. Luke put his arm around him. 'Don't cry, Royce.'

'I can't help it. I don't know what the fuck's the matter with me. It's OK for you, your mum's here.'

'My mum is dead, so is my dad. Jennifer is my stepmother.'

'Oh yeah? You two don't seem to be getting on too well.'

Jennifer sat on the outside of the group, half turned away and staring out into the gathering darkness of their fourth night. Her hands were blackening with frostbite and she shivered uncontrollably.

'No, not really.'

'Why?'

Luke fell silent. 'I don't know,' he answered.

MARION

Fourth night over, and daylight broke across the fifth day. The snow kept coming, the cold unrelenting. Marion and Mike huddled closer than might, in other circumstances, be construed as appropriate.

Jennifer's frostbitten hands were getting worse. Buddy's broken arm was turning a shade of blackish green and he was shivering with a fever that was making him hallucinate.

Her own feet were numb and she was too scared to look at them. She simply could not work out why they were not being rescued. The flight would have had a flight plan tracked by GPS, and the Kin on board had a tracking device in its arm. To be lost was inconceivable. Something had gone terribly wrong.

It was fairly clear as the fifth day inched into the sixth night, that no rescue was coming. None of them were prepared for the conditions, nobody knew how to make a fire even if they had the right tools or materials. All they could do was huddle together, shivering, waiting. They were going to freeze to death long before they starved.

'I'm going outside,' she announced to the small group and stood up.

'Don't you even think about it,' Mike said, 'I'm coming with you.'

The two of them went outside into the snow. The wind was picking up. Most of the plane debris was gone, vanished under a blanket of white.

'We're going to die here, Mike,' she said, and started to cry. Her tears froze instantly to her dark red, chapped cheeks.

'No, we're not,' he replied, but he sounded unconvinced, even to his own ears.

'Jennifer has bad frostbite, and the boy isn't much better. Buddy is obviously going to die, and I can't feel my feet. I'm too scared to look.'

'Not how you envisaged ending up, is it?'

'No,' she wept, 'it isn't.'

'You changed the world you know. Your plan, your determination. You have a legacy far greater than any singer or politician.'

'Fat lot of good it's doing me out here.'

'That's the thing about a legacy, it's supposed to outlive you.'

The two of them kissed in the driving snow. It might have been passionate but Marion couldn't feel her face. They broke it off.

'Sorry,' she said.

'It's OK. We'll try again later, when we're warm again.'

They both laughed.

'I wish-'

'What?'

'I knew a guy once. He always knew what to do, somehow. How to approach things. I wish he was here.'

'I bet he'd just love to be stuck on a mountain with you. I'm not sure even he'd know how to get out of this one.'

'It's not that he'd know how to get us out necessarily, he'd just know how to... cope with it better I suppose. I'm sorry. I'm not really myself. All I'm saying is - I think we need to move. We can't stay here and wait to die.'

'And go where?'

'I don't know. Pick a direction. Try and find civilisation. It might not be that far away.'

'If it wasn't far away someone would have seen the plane go down. Nobody saw it.'

'I don't care, Mike. I'm not going to sit here and freeze to death.'

'Spoken like a true pioneer. What's your plan?'

'I don't have a plan. Start walking, I guess.'

'OK, that's a shit plan. We need to put it to a vote, those who want to stay can stay, those who want to go can go. Then we pack up what we can, although none of us are going to get very far without food. Drinking snow isn't going to cut it.'

'I know, but it's got to be worth a try. Do I take it that you are coming with me then?'

'Sure thing. Let's blow this joint.'

'What?'

'Nothing.'

LUKE

The evening had turned surreal, even by the high standards set by the previous few days. First of all Royce Brims, hard-ass rap-gangsta, had burst into tears and rested his head on Luke's shoulder and fallen asleep.

Then Marion Crandall from the news and the lawyer guy went outside and came back after ten minutes and told them that they were leaving in the morning and that whoever wanted to come with them were welcome. Very informal, like they were going to the pub.

Royce immediately said he would go with them and after nearly hacking up a lung, so did Royce's agent Buddy whose arm was definitely starting to smell really bad.

Luke wasn't really sure what to do, but he sure as hell didn't want to stay here on his own with his step-mother, so he agreed to accompany them. Jennifer said nothing, just looked up briefly and gave a short nod.

He was finding her silence really unnerving. She didn't respond to anything or say a word, and even though her back was turned to him the whole time he couldn't shake off the feeling that she was watching him. It was weird.

Even more weird was when Mike and Marion raised the subject of food and how they wouldn't get far without it.

'What do you mean?' he asked, confused. 'There is no food?'

The two of them paused, then the agent spoke up. 'They mean to eat a person. A human being.'

'What?' Luke said, incredulously. 'You can't be fucking serious?'

'Meat is protein. Energy,' said Mike.

'No fuckin' way,' said Royce. 'No fuckin' way. I'd rather freeze to death.'

'Well, that's the other option. We're not going to force it on anyone,' said the woman from the news, Marion Crandall, 'but our best chance of making it out of here is to eat. If it works, we'll be saved and we can thank our lucky stars that statistically we'll never have to do it again. If we die, then it makes no difference.'

'You're fucking crazy.' Royce again.

'OK,' Buddy Tucker spoke up, 'I'll do it. I don't want to die here.'

Luke and Jennifer were silent.

'It's OK, you don't have to make up your minds yet. We'll find something in the morning and set off immediately afterwards,' Marion said, and they sat down in a flurry of snow and huddled with the group. The temperature was dropping again. All they could do now was hold together and try not to die.

Luke sat as close as he could to Royce Brims and as far from Jennifer as he could get. He couldn't sleep at all. He was dreading the next day. Secretly he thought he'd rather stay and die than become a... what? Cannibal? The word whizzed around his brain as it turned from a sick joke into a very real possibility. He started to feel queasy and more terrified than at any point in this whole fucked-up ordeal. He started to sweat, which froze into a thin layer of ice on his face. He wiped it away. His breathing became faster, more laboured and forced. He felt faint, stars danced in front of his vision. The world was spinning around him.

He passed out.

JENNIFER

Luke had never known a world without the Kin, or with the world wide web. Jennifer missed her social media but had never been so invested that she suffered when it was taken away. What had replaced it was in her opinion better, more visible, less open to misinterpretation and misuse. It had helped the world regain it's balance.

A combination of old, existing and new technology had evolved throughout Luke's life that enabled him to stay in touch with a wide circle of people, update them, swap stories and share interests. The new social network had grown up within a few weeks of the death of the internet and Luke had grown up with it. At fourteen he was highly regarded in his circle. He was diligent and loyal, a regular contributor. His status was exemplary, and the most important thing in his life.

She held a newspaper fashioned into a bag over his face to slow down his hyper-ventilating and knew that of them all, the boy was going to struggle with the idea of cannibalism most. If they survived the story would inevitably come out. It wouldn't matter what an amazing, entrepreneurial, altruistic life he might lead after this event, he would forever be the boy who ate human flesh.

His breathing slowed and he passed from agitated unconsciousness into sleep, his head on her lap. The others said nothing. She stared at his face. The last time she had stared at it she had seen the face of her dead husband. The two of them did look very alike.

She moved him closer to the others for warmth. She was going to do it, and if she had to, she would force him to do it too. She was still responsible for what happened to him if they lived, and she was going to do everything in her power to make sure that he faced up to what he had done.

MIKE

Mike stood over the frozen corpse of a human being, a piece of jagged metal in his hand like a carving knife. The body looked broken and not like a human being at all, half buried in snow, but still Mike stared, gulping every few seconds like a goldfish drowning on a surplus of oxygen. He and Marion had found body parts, but couldn't bring themselves to touch them. For some strange primal reason it seemed easier to select a body that still looked intact and try to hack it apart. They found a male corpse still attached to a seat, lying on it's side. The neck was broken and the head lolled like a broken doll but the body otherwise looked reasonably intact, so they dug it up and dragged it into the open and Mike found some metal to use as a carving knife. But for all his bravado and talk the previous evening, he found he couldn't do it. The group stood in a silent circle around the corpse lying face down in the snow.

Marion snatched the metal from Mike's hand and peeled the frozen business shirt away from the man's lower back and side. His skin was the colour of a pale blue flower. Marion stabbed the man in the side and started sawing at the flesh. She ripped out a chunk, then another and another. It shredded slightly, like dry chicken. She took a piece and lifted it to her mouth. The tip of her tongue licked it, then she gagged and retched phlegm over the snow.

'Shit. I don't think I can do this,' she said.

'Then you'll die here,' Mike replied and took some meat. He raised it to his lips and pressed it against his closed mouth. To the others it looked like his lips had a life of their own, refusing to open and let him chew on the meat, locked together in their own private battle.

Finally he dropped it and stormed off. 'Fine!' he shouted. 'We'll all die out here, frozen and starving. Let's just go, let's walk.'

'*Wait!*' shouted the agent, Buddy Tucker. 'What about-'

BUDDY

'-that?' Everyone's gaze followed where he was pointing, which was a small raised bump of snow just outside and to one side of their makeshift shelter.

There was a short silence. Then Marion Crandall said: 'No.'

'Why not?'

'Because we have no idea what they're made of. It's probably poisonous.'

'But it might not be. It has to at least be, you know, organic?'

'Its too dangerous.'

'Why?' Mike had come back. 'If they were poisonous wouldn't we know about it by now?'

'Not really. There are millions of poisonous creatures that are harmless unless ingested. Nobody has ever seen inside one of them, that's where I was headed on this flight, ironically. It's far too risky.'

'But easier, though. Easier than eating... him-' Jennifer spoke up, looking down at the abused corpse on the snow.

'Morally, probably. Psychologically, most certainly. But potential suicide. At least we know that human flesh contains proteins and iron that might keep us alive out here. We don't know anything about Kin physiology except from what they have told us and that could be hugely misleading. It was part of the agreement, the very first manifesto fourteen years ago, to wait until we could examine one naturally.'

'Bet you're regretting that now,' Royce said.

'Yes Royce, if I had known I was going to starve to death on the side of a freezing mountain unless I ate one in a fucking *pie* I might have been more persistent about that point.'

'Alright, jeez.'

'But you know what would have happened?' She was

really shouting at Royce now, 'you know what? Hatred, death and violence, probably. You think the Kin came down here defenceless, ready to lay down arms and submit? They needed a place to stay and we gave them one peacefully, otherwise the whole fucking world would have ended up like one of your wretched films where the world is covered in skulls and it's always dark and humanity is circling the fucking plughole. Everything that happened to black people and gay people and minorities throughout the goddamn centuries - generations of hatred - would have happened all over again, but worse. Much fucking worse. No-one would have had the money to buy your stupid fucking records, because they would have all been dead, or more interested in actually feeding their children-' she was crying now, and her voice trailed off. 'Is that what you want?'

'My film was a comedy.'

Marion turned away, her head in her hands.

'Are you saying-' asked Jennifer, 'that the Kin would have attacked us if we hadn't let them stay?'

'No. Not as such,' Marion's voice was hitching and squeaky as she tried to regain her composure. 'But they needed a new home. Once the signal was answered they were coming, with or without our permission. Without the manifesto, without the plan, we would have construed their arrival as a threat and attacked them, for sure. They would have fought us for the right to stay. I don't know how that would have worked out, but it wouldn't have been pleasant for any of us.'

The group fell silent.

'I'll do it.'

They all looked at Buddy, who repeated himself. 'I'll do it.'

'Do what?' Hennessy asked.

'I'll eat the Kin.'

'No,' Marion said again.

'I'm dead already,' Buddy replied. 'I can't feel my arm. It's turning black. It probably stinks but my nose is an ice cube. I won't make it far if we leave anyway. Let me try it. If I die, don't eat it. If I'm OK, then you don't have to face being cannibals.'

'That's a good idea!' Luke said, far too eagerly. The rest of the group stared at him and he averted his eyes, looking down at the snow. 'I mean, it must be worth a try, right?' he mumbled. Royce punched him on the arm.

'That's my agent you're throwing to the wolves man,' he grinned.

'Sorry,' Luke mumbled back.

'S'OK, that's what agents are for, right Bud?' Royce said to Buddy, who smiled weakly at him.

'Do what you want,' Marion said eventually, 'I want no part of it.'

To her surprise, Mike helped the others uncover the Kin from it's resting place next to their shelter.

They all huddled around it for a moment. Marion could see that it had turned completely white, it's distinctive blue markings faded away, the body almost invisible against the snow.

To her surprise, again, it was Jennifer who wielded the makeshift knife. She pressed it to the thigh of the dead creature and started to saw a piece from it, with the others watching closely. It must have been tough or frozen, because she hacked and sawed for a full minute before she had a thick cut of the thigh in her hands. The meat looked to Marion like a large white fish. It dripped gelatinous white blood.

Buddy Tucker was watching over her shoulder and she held it out towards him in cupped hands like she was making an offering to a deity or a monarch. Buddy accepted the flesh in his one working hand.

He stared at the dripping white meat. Sniffed it. Then he opened his mouth and took a bite.

PART FOUR

DANDRIDGE

The squat, black-brick house didn't have a garden or fences or any boundaries as such, except for the active volcano that loomed thousands of feet over it, casting it in permanent shadow. The house just sat there, buffeted by the almost constant wind that came whistling down the rocky slopes behind it, blowing around the corners, under every door and window-frame and through the rotor blades of the small bubble-shaped Hughes TH-55 Osage helicopter that was lashed down under a cover alongside the building.

Dandridge didn't notice. He had long since stopped noticing the noise of the almost constant wind against the exposed house, just like he never used to notice the weird, piercing screams of mating foxes in the garden of his house in Gloucestershire.

The occupants of the house lived peacefully on their own. The helicopter took them to and from the nearest small town forty miles away and there were two motorcycles stored in the basement for emergencies. The remoteness suited Dandridge. He loved living off the map, although he did occasionally think about the house in Gloucestershire and hoped that Josh would have taken the hint and moved in, perhaps with that delicious pilot of his, Perron.

Dandridge had wandered for a long time, watching as the world changed and grew and developed in the most amazing and fascinating ways no-one could ever have predicted. Since the Kin arrived it was like being back in the early days of aeroplane travel in the nineteen fifties and sixties; boundaries had fallen, restrictions loosened. You could turn up, pay a fare and get on a plane to wherever you wanted to go, and it was so much easier to travel unnoticed.

In Iceland he had learned of a commune of the aliens living in a remote seismological and meteorological station near a volcano and had come out to visit, hiking and camping the whole way. The station had turned out to be a rather ugly small house. The three Kin who lived there had welcomed him in without hesitation. They all did, everywhere. To the Kin, he was well-known, a hero almost. To humans, a stranger.

A year later, he was still living with the three of them. He and the Kin worked the station each day, recording seismic activity and reporting any undue wobbles and grumbles in the earth beneath them. The world on the surface may have changed, but the planet was still very much the same.

He and the Kin talked of many things. He learned about their lives on their own planet, their jobs, their families. He asked them how they reproduced in a sexually ambiguous, apparently mono-gender race. He asked them why it was widely reported that they were not reproducing on earth. They fenced his questions for a long time, countering with their own questions about human sexuality. Dandridge happily told them everything they wanted to know in excruciating detail, recounting each of his experiences and partners starting from his first when he was sixteen. The Kin listened avidly to all his stories.

Their blue markings were all very different from each other and he discovered that despite all having the same voice they had very distinct personalities, so he gave them human names. He called them Belle, Maisie and Daniel. They asked him why two of them were female names and one was male, but Dandridge didn't really know, it was just that Daniel seemed, somehow, more of a bloke.

They didn't eat or excrete or even sleep as such, although Dandridge knew that there were hours in the night when they would enter a strange 'slow-down' period and struggle to be able to respond to him or move very quickly.

So they lived together contentedly. It was almost a year to the day since Dandridge had entered the little house when he was lying in his boxer shorts on his bed reading a Clive Cussler paperback he had picked up from the local bookstore at the tiny local town. They didn't have much in the way of English language novels but for some reason seemed to have a steady supply of Cussler. He turned the page and glanced up to see all three Kin awkwardly crowding the doorway of his bedroom. He rarely closed the door.

'Hi guys,' he said, surprised. They had never disturbed him when he was reading late at night.

'Richard,' said Belle.

'Yes? Are you alright? What's up?' he put the paperback down next to him, face down and open at his page.

'You once asked us why the Kin are not reproducing. We might have an answer for you.'

'OK. Right now?' Dandridge sat up, paying attention.

The three of them came into his bedroom and sat down on his bed. He started to feel slightly nervous and a little buzzed, as if he had drunk a glass of champagne on an empty stomach. For some reason he suddenly noticed the sound of the wind gusting through the rotor blades of the helicopter parked underneath his window and felt the looming presence of the volcano above them.

'Our species has existed for a very long time, much longer even than yours,' Belle began. 'We communicate like you do, via altering sound wave frequencies emitted from a voice box and received using auditory sensors.'

'Ears?'

'We talk and hear with mouths and ears, yes. We do not possess the power to communicate any other way.'

'OK. Although I think I know that.'

'You do. But our species can communicate in other, non-verbal ways. Ways that are harder to explain. The closest human word I can find is 'empathy', but this is still not quite accurate. For example, if one of us dies, we all feel loss and grief, even if we had not witnessed or been told of the other's passing.'

'OK. A kind of familial cellular-level sympathetic vibration? Like on earth, it has been reported that some identical twins can feel what the other is feeling, even if they are hundreds of miles apart.'

'Possibly. On our planet, within our own community circles, we would hold a grief ceremony. We would celebrate the grief and pain we felt.'

'Like a funeral?'

'Yes, like that.'

'That makes sense. But what does that have to do with reproduction?'

'During the ceremony, our feeling of grief becomes the need to reproduce.'

'Holy shit - you have a fucking great big orgy?' Dandridge laughed. The Kin, who often found Dandridge very funny indeed, said nothing. Dandridge fell silent, slightly embarrassed. 'Sorry.'

'That is OK. Thanks to you, we do know what an earth 'orgy' is, and I suppose that it might be deemed similar. But our 'orgy' concludes with the birth of a new Kin to replace the passed.'

'Oh, right - so there is no incubation period?'

'No. A new Kin is created the same day. We never reproduce at any other time.'

'So that keeps your population in check. Do you ever want to reproduce at any other time, for recreation?'

'No. The feeling occurs only and soon after a passing.'

'How? How does it work? You guys seem to have no genitalia or any kind of aperture to expel a new life.'

'Richard, one of our race has died recently. We can all feel this quite clearly.'

'Oh shit. Oh crap. I'm really sorry, I should have realised. That's why you are telling me. So how long does the grieving take, before the... er... fucking?'

'It can vary greatly, but the first cycle is ending, which is why you must now leave,' Belle said.

'Leave? Really? You want me to go?' Dandridge got the weirdest feeling that although they were asking, they didn't really want him to go.

The Kin looked at each other. At least Dandridge thought so, given they had no eyes it was hard to tell.

'You have become part of our circle, and it pains us to ask.'

'Then why?'

'It will be safer for you.'

'It will? But I feel safe around you all. I trust you. Besides, you guys are useless at changing the spool on the barometer. I won't interfere or get in your way, I promise. I'll stay in my room if it helps.'

Maisie and Daniel got on their knees either side of his bed, like they were going to say their evening prayers, and took hold of Dandridge wrists, pinning him to the bed.

'Guys? What's going on? Seriously, it's OK. I've changed my mind. Of course I'll go. I'll stay in the village for a few days, I just need to find the helicopter keys.'

Belle took hold of his boxer shorts and pulled them down his legs, over his ankles and off. 'Fucking hell Belle, please don't do that. It's not necessary. I'll definitely go, you've made your point. My apologies. I'll go, right now tonight. I promise. Forget the chopper, I'll take one of the bikes.'

Belle climbed over him, supporting herself on her arms and toes so she was directly over Dandridge without touching him.

'Belle, that's enough, stop it right now. *Stop*. This has to stop. I'm sorry. I'll leave, right now, OK? *OK?*'

Belle's blank white face stared down at him, her jagged blue markings that started on her forehead and ran all the way down to her smooth groin seeming to shift slightly, to move. He looked down, in a real panic now.

'Maisie, Daniel? Please let me go,' he started to struggle but the Kin held him down securely. '*Please.* Whatever it is you are going to do, *please, please don't-*' then he felt Belle push her groin down against his penis. He was utterly paralysed with fear, his heartbeat pounding in his ears. He looked down. Belle's Ken Doll groin area wasn't smooth and flat any more. Belle was growing a kind of white fleshy tubular protuberance from her groin, a Kin-white cylindrical appendage with flecks of her dark blue markings across it. It grew outwards from her body and pressed itself around Dandridge.

'Jesus, Belle, please - no. Just no. Please stop this. *Everybody stop, right now. Fucking stop this!*' he shouted, realising that for whatever their reasons the Kin were now including him in their ceremony and as a result he was about to be raped by an alien species. Belle did not move or speak as her flesh-cylinder tightened up around Dandridge's terrified, shrivelled penis.

He was starting to hyperventilate with fear. He knew he had to stop struggling against his captives and fight to control his breathing. He slowly began to feel a very slight vibration emanating from the Kin above and around him, like a heat shimmer. He opened his eyes and looked down. It was now feeling very warm down there and the vibration had started to subtly increase and decrease in waves. Dandridge stared down at his trapped body and felt his penis involuntarily stiffening into the tube, which clamped itself tighter around him.

It wasn't just his genitals starting to respond to the Kin, his breathing had slowed and his mind was wandering, his consciousness expanding in ways that no drug he had ever ingested had been able to achieve. He felt an overwhelming sense of pride and confidence; that there was absolutely nothing he couldn't do, nothing he couldn't accomplish and he now understood exactly how he wanted to live from this moment forwards. He started to laugh.

Belle's flesh tube was now pulsing against his erection, the inside absorbing and adapting to the slight thrusts of his hips against her.

The other Kin had released him and left the room, but he hadn't noticed. He took hold of Belle's hips and pulled her body down and closer to him. Her body seemed to give slightly, allowing him more access into her. He laughed again, exultant with ideas, thoughts, colours and energy.

He had a brief flash of panic when he realised that he was almost definitely going to come, before immediately submitting to it and clamping his arms and legs tightly around Belle, grinding himself against the tube as hard as he could, desperately milking every second of pleasure he could, the vibrations against him increasing to a fever pitch exactly at the right time and exactly as he willed it, perfectly prolonging the most powerful and lasting orgasm he had ever experienced.

His comedown was gradual. First his arms then his legs released her and he shuddered with gentle aftershocks. His head was thrown back on the pillow, now damp from his sweat. He felt his penis released. Belle sat back between his ankles, the flesh tube retracting inwards until her groin was smooth and featureless once more. Dandridge sat up and reached to her, pressing his hand between her legs. 'Dry. Where's the semen?' he asked.

'I have absorbed it. Don't worry, we are not physiologically capable of fertilisation.'

Dandridge lay back on the bed. 'Holy shit, Belle. Why did the hell did you do that to me? It was unbelievable. I feel - really high, if I'm honest.'

'High? As if you have ingested drugs? That is curious.'

'How was it for you, Belle?' Dandridge laughed again. He had never felt better or healthier or more alive. Even his black-walled room seemed more vivid. 'Did you actually feel any pleasure from that?'

'I did, although perhaps not in the same way you experienced it,' Belle replied.

'If you had, you'd be smoking a fucking cigarette right now.'

Even though he felt physically exhausted, Dandridge leant up on his elbows. 'That was a neat trick, that tube thing. Pretty amazing. What else you got down there?'

Belle's head cocked to one side slightly, and Dandridge distinctly sensed her amusement. From the smooth white of her groin something began to grow. Not a cylinder this time, but a solid tube of white flesh, flecked with blue. Dandridge's grin grew wider as it grew longer.

Belle pushed Dandridge back down to the bed and knelt between his legs. And his mind was blown apart for the second time that night.

BUDDY

Buddy felt distant from the others, like he wasn't actually on a cold mountainside surrounded by a small band of survivors and a lot of dead people at all. He knew that he *was*, he just didn't consider it such a big deal any more. And the mountains were just so *beautiful*.

He was dreaming, planning, mapping out exactly what he was going to do. He was going to make Royce the next Henderson Mulcahy. He laughed excitedly, looking forward to the challenge, to the future.

Mike was staring at him. 'He looks high,' he said to Marion.

'I don't really know what high looks like.'

'No, Mike,' said Buddy, 'you're wrong. I'm not high. I feel shitloads better, but I'm not high. I think... I think I can walk off this mountain *right now*. And my arm feels better. Well, I can actually feel it now anyway.' He took off his shirt and looked at it. The bone below the elbow was still horribly, visibly broken, the flesh over the elbow and down to his hand dark mottled grey, but he flexed the arm out and in, with only a slight flinch. Luke looked away, nauseous.

'OK,' said Mike, 'if he's still alive tomorrow we'll eat, pack some up and leave at first light.'

The others all nodded and kept staring at Buddy, who had put his shirt back on and was smiling broadly, gazing at the mountain like it was the very first time. Then he disappeared into the shelter and fell into a contented sleep.

JENNIFER

Royce's agent was acting very strangely, but he did seem much better. He had slept through the night, the only one of them to do so, and was now busying himself around the shelter. The others huddled together, weak and exhausted. The body of the Kin lay in the snow nearby. They all felt a sense of nervous anticipation, knowing they were soon going to have to eat some of it, provided Buddy hadn't dropped dead by then.

Jennifer crunched and struggled through the deep snow away from the others and looked around her. It was a shame they were freezing and starving, as the area where they were stranded was breath-taking. Mountains towered above them on all sides, cold sunshine glinting off mile upon mile of glittering snow which would remain forever unspoiled. Her breath billowed out of her and drifted upwards, disappearing in the freezing air. She heard someone approaching and half turned, keeping her feet and legs buried in the snow where she stood, without enough energy to actually turn around fully. It was Luke and her heart sank.

'I don't want to talk to you.'

'Why not?'

'Is that a trick question?' she replied. 'I'm just not ready to talk to you. We need to survive this if we can, and then we'll have a chance to talk. So leave me alone.'

'What if we don't survive?'

'Then we'll take it to our graves and thank god for that.'

'Take what to our graves?'

'Another trick question, Luke? I don't have the energy.'

'It's not a trick question.'

'You want me to spell it out for you? You raped me. On the plane. You fucking *raped me!*' she shouted, her anger flaring up in exactly the way she had wanted to avoid. She started to cry.

Luke stepped forward and placed his hand on her shoulder. She shook it off and stumbled a few steps away in fury.

'No-' he stammered. 'I thought, I thought we both... I thought you wanted... we were going to die... I thought-'

'Fuck off, Luke. I know you too well. There's a tiny, minute chance we might actually get off this mountain and you're testing the water to see how I feel before we do. I'm not playing with you any more. You're old enough to rape me, you're old enough to face up to your actions. And you will.'

She stomped off, as best she could in thigh-high snow, leaving him standing and staring at the exact same view she had admired a few seconds before.

DANDRIDGE

He hobbled to the bathroom and stood under the hot shower. He was physically exhausted yet he thought he could probably go again with Belle. Maybe more. A lot more. He wanted to run a marathon, he wanted to abseil inside the volcano, he wanted to do everything. He had never felt this way before; so raw, so exposed, so confident in himself and his own destiny. He felt like the best of him was still to come, and the anticipation of it all made him giggle and laugh to himself in the shower. The water cascaded through his hair and over his shoulders and he felt his penis stirring again, which after two of the most bizarre and intense sexual experiences he had ever had, was nothing short of a goddamn miracle.

Hurrying in case she had lost the urge, Dandridge hopped out of the shower and crossed the hallway naked and dripping wet to the bedroom the three Kin shared.

He stopped in the doorway. Maisie and Daniel were on the bed, still connected. It looked like Maisie had extruded the white flesh cylinder and Daniel had grown the solid white erection that was encased within it, but the connection had spread across their whole torsos. They were pressed together, moving backwards and forwards, and with each pull backwards Dandridge could see that they had fused together, the two Kin completely joined by elastic looking, white connective tissue, thin and opaque. As they pushed together and pulled apart, he watched as the flesh pulled and stretched. It looked they were fighting to separate, to break the biological connection between them. Blue markings were rippled along the length of the new flesh, a combination of both Daniel and Maisie's own markings. The two of them were pressing together and pulling apart over and over again, and each time they pulled, the connective tissue became less translucent and elastic and more solid, more flesh.

Dandridge's penis was hard and straining as he watched the two Kin. He took Belle's hand.

After a short while - he had completely lost track of time - the two seemed to be really struggling to pull the now almost solid length of flesh apart between them. There were now very distinct arms and legs protruding from the mass of white flesh. Finally, they seemed to gather themselves for one last effort, pressing together for a few moments before ripping themselves apart.

With a weirdly squishy, gurgling, ripping, tearing noise the two fell away from each other. Dandridge's heightened emotions could somehow sense the sheer effort, pain and pleasure from them both.

Maisie fell off the bed and was caught by Belle. The whole of her front was a deep blue. On the bed, Daniel placed his hand on the new Kin, arms and legs now fully grown. It sat up, the head growing into place, the blue markings growing upwards like vines over and across its head. It stood up.

Belle took it's hand and joined Maisie and Daniel. The four of them held hands, head bowed, like a prayer circle.

The sun came up from behind the volcano. Dandridge watched the four of them as the light hit them, dust motes filling the slant of new sunlight. This was a new dawn, a new beginning, for them all.

MIKE

'What if he is slowly turning into a Kin?' Marion said to him. 'Look at him now.'

Buddy was whistling as he collected together all the newspapers and material and assorted debris that might help their walk off the mountain.

'It's unlikely. The worst that might have happened was an unpleasant death by poisoning. Which seems not to be the case.'

'Yet.'

'Yet. But its been eighteen hours. It would almost certainly have happened by now.'

'I guess.'

'He is acting really weird. I never seen him like this before,' chipped in Royce, his arms wrapped around himself as he shivered uncontrollably, stamping his feet in the cold and sinking further into the snow.

'Royce, you've probably had more experience with drugs than us, does he look high?'

'That's really fucking judgemental. I'm a black man so I must have taken drugs?'

'No, Royce,' Mike said. 'it's because you're a young, rich celebrity and photographs of you snorting cocaine were in most of the entertainment and gossip newspapers less than a month ago.'

'You as bad as she is.'

They heard raised voices and watched Jennifer stomp back to the more compacted snow around their shelter. She joined the group, cupping her hands around her mouth to warm up her face.

'Everything alright?' Mike asked.

'I'm fine. Let's eat and get off this fucking mountain.'

Luke slowly followed her back to the group and once again they stood around the corpse of the alien which now lay face up, the edges of the wound in its thigh dried with white fluid that looked like classroom glue.

Buddy was still alive. More than that, he seemed healthy. He was the only one who had slept through the night. He was confident and positive, chivvying the others along as the sun rose and they slowly stretched and emerged from their freezing shelter. Luke found him unbearable. He wondered if the meat would make them all like that. He felt nervous and nauseous again.

Mike cut five small pieces of meat from the same leg and handed them out. Luke sniffed it and held it away from him like it was a live grenade. Buddy snatched his from Mike's hand and took a big bite, pulling the white, elastic flesh with his teeth, tearing it off, chewing noisily and swallowing with delight, the white fluid dribbling over his hand and down his chin. Within a few chewy bites it was gone.

Mike had closed his eyes and was pulling the flesh with his teeth, pulling off a tiny corner, chewing and swallowing quickly. The others followed his lead, and soon all but Luke had taken a tiny nibble.

'Go on,' Jennifer said to him, 'try some.'

'I'm scared,' he said.

'We're scared too, but actually it's not too bad. In fact, it tastes a little bit like-' she smacked her lips together and ran her tongue around her teeth. 'It tastes a little bit like fudge.' Jennifer took a larger bite from the meat, tearing it off and chewing through the gristle slowly, before swallowing. 'Yeah, like vanilla fudge.' She took another bite.

Luke looked at her in disgust.

'She's right Luke, although it's more chocolate-y than fudge I think, sweeter somehow,' Marion had a mouthful, and the white liquid ran down her chin. Luke's mind flashed to a porn image he had seen in a magazine once and was slightly repulsed. Mike had finished his piece of meat, in fact he had stuffed the last, larger piece straight in to his mouth and was chewing slowly, savouring every last drop of the juice. He swallowed, thinking the two women were crazy. The meat didn't taste like chocolate, it wasn't even sweet. It was smokier, earthier. The meat itself tasted of nothing really, but the burn it left on the back of his throat as it went down reminded him ever so slightly of whisky.

DANDRIDGE

Frustratingly for Dandridge, the moment the new Kin was created seemed to signal the end of Belle's willingness to indulge him sexually.

'I am sorry Richard. I am unable to comply to your wishes, although it was a very interesting experience. We have a new Kin, which means our cycle of replication is complete.'

'And you can't, you know... get an erection or a... tube-thing... just by willing it?'

'No.'

'Fuck.'

'Sorry, Richard.'

'That's OK. I think I need to finish my shower.'

Dandridge ran the hot water again and stepped back in. He was still buzzing with excitement at what he had witnessed. His erection wasn't going away any time soon, so he finished himself off under the spray of water. His third orgasm of the night was almost as great as the first two.

He went to bed alone and slept deeply, dreaming the most wonderful things he was going to do when he woke up. He slept for eight hours straight, three hours more than usual.

When he opened his eyes and sat up there was no residual sleep in his head. He smiled to himself, feeling more energised than he had in years.

He pulled on his running shorts and a T-shirt. There wasn't a clock in his room, but the one on the microwave in the kitchen read 16.46.

He opened the back door and stepped out into the wind whistling down the slope from the volcano. He bent down and tied the laces of his running shoes before stretching his legs, which seemed pre-stretched and warm and ready to run. He also noticed that his back felt absolutely fine, even though it usually ached and groaned in cold weather.

He started his run, which took him up and around the very foot of the volcano just to the point on the ascent before it would necessitate climbing equipment to proceed. He ran for two miles before his body began to feel too warm and restricted, so he pulled off his T-shirt, leaving it on the black scree and carrying on running, feeling freer than ever, exultant as the crisp wind dried the sweat from his skin. As he ran it became perfectly clear to Dandridge that he was still too warm. He removed his shorts and shoes and carried on running completely naked around the volcano, laughing with joy at his exhibitionism and wondering why everybody didn't run this way, even as the dark shale and rock cut into the soles of his feet.

Then he came to a dead halt, standing absolutely still save for his hard breathing. His joy evaporated with his sweat, his thoughts whirring ceaselessly around his head. Then he turned on his shredded heels and began to run back the way he had come.

Twenty minutes later, naked, sweating, panting and covered in black volcanic dust, he burst through the red kitchen door. His feet had been cut to ribbons and poured blood. Leaving bloody footprints he took the stairs to the large attic room two at a time and burst in.

The four Kin in the room, surrounded by the seismological equipment, turned to face him.

'Richard,' said Belle, 'you are dressed inappropriately for the laboratory.'

'Sorry,' he panted, 'I need to ask you something. Last night, just before we all had sex, which was amazing by the way-'

'Thank you.'

'-you told me that since the Kin had come to earth, none of you were part of specific circles any more, that your ancient societal patterns had been destroyed along with your planet. All the survivors have formed into just one circle.'

'That is correct.'

'So your biological clocks, if you like, have been interfered with, messed up. You could feel the death of the other Kin and were obliged to have the ceremony, to mourn and reproduce.'

'I do not-'

'So does that mean that *all* the Kin mourned at the same time? Which would mean-' his mind started whirring, calculating.

'I understand where your thought process is taking you, Richard. You may well be correct.'

'Eight million Kin, all reproducing at once. Well, an awful lot of them. A possible extra four million Kin, give or take. And if any more of you die another six. Then nine, for a total of 27 million Kin. And that's just two more deaths. And the more of you there are, the chances of more deaths go up exponentially.'

'That may not occur. We have never reproduced in such numbers, not for thousands of generations.'

'I know, I know. But the strain on the Earth's resources could be unimaginable. I need to go. I need to see Marion. I mean, she probably knows by now anyway, but just in case. Will you come with me, Belle?'

Belle hesitated and turned to his three companions, including the new-born Kin who was now exactly the same height as the others. They all nodded.

'I will come with you, Richard, but please tend to your feet and take a shower first.'

Within an hour they were in the helicopter and airborne.

JENNIFER

'Luke, you have to eat if you're going to make it out of here. We all do. I promise it's OK. I feel much better with something in my tummy,' the fudge-y taste was lingering pleasantly in her mouth. She licked her lips. 'Come on, Luke. We're all waiting for you and we need to get going.'

All the group except Luke had now eaten their portion of the meat and all were feeling much better, more awake and alive than they had for days, hopeful that they might actually get off the mountain.

Luke just stared at her.

'Luke?' asked Royce, 'man, come on. This stuff is the shit.'

'Really?' Marion said. 'Mine was more chocolate-y.'

'No man, *'the'* shit, not 'shit'. It wasn't chocolate, it's definitely meat, but more like hamburger I think. Like proper hamburger from the kebab shop, with onions. Seriously man, you gotta do it. We need to go.'

Luke felt his heart start to pound in fear. The group all stared at him, their eyes shining. They looked possessed. .

'Come on, Luke,' Mike chimed in.

Luke dropped his portion into the snow and backed away.

'No. I'll be OK, I'll come with you, but... I'm not hungry, really. I'm feeling fine. I'll make it without eating.'

'You won't. You'll die within a day of walking out of here. You have to eat.'

Luke carried on backing away, and the others moved forward.

'Stop following me, alright? You're creeping me out. *I'm not gonna eat the fucking meat!*' he shouted, and backed off up the slope, struggling to get away.

'What are we going to do?' Marion asked, 'we can't-'

'Force him.' Jennifer said. 'We pin him down and force it into his mouth. Even a little bit should be enough energy to keep him going for a while. And he's younger than us. He won't need as much as we do.'

'Are you sure?' said Mike. 'Forcing the boy to eat it against his will is extreme.'

'We're going to run out of daylight if we keep discussing it,' Jennifer said, 'so lets do it now and get out of here.'

She felt ready to go home. Her head was clearer, her anger with Luke more defined, crystalized in her mind. She had never felt more determined to bring someone to account for their actions.

She had lost all the people she loved and left with the one person she didn't. She also knew something else now, unequivocally and without a shred of doubt in her mind, even though it had only been a few days since the assault. She was pregnant.

JOSH

The evening before Marion had left on her trip to Argentina, she visited Josh at the house. They had tea and joked and laughed like old friends, although they had only seen other sporadically over the last fourteen years. As Josh was telling Marion all about their wedding the previous year, Ezra returned home, placing his airline pilot jacket over the back of a chair in the kitchen before kissing Josh on the forehead.

'Congratulations, you two. Is it Perron, or Honeyball, or both?' she smiled, 'Perron-Honeyball' has kind of a ring to it-'

'It's Perron,' Josh said quickly, glancing at his husband. 'Neither of us were ever all that keen on 'Honeyball' except for my Dad, but he'll come round.'

Ezra made them dinner, a chicken and chorizo casserole and mashed potatoes which might have been Marion's first home cooked meal for years. Late into the evening and just a few hours before she was due to fly, Marion stood up to leave.

'I want you to look after the Shack until I get back. I want you in charge,' she announced.

Josh blinked rapidly, unsure he had quite heard her correctly. 'What? Me? No. Why?'

'Because I haven't been away from it for nearly fifteen years. Fifteen years, Josh. Every day, save for the occasional weekend. And the only person who was ever going to run it if I wasn't there, was you. I just never got round to telling you. Sorry.'

'In fifteen years? Jesus, Marion. What am I supposed to do? There must be better qualified people around there, surely?'

'Turn up, use my office. All access and permissions have been transferred to you. Most of it runs by itself now, but there are always problems, issues, certain elements that can't quite play nice with another species. The research and tech development is still ongoing too, which I know you'll find particularly fascinating, but we're probably decades away from finding a way to fuse and implement Kin knowledge with existing human tech.'

'How long are you going to be?'

'I'm not sure. Just a few weeks I think, maybe more. I'll keep in touch.'

'You'd better.'

'You can start on Monday. Please do keep it safe till I get back,' she said, and they hugged tightly.

Josh was speechless with shock, a condition he remained even as he found himself at eight thirty the following Monday morning trying to get comfy in someone else's chair and working out how the computer interface worked, searching for the instruction manual to one of the most advanced facilities in the whole world. The phone rang. His heart sank at the thought of having to have a sensible conversation with someone when he had not a single clue what he was doing. He wasted a few rings to see if would go to voicemail, but it kept ringing. He picked up the receiver carefully.

'Hello?'

'Mr Perron?' A female voice.

'Yes?'

'Why did you wait to pick up? I can see you, you know.'

The floor to ceiling window to Josh's left looked out across a view of the large reception area. A woman wearing a headset and a bright fuchsia pantsuit totally at odds with the stern glass and chrome building sat at the huge desk waving at him. 'I'm Holly, the receptionist. One of them anyway.'

Josh suddenly felt very exposed and idly wondered if the acres of glass surrounding them was some kind of subconscious response to the years Marion had spent in a windowless basement. 'Hello, Holly. Sorry.'

'That's OK,' she replied, 'I'm here to help if you need anything. Marion didn't have a PA but she said I could organise one for you if you wanted.'

'Thank you. Holly. Was that all?'

'No, there's someone here to see you.'

'Who?'

The figure sat on one of the reception chairs with his back to him stood up and turned around. Josh's heart leapt.

'Show him up,' he said.

A minute later, he and Dandridge were embracing warmly by the lift that had brought him up one floor from reception. Josh had tears in his eyes.

'What the hell are you crying for?' Dandridge said as they embraced, although he felt quite close to tears himself. 'How's my house? Broken anything? You won't get your deposit back.'

'Fuck you, Dandridge,' Josh cursed, amazed that he fell so easily back into calling him by his surname. 'Where in God's name have you been?'

'Here and There, and Back Again, to paraphrase Tol-'

'I don't give a fuck about Tolkein. Where have you been, Dandridge?'

To Josh, Dandridge looked older, wiser, slightly greyer, perhaps leaner, but still childishly energised and exuding a sense of excitement that was almost palpable.

'There's time enough for stories, Honeyball. What's going on?'

'It's Perron now. Ezra and I got married, so I changed it. Better than 'Honeyball'.'

'No, it's not. Congratulations. Anyway, I need to see Crandall really urgently but the reception girl told me she's gone on holiday and you've taken over. First day?'

'Yes.'

The two of them had retreated to the office and Josh took his seat behind the desk, while Dandridge sat opposite him on the visitors chair.

'How's the back?'

'Fine, thank you. Almost never notice it any more. Do you know how to get hold of Crandall?'

'Yes, she's going to be at the Clinica Belgrano in Buenos Aires in a day or so.'

'Why?'

'To attend the autopsy of the first dead Kin.'

They were interrupted by a Kin entering the room. It stopped when it saw Dandridge, the head cocked slightly to one side.

'Mr Perron, Mr Dandridge.'

'Hello, Kin,' Dandridge said.

'Mr Perron, I would request that you accompany me to the labs immediately. Some information has come to hand and I would prefer to discuss it there than pipe it to your desktop.'

'What is it?'

'Come with me, if you would.'

The three of them walked through bright glass corridors with a view of the Kin ship, past groups of men and women dressed in white lab coats, all of whom stared at the three of them as they passed by. They followed the Kin down an elevator about twenty floors beneath the surface and into another complex of clinical white tunnels into a dry, cool control room dominated by a huge screen at one end. They were the only ones in there. The only sound was the soft hum of a discreet air conditioning unit.

The screen was displaying a map of the earth covered in blinking symbols dotted around it.

'What are we seeing, Kin?' Dandridge asked.

'This is the global tracking information of the Kin species,' the first Kin replied. 'I will demonstrate.'

It used gesture control to zoom into the UK on the digital map, increasing the zoom over Gloucestershire and the Shack. Two blips showed. The Kin cocked his head again. 'There are two Kin. Myself and one other. I was only expecting one.'

'There's one waiting outside,' said Dandridge. 'I'll explain later. Zoom out to the globe again, Kin. How many Kin markers should be marked on the screen in total?'

'All of us. Eight million, four hundred and fifty six thousand. Pardon me, four hundred and fifty five thousand. I regret to say that one of us has died very recently.'

'But there aren't nearly that many markers on the screen. I would say... less than a million.'

Josh stared at Dandridge, whose eyes were flickering over the screen restlessly. There was definitely something odd about him.

'How the fuck can you tell?'

'You are correct, Mr Dandridge,' the Kin said.

'Just Dandridge.'

'There are nine hundred thousand, seven hundred and four. In total. I have individual totals for every country.'

'So where are the others?' Josh asked, with growing panic.

'I don't know, Mr. Perron. They're gone.'

'But how can eight million Kin just disappear?'

'They haven't disappeared,' Dandridge said, 'they're still there, it's just that for some reason we aren't tracking them anymore, at least 91.2 percent of them. Which means we potentially have a much larger problem than I thought.'

'Mr Perron, I'm afraid there's more news. We recently received an emergency radio message from a passenger aircraft.'

The Kin brought up a different display on the huge screen which appeared picture-in-picture at the top right of the tracking map. It was a image of a soundwave. The Kin hit the spacebar and the scared, confused but calm voice of a pilot was piped loudly into the glass office. The message was fifteen seconds long, and was difficult to listen to. It cut off with a short scream before dead silence.

'Well, that was awful. Why were we listening to it?'

'That was the pilot of the aircraft carrying Marion, my Kin colleague and the Buenos Aires contingent. All contact was lost with it about two hours ago.'

'Holy shit,' Josh's blood ran cold. He was becoming aware that he had stumbled into possibly the worst first day of a job in recorded history. He rubbed his knuckles into his eye-sockets, praying that when he removed them it would all go back to normal. No such luck. 'How did it happen?' He sounded as scared as he was confused.

'Unknown, so far. We understand an investigation and search and rescue mission is underway.'

'Did the huts pick anything up?' asked Dandridge.

'The huts are pretty much automated now, only essential messages get recorded. We could go and take a look.'

'I'll go and check it out. Looks as if you might be busy for a while,' Dandridge said.

Josh nodded glumly, unwilling to let Dandridge go again.

ROYCE

Royce was the absolute fucking *bomb*. He knew it with utter certainty, and even though Buddy had been telling him so for the last twelve hours, babbling about the music and destiny and all that shit, Royce hadn't really listened. But he did now. He and Buddy were going to become the next Henderson Mulcahy. He just knew it. He couldn't wait. But he had to get off this mountain first. And to do that, they all had to get off. And for them all to get off, they all needed to eat.

He told himself all this as he put a comforting arm around the kid. Then, in a long-dormant schoolboy manoeuvre, he hooked his leg behind Luke's and tripped the boy up, pushing him to the snow. Luke fell back with a cry. 'I'm really sorry, kid,' Royce mumbled as he held one struggling arm down while Buddy took hold of the other. Hennessy took a leg and Crandall took the other and his step-mother - *Jesus Christ she looks like she's enjoying this* - held out a small morsel of the white meat towards him.

The boy struggled really hard, more than Royce had ever seen a human being struggle. But the others in the small group were fed and strong and determined. Luke had clamped his mouth shut, pressing his chapped lips tightly together but Jennifer pressed her hand over his nose and after a minute he was forced to open his mouth to breathe and she jammed in a jagged piece of wreckage to lever his mouth open. They all heard his teeth as they clanged against it. Jennifer forced some of the white meat into his mouth, using the metal to push it down his throat. He tried to spit it out but she kept pushing it back in. He kept struggling the entire time, never letting up, gagging, choking, retching and screaming hoarsely at them against the metal.

Royce and the others held him down, and after two or three terrible, intense minutes it was over. Luke swallowed involuntarily, the meat slid down his throat and he slowly calmed down. He coughed a few times and retched, but the meat stayed down.

They let him up and he climbed unsteadily to his feet and stumbled away, sobbing and distraught, mumbling incoherently, blood dribbling down his chin from a deep cut on his lip from the metal shard. He disappeared into their shelter.

'OK, so that was fuckin' horrible,' Royce said, to break the silence. 'but he knows it was for his own good though, right?'

'He'll come around,' Jennifer said. 'Now we can get going. Let's gather what we can and get out of here. Luke can cry it out on the way.'

Royce and the others looked nervously at each other, taken aback by her directness, but all agreed. They were all fired up, good to go, eager to get off the mountain, eager to survive.

'I'll carve up the Kin. Royce, fetch me some paper,' she said as she bent down to the dead creature, 'we'll wrap some up to take with us.'

She lowered her head and slowly ran her tongue along the exposed wound, lapping up the leaking white flesh with her eyes closed, a dreamy expression on her face like a kitten's first taste of cream. She gripped her makeshift knife and pierced the flesh at the groin, pulling the knife down and through the leg to meet the existing incision. The flesh tore open and more juices ran out. Royce, almost without thinking, knelt beside her and lowered his head to lick it up before it could get lost in the snow. He ran his tongue along the edge of the new incision and bit down, feeling the rich, fleshy meat squirt blood into his mouth. He tore a piece off with his teeth. It was quite fibrous and he had to pull hard before it tore away. He chewed through sinew and gristle as the flavour flooded through his deprived system. He tore more flesh from the legs, and was only vaguely aware of Jennifer doing the same. He took a third bite, and moved upwards from the wound, taking the knife from Jennifer and plunging it into the Kin's stomach, lowering his mouth to the stab wound and sucking up the white blood as it flowed out, burying his face into it as far as it would go. The knife was snatched away from him.

He looked up to see Mike attacking the opposite leg, hacking and tearing away a huge strip of meat and biting down. Marion was sharing his cut and they kissed each other every time they turned their heads after taking a bite. The flesh was caught between their teeth, the juices leaking down their chins and smearing over their faces as they snogged passionately, unashamedly. Soon the large hunk of meat was gone and they forgot about the knife and attacked the body with their bare hands and bared teeth.

LUKE

Luke's stepmother was running her cheek up and down the untouched smoothness of the dead Kin's inner thigh like it was pure silk, breathing heavily, her eyes closed. The mutilated leg rested over her shoulder as she moved up and down before shifting further upwards, licking up the missed smears of blood until she reached the joint where the leg met the groin. She clamped her mouth over it and bit down. White blood spurted out from between her teeth as she chewed and ripped and pulled. The dead creature was now grotesquely spread-eagled as Royce gnawed the other leg. Jennifer chewed and pulled and fought and the leg came away. She and Buddy Tucker fell on it like ravenous wolves.

Luke watched from the safety of the shelter, trembling and scared, holding the back of his hand against his cut lip. He watched as the group apparently lost control of themselves, ripping apart and devouring the Kin body, utterly overwhelmed by the effulgent sweetness of the flesh.

He placed his hands over his ears to muffle the sound of tearing flesh, of chewing, of the grunts of effort and pleasure as Mike and Marion began to fuck in the pooled blood of the creature, both now seemingly immune to the freezing wind that had sprung up and the sleet that was slowly covering the compacted snow around the shelter.

As the meat he had been force-fed digested in his stomach it fizzled and burned and popped and spread and exploded through his body, already filled with churning adolescent hormones. Even as he fought it, his conscious mind began to open and expand, filling him with dizzying visions. He fell to his knees, buried his head in his hands and rode out waves of entirely new and overwhelming feelings of lust, hope, terrible sadness, joy, regret, grief, ambition, frustration and love that hit him one after the other and then all at once, a tumultuous wave that threw him to the floor and wracked him with almost physical pain.

He shuddered and screamed and cried, writhing on the filthy floor of their shelter, his body craving more even as his mind screamed for it to stop. He felt his soul reaching out to the stars and his future stretching out before him so bright that even shades wouldn't make a difference.

He knew it was the meat freeing his mind and allowing him this perfect clarity, to see the colourful strands of infinite futures opening up before him, looping and twisting and rushing and stalking and coiling around each other before vanishing into the distance towards an unknowable end. He was held aloft by the strands of his own endless possibility.

And despite his altered state, or perhaps because of it, he began to understand that not devouring the Kin like a feral animal with the others would be what separated him from them if they actually did come out of this.

He tried desperately and reluctantly to gather the leaping threads of his mind and pull himself back to the present. In his current timeline he was still stuck on a remote mountainside with his stepmother he had raped, a group of people he didn't want to know and Royce Brims.

He crawled out of the shelter on his hands and knees.

The Kin was gone. Head, body and limbs. Royce and Jennifer were fully dressed but entwined, Royce with a broad, satisfied smile on his face. Mike and Marion were naked and covered in the Kin's juices, curled up together like they had just made love and fallen asleep on a goose-feather duvet. Buddy was on all fours, hoovering up the remaining flesh and stuffing it into his mouth.

Luke felt exultant, triumphant. He got to his feet and raised his head to the grey skies, his face turned into the driving sleet and snow, his tears freezing to his face. He screamed and screamed into the mountains, his voice echoing and bouncing around the snowy, rocky landscape. He screamed until his throat was raw. Every emotion tearing relentlessly through him was held in the scream which echoed around them for minutes.

He had never believed he was going to die, but in those moments as his scream echoed around the empty mountains, he finally knew how he was going to live.

PART FIVE

JOSH

Josh opened the front door. Dandridge and the two Kin followed him inside. Dandridge delightedly explored every room and then sat down in the middle of the garden for ten full minutes, a garden that had been carefully tended and maintained in his absence in a way he had never found time to do. Josh made tea and talked with the two Kin, Belle explaining to Josh where Dandridge had been for the last year.

'Iceland?'

'Yes. We do very important work there. It is very fulfilling.'

'I'm sure it is. The Huts monitor all the reports from Nordic seismological stations.'

'It is reassuring to know that somebody does.'

'Does what?' Dandridge came back into the kitchen, stepping through the new double-glazed back door Josh had replaced a few years earlier, and nodding approvingly as he wiggled the handle up and down.

'Monitor the Nordic seismologi-'

'Yes, yes of course,' he said impatiently. 'Come on, lets go and sit down. Is that my Crunchie mug?' he said as he accepted a tea. 'Thanks for looking after the house, it's like an actual, proper home now.'

'Are you going to kick me out now or something?'

'Not yet, although I'd like to stay for a few days. Can we use the spare room?'

'Of course, I made your bedroom the spare room. And by we you mean-'

'Belle and me.'

'Huh-' Josh felt slightly nonplussed, but in the presence of the alien he felt it best not to pursue this line of enquiry with Dandridge just yet.

'Quite a first day for you in charge of the Shack, eh? Losing all the Kin like that. What would Crandall say?'

Josh flushed, and felt anger rising. 'Dandridge, Marion is probably dead. You heard the recording. Why are you back? Why now? What do you know about the Kin disappearing?'

Sitting in the hospitable surroundings of the living room, cosy in the way it had never been when Dandridge was the sole occupant, with cups of tea and stacks of jam on toast, Dandridge, Belle and the first Kin explained to Josh the recent mourning and reproduction processes of the Kin.

'You know, sometimes I genuinely forget that you are aliens,' he said.

'Me too,' agreed Dandridge, 'it's amazing how something that seems so bizarre can become just another part of the fabric of the world, isn't it? Well, to answer your question about why I am here - well, after we had sex, I really had an urge to go for a run, and so-'

'Wait. Hold on a second. You just told me that you have spent a year living with three Kin, and that a few nights ago you watched them reproduce.'

'That's right.'

'So who did you have sex with?'

'You mean *'with whom did I have sex?'*

'Dandridge-' Josh stuttered, eventually. '-I kind of need to ask, and at the same time I am not sure I really want to know, but did you and this Kin have some form of... sexual encounter?'

'A sexual encounter is actually an apt description, Mr Perron,' Belle spoke up. 'The intercourse, albeit not conventional, was very clean, very interesting and highly satisfactory.'

'You had sex with a Kin. I just don't believe it. Is there simply *nothing* you won't shag?' Josh spluttered. 'I feel like I need someone to scour my brain clean.'

'In Richard's defence, he needed a lot of persuading, at first.'

'At first? You've done it more than once?'

Josh got up and went into the kitchen, where they could hear him clattering around, cleaning dishes, making more tea.

'Perhaps this was too much information,' Belle said.

'I'll go and talk to him,' Dandridge said and followed Josh into the kitchen.

'I really like the new cabinets,' he said.

'They're from Wickes. Cheap, but pretty good.'

'That should be their marketing tagline.'

'Fuck the new cabinets, Dandridge. You're like a real life Captain Kirk. Are you seriously saying to me that the act of you fucking – apologies - having a *sexual encounter* with a Kin has somehow deactivated all the tracking devices?'

Dandridge waited patiently for Josh to connect the dots. Josh leaned against the draining board, staring out at the top of the Kin ship in the distance as he had so many times before, his thought processes processing.

'It's not you. Of course. Belle still showed up on the tracker, as did the first Kin. All the others... it must be all the others who *did* reproduce... which means that the act of reproduction must have somehow shorted out or affected the tracking devices somehow.'

Dandridge nodded. 'That's right. And Josh, remember that the Kin only have sex to reproduce, they don't do it for fun.'

'So if all the Kin who have vanished have reproduced, then we potentially have a Kin population explosion. Millions more, all unregulated.'

'Yes. I've witnessed it, it's quite remarkable.'

'If you're not careful there's going to be a mini-Kin/Dandridge running around. Kindridge.'

Dandridge laughed as they returned to the living room.

'So,' Josh said to the first Kin, 'Dandridge just told me that you only have sex to reproduce and not for fun. As all the trackers have vanished, they must have been short-circuited somehow by your act of reproduction. So we can speculate that just under eight million Kin have just reproduced, which means we potentially have another four million Kin on this planet, with no means to track them. Kin, did you feel grief and the need to reproduce when the other Kin died, the one Crandall went off to see?'

'I did,' replied the first Kin, 'but there are no other Kin here, and so my grief manifested as anger. I took it out on Marion before she left. I felt the need for connection but could do nothing. And before you suggest it Mr Dandridge, masturbation is not an option for Kin.'

'Wow, he's known you for two whole hours and totally has you worked out,' Josh said, and took a deep breath. 'We need to get the full passenger manifest from Marion's flight. We need to know if there was a Kin on board.'

'We have not felt another death among the Kin,' Belle said.

'OK good, but let's check anyway. It's possible the Kin survived the crash. The more Kin there are then statistically there are more chances of one dying accidentally and the reproduction process begins again. In the morning we will need to notify the Prime Minister and then all the Shack reps around the world. We need a plan to re-implement the trackers or request that all Kin, classic and new recipe, be registered somehow. We must be able to keep track of numbers or else there is going to be serious strain on resources here.'

'I understand, Josh,' said the first Kin, 'I will head over to the Shack now and begin preparations. May I borrow your bicycle? I do not require a lift.'

Josh nodded and the Kin took Ezra's bike from the hook in the utility room. It wheeled the machine outside and clicked the back door shut behind it.

EZRA

It was past two in the morning when Ezra Perron drove onto the gravel and saw Josh's car and a hire car sitting in the drive. The hire car had been pulled right up to the house, allowing him to drive his jeep all the way in and park alongside without any of them being blocked in. Somehow, he already knew who was indoors.

'Dandridge,' he said, his hunch confirmed as he saw the three of them - Dandridge, Josh and a single Kin sitting in the living room.

'Perron,' Dandridge replied, embracing him with a kiss on both cheeks, 'left the Air Force I see. Civilian life treating you well?'

'Well enough,' he replied. 'excuse me, I need to take a quick shower. If there's any red wine left, I'll have a glass in a few minutes.'

He went upstairs and turned on the jet of hot water, filling the colder air with steam. In the bedroom he shared with Josh he folded his uniform carefully and hung it up on the door of their huge antique wardrobe. He stepped back to the en-suite and wriggled off his underwear, stepping under the water and running his hands through his wet hair, his face turned towards the shower head. When he shook the water from his eyes, Josh was standing next to the tub.

'You OK?'

'Fine.'

'He's not here for me, you know. There's a problem, with the Kin.'

'It's only your first day on the job. I take it that it didn't go so well if you had to call him for help.'

'I didn't call him, he just showed up.'

'What a coincidence.'

'Just a coincidence, although he had some information that happened to relate to something that happened today. You've never been jealous before, Ez. I don't get it.'

'We live in his house, and don't think I don't know that you think about him all the time.'

'I think about him a lot, not 'all the time'. I'm not going to lie to you. We worked together a long time, went through some shit together. Then he just fucking vanished, after I'd helped him through a massive life-changing car wreck.'

'You were injured in that crash too, but somehow I never hear about that. It's always about him.'

'He got it worse than me. You still sound jealous.'

Ezra was still standing under the jet of water and ran his hands through his hair again, away from his eyes. 'I am jealous, Josh. I'm sorry. I can't help it.'

'I love that you're jealous. I love you and nothing is going to change that. Not him, not anyone. We're just house-sitting for him, you know that. But now he's back, so what do you say we start house-hunting?'

'Really? Our own place? Finally?'

'Yes.'

'You really love me? Crap, I sound like a goddamn love-sick puppy.'

'Yes, I love you.'

'Prove it.'

Josh climbed fully clothed under the jet of water and proved it.

DANDRIDGE

'Slightly longer than ten minutes fellas, but we saved some red for you.'

'What do you mean *we*? Kin don't drink alcohol. You mean you actually showed some self-control,' Josh said as he sank into the sofa.

'True enough. Did you decide to take a shower too, Josh? Your hair's all wet.'

'It's good to see you, Richard,' Ezra said as he poured himself a large glass of Shiraz.

'I'm pretty sure you don't mean that Ezra, but it's OK. It's nice to be back.'

The four of them sat and talked and the night quickly ran out. It was past five in the morning when they all retired to bed, the dew of the new day settling across the three cars in the drive.

Dandridge lay down in his own bed for the first time in twelve years. Belle lay down next to him. The mattress sagged slightly and his back ached. He grimaced but was too tired to be kept awake and he drifted off almost immediately.

About an hour later, the sun fully up, he felt Belle shaking him gently. He opened his eyes and the Kin's face was right over his. 'Belle, you know I really do want to do it again with you, but now probably isn't the best time. Red wine-'

'I have to go, Richard. I have to go now. I have to go to him. It has happened again.'

'What? What has happened again?' Dandridge eyes opened and he sat up, pushing Belle off him. 'What do you mean? Another death?'

'Yes. Perhaps the Kin in the aircraft with Marion Crandall, or perhaps another. But I have to go to the Shack, now.'

'You can't Belle. You know what'll happen. Besides, the

first Kin said he wasn't affected.'

'Because there were no other Kin around. I need it to happen. I need to grieve with the first Kin, in our own way. I will see you soon Richard.'

'When? How? How did the other Kin die?'

'I do not know, but it was not long ago.'

Belle left the bedroom, shutting the door gently behind her. Dandridge collapsed back on his pillow, his back aching again. He felt pangs of jealousy, and as his eyes traced the familiar lines and curves of the plasterwork ceiling, the jealousy turned to anger. He screwed up his face and fought the tears of rage and hopelessness that had begun to creep over him. Another Kin dead. His mind whirred with the numbers. The first dead Kin would have triggered the reproduction process of eight million original Kin. Presuming that most would have coupled up, give or take a hundred thousand or so according to the remaining trackers, it would have generated an extra four million, to make twelve million in total. Which meant that a second dead Kin would mean that new and old Kin would couple up, six million on each side creating another litter of six million extra Kin, give or take half a million or so, the ones alone or unable to reproduce for whatever reason. His mind started adding up the numbers until he reached twelve dead Kin, potentially an extra billion aliens. And with that many, the death rate would increase exponentially. They were going to be overrun.

Something needed to be done, but as the night wore on and the anger exhausted him, a wave of loneliness spread through Dandridge, as powerful an emotion as he had ever felt. His tears flowed hot down his cheeks.

He stumbled from the bed, the thought of being alone any more too much to bear. He opened the door of the other bedroom and saw Ezra and Josh in the bed, Perron's arm flung across Josh's chest. Josh was awake, and sat up as Dandridge stumbled in, unable to hold back his tears.

Without a word he drew the covers from the Queen size bed for Dandridge to climb in. He did so, weeping uncontrollably, and curled up against Josh who held him tightly until they both fell asleep hours later.

EZRA

He had never really liked Dandridge. The man was overconfident to the point of arrogance, didn't like being wrong in any way and held some mystery sway over his husband that he didn't completely trust. Quite what Josh saw in him was a mystery. But this was different. It was like there were two Dandridges; the cocky annoying one and his depressed twin. Dandridge was having a breakdown, and Ezra wasn't sure what to do. He and Josh had both cuddled him for most of the day after Belle's departure, talking in low whispers across his fitfully sleeping form.

Ezra was not rostered to work and reluctantly took over as primary carer when Josh extricated himself and left for the Shack. He was in the kitchen making a green Thai curry when Dandridge finally came down at half six in the evening. He looked broken, shuffling like an old man, his eyes bloodshot and hair sticking out at all angles.

'Where's Josh?' he croaked.

Ezra placed a large glass of water and four vitamin tablets on the worktop next to him. 'Take these. I'll make you an omelette. I think the curry might finish you off.'

Dandridge sat down on one of the stools at the breakfast bar and obeyed, swigging down the tablets. He had shakes that he couldn't control, he had never felt so utterly raw and wretched. He ate the omelette and immediately felt better, then ran into the toilet and threw it up. He started to cry again, lying on the floor of his own downstairs toilet, utterly desolate.

Ezra gathered him up. Dandridge curled up against him, reaching for the security and warmth of contact.

'Dandridge, what the hell is the fucking matter? Man, I don't know you that well, but this isn't you. What are you on, man? *What are you on?* We can help you. We aren't going to leave you, OK? Josh and I, we're here for you. But you gotta tell me what you've been taking.'

'Not taken anything. I think it's-' his voice was ragged with tears, '-I think it's because of... the Kin-' he hiccuped and his chest hitched like a child as he took in air and tried to control himself, '-a side-effect of the Kin. Some kind of... heightened emotional response... maybe...' he curled up tighter, and Ezra could see him fighting back more tears.

'Come on, lets get you back to bed.' He helped Dandridge to his feet and took him upstairs, laying him down in his own bed. Dandridge slept.

Later that evening as he and Josh were eating the green curry and sticky coconut rice, Ezra told him what had happened. 'I don't know what the fuck he's on, but he needs help and we can't do it here, not with everything that's going on. He needs a rehab facility.'

'I don't think he's on anything. He had sex with a Kin,' Josh said eventually, 'and I think it might have messed him up, somehow.'

'What? *Jesus fucking Christ*. How is that even possible?'

'He said it was the most mind-blowing experience of his life 'no offence'.'

'Well, he's now coming down from his so-called *mind-blowing experience* and there is either something seriously wrong with him or he is just the biggest pussy ever at handling break-ups.'

'Well, neither Kin were around today. Belle and the first, both gone.'

'Did you check the tracker?'

'Yes. Both gone, vanished. No Kin anywhere within a hundred miles apparently. And from yesterday, we are down another two hundred thousand trackers. Also, I received the passenger manifest from the missing plane. There was a Kin on board. A search and rescue is underway. So I can only assume they're all dead, and unless there's been a death we don't know about I assume the Kin who died in the plane is the one who kicked this new sequence off. Jesus, Marion left me in charge of all this and now she's-' tears sprang to his eyes and he wiped them with a napkin. 'Guess who else was on the plane?'

'Who?'

'Royce Brims.'

'No shit, really?'

'Yup. I hated his last album though.'

'Dying in a plane crash is probably too severe a punishment for a bad album. Did you call the Prime Minister about all this?' Ezra asked.

'No, I did something even better.'

ADLER

Adler was sitting on the terrace of his new apartment in Amsterdam drinking coffee and watching the tourist boats on the canal chug past when his phone rang. It was the Shack. He hit the green handset button on the screen.

'Marion.'

'Hi Ernest, it's me actually - Josh.'

'Honeyball.'

'It's Perron now, but you can call me Josh. No need for last names.'

'Everything OK over there, Perron? Is Marion finally taking time off?'

'She took a flight to witness the autopsy of the first dead Kin.'

'Really? I bet she was excited, in her own way.'

'Yes, she was. The thing is... the plane... it's missing, presumed crashed, somewhere really inhospitable.'

Adler sat up, placing the coffee cup he was holding back onto the silver tray on the table next to him. 'The plane that's on the news right now?'

'Correct.'

Adler paused momentarily. 'And what can I do about this, other than pray for her safe return?'

'I think we have a larger problem. And I need your help.'

He took a deep breath, looking out across the peaceful canal in front of him, a long, brightly coloured houseboat chugging gently past, two young boys playing on the roof while their father steered and mother drank a mug of something hot. The father at the tiller waved to him, and he waved back.

Eighteen hours later, Adler presented himself in Marion's office at the Shack.

Nineteen hours later, he and Josh were in a car on their way to London.

DANDRIDGE

Belle reappeared three days later. She was accompanied by another Kin he assumed was her offspring with the first Kin. He had returned to the Huts, which now sat virtually unused and dwarfed by the alien ship on the site of the old RAF base. He was lying beneath the main console, re-wiring the dust covered CUBESat. He came up for air and she was standing in the doorway to Hut Three. The moment he saw her his heart leapt, but he had recovered enough composure to realise what was happening to him and fought to keep his emotions under control.

'I looked for you at the house. I spoke with Ezra Perron. It was a mistake to accompany you, Richard,' Belle said, not moving from the doorway.

'No, it wasn't. The very opposite of a mistake. I think once I, once we, recover from this, it will be a fascinating and brilliant discussion point. But for right now, everything just hurts. My *soul* hurts. I never thought such a thing could happen, if I even *had* a soul. But now I know that I do, because it hurts so fucking much.'

'Are you in love with me, Richard?'

Dandridge tried to fight the tears - the fucking, constant, burning tears - and blinked them away. 'It appears so. But my feelings seem to have transcended all appropriate human response parameters.'

'Is that so?' Belle said, her flat, inflectionless voice somehow sounding amused. 'You sound like me. I was unaware that human responses had parameters. Are you sure that perhaps you have just never been in love before?'

'I've been in love,' he replied, and it was true. He was sure he had. Positive. 'But trust me, this is different. You know I said I felt high after we were together?'

'Yes.'

'Well, I think I'm coming down, and I'm struggling to cope, Belle. I just want to be with you, all the time.'

'It is not possible. I shall leave.'

'No, don't. I'll get over this. I want to travel with you, to see the world through your eyes.'

'I will leave for three days. On my return, we will see how you are feeling.'

'Three days?'

'Three days.'

'OK. I'll be here.'

The two Kin left and Dandridge's heart sank again. His bruised psyche took another battering as he forced himself back to work, his hands shaking, linking up some machines and re-connecting a digital antenna. The place needed some serious upgrading.

He boiled the old kettle and poured himself a cup of black tea with a thin film of limescale floating on the surface. He took a slurp. Not bad.

He stood outside the Hut and gazed upwards at the alien ship, the dark, quiet, rusting pizza slices. The best engineers and technicians in the world had been taken round them, had investigated every nook and cranny of the dark insides, explored and taken photographs, recorded and learned. The ships had all stopped functioning, the power units dead, deprived of the materials required to run. All photographs taken of the inside were classified but Dandridge supposed he could look at some if he asked Josh. Belle had come out of a ship that had landed in Iceland, but by all accounts they were all identical. He had never seen inside one for himself.

He decided it was time for some exploring.

ADLER

The Prime Minister was wearing his solemn face, the one he usually reserved for state funerals. 'I'm sorry about Marion,' he said, 'I know the search is still ongoing. It's a complete mystery.'

'Thank you Prime Minister.'

Adler, Josh and the PM went through a set of double doors and into the large Cabinet briefing room at the back of No.10 Downing Street. It was extremely wide and very ornate. Ancient portraits of Prime Ministers past stared down at the highly polished antique meeting table surrounded by all twenty two Cabinet Ministers, the men dressed in dark suits and ties and the women all in dark-hued, austere business attire.

'Sorry for the informality but you didn't give us much notice,' the PM said as he took his seat between the Deputy Prime Minister and the Minister for Kin and Human Relations Nile Cody, the Northern Irish back-bencher selected by Adler himself to handle the public face of human and Kin development.

'OK, so Nile has filled me in on the details and we have a report here.'

'Already?' whispered Josh. 'You only spoke to him an hour ago on the phone.'

'They have great typists here,' Adler whispered back.

The two of them sat at the very end of the long table, the Ministers on either side of the PM along one long leading edge. There was silence for some minutes, punctuated by the shuffling of paper as each minister turned pages. By the end of it, there was a palpable air of concern in the room.

'What do you think we can do about this situation, Adler?' the PM said, tapping the report with his fingertips. 'Two Kin are dead already so we have an extra ten million or so walking around. I'm probably not the only one here slightly apprehensive by these numbers.'

'In the scheme of things, ten or eleven million extra bodies isn't a huge volume,' Adler said. 'It means that in terms of total population the planet has skipped forward a generation or so, which *sounds* bad, but bear in mind that Kin don't really eat or consume in the same way we do and so far have not indicated any substantial desire for personal accumulation. Global manufacture and agriculture hasn't been unduly affected. I don't think it'll make a huge difference, environmentally. The hardest task of course will be housing them all, so we face some tricky local council negotiations to free up more affordable homes and we need to impose a limit on how many jobs they can take up in any given area. I agree that we need to try and track and monitor their numbers as best we can. I am not sure they will subject themselves to another tracking device as it was a sticky point of contention the first time - plus we actually need to produce millions of the things, which will take some time.'

Josh sat eating biscuits and listening. They had had the same conversation in the car from Gloucestershire.

'I have had reports coming in from all the Shacks of unusually high numbers of Kin requiring location and fresh integration,' Adler said. 'Most of the trackers have now gone off-line and so Shack leaders have no idea that we have been dealt a fresh hand. They don't have enough intel or resource to cope with the extra demand. I've allowed the allocation of more personnel into the Shacks for the more populated Kin areas, the American Mid-West, Japan, China, Spain, and we may need to open up the temporary accommodation again.'

'But Adler, what about long-term? the PM said. 'What's to say that as their numbers grow that they won't slowly become the pre-eminent force on this planet, reducing humans to a secondary species, a subordinate? What's to say, Adler-' the PM leaned forward as the thought occurred to him, and jabbed his Bic in his direction. '-that this wasn't their plan *all along*?'

'Precisely,' said the Deputy PM, sitting on the PM's right and banging a clenched fist on the polished desk to emphasis his point. Adler flinched. 'What if it really is an invasion, a slow, insidious unstoppable invasion?'

Nile Cody spoke up. 'Enough of this. It will get us nowhere. The very preservation of our way of life is at stake now. We cannot afford to let this pre-emptive line of thinking cloud our judgement. In fourteen years the Kin have been nothing but compliant with our wishes, not so much as a squeak of a complaint, other than the usual day to day territorial issues.'

'*Living in Kin.*' said Josh, and smiled to himself. The entire UK Cabinet turned to stare at him and he blushed.

'Do you have something to add, Mr Perron?' the PM asked.

'Er, not really. I agree with Mr Cody. If word gets out that the Kin are able to add a third again to their number each time a single one of them dies, even the smell of conspiracy about incremental invasion would be catastrophic. The conspiracy papers are already gaining in popularity, right behind the gossip and porn ones.'

'Josh is correct,' Adler said, 'the big sellers are still news and gossip, but the conspiracy papers are gaining traction in large numbers. There are three new ones that I know of, all trading on supposed tensions between human and Kin. Gentlemen, you know as well as I do that the media thrives and revolves on the big stories, big events, wars. It always has. But since the Kin arrived it's gone quiet, even in the Middle East. I fear that this information will set the cat among the pigeons.'

'And by 'the cat', you mean '*civil unrest on a massive, global scale*', and by 'pigeons' you mean '*society as we know it*',' said Josh.

Adler glanced at him. 'We have no idea, no clue that this

is their intention. One of the Kin has become a close friend to Richard Dandridge and is insistent that they had no idea that this would happen.'

'Well, he would say that, wouldn't he,' said the DPM. 'And where has Dandridge been for the last decade? I am not sure his testimony can be trusted.'

'You've never met Richard Dandridge, have you?' Adler asked. 'If you had, you wouldn't be questioning the veracity of his character.'

'And why should I not question yours, Adler? You were first contact. You and Crandall. The two of you have guided and influenced us all from Day One. Perhaps they convinced you of their plan and you're going along with it. I'm just playing devil's advocate here.'

'Playing devil's advocate is all very well, Deputy Prime Minister, but if you start questioning my loyalty now I can assure you that this situation will spiral out of control quicker than you can possibly imagine.'

'I don't doubt it. What do you suggest then, Adler? You're a solutions architect, so what's the solution?'

'The best we can do right now is convene a private, confidential forum with all Kin Community leaders and Shack leaders and talk it out, voice our concerns, get their input. I'm not even sure that they know what's happening.'

'They're not going to just come out and tell us their plans!' The DPM's face was red, beads of sweat lining his upper lip. 'They don't even have faces so we have no idea *what* they're thinking!'

Adler stared at him impassively. 'I have a face. Can you tell what I'm thinking?'

'Enough,' the PM cut in. 'If we ask, they might very well just tell us their plans, for better or worse. And if they do, perhaps we can prepare. Adler?'

'I agree, sir. Prepare for the worst, hope for the best. We can do nothing without knowledge. Hard facts, numbers, so we can revise terms, come to agreements-'

'Revise terms? You do realise that the only possible direction their numbers can go is up? What if they don't want to negotiate any more?' The DPM's face was reddening further with anger, and spittle flew out of his mouth with every word. He turned to the PM next to him. 'We need a contingency plan, Prime Minister.'

'Give me a month,' Adler responded. 'We'll collate new learnings, get clarity.'

'OK, you've got a month to get your hard facts, Adler - you and Perron here. Let's talk again in two weeks to catch up, keep me up to speed.' He stood up. The DPM remained sitting and shuffling his papers, looking quite pale and unwell beneath his red-faced anger.

They all left the room, Adler and Josh shaking hands with each of them in turn. Adler's car had been parked outside No. 11 and they drove out.

'Got plans later? Josh asked. 'I don't get to town much, I might find somewhere nice to eat.'

'I'm meeting a friend tonight. I'll drop you off at the hotel.'

Josh disembarked the large car and disappeared into the Dorchester, leaving Adler to drive alone through rush-hour London, the streets so clogged he was rarely out of first gear, until he reached his destination; a nondescript looking suburban home in North London with a low black gate and nicely trimmed trees lining the perimeter of the modest front garden. He parked across the road from the house, the large engine idling quietly, watching the house patiently for an hour until a black Jaguar saloon pulled into the driveway. He waited another ten minutes before opening the car door. He left it ajar.

He opened the low gate and quickly approached the grey front door. He rang the doorbell.

It opened and a man looked at him. 'Adler? What do you want?' The Deputy Prime Minister asked him. He was still in the suit he had worn to the meeting, but the shirt was unbuttoned down to his large gut which stuck out and hung down over his belt buckle, a grotesque assertion of wealth.

'I wanted to talk to you about the Kin problem,' Adler said.

'Ah, so you finally acknowledge it's a problem,' the DPM said and ushered Adler through to the large beige living room.

'Drink?' he turned to indicate an antique silver drinks tray in the corner laden with bottles, and as he did so Adler raised a small automatic with a long silencer and put a bullet through the back of his head.

A chunk of his brain pan pinged off the pewter tray of the drinks trolley with an audible 'clink.' He dropped to the carpet in a spray of blood, gurgling and gasping, his body twitching uncontrollably on the deep beige shagpile. He had fallen onto his side and his desperate, panicked eyes tracked Adler who stood over him, straddling his body. Adler fired another silenced shot into his head, and another into his heart.

He cast his eyes around the room as he unscrewed the silencer from the gun and placed the hot metal cylinder in his pocket and the gun back in his shoulder holster. On the pine coffee table in front of the television was a set of keys and a stack of the day's newspapers. There was the normal selection, news, politics and entertainment, but it was one of the new conspiracy papers that lay open. Next to it was a small vial of white liquid with a tiny cork stopper. Adler picked it up and stared at it. It had the consistency of semen but whiter, more like paper correction fluid. It was, without a doubt, the blood of a Kin.

Adler put it in his pocket and left the house, clicking the front door shut, returning to his car and driving away without looking back.

JOSH

What you doing? The text message from Ezra blinked onto his phone screen. Josh was seated alone at a restaurant in London in front of a starter plate of Confit of Duck. He put down his knife and fork and typed out his response. *Eating. Really expensive.*

Put it on xpenses Hw dd it go with PM
K. Scary. Lot of work to do
R kin gonna take over the world?
don't know

Josh took a bite of the duck. It was pink, succulent and delicious. He chewed and texted as Ezra's next message pinged in.

Dandridge gone. Didn't come home last night

Josh felt a pang of worry and disappointment.

He be back
Maybe. Love you

Josh ate the rest of his meal in a slightly despondent frame of mind. He was finishing with coffee and reading an entertainment paper when Adler slipped in opposite him.

'How did you know I was here?'

'I know a lot of things,' he replied. 'How's the food?'

'Great, I think. I didn't really taste it. I feel a bit... not sick, but really nervous. Like we're on the brink of something but I don't really know what.'

'Nobody knows what,' Adler said, before ordering a bottle of mineral water and a black coffee. 'You did well in the meeting today,' he said.

'I thought I came over rather badly,'

'On the contrary, you were great. Politicians sometimes forget how to cut through the bullshit. It's good to have a fresh voice in there.'

'I don't think I can be the new Marion.'

'You don't have to. Be the old Josh.'

'The Deputy Prime Minister was getting pissed off with

us I think. He seemed to be trying to incite some kind of argument.'

'He's too dangerous a man to be a direct influencer on policy, especially regarding the Kin. Do you know what this is?' Adler placed the vial of blood he had found on the table in front of him.

'No,' Josh picked it up and examined it. 'It looks a bit like shampoo. Have you been stealing from the hotel?'

'It's not hotel shampoo, Josh.'

'Oh god, it's not... you know-? That's really disgusting.'

'No it's not human ejaculate either, if that's what you are suggesting. It's blood. Kin blood.'

'Shit,' Josh swirled it around in the light of the candle flickering on the table. 'Where did you get it?'

'I acquired it. Someone seems to be dealing black-market Kin blood.'

'You are fucking kidding me. What the hell for? Does it taste nice?'

'I'm not sure. I need to find out where it came from. Stop the supply. We can't have any more dead Kin than necessary. Regrettably my only lead has gone cold.'

'Cold?'

'Yes. Come on, we need to get back to the Shack and get this analysed.'

'Now? I've just drunk a bottle of red-'

'You can sleep it off on the way.' He waved the waiter over and paid the bill, downing his scalding hot cup of black coffee in two gulps.

The two of them walked around the corner to where the rental SUV was parked in a side-street, almost blocking the entire thoroughfare. They climbed in, Adler gunned the engine and they set off back to the Shack.

DANDRIDGE

There was no way into the alien ship at ground-level except via the Shack, so instead of risking the wrath of Shack security he worked out where the first Kin had originally exited and laboriously climbed up the outside of each of the towering pizza-slice sections, stopping for few moments between each section or when a spotlight swooped across the surface. It took a long time. He still had the shakes, and was struck by waves of loneliness and paranoia he was simply unable to control. He had lost track of how far he'd climbed when he finally reached the pizza slice that had the ragged tear in the hull where the first Kin had emerged. He climbed across the narrow flat surface towards it, the metal creaking and groaning as the structure was pushed and pulled against the gusting wind. He had no idea it moved so much in the wind and staggered slightly against it. He felt like he was exploring an undersea wreck.

The ship was utterly deserted but his torch cut through the pitch blackness like a nail through a tyre. He entered with his rope still tied around him and soon found an upright structure he could lash it to. He kept hold of the coil, unravelling it as he went.

Although he knew that the upright structure was triangular, its almighty girth meant that it was impossible to make out what shape it was from inside it - the beam from his torch unable to reach the far side. There were dozens of blank, smooth consoles like black glass gleaming along all three walls but it was otherwise just a huge empty space, the largest empty space he had ever seen. The creaking and groaning of the metal in the wind echoed and amplified across the emptiness like it was trying to tell him something.

There were signs from previous explorations, markers on the floor, little numbered yellow plaques to indicate areas of interest to photograph, like a crime scene. He ventured further in but there really was nothing else to see.

He followed the wall around and found a narrow staircase that lead down to another vast empty triangular space identical to the first. Then another and another. The fifth staircase opened into another vast space but with no glassy blank consoles. Instead, the floor was pitted with individual Kin-sized shallow indents, hundreds of dark grey metal bathtubs set into the floor. There were more photographic markers.

Dandridge started crossing the floor, hopping across on the sides between each dip. He quickly realised it would take hours to make it to the other side, so instead he stopped and lay down in one, and imagined Belle resting in one alongside thousands of her own kind.

It was deep enough so that he was just under the surface. He listened to the creaking metal of the giant ship and tried to understand what it might be saying to him, feeling the silence and emptiness all around him. He started to cry silent tears again.

He'd had enough. The thought hit him like a punch in the gut, making him gasp. He wasn't getting over it. He had made a huge mistake and he had no-one to blame but himself. Just what had he been thinking? There was no way out of this, no future in pining for a fucking *alien*. He had fucked up, and now he was a laughing stock. He remembered his father, always doodling, always drawing something, never giving up, unable or unwilling to do anything else even as his family struggled desperately to get by, until the charming little cartoon that had made his fortune. *Little Dickie Dandridge* and his constant dreams of the stars, the little boy with a rocket made out of cardboard and paper glue, running around and breaking things but never, ever giving up on his dreams.

His father had died after a long battle with stomach cancer, but before he died he had drawn a final Dickie Dandridge strip that ran in all the newspapers the day after his funeral. In it, Dickie was a grown man, floating free from gravity in his real spaceship, looking down at the earth shimmering far beneath him, a beatific smile on his face.

Dandridge scrambled out of the grey tub and ran full-tilt back up the stairs to the opening in the side of the ship. He looked out at the night. It was dark but the lights of the Shack and the occasional sweeping spotlight lit up the giant ship. He was at least forty stories up, not nearly at the top, but the view was still beautiful. Dandridge took a step to the edge and looked down. He was on the wrong side of the ship to see the Huts down below, but the glass roof of the Shack was lit up. He would miss it by about twenty feet. He took a deep breath, the sharp wind drying the tears instantly on his cheeks. He felt calmer now and more at peace, looking forward to not having to think so fucking much.

He raised his arms and lifted his right foot over the edge, trying to think of a coherent final thought that didn't include Belle.

Then there was a noise behind him and a hand on his shoulder and he was yanked backwards. He stumbled to his arse, yelling in surprise. 'Jesus, *what the fuck*!'

'Dandridge.'

'*Adler?*'

Adler was dragging him, literally kicking and screaming, back into the ship. 'What the fuck are you doing up here? Are you trying to kill yourself?'

'How did you find me?' Dandridge gasped, trying to stand up but only making it half-way, doubled over, his hands on his knees.

'I got back from London about three hours ago and security told me you were climbing up. I told them to leave you to it.'

'You knew? How did you get up here?'

'There's a ladder, idiot.'

'Oh. So what do you want? I'm trying to kill myself here.'

'I need your help, Richard.' Their voices echoed off the

walls.

'What with?'

'You've had some recent experience with Kin.'

'Don't fucking remind me.'

'Do you know what this is?' Adler held up the vial of Kin blood in the beam of his torch. Dandridge took it and examined it in the bright beam of light, tilting it backwards and forwards.

'It's Kin. Where did you get it?'

'Don't ask. But I want to know where it came from. I need you to find out for me.'

'Me? No.'

'I need someone I can trust, someone who can work quickly, think on their feet. Someone who can get stuff done, and who, to be frank, isn't actually busy right now.'

'Charming. What's your play?'

'The person I took this from had to have got it from somewhere. I am assuming that there is a black market for this stuff, that somebody out there is profiting from some perceived positive effect or health benefit from drinking Kin blood. We can't let that perception continue, which means we need to shut it down, as soon as possible.'

'And where am I supposed to find this black market Kin dealer?'

'Go to London. Bars, nightspots in trendy areas. Where rich people hang out. Ask around, carefully. See what information you can dig up. Something's going on, something not good, and I really need to know what, especially in light of the recent wave of new Kin arrivals.'

Dandridge put the vial into his pocket. 'How do you know I won't drink it?'

'You want to have another meltdown on the floor of your kitchen again?'

'Not so much.'

'Then don't drink it. You want to stand at the precipice of this alien ship and try to off yourself? Do it on your own dime, Dandridge. For right now, we need you.'

Dandridge shrugged. 'Fine. I'll leave tonight and be in touch when I find something. Now, where's that ladder?'

JOSH

Josh sat in Marion's office reading the first of the day's newspapers. They all lead with the same story about the death of the Deputy Prime Minister, even the gossip ones. He was fairly positive that Adler had something to do with it, although he wasn't sure how to broach the subject and he hadn't actually seen him face to face since they had returned from London two days ago.

Josh had re-opened the temporary housing block to accommodate the slow trickle of new Kin requiring induction and a fresh integration program. The block had been undergoing a process of conversion into affordable, modern apartments so there was scaffolding covering the entire long building, but fortunately for him the interior was still virtually intact and there were a number of Kin now living on-site for the first time in about five years.

He had a daily call with the Prime Minister, the novelty of which was growing increasingly thin. The fact was that Adler was doing all the hard work and he was just about coping with a small number of new Kin in a single location. He felt slightly helpless.

He carried on reading the newspaper which reported how the DPM had been discovered by a cleaner. Two gunshot wounds to his head and one to his heart. There was nothing else disturbed and nothing stolen which indicated he had known his murderer. His time of death was estimated to be about seven thirty in the evening. Josh calculated in his head the time between Adler dropping him off and the time he had joined him at the restaurant. His blood ran cold and he shivered.

All the newspapers worked on a tacit agreement not to overtly encroach on each others remit, but even the factual titles were speculating a number of wild theories; that the DPM had been murdered by a jealous gay lover, he was a drug addict, he was involved with underworld figures. Josh closed the papers and closed his eyes. The phone rang. He stared at it for a few rings and glanced over to Nancy at reception who gave him the 'thumbs up' sign.

Josh picked up.

'Perron,' Adler said. 'Everything OK over there? What are the numbers?'

'Two hundred and twenty two so far. All the twos.'

'You got lucky, North America got over three thousand so far, Spain about five. People are really starting to get suspicious.'

'I'm sure. Adler, about the DPM—'

'Tragic news indeed.'

'Do you know anything about it?'

'I don't know everything, Josh. Just keep focused on the job in hand. If you get any calls from the press about the Kin, stick to the company line.'

'I will. Where are you?'

'Peru. I'll be back at the end of the week.'

'OK.'

'Thanks Josh. Be careful.'

'Why would I need to be careful?'

But Adler had rung off.

There was a buzz on his computer console. Two more Kin were at the Shack, requesting integration protocols. Two hundred and twenty four.

PART SIX

LUKE

They were picked up four days and nearly a hundred and fifty miles after they had set off from the crash site. Luke had spotted the helicopter first and had shouted and screamed until his throat was raw, waving his arms frantically up and down. They had all run to the top of a small rocky outcrop, shouting and screaming and waving together. At first it looked as if the tiny buzzing dot against the skyline wasn't going to see them and vanish into the distance, but incredibly and unbelievably and with a crashing feeling of relief and joy so overwhelming he thought he might pass out, the bright red machine changed course and flew towards them, then right over them, the pilot and co-pilot both grinning and waving from the cockpit.

The survivors were all hugging and leaping around and weeping with happiness.

They had walked for nearly ninety-six hours straight with very little rest or respite. None of them wanted to stop.

Luke suspected it was possible that they couldn't stop even if they had wanted to. They had left the crash site running and laughing like they were schoolkids off to the park to play on the swings. Luke had followed them, casting a glance back to the spot where the Kin had lain, an area of compacted snow and white blood soaked into the ground.

Hennessy and Crandall would have skipped off the site naked if he hadn't insisted they put their clothes back on, their pale goosebumped bodies still caked in congealing Kin blood and both unashamedly aroused from the euphoria coursing relentlessly through them both. Luke tried to avert his gaze, but they didn't seem to care. The only slash of colour against the freezing paleness of Crandall's skin was her red, swollen labia, while he was fairly certain they could have used Mike's straining, glistening penis as an SOS beacon.

He wasn't immune to the effects of the white flesh he had been forced to eat and felt an eager anticipation of his life ahead that was so keen it was like a razorblade slicing open the fabric of the world in front of him, ready for him to step through. He was surrounded by snow yet all he could see was colour. But he had enough control of himself to realise that the only thing standing between him and his new life was this fucking mountain.

His step-mother and Royce Brims were chattering excitedly, unable to contain their bubbling enthusiasm, their hopes and plans and dreams and fantasies. When Luke tried to corral them all together Jennifer turned round and snapped at him with a vehemence he never knew she possessed. Hate blazed in her eyes, her upper lip curled with undisguised contempt. He took a step back in shock, but Royce had already distracted her with another fanciful idea about running for office.

And so, after an hour of cajoling and encouragement and without any real fanfare, the mountain echoing with the sound of chattering, excited voices, they had simply walked away.

MIKE

He felt strong, that was all he could remember later of the walk itself. There was never a point where he didn't feel as if he could have carried on walking. It felt like he didn't actually need rescuing, he was just going to walk all the way back to his South London flat. Through the exhilaration of his confidence and undiminishing lust for Marion Crandall he could feel a vague background noise of his body fighting hunger, and both his feet struggling with the pain of frostbite inside his black patent-leather work shoes, but he was easily able to shrug it off and keep going.

Once they had actually started they fell into a rhythm, Mike heading up the procession with Marion, Buddy, Jennifer, Luke and Royce following behind, crossing mountainous terrain through snow storms and bitter nights in an unchanging order, climbing where necessary, across narrow ledges, precipices and almost impassable terrain, none of them afraid of falling or losing their grip. Their confidence was unwavering despite not one of them having any survival or mountaineering experience.

On one occasion Marion, climbing right behind him, did slip slightly and began a slide downwards that might have taken down everyone behind her, but as soon as she lost her footing Mike had already reached down and caught hold of her as if he was one step ahead of fate itself.

The focus of Mike's impatience to get rescued was to have more incredible, mind-altering sex with Marion. Mike was normally quite prudish and conventional when it came to sex, but he felt no embarrassment or shame at having abandoned himself to his desire in front of the others. If anything, it aroused him more.

He wasn't exactly sure how long they had walked when Luke, the boy doggedly and silently trailing in their footsteps, spotted the helicopter in the distance and started shouting wildly. He frantically climbed to the top of a low ridge and waved his arms up and down. Mike and the others followed him and they all started to scream, and then the miracle happened and the machine flew low over them, the pilots both waving as they passed overhead. Royce Brims stood next to him, waving and laughing the hysterical laughter of someone who knows full well he has cheated death.

ROYCE

The co-pilot of the small red helicopter leaned out of the window and fired a bright orange flare marker into the snow which immediately started to belch out great billows of orange smoke. The helicopter flew away again with a reassuring wave from the pilot.

Royce found himself unable to stop laughing and crying at the same time. He had no idea how long they had walked, but they had made it. He had made it. Kai hadn't, but Royce made up his mind there and then to see Kai's mum and pay for his funeral, maybe buy her a house. He hugged Jennifer tightly, hoping he could spend some more time with her when they got home. She was so cool, even though she was older than him and her stepson was kind of a dick.

A much bigger white and yellow helicopter appeared on the horizon and gradually increased in size and noise to where they were all still balanced on the rocky ridge, standing in a row like the world's filthiest identity parade.

It hovered above them, the downdraft of the rotors blowing the rest of the snow off the ridge. The group stood with their arms across their faces, protecting themselves from the wind and billowing snow. There was nowhere safe to land, so a rescue team member in orange overalls winched down ready to hook them one by one into a padded harness. Marion went first, then Luke, then Jennifer, then Buddy and then Royce, who watched from safety as they hauled Hennessy up into the windy, loud machine after them. Once they had unhooked, the large side door was slid closed and the comparative quiet was deafening.

All at once the survivors felt strangely protective of each other and huddled close, not really responding to the rescue crew's efforts to engage.

There was a medic in the helicopter who peeled away Buddy's shirt sleeve to check his broken arm. To Royce, the black, mottled area that had stretched from his wrist to just above his elbow was not nearly as extensive at it had been four days ago, but it still smelt like rotting meat. The medic bent the arm back and forward slightly and Buddy didn't flinch. The medic checked each of his pupils in turn with a penlight.

'Are you OK?' he asked. 'Does this hurt at all? You seem a bit out of it.'

'I'm fine. It hurts, but I think I must just be in shock,' Buddy said.

The medic said nothing and looked over each of them in turn as the large helicopter sped past mile upon mile of white. Royce decided it would be a long, long time before he took another skiing holiday.

The medic removed one of Marion's thin shoes, the sole completely destroyed. She must have been walking in bare feet for the last two days at least. Her soles were broken and bleeding, her toes blackened. The nail of her left big toe was hanging away as her sock was cut away. She grimaced slightly, but it was more a grossed out reaction than a painful one. Royce was slightly disgusted to note, with perhaps a touch of admiration, that Hennessy adjusted the crotch of his business trousers as Marion's leg came into view, despite it ending in black toes and a torn-off nail. The medic wrapped a temporary gauze bandage around her foot.

He checked Jennifer over next, going over all her blackened fingers and toes.

'How do you feel?' the medic said loudly over the sound of the engine. She shrugged. He then looked at Luke, who seemed fine, but more tired and sleepy than the others, more in shock. The medic strapped an oxygen mask over his head then turned to Royce, who waved him away.

'I'm fine,' he said. 'I can wait till we get to the hospital.'

The medic nodded and sat back against the forward bulkhead of the helicopter. He looked for a bit longer at Royce and then produced a pen from one of the many exterior pockets of his flight suit. From another came a CD. It was Royce's album 'White, Blue and Red'. He silently held them out to Royce, who took the pen and slid out the paper insert from the transparent case of the album. Leaning on his knee, Royce wrote *'Thanks for rescuing me. Keep doin' what you're doin'. Royce Brims.'* He then handed both back to the man who nodded his appreciation and stared at the words before sliding the CD back into his pocket, his grey eyes calmly watching his passengers.

MARION

Her foot looked absolutely horrible, but the pain wasn't as intense as she thought it would be. She hoped to receive a large dose of painkillers by the time it hit her later on. She looked across at Mike, who was staring back at her. She felt a wave of desire. It was as much as she could do not to crawl on top of him right there and then.

The machine was slowing and preparing to set down. She stared out of the small window and could see a basecamp of some sort, lots of tents, a couple of large temporary looking portacabins and two or three helicopters parked at one end, including the little red one that had spotted them. There was a small group of people standing and watching the helicopter as it approached.

The large machine landed gently in the middle of the 'H' and the pilot shut the engine down, leaving only the *whumph* of the rotors still spinning above them, slower and slower.

One by one, they stepped down into the chill wind to the sound of applause from the rescue group. There were five gurneys lined up in a row in front of the helicopter's side door and as they disembarked they were each directed to hop up on one. They smiled and waved as they were wheeled through the small crowd and through the double doors of the temporary grey building, where they were split into separate rooms.

She was hooked up to a saline drip to rehydrate her body and a cluster of doctors and nurses helped her remove her clothes and into a hospital gown. She felt perfectly fine. She knew she was tired and that her feet needed some treatment, but there was nothing that a night's sleep and perhaps a large steak and chips wouldn't fix. Perhaps some mustard.

She was examined from head to blackened toes. It was getting dark outside when they left her alone to her own, marvellously lucid thoughts. She drifted off to sleep, awoken some time later by Mike opening her door. He wheeled himself in on an ancient looking wheelchair and locked the door behind him.

He climbed up on the bed next to her and slid his hand up the thin material of her hospital gown. His own identical gown did not leave his intentions to her imagination. They kissed deeply, his hands all over her, both gowns riding up above their waists. He entered her urgently and her legs wrapped tightly around him. She gripped his buttocks and pulled him inside her as deeply as possible, feeling every millimetre as he pulled and pushed inside her. She had never felt so physically and emotionally connected to another person before. She had completely surrendered to him; a hedonistic, utter freedom of body and mind, a submission and fearlessness between two people that had brought her pleasure unlike anything she had ever experienced.

As she felt Mike move faster her back arched and she came, her mouth clamping on his neck to stifle her moans, her fingernails raking his back. He didn't last much longer.

He pulled out of her and they rested side by side for a long while, drifting in and out of sleep. As light came up, she opened her eyes to see him staring at her.

'It was great, but not the same. Was it for you?'

'No. It felt more like... just sex.'

'Thanks a bunch.'

'No, it felt like amazing sex, but not the same. I think maybe we were high before.'

'High on what? The meat? The Kin?'

'Yes.'

'We need to get together with the others. Nobody can know what we did.'

'We didn't just eat it, Mike. We fucking devoured it, and you and I had sex in it's blood, right in front of the others, even Luke. It was horrible, what we did.'

'I've done worse things in my time.'

'You have? Worse than eating a Kin and then having sex in front of a group of strangers and a kid? I can still feel it in me, affecting me. Can't you feel it?' Marion had started to cry. Mike gently kissed her tears away. 'I can, yes. But it's the reason we survived, isn't it? The reason we are still here, alive, you and me. We had to eat it.'

'I suppose.'

'Come on, lets go and talk with the others.'

'I need a shower first.' Together, they went into the small shower cubicle attached to her room and pulled the curtain across. As they soaped themselves Mike took her again and the sex was as passionate as the previous night without ever attaining the heights of the pleasure they had achieved on the mountain.

They stepped out and dried themselves, getting dressed back into their identical hospital gowns. Mike wheeled himself out and they gathered the others together in his room.

BUDDY

'I've got to show you something,' Buddy said as they gathered in Hennessey's little hospital room.

'What?' the boy said, nervously. 'I don't want to see anyone else naked,' he glanced at Mike, who had regained the fortitude to blush slightly.

'No, it's OK. I'm not going to get naked.' He unbandaged his arm. The medics were treating the frostbite before they placed the broken arm in plaster. But the mottled, stinking, rotting flesh of Buddy's arm was practically gone. The area around the break was red and bruised, but there were only traces of the dark rot in his veins. For the most part it was gone.

'How?' Royce said. 'It looks almost better. Holy shit.'

Buddy flexed it back and forward.

'Even the break doesn't hurt much any more. What about you guys? Jennifer, you had bad frostbite on both hands and your feet. Lets see.'

Jennifer's hands were clear, her fingers pink and healthy. She unbandaged her feet and showed the group traces of frostbite on three toes on her right foot and two toes on her left. 'He's right. This was much, much worse on the mountain. I was sure I was going to lose a foot, at least.'

'What does this mean?' Luke asked, as he unbandaged his own feet and revealed practically healed, healthy toes.

There was silence for a while as they all compared their injuries, or lack of.

'This can't come out,' Marion said finally. 'We can't tell a soul. This has to stay between us. Firstly, that we ate a Kin. Secondly, that it seems to have somehow given us enough energy to walk down from a mountain and then heal us. This information could have potentially damaging consequences.'

'Then we need a cover story, for how we escaped being on a freezing mountain for days on end with barely a scratch,' Buddy said. 'They know roughly where the plane crashed now. They'll find the site. They'll know.'

'Then the story needs to be convincing. And everyone on this whole site needs to be on the same page. We can't start a riot by claiming that the Kin can cure cancer or something. I'll make some calls,' said Marion.

'Make some calls?' Royce said suddenly. 'Really? You can just brush the truth under the carpet as easy as that?'

Marion looked sharply at him. 'What do you mean?'

'It was your manifesto that took away the internet, that took away free speech, that caused thousands of people to die. What else weren't you telling us?'

'Royce, the Kin are here because we negotiated their safe arrival and integration and avoided a conflict. It's worked out OK so far, wouldn't you say?'

'By taking away our free speech.'

'So you keep saying, but free speech is alive and well, it always has been. Maybe its even freer now than it was before, now people have to actually fucking think before saying shit.'

'We're getting off the point,' Mike interjected, 'which is that the Kin flesh seems to have opened our minds and healed the worst of our injuries. And I don't know about you, but I have felt great since we-'

'-tore it apart with your bare hands?' Luke said.

'Yes, I suppose so. It got a little crazy up there.'

'OK, so for now, we stick to a basic story,' Marion said. 'It'll be the easiest to repeat. We survived on food we found from the aircraft then packed it up and walked till we were rescued.'

'They'll search the site and know that no food was recovered,' Buddy said.

'Yes, but until then we have no option. The story will hold if we stick to it. Plausible deniability. Plus there's no other rational explanation.'

'Only the irrational one, that Kin flesh is magic and

healed us all,' Luke muttered.

'Luke, if a single word gets out about 'magic Kin flesh' there will be massive trouble, I promise you. Trouble you can't even begin to imagine. Please, please stick to the story. There's going to be press. Lots of press, media, TV, all the papers. The news ones, as well as a couple of the fringe papers, the conspiracy and political types. Stick to the story. Basic details only.'

Buddy flexed his arm up and down some more. It twinged, but it wasn't too painful. He smiled with happiness.

'Agreed,' he said, chiming in with the others.

JENNIFER

The meeting adjourned, they all returned to their own rooms. Jennifer lay down on her narrow bed and her brain started whirring with the enormity of what was happening to them. Then she had to get up and rush to the small chemical toilet to vomit.

There wasn't much in her stomach. She threw up a greenish white mucus and watched it slide down the bowl. She stayed on her knees, her head and hair dangling towards the foul-smelling gloop in the pan. That was how a nurse found her ten minutes later before escorting her back to bed.

Doctors and nurses continued to come in and out of their rooms throughout the day. Jennifer lay unmoving and unspeaking, only answering direct questions and submitting to their tests.

In the afternoon, a doctor wheeled a gurney into her room, and indicated she should climb up. Outside her window she could hear a helicopter's engine start to wind up with a whine.

'Where am I going?' she asked, climbing up onto the gurney.

'To a hospital,' the doctor replied in a thick Spanish accent. 'None of you are really safe to move right now, but you need more care than we can give.'

'What about Luke?'

'He will follow with the others once we fully ascertain the extent of their injuries.'

'He should come with me,' she said but even to her own ears the words sounded hollow.

'He will stay here one more night, if you consent. He can join you at Llulaico National Hospital tomorrow.'

'OK.'

She was wheeled down the short corridor and past the other rooms to the main double doors and into the cold sunshine. She was facing backwards and saw Marion staring out of her window at her. Marion waved at her before the gurney was lifted into the helicopter and strapped in securely. The doctor sat next to her, smiling reassuringly.

The rotors were at full dizzying speed and as the side door was slid shut it lifted off. Jennifer lay and stared at the curved cabin ceiling as it carried her further and further from the base camp, and Luke.

The further away she got the better she felt.

Some time later they touched gently down at Llulaico National Hospital and she was wheeled inside. It was clean and quiet and smelt of disinfectant and bleach just like a hospital should. Her room was smaller than the one at the basecamp but better equipped. She was lifted onto a narrow bed and relaxed back under the clean starched white sheets and closed her eyes.

When she opened them a Kin was standing over her. She started and let out a short scream before clamping her hand over her mouth in shock.

'My apologies, Mrs McDonald. I startled you.'

'No,' Jennifer croaked, 'it's OK. I just woke up, that's all. What are you? Are you a doctor?'

'No, Mrs McDonald. Although a number of us have qualified as physicians, I work here as a porter and nursing assistant. I am here to ensure you know how the call button and the bed operate.'

To demonstrate the button that raised the bed to a sitting position, the Kin reached across Jennifer and the bed started to lift her slowly towards it's pure white chest. Jennifer felt a thrill course through her entire body and she lifted her face to meet it, pressing against the warm dry flesh and breathing in deeply. The Kin pulled back.

'Mrs McDonald? Are you alright? Should I fetch a doctor?'

'I'm fine,' Jennifer said. Her heart was thumping with the effort it was taking her not to lick the Kin's chest, not to reach over and grab it, to close her mouth around it's muscular upper arm and squeeze all the juice out of it. Her body was quivering with lust and abject need for the creature. She forced her eyes closed.

'I'm just tired. Please leave.'

'I understand. I will leave you to rest. Press the green button if you require attention. The Doctor will make her rounds at three o'clock.'

The Kin stepped out and left Jennifer in the bed, her toes curled, her fists clenched, her whole body pulsing with the memory and taste of Kin, the feeling as she had torn off its leg and taken huge, overflowing, decadent mouthfuls. Something inside her twitched and she placed her hand on her stomach protectively.

She started laughing out loud, huge gales of laughter. She couldn't stop, didn't want to stop. She was going to have a baby! *Luke's* baby. She was so angry, so full of blistering hatred. A loathing of him so strong it could peel paint.

And at the same time she knew that she wanted this baby, regardless of how it was conceived. She had no option but to laugh; laugh or die. So she laughed even harder, the taste of the Kin on her tongue. She kept on laughing as three nurses ran into her room to find out what was happening. She couldn't stop laughing as one of the nurses slipped a needle into her arm and slowly pressed the plunger. Her laughs turned to giggles which turned to helpless hitches of breath before she drifted off to sleep, feeling her baby twitch and move deep inside her.

MARION

Jennifer was loaded into the waiting chopper and Marion watched as it lifted off and dwindled in sight and then sound over the horizon. She went through to Luke's room.

'Why is your stepmum leaving?'

'I don't know.'

'Didn't you two speak about it?'

'We don't really talk much.'

'No, but still. It's odd that you didn't go with her.'

'I guess.'

'How are you feeling, Luke?'

'Fine. I still feel pretty good. From the meat, I mean. I'm ready to get out of here.'

'Me too. Listen, about the mountain, what you saw-'

Luke blushed as the image of Marion's vagina flashed unwanted across his memory.

'Forget it,' he mumbled.

'I can't. The Kin made us all feel crazy. Uninhibited. I would never normally- What I mean to say is that we should have been more discreet.'

'I know.'

'Now we're safe it all feels so bizarre and ridiculous. I'm so sorry that you had to be a part of that.'

'I *wasn't* a part of that. I wanted no part in it. You forced me to eat the Kin and I *hate* you all for it. But I guess I owe it my life. The rest of it was all you. You and Royce and Buddy and Mike. And *Jennifer*,' he spat out her name. '*You* all went crazy up there, having sex and eating the Kin, not me.'

Marion stared at him, slightly taken aback by his outburst.

'You need to keep it all a secret Luke. You know that, right? All of it? Even if you weren't part of it. All your social networks? Not a word. It's our secret.'

'I know, you told us.'

'I know I told the group, but you're the one who has the most social connections, not us. And once we get out of here, you'll be famous.'

'Don't worry, I won't say anything.'

'Good. Thank you. And I'm sorry again.'

She left Luke's room and went in to see Mike. He was dozing, but stirred when she clicked the door behind her.

'What's up?'

'It's Luke. I think this is going to get out. Maybe not in the next week or so but almost certainly at some point. Either Luke or Royce. We need a back-up plan.'

'That's not really my area of expertise.'

'Nor mine.'

'I'm horny again,' Mike said, indicating his tented hospital gown, 'I don't know what's wrong with me. This never happens. I'm a once-a-night guy as a rule. We've done it twice already today.'

'Me too. It's the meat, it's still affecting us. It's like a mental and physical viagra.'

'For us maybe, but the others didn't feel the same way. I know that Buddy and Royce just felt kinda powerful, like they were ready to take on the world. Jennifer looked determined about something, confident too. I don't know what Luke was feeling.'

'He didn't eat as much as we did. I know he feels ready to go home. He's definitely still got some arrogance about him.'

'Perhaps it enhances what you naturally feel, amplifies your normal psyche, but I don't know if it's the meat or his normal attitude,' Mike mused.

'Maybe it brings out long suppressed emotions. I just don't know. Maybe all of it. Whatever the explanation, you and I were always going to get together. I had every intention of having you when we got to the hotel in Buenos Aires anyway.'

'Oh really?' said Mike, laughing.

'Absolutely. With or without the Kin, I usually get what I want.'

They laughed, and kissed, and then Marion locked the door.

ADLER

The black and white webcam footage showed the entwined couple in an intense, oblivious, almost frantic session. There was no audio over the picture, a live stream from Mike Hennessy's room. Adler sat on a wooden folding chair next to the Basecamp Rescue Team Leader Alex DeSouza, a man whose stubble was millimetres away from a full beard and whose jet black perma-tousled hair and rugged looks could have equally suited the side of a mountain or in GQ dressed in a dinner jacket. He was dressed in a plain white T-shirt and blue jeans with flip-flops. Adler wore a thick, black puffer jacket, a large red bobble hat and insulated thermal trousers. He was not a fan of the cold. He stared intently at Mike and Marion having sex.

'OK, Alex. If you are asking my opinion, I think that this is a bit unpleasant, slightly creepy and I am thinking about reporting you.'

'Mr Adler.'

'Just Adler.'

'You are missing the point,' DeSouza replied in his heavy Spanish accent. 'These two people are having sex. This is the third time today that they have had sex.'

'Your case is not improving.'

'Have you been on the side of a mountain, Mr Adler? Or scaled one?'

'No.'

'The conditions can be very harsh, very unpleasant. Almost certainly fatal without adequate clothing, protection, equipment. Minus thirty degrees most nights, a wind so cold it will freeze the marrow in your bones. Snow so deep you could drown in it. These people had nothing. They stuffed newspapers into their city clothes to keep warm. The man there-' DeSouza indicated Mike's buttocks on the screen, '-was wearing a business shirt and fake leather shoes.'

'OK.'

'We have located the crash site now based on their reports. It looks like they had a shelter, a rudimentary section of the destroyed fuselage. They were there four days, and walked for three. Seven days.'

'Right.'

'Seven days at temperatures and conditions they would never have experienced before, in shock from the plane crash, with no equipment.'

'Continue.'

'It is possible they could have survived at the site. But then to walk well over one hundred miles across the terrain they did? Impossible.'

'Yet here they are.'

'Here they are. Having sex three times a day. And Mr Adler-'

'Just Adler.'

'They hardly have a scratch on them.'

'What do you mean?'

'This one, Tucker-' he pressed a button on the keyboard of the PC and a webcam image of Buddy pacing his room replaced Mike's buttocks, '-this one had slight frostbite and a broken arm. After seven days in sub-zero temperatures, the fracture would have mortified and become infected. We would have had to amputate, no question. Instead, we have treated the frostbite and plastered the arm. According to their accounts the boy and his stepmother were stranded on a piece of the plane overnight with no protection whatsoever, unable to move because it was sited precariously near an ice fissure. That one night alone should have resulted in irreparable damage to their extremities. Their hands, fingers, toes and feet would be black with frostbite. It's there for sure, but barely.'

'Where is the woman?'

'I sent her to Lullaico. Our tests indicate that she may be pregnant.'

'What?'

'We think she's pregnant. Very early days. Maybe three weeks, maybe even less.'

'Holy fuck.'

'She knew it too. Adler, I don't know what the fuck is going on here.'

'I don't know either. DeSouza, I want you to round up your entire team, every last man and woman, for a meeting in the canteen block at twenty-two hundred, and don't breathe a word of any of this until I speak with them.'

'Understood, but the medical personnel are as confounded as me. They will have spoken about it.'

'Fine. Twenty-two hundred.'

Adler walked out of the small office and DeSouza, with a mildly guilty glance behind him, switched the camera back to Mike's room. On the screen, Marion was pulling her hospital gown back on. Mike was in the bed, adjusting the sheets.

Alex DeSouza watched as they both looked towards the door in alarm then back at each other. Mike got out of bed and unlocked and opened the door as Marion stood hiding behind it, out of sight. He watched as Adler stepped into the room, Marion appearing behind him and throwing her arms around him. They embraced briefly and he closed the door again, glancing up at the hidden webcam, but otherwise ignoring it. Adler pulled up a chair and the two survivors sat on the bed next to each other.

After talking with them both at length he visited Buddy Tucker, then the rapper guy Royce and lastly the boy, all of whom related a vaguely similar story to him about their survival on the mountain, living off aeroplane food. They told it convincingly enough, and on the surface at least there was simply no other explanation.

After gathering the stories of all the survivors he made his way to the canteen area and sat down. There was a small crowd gathered; pilots, rescue team, climbers and medical staff. Alex DeSouza sat on a chair next to him, his two black Labradors, Lionel and Fernando, lying at his feet.

'OK everybody, thanks for gathering round. My name is Ernest C. Adler. I work for the United Kingdom Foreign Office. Together with one of our survivors, Marion Crandall, I was partly responsible for the peaceful integration with the alien species known as the Kin.'

'What does the 'C' stand for?' asked De Souza, and Adler shot him an irritated look.

'Gentlemen and ladies. You have conducted yourselves impeccably. The media is hammering on our door for answers, but we need to make sure we are all on the same page before we release our survivors to the outside world. Flight PK3210 crashed a week ago, taking the lives of two hundred and thirty three people. We have six survivors and I understand it is unlikely we'll find any more.

'As I understand the situation, the six people currently recuperating across the way were stranded alone on a mountain for four days in sub-zero temperatures with little to no food and endured a hundred mile or so trek to safety through perilous conditions and terrain.'

The room was silent.

'On top of that, the woman, Jennifer McDonald, is also pregnant. She is currently under surveillance at Lullaico, but I have been informed that she has suffered some sort of breakdown and is under sedation. That aside, the facts as we know them do not add up, and we all know it.'

'So what did happen up there?' one of the pilots asked. 'Do you know?'

'They found decent shelter, consumed the food from the plane and then made their way south until they were picked up. That's it. That's the story.'

'It's not possible,' the pilot said.

'No, probably not. But when the media gets here, you will stick to that story without hesitation.'

'Why? They are obviously lying to us. I've been to the

crash site, I've been recovering bodies for two days now.'

The pilot pointed at the large blue schematic of the aircraft that was blu-tacked to one wall of the canteen. 'There is no sign of the cockpit to about this point here, and that's where the galley was and the stores were kept. I suspect it's down that ravine with much of the rest of it.'

'So what do *you* think happened?' Adler asked.

'I have no idea.'

'Not good enough. We all need to be on the same page here.'

'Why?'

'We all know something strange is going on, but none of us know what. Royce Brims and Marion Crandall are well known public figures. We can't have them being asked awkward questions because someone in this room leaked some bizarre theory that they should both, by any natural law, be dead. Until we find an answer the press must have the standard rescue story.'

'I still don't really understand,' one of the female paramedics said, 'why it's so important that we need to stick to this story? Why aren't we trying to find out the truth?'

'Because I suspect that the actual answer may have further reaching consequences than any of us here can imagine. And I need to nip the head from that bud, right here and right now. I have no answers and no explanations for you, but I need your help and trust on this.'

There was silence in the room broken only by the panting of the two dogs at DeSouza's feet. 'I hope you all understand,' Adler continued, 'I speak with the full authority and backing of the United Nations. We must stick to their story, just as they are doing.'

They all slowly nodded agreement and gradually began to disperse. Adler sat back down next to Alex DeSouza.

'Are we in any danger, Mr. Adler?' he asked, scratching one of the dogs behind the ears.

'I don't think so. In fact, we're probably in the safest

place to be right now.'

Adler's phone chirruped and he read the message on the screen. It was from Dandridge, and it read 'Sugar and Spice'.

Adler read the words two or three times.

'Are you OK?' Alex asked him.

'Yes. But you need to be vigilant over your people, Alex. Stick to the story. It's vital.'

ROYCE

After two days decompressing and recovering at the basecamp, the group were airlifted to Lullaico Memorial Hospital. Royce shared a helicopter with Buddy, who seemed awkward and agitated for the entire two and a bit-hour flight.

'You're still up for it yeah? Roy?' he kept saying, his knee jiggling urgently up and down and his fingers tapping out a constant beat against the armrests.

'You and me, Roy, yeah? You and me against the world!' Occasionally he would giggle to himself.

Royce was still feeling pretty positive. Not as much as on the walk, when he was absolutely, definitely certain he was going to walk all the way from the mountain straight into his Bethnal Green loft and start playing Nathan Drake on his PS4, but still pretty damn good. He was sure that Buddy was experienced enough to guide him to the superstardom he seemed to think was possible, but he had started to wish that the little man would just shut up about it.

He thought of Henderson Mulcahy in his huge chrome and glass tower like a kind of hip-hop Tony Stark. At the thought of Henderson, he shivered.

'You alright, Roy? You alright? Don't want to get sick now, you know... your public awaits.'

'I'm not getting sick and stop calling me Roy,' Royce leaned forward, 'Buddy, you've been with Henderson for a while now, right?'

'Fourteen years.'

'OK. So what do you think of him? Do you like him? How much do you know about him, really?'

Buddy sat back on his seat against the side of the helicopter and looked at Royce, his jiggling knee pausing its frantic movement.

'Roy, you know that Henderson is a powerful man,

don't you?'

'Yes.'

'It's vital that we don't get on his bad side or say things that would make him turn against us. Do you understand? What we're going to do we have to do with his full backing and co-operation.'

'Yes, but if we do that, then we won't be breaking away from him at all, will we? We'll still be his property like everyone else. Isn't the point of forming our own label to make our own decisions?'

'Up to a point. For a start, you are still signed to his label. In order to break that contract and start over you'll have to pay him off, and the only way to do that is to promise him a percentage of the profits of your next album, and the albums of any other artists we sign. And the merchandising. We'll be free from him eventually, but we need to work at it, chip away at it a piece at a time. And you can't open your mouth and tell anyone anything you might know about him that might jeopardise that. He'll destroy you. And me, by association.'

'Destroy? That's a bit strong isn't it? He's not going to murder us.'

'There's a lot more ways to destroy a person than murder. You were his favourite for a long time Royce, so that bridge is strong, thankfully. When we do this, it'll be with him and not behind his back. It's the only way.'

The helicopter was passing over suburban settlements. They were descending towards a rooftop helicopter pad. Below them was a field of press, every camera pointed up at the helicopter above them.

Royce was used to the press. He loved them and they loved him. But this time he felt a little different. He felt a stirring of unease and something else, something unidentifiable in his gut, a feeling of need which felt slightly like wanting his mother. He hadn't wanted his mother for years now and although he had telephoned her to say he was safe, he had become impatient with her when she had started to cry with relief and so now he felt mildly guilty too.

The helicopter came to a perfectly gentle halt and he and Buddy were pushed in their wheelchairs by two waiting porters to a lift and taken down three floors. The lift doors opened onto a clinically white corridor. The quiet was eerie. A line of nurses waited either side of the lift doors like a terrifyingly stern, unsmiling wedding tunnel. They all applauded lightly and as Royce was wheeled between them he half expected to get showered in confetti.

He was taken to a private room and examined top to toe by even more stern, unsmiling doctors before being left alone. Royce figured they didn't appreciate being told to empty out half the hospital for just a few people. The doctors gave him a shot of something. It was making him woozy.

He lay quietly on the bed, the unease and worry and guilt slowly melting away as he fell asleep.

DANDRIDGE

Dandridge did as Adler asked. He travelled to London, asked the right questions, shook the right hands, found the right bars, made the right connections and fucked the right people. It hadn't taken him as long as he had expected. It seemed there was a growing and silent clamour for the substance he had been tasked to track down.

In his third week in London he found himself on the arm of a dapper Italian man with a long gelled quiff dressed in a white suit, trying to talk his way past a red velvet cordon into the VIP area of an exclusive North London nightclub. Loud dance music was pumping from inside, and the two large bouncers were listening but looking over his shoulder and acting as if he didn't exist in that infuriating way most bouncers learn on day one in bouncer school.

Eventually, miraculously, the red silk rope was unhooked and the two of them made their way through to the back of the club towards a man sitting in the middle of a huge burgundy leather sofa. There were three blonde Russian prostitutes draped over him with some inevitable overlapping and intertwining of long, toned limbs, two bottles of Cristal in buckets on a table in front of him and a brand new matte-black Beretta M9 handgun on the table next to the champagne. As Dandridge and his companion approached, the man tilted his head to the right and they diverted course to a curtain that lead to an area even further back behind the main club.

Behind this curtain was a smallish room, walls of burgundy flock with a deep gold carpet. In the middle was a wooden desk and behind the desk sat another man, an older man with wild curly white hair and a scar that snagged the left side of his mouth upwards towards his cheek in a permanent sneer.

'Gentlemen.'

'Mr. Armitage, sir,' said Dandridge's companion, 'we are

here to purchase some of your product. I am told it is the very best around.'

'You are misinformed.'

'Sorry?'

'It is the *only* product around.'

'Ah, of course.'

'People go to great lengths to get this product. Your friend here-' he nodded to Dandridge, '-has been asking around for a couple of weeks now.'

Dandridge heart sank. He replied, 'Am I the only person interested in sampling something new? You're gonna be out of business if that's the case.'

'You are not the only person.' He stood up. 'But not everyone is Richard Dandridge, the man responsible for deciphering the transmission and credited with first contact with the Kin species.'

Dandridge's Italian date in the white suit stared at him and shuffled away, distancing himself as much as he could in the small room.

'I had help.'

'I'm sure. Why are you here, Mr. Dandridge? We don't want any unpleasantness.'

'I'm just here to sample the product.'

The man called Armitage pulled a vial of the white liquid from his pocket and placed it on the table between them. 'Why?' he asked.

'I've tasted it before. Kind of. I know how it made me feel. I want to feel that again.'

'Do you? I have learned that it makes people feel things in different ways. How did it make *you* feel?'

Dandridge paused. Armitage watched him carefully with his bright grey eyes. 'Well?'

'I fell in love.'

Armitage laughed uproariously, long and loud.

'You fell in love? That's fucking priceless!' He laughed, even longer and louder, tears rolling down his cheeks. 'You are an amusing man, Mr. Dandridge. Do you think that this will make you feel love again? Are you so stoic that you believe that you are unable to feel love without it?' His laughing was reduced to the occasional giggle and hiccup.

'Maybe.'

'Maybe. But I don't really believe you, Richard.'

'Just Dandridge. You don't have to believe me, you just need to sell me some.'

'Dandridge, I really do want to believe everything my clients tell me, otherwise there is no trust in the partnership. Trust is everything. I believe that your companion here simply wants to get high, to experience something wildly different. Fair enough. But you. You I do not trust. I think you want to stop me from dealing this product. Am I correct?'

Dandridge nodded. His brief was to either buy some product or find out where it was sold and report straight back to Adler, but it seemed that he might have to improvise a little.

One of the guards masquerading as friends from not-quite-the-back room stepped up to Dandridge's companion and hit him across the side of his head with a brand-new looking cricket bat. The contact made a hideous crunch and his head snapped sideways and lolled back alarmingly before he crumpled to the carpet, blood leaking out of his ears.

Dandridge leapt away.

'*Jesus!* What the *fuck!*' He was restrained on either side by two other men as Armitage stood up.

'That one was definitely a 'six', Baron. Although we will have to replace this carpet tonight. Send someone to the Old Kent Road for more carpet. Nothing gold this time, a darker colour maybe. Burgundy.'

'Yes, sir,' the man called Baron replied, wiping the bat down with a blue checked J-cloth.

'And now what am I to do with you, Dandridge? I don't

want to kill you but I am not sure you've given me much choice. At least I respect you enough to kill you nicely, and not like *that*. I do hope you two weren't close.'

Dandridge struggled against the guards, but they held him securely.

'Tell me out of interest,' Armitage asked, watching as a large patch of his carpet slowly turned a rusty colour, 'do you know anything about the death of the Deputy Prime Minister? I am informed of every non-accidental death in London but his was a surprise to me, and a mere day after I had spoken with him. What a coincidence.'

'I don't know anything about it.'

'No. You're not a killer, I can see that. But I think you know who did.'

He spoke to Dandridge's captors. 'Take him out the back. We'll find out what he knows and then, with regret, we'll have to do the necessary.'

Dandridge was taken through a narrow hidden door in the back-back room out to a small courtyard, surrounded on all sides by the dirty brick walls of the club, a kebab shop and a Tesco Local. The heavy referred to as Baron pushed Dandridge hard and he stumbled to the concrete floor among the half smoked cigarette butts.

'Baron, you don't have to do this.'

'Shut up.' Baron aimed a kick at Dandridge's head. Dandridge rolled away in time but straight into the path of one of the other heavies, who planted a steel toe-capped boot into his midriff. He curled up in pain, the breath whumphed out of him.

'*Stop-*' he gasped, '*-listen to me-*' He rolled away from another kick, and then another, and staggered to his feet, backed up in a corner as the three heavies, lead by Baron, advanced on him with the gleeful anticipation of giving someone a good kicking shining bright in their eyes.

'-it doesn't matter what you do to me, there's more at stake here-'

'Well that's lucky then,' Baron said as he theatrically slammed his fist into his palm as he advanced.

The odds were not good. The three men were larger, younger and harder than Dandridge who hadn't been in a proper fight in over twenty years. These guys looked like they had fights over breakfast. He reached into his pocket and his hand closed around the small vial of white liquid he had palmed as he had been lead from the room.

He didn't really have a plan at that point, and had mere seconds before he was evidently going to be very badly beaten. His thumb flicked off the tiny cork stopper of the tiny vial and in one movement he poured it onto his tongue and swallowed it.

The three men stopped.

'What did you do?' Baron asked. 'Did you just take the Kin blood?'

Dandridge stared at them.

'It doesn't matter,' one of the other goons said, 'there's three of us.'

The buttery liquid rolled from Dandridge's tongue down his throat. He could feel its gradual path downwards. One of the goons hit him twice, the first punch across his face, a brutal right hook that opened up a cut and swelled the eye up almost immediately. The second was to his gut, doubling him over, gasping for breath. The side of his face throbbed and poured blood down his cheek, stars dancing in front of his eyes. He struggled to breathe.

He registered all of this activity in the periphery of his consciousness. The rest of him was experiencing a rush of feelings marching through him one by one like a parade of his greatest hits. First, there was relief that he was not going mad, confirmation now coursing through his veins that the Kin had definitely affected him, his moods for the last month not entirely of his own governance. Following the relief came the love for Belle and for life, for all the potential they had together as partners. After that came the hope. The hope that all this was going to turn out OK, that they could not only be together but that they would usher in a new age of tolerance between species that would last for generations. He looked up and locked eyes with Baron. Dandridge smiled at him, a genuine, happy smile, his teeth shining red with blood.

And then, after being held upright and punched a few more times in his stomach and face, came the white-hot rage.

PART SEVEN

MARION

A few hours on a train and a short taxi ride from Lullaico she finally arrived at her original destination. From her office back at the Shack in England she had booked a room at a small hotel on the outskirts of Buenos Aires within spitting distance of where the body of the first dead Kin was stored. Nearly a month late, she checked in. She was the only guest.

The room was cool and shady, her view across a landscaped garden to the deep blue sea sparkling behind it as pretty as a screensaver. The bed was extremely comfortable and climate control maintained a perfect temperature, yet on that first night Marion tossed and turned and could not sleep a wink. Not a single second of sleep could she get. She tried everything, from reading to going for a short walk and then a swim, to masturbation and then counting sheep. She felt so tired, but rest hovered just out of reach, dancing beyond the ragged grey fringes of her vision.

Marion's whole sense of self had been completely altered by what had happened to her on the mountain. What remained of old Marion was appalled and disgusted by what she had done, unable to even feel relief at having survived. The new Marion was awake and aware, could feel the very planet around her as a living, breathing, thinking entity and was excited and desperate to know her part in it.

At five o'clock she finally gave up trying to sleep and went for a jog before taking a shower, getting dressed and calling for a taxi.

The biopsy of the first dead Kin had been placed on hold during the search and rescue operation. Now, selected physicians, medical professionals, bio-engineers and scientists were all assembling, ready for the dissection and examination to be held in the amphitheatre at the Clinica Belgrano, Buenos Aires most prestigious teaching hospital.

Marion arrived at ten past seven, three hours and fifty minutes early. There was nobody on reception so early so she banged on the double doors for a few minutes until a night porter reluctantly let her in.

She took a seat in the waiting area, sitting primly on the plastic chairs. The only vending machine offering hot beverages had been unplugged. She plugged it back in and the scrolling red digital display informed her it was warming up, but then stubbornly refused to progress from that status. After twenty minutes and seeing not a single other person she got up to stretch her legs and try to find the auditorium.

She went down a flight of steps, along a corridor and through a door at the very end where she found a small semi-circular amphitheatre with seating for perhaps a hundred people in steeply tiered semi-circular rows. The seats overlooked a stage that completed the wedge. The stage had already been prepared with a lethal array of gleaming coroner's tools laid out neatly in three rows on a metal trolley.

She sat down at the back and closed her eyes for a second. Then she blinked and started in surprise, pushing herself upright on the wooden bench and looking at her watch. It was 10.45, fifteen minutes before the autopsy and the auditorium was half full, the noise of chattering academics filling the room. She stood up, trying not to look as if she had just woken up, smoothing down her hair and then her skirt, and made her way to the front where a seat had been reserved for her. She sat next to a Kin, who introduced itself.

'Hello Marion. I am the Kin representative from the Buenos Aires Shack. I am very pleased to see you again. I hope you have recovered from your terrible ordeal.'

They shook hands.

'Yes, thank you,' she replied. 'How has it been here? Have you learnt any Spanish?'

'*Pero por supuesto*,' it replied. 'All the Kin have tried to learn local languages and dialects.'

'Yes, of course. I know that,' Marion smiled. 'I am sorry that we have to meet under these circumstances.'

'Indeed. But this death was an accident. We wish to contribute in any way we can, and understand the need for learning and continuous development. Our two species would not have integrated so well if this had not been the case.'

Marion nodded. She was struggling to concentrate on the Kin's words. Her heart had started to beat faster, her eyes darting from the gleaming coroners tools to the Kin's bare white chest, its tiger-stripe blue markings running from the side of the featureless head down its neck to the groin. She could actually smell the sweet white flesh and the more bitter blue markings.

She had started to become acutely aware of the room around her. She knew that one hundred and twenty people were seated and fifteen still stood and chatted. One person was drunk, another thirty two had pungent body odour, six had head-colds. The lights illuminating the stage in front of her were too bright.

'Marion? Are you alright? Would you like some air?' asked the Kin. She shook her head.

'No, I'm fine.' She concentrated on breathing. She squeezed her eyes shut and could practically hear the thoughts of the assembled crowd, the excitement. She was sure she could hear words, phrases, emotions that weren't her own.

A porter pushed a gurney onto the stage, the outline of a figure covered in a pristine white sheet laid out on it. The chatter in the room stopped and everyone sat down in a hushed silence. Marion exhaled loudly, a rush of blood to her head and her privates making her light-headed. She placed her hand on the Kin's leg. It turned its head towards her.

'Please reassure me that you are feeling alright, Marion. You are worrying me. Would you like some water?'

Her eyes were still squeezed tightly shut and she was afraid to open them.

'I'm fine, really. Just nerves.'

'You have recently endured a very traumatic event. Please just give the word and I will take you outside for fresh air.'

The thought of the Kin carrying her, his skin pressed against hers, made Marion's toes curl. In the darkness behind her eyelids she felt sad, intoxicated, excited, horny, nervous, furious, the emotions roiling unwanted inside her in an uncontrollable whirlpool. Her hand on the Kin's thigh tightened.

'Marion, I must insist-' the Kin started, just as the Doctor and the pathologist entered the auditorium, rubber gloves already snapped on ready to begin the proceedings. The sheet was pulled from the corpse of the Kin. Like the one from the mountain its blue markings had faded away almost completely, leaving a white figure with a long open wound from left collarbone area to right hip where it had been fatally struck by a collapsed gantry on a local building site.

As Marion saw the body she twitched and convulsed involuntarily, a muscle spasm over which she had no control. She could feel one hundred and thirty five eyes staring at the back of her head, confusion and interest going up a notch in the emotional awareness she had somehow unwillingly latched onto. The Kin representative from Buenos Aires stood up.

'Gentlemen, I think Ms Crandall has been taken ill-'

'I'm fine,' Marion gasped. The Kin took her upper arm.

'Please come with me, we will get you some water.'

She stood up and gazed at the body of the dead Kin lying exposed and vulnerable on the gurney.

She stepped up onto the small stage. The coroner was standing, scalpel in hand, ready to make the first incision.

'Señora, qué esta haciendo? Por favor bájese del escenario.'

Marion could feel the buzz in the room increase as she bent her head down to the dead Kin. The doctor put the scalpel back onto the trolley and took hold of her shoulders, trying to pull her back, but she shrugged him off. She inhaled the familiar soft, sweet smell of the exposed Kin flesh. Her fingers traced the line of the fatal wound along its torso.

The doctor took hold of her shoulders again, more forcefully, and a wave of frustration crashed over her like a wave breaking over the head of a surfer. She wheeled around towards him with hands raised. Her nails, which fortunately weren't long, slashed across his eyes and face. He screamed and staggered backwards. She pushed and he toppled backwards off the stage into the lap of the first row spectators. She clearly heard a bone in his ankle snap as he tried and failed to land on his feet, screaming again in pain. The local Kin representative tried to catch him but they both toppled over to the floor.

Marion didn't stop to see what had happened to them. She straddled the gurney, her skirt riding up to her waist, grinding herself against the dead Kin's groin, revelling in the soft, cold contact. Then she pushed her face against the wound, burying in as far as she could before opening her mouth and letting the fridge-cold Kin juice flood her mouth, the power and energy and love and strength filling her up once more. For the second time in her life, the real and true purpose of her existence crystallised in her.

Then she felt hands on her and she was torn away from her bliss and dragged roughly off the stage into a heap on the auditorium floor. Everyone in the lecture theatre was on their feet trying to get a better view of what was happening at the front.

The porter, the Kin and one of the coroners were all trying to hold Marion down, but all three of them taken by surprise with her strength and energy as she fought back against them.

The porter caught a foot in his stomach and was kicked across the floor as easily as if he was inflatable, cracking his head against the raised stage. When Marion lifted the coroner off her, she was only vaguely aware of his weight on her arms, watching with mild interest as he floated upwards as if supported by the force of her will alone. She flung him aside and he crashed across the stage into the gurney, which rocked precariously before gravity took over and it toppled, the body of the dead Kin body tumbling unceremoniously across the stage floor and over the edge.

The BA Kin representative was still trying to subdue Marion. When its dead brethren rolled off the stage it reached with both arms in a futile gesture to catch it and retain it's dignity, but Marion took the opportunity to push the Kin off her and it slammed backwards into their vacated front row seats. The dead body fell right on top of her. She wrapped her legs around it, pulled it close into an embrace and took a huge bite of the sweet flesh from its neck, pulling hard as the elastic skin stretched and tore. Her skirt was still up around her hips exposing her plain white underwear, and this excited her. She took another bite.

Then at least five men and the Kin were on the body, pulling it away from her, severing her connection with the sweetness, pulling it away as cold white blood oozed and ran over her from the fresh wound in the neck. She leapt up after it and knocked three of the men down as if they were bowling pins and she was a sixteen pound ball rolled by a league player.

The remaining two dropped the dead Kin to the floor and faced her, a futile human barrier standing between her and what she wanted.

Why didn't they understand?

She leapt on them, kicking and punching, and soon they were all lying dazed on the ground, bruised and bloodied, unwilling to go near her again. The Buenos Aires Kin grabbed her in a bear hug, trapping her arms by her sides, but it was facing her and too late felt it her teeth bite down, felt her take huge shredding bites of its neck, stronger and harder than it had ever thought a human should bite. It pulled her off, feeling Marion's teeth tear more flesh as she was ripped away.

The Kin pushed her away, but she immediately came back towards him, straight into the Kin's blow, as hard as it could muster. It connected to the side of her head and she staggered backwards, dazed.

A doctor banged open the doors of the amphitheatre and ran towards them but slipped on the mess of spilled white and red blood on the wooden floor. He slid onto his arse and the syringe he had been carrying skittered along the ground, ending up at the Kin's feet.

Marion was almost completely covered from head to toe in the white blood. The gash on her temple where it had hit her was oozing blood that mixed with the Kin blood and ran in pale pink rivulets down her face.

The Kin picked up the dropped syringe and stuck it into the bite marks in its own neck, pressing the plunger and feeling its body absorb the drug.

'Kin, I'm fine, really. You just don't *understand-*' Marion said and closed her mouth around it's neck once more, feeling the strong white arms folding around her in a gentle, comforting embrace. After a few moments of silence around the entire auditorium as she sucked and fed, her embrace loosened, her feeding slowed and she slid unconscious to the floor.

And in those few seconds that Marion fed, it realised. She was right. The Kin finally understood.

MIKE

Mike Hennessy sat on his sofa staring at the open newspaper on the coffee table in front of him. Covering an entire centre-spread were a number of blurred, fuzzy and out of focus photographs of what appeared to be a fight in some kind of theatre involving a number of people and a Kin. In one of the photos, the face of Marion Crandall could be seen clearly, snarling at two people and covered in... what? Sweat? Mike couldn't make it out but it didn't look good. His hands were shaking as he picked up the phone.

'Joy, it's me. How are you? Good to hear. Yes I know, it's been crazy, properly crazy. Thanks, but I really don't think I come across all that well on TV. Joy, I think I might be in a bit of trouble. Marion? Yes, I think it's related. The papers are full of pictures that don't show that much, but I've not heard from her or her government friend. I've left dozens of messages. Can we meet?'

In the early days of his sobriety Mike had woken up every morning with a desperate scratching feeling at the back of his mind, a constant irritant, an unwelcome reminder from his body to his brain to supply it with the fortification it needed. By lunchtime, he would have a raging, unslakeable thirst that no amount of talk or food or television or cigarettes could resolve, a thirst that required him to be physically restrained. And now, as he sat in his small shabby flat in South London, a place where he could usually find comfort and peace, he was restless and unsatisfied. Worse, he could feel a familiar scratching at the back of his mind.

He set out on foot into the darkening evening and persistent drizzle, a two and a half mile walk to a cafe in Greenwich, a greasy-spoon that brewed builders tea just how he liked it. He found a seat in the corner and ordered.

He was pouring white sugar from the clogged nozzle of the dispenser into his teaspoon when Joy walked in. Given there were only two other people in the place she picked him out easily and went to join him. He dipped the teaspoon of sugar in his mug and stirred it in as she shrugged off her wet coat and placed her bag on the chair next to his. Then he rose, and they hugged tightly. The waitress was hovering and she ordered a coffee.

'Jesus Mike. I haven't seen or heard from you in fucking weeks, and then there you are on national fucking television, survivor of a fucking plane crash. What the *fuck* happened?'

'Didn't you see the press conference?'

'Yes, but Mike. Holy shit. What the fuck were you doing on that plane in the first place?'

'Your language hasn't improved I see. I was there because of my work with the Kin. I only do small time stuff; getting them places to live, work, making sure the terms of integration are adhered to, that's all. But they nominated me to go and witness the autopsy on the first dead one to make sure no laws or terms were broken, that kind of thing. I have no idea why they chose me.'

'They needed a lawyer for that?'

'You need a lawyer for everything, Joy.'

'And you saw the pictures in the papers yesterday? Of Marion Crandall?'

At the mention of Marion's name, he teared up and took a slurp of the tea to try and cover it up. 'Yes.'

'Mike, what's going on? You have to tell me. You have to tell me everything or I can't help you.'

Mike looked at her. 'I can't,' he whispered, 'there's more at stake here than just Marion and me, or any of the others.'

'What happened up there, Mike?'

'I can't tell you. It was bad. Really bad.'

'Is that why you're drinking again?'

Mike stared at her. 'You think I'm drinking again?'

'You're acting like it. And Mike, I've got to tell you - I can't go through it again. I have daughters now, a husband. My own life. You have to stop relying on me.'

'I'm not drinking again, I promise.'

Joy was silent for a moment as she sipped her coffee and regarded him.

'OK. So you're not drinking. But something is wrong. You look fucking terrible.'

'Cheers.'

'Do you think how you're feeling is the same thing that might have affected Marion Crandall?'

Mike nodded. 'And the others, probably.'

'According to the papers Royce Brims has just embarked on a world tour, the other woman is still in hospital, I don't know where her son is and Crandall has just lost her fucking marbles.'

Mike's hands shook as he took another slurp of the hot tea. 'I think I'm losing my marbles too,' he whispered, somehow ashamed.

'I can tell, but there's fuck all I can do if you don't tell me what's happened or why you called me.'

Mike finished his tea. 'OK, let's take a walk, we can get your coffee to go. But I need to tell you something before we do. Once I tell you what happened that's it - you're in this and there's no getting out. So if you really don't want to know or don't want to help, I understand completely. Just get up now and leave. I'll still love you.'

'You're scaring me.'

Mike sat, staring at the dregs in his mug and saying nothing.

'You've not given me any choice have you?' Joy said, her anger making her already red cheeks redder. 'You know that, right? By calling me and getting me out here, and looking so fucking miserable. How could I say no, right? You always were the best at getting what you wanted.'

'I didn't want this.'

'Not what's happened, maybe. Not the crash. But everything else, all the people around you. Even that girl you met in rehab, Alice.'

'Alice wasn't beholden to me. She had her own life, her own problems.'

'Yes, but she knew, didn't she? She knew that the longer she stayed the more her problems would be suffocated by yours, just like mine. You're a fucking selfish arsehole Mike, you know that?'

Mike stared into his tea, close to tears again. He was angry at her words, but he knew she was right, of course. She was always right.

'Well, come on then if we're going,' she said eventually. 'We'll take the Thames Path. The Maritime Museum looks lovely lit up at night.'

They got up to go, shrugging on their winter coats, and Mike dug a crumpled five pound note from his pocket and left it on the table.

As they left the dingy cafe and stepped into the dark evening, one of the other two people inside, a black man with a shaved head and an aggressive goatee took out a phone and dialled a number.

'It's me. Yeah, he's telling his ex-wife. He seems pretty desperate. OK, will do.' The man stood up and followed them out of the cafe.

ADLER

'Follow them, but don't let them see you and don't interfere. I think he's going to go and stay with her, in which case he should be fine for the time being. She'll look after him. Let me know where they end up.'

Adler hung up and slid the phone back in his pocket. His response to the man in the cafe was spoken louder that he would have preferred, although there was little chance of being overheard given he was currently standing at the back of an arena which was slowly filling up with people. The entire auditorium was bathed in strange artificial light, the slack period between the support act and the main act as roadies busied themselves swapping equipment over, pyrotechnics for the main act were set up, lighting adjusted. The crowd who had turned up for the support had mainly dispersed to run to the toilets or to refill their plastic cups with overpriced lager, but there was still a couple of thousand people milling about. The crowd were mainly teenagers dressed in an eye-wateringly vulgar display of hip-hop inspired fashion; loud, brash, confident, excited. A few were accompanied by parents who made grateful eye-contact with each other in shows of parental solidarity.

Adler lingered at the back. Half an hour later the auditorium was packed, all seats taken, all standing room occupied. The lights went down and the crowd gave a collective but premature scream of excitement. Another half an hour later there was a fervour in the room, anticipation so high and an atmosphere so tense that Adler wanted to bottle it and release it in a library just to see what would happen.

There was a dramatic click of amplified drumsticks and a backing band started to play, the sound blasting so loudly from speakers so massive Adler reckoned that these kids were going to be deaf for at least a week. The music drowned out the screaming and roaring. Then the first line of the first song was sung and the screaming somehow managed to get even louder. A single spotlight *clunked* on, illuminating a single figure standing alone on the wide stage, his back to the crowd, dry ice swirling around his legs, his hand holding a microphone aloft. The figure wore a bright red leather jacket and black leather trousers. He spun around and the crowd went ballistic.

Adler left through the black double doors at the back of the arena and threaded his way along the now deserted corridor alongside the auditorium, the music ringing in his ears. He went through a door marked 'Private' and climbed some stairs, along a second corridor and up more stairs, through more doors marked 'Private' until he came to another door, unmarked but which had two heavy-set security guards standing against it. He showed his Foreign Office pass, a pass that would get him through practically any door marked 'Private' on the planet. But not this one. Politics and entertainment, two different worlds. The two men stepped closer together in formation, barring his progress. So Adler dug out his 'All Areas' pass instead and they grudgingly stepped aside. He smiled to himself and went through.

It was another corridor, but less concrete and more luxurious; a beige carpet, lightshades over the bulbs, pictures of all the various artists who had performed on the stage decorating the walls. Adler could feel the bass of the music through the walls where he stood.

He made his way along the corridor and past a number of doors to Royce's dressing room. There was nobody around, they were all down in the wings watching the show. He opened the door to a room much larger than he imagined - all the doors he had walked past opened into the same, long space. Adler presumed that the room could be partitioned off into a number of smaller areas, but Royce Brims had the whole thing. At one end were tables covered with food, a Hogwarts feast of fruit, meats, cheeses, dips and canapés, virtually untouched. A number of empty bottles of Cristal were scattered around the room.

Adler glanced around. A few spliff butts on the carpets, nothing too incriminating. He went into the main bathroom, all chrome and glass and rolled his sleeves up. He plunged his hand into the toilet bowl and felt along the bottom of the porcelain. He could feel tiny fragments of broken glass. He pulled his hand out. It wasn't definitive, but a fairly positive indicator. He washed thoroughly in the basin and was about to leave the bathroom when he spotted the tiny discarded cork lying in the corner of the bathroom. There was a small marking carved along the top. He sighed, wishing he had seen it before he had felt along the bottom of Royce Brim's toilet bowl, but at least now he was certain. Somebody who had been using this toilet was taking the blood. Kin blood sourced from a known London supplier. A supplier temporarily disbanded thanks to the information received from Richard Dandridge and his unexpectedly violent intervention.

The addictive properties of Kin blood were, for now, still something of a myth and Adler was doing everything he could to prevent the knowledge filtering out. But Royce Brims was hooked on it and he was very high-profile indeed. Adler would have to keep a close on eye on him.

LUKE

Luke clenched his right hand into a fist, his bicep flexed, knuckles white, lips pulled back from his gritted teeth in concentration. Stars of white pain danced in his vision as he slowly drew the serrated edge of the Ikea bread knife across the flesh of his upper arm.

His left hand gripped the plastic handle, shaking slightly, every natural instinct he possessed telling him to drop it. He doubled down and squeezed his eyes shut, forcing himself to keep it moving until the new cut crossed paths with an older one just beginning to heal. The jagged blade pulled apart its edges as it passed and the pain intensified, a deep, throbbing, excoriating burn. He refused to allow himself to stop until the cut was four inches long and blood poured down his arm onto the red towel he had placed on the side of the bed in careful preparation. He dropped the knife and pressed tissue paper to the gushing wound before laying back and shaking in pain, tears stinging his eyes.

Living with the parents of his step-mother's dead first-husband was about as far as where he wanted to be as it was possible to get. Both his dead real mother and dead father were, like him, single children and he had no grandparents. His dead mother's parents had taken off years ago to Florida and had lost contact with their family on purpose, and his father's parents were both also dead.

There were a lot of dead people hanging from his family tree and sometimes he wondered if loneliness was hereditary. He supposed it was. If it was possible he even missed having Jennifer around to ignore. He had been told that she had suffered a breakdown and was being kept in isolation and observation at the hospital back in South America. He was not allowed to see her, and he didn't much feel like pushing the point.

He found himself placed with his... what? Step-grandparents once removed? He didn't even know what the fuck to call them, yet they were fucking impossible to ignore. They wouldn't leave him alone, seemingly oblivious to his rude rebuffals of their relentless flood of generosity. The late Stephen Jones parents had been the only people to step forward and take him in when social services were forced to place him in a temporary foster home on his return from South America.

Their home was a nicely kept, slightly twee but tidy detached house at the far end of a cul-de-sac in a small corner of South East London near Orpington. Luke absolutely and without reservation detested Orpington with its busy self-important atmosphere and unending selection of curtain fabric shops. He would often expound his expletive filled opinion on South London to his two carers who would press their lips together and smile through his torrent of hate about the town and its inhabitants.

'Oh, it's not that bad,' they would say, 'we have a nice big Tesco Extra now,' and Luke would stare at them, amazed that their happiness could be dictated by the arrival of a giant supermarket in their midst.

But the worst thing about them wasn't their love for large multi-national chain grocery stores, it was that they listened to folk music. A lot. All the time in fact. Whenever Luke took his headphones out of his ears, which wasn't all that often, all he could hear was old people singing about unrequited love, lakes, red skies or the demise of the Liverpool shipping industry. It drove him crazy.

It was only the pain that got him through, the constant burning throbbing pain that blocked out the white noise and uncertainty that had threatened to overwhelm his thoughts ever since he returned from the mountain. The knife that sliced open the tender flesh of his upper arms and thighs was a conduit to recapturing those feelings, that absolute clarity, the elation in the knowledge that he simply understood more than everyone else. That somehow he was the key to something bigger and better and more significant than anyone else could possibly comprehend.

The Jones' figured that this was pretty much the typical mindset of a fourteen year old boy.

It had started with his inability to sleep after he had moved in. For the first few nights, he simply could not close his eyes for longer than a few minutes at a time; not a jot, not a single minute of rest. He lay awake for hour upon torturous hour, unable to concentrate enough to read, watch TV or jerk off, able to only thrash about in his own confused and withdrawn psyche.

Until he cut himself on a cutlery knife one afternoon while making a sandwich. A small pinprick of pain and a brief precious few seconds in which he could only concentrate on the blood oozing from the tip of his index finger. Taking the knife upstairs he had started with small experimental nicks on his fingers, tiny enough for a fleeting piercing burn and to taste his blood, which he had read was supposed to taste coppery but seemed to him sweeter somehow. He had slept better that night, three or four hours of dreamless sleep as his fingers throbbed and healed.

The cuts gradually became longer and the pain more intense as he craved more relief. During the long days he would wander aimlessly around Orpington with little energy and no inclination to re-engage with his social network or connections, eagerly anticipating the late evenings when the house was asleep and he could sit in his boxer shorts on the edge of his bed and drag the new knife across his arms and legs. Within a fortnight both his upper arms and thighs were criss-crossed with raw, red wounds, cuts and scabs.

He knew what was wrong with him. He wasn't stupid. Jennifer had gone off her rocker and now apparently so had Crandall, if you believed everything the newspapers had to say. The more time he spent in Orpington the more certain he felt it was going to happen to him too.

As he lay dozing on his duvet, sweating profusely despite the cool evening, as blood dripped down his left arm onto the red towel he had bought specifically for that purpose, Radio 6 was being piped through his earbuds and the hipster DJ played a song by Royce Brims. It wasn't the first time that the song had been played or the first time he had heard it, but it was the first time that his mind felt clear enough for some dots to suddenly connect in his mind. Royce was on tour and seemed to be doing just fine. Luke had seen him on BBC Breakfast with the agent, Buddy Tucker, talking about the crash and the new tour. He had been funny and cool and they both seemed really together.

Luke didn't waste time or any further idle thought. He dressed quickly and threw a spare t-shirt, underwear and toothbrush into his Fjallraven backpack. After a moment's hesitation he added the kitchen knife and slipped out of the house quietly, leaving the front door ajar but clicking shut the double glazed porch door securely behind him. It was both too late and too early for buses, so with heat burning from his arm and feeling the satisfying drip of blood from his fingertips, he threaded his way over dark front lawns until he came out onto the main road and started to walk, towards London and Royce Brims.

ROYCE

The tour was the biggest and most successful Royce had ever attempted. His stock was sky high. The publicity he had got from the crash had launched him to the next level. Buddy was true to his word and pulled together the most amazing itinerary, taking in the world's best venues with dancers, pyrotechnics, set dressers, special effects - an arena tour for the ages. The tour was called 'Survivor' and although Royce had worried the name was too much of a cliché, it had sold out in minutes. He had never before played to such huge crowds and he was in demand on every chat show in every country he was due to visit. His album sales had exploded and the record company presses couldn't print enough of the shiny red disks.

He and Buddy opened White Mountain Records for business and had already signed two very promising young hip-hop artists to the label, both supporting him on the tour. He had played the first London date already and he was having the time of his life.

The O2 arena was sold out for three nights solid, with another night about to be announced due to demand. Royce and what was left of his entourage were staying at the Mandarin Oriental hotel on Piccadilly, the most opulent and well-catered hotel he had ever experienced. On his previous tour he had slept on the tour bus more often than not and felt lucky if they could afford a Travelodge and a Ginsters from the petrol station.

The Mandarin Oriental was host to the A-List, currently other occupants included Will Smith, Victoria Beckham and the President of Uruguay, among others.

The trained staff at the hotel took his appearance in the breakfast room at three in the afternoon in their stride, ushering him to a corner table and laying out porcelain and cutlery so fast that he had to lower his sunglasses and peer over them to affirm that the table had indeed just been set.

He wore huge Dirty Dog sunglasses over bleary eyes, the result of a long after-show party that had ended about two hours previously. Steaming, fresh coffee from a silver coffee pot was poured and a menu provided. Royce raised it to his eyes and scanned the options. He didn't feel at all hungry, in fact he hadn't felt hungry for days. He sipped the coffee and vaguely registered a slight ruckus at the reception desk. Somebody was shouting his name and other voices were trying to hush him. Royce couldn't see what was going on, so he stood up to get a clearer view. Three smartly dressed doormen were in the process of removing a boy from the hotel. A boy he recognised. He called out.

'*Hey*! Don't you know who that is? Leave him be. He's my breakfast guest, you bitches.'

The staff reluctantly released Luke and Royce watched him as he cautiously entered the plush surroundings of the breakfast nook. He looked terrible; filthy, pale, frail, ill. He took the seat opposite Royce.

'How did you know I was here?' Royce asked. Luke held up three different, thick newspapers, two gossip and one conspiracy, all of which had a picture and article about him and showed a photo of him from the previous day, shades in place, entering the hotel.

'Ah. I never read the conspiracy ones.'

'No, I'm not allowed either, but my step-grandparents do.'

'Your step *grandparents?* Shit man, that's fucked up. Where's Jennifer?'

'As far as I know she's still back at Lullacio but no-one will tell me for sure, although my social worker says they'll take me to her in a week or two.'

'That's fucked up too.'

Luke watched Royce as he ordered two full English Breakfasts and a coffee refill.

'Where's Buddy?' he asked when the waiter had taken the order and slid silently away.

'Staying at the Hilton in Canary Wharf. I like Buddy, but I prefer it when we don't stay in the same place. I don't like him keeping an eye on me. He's closer to the venue, that's how he likes it.'

'How's the tour going?' Luke felt weird asking one of the most famous men in the music industry how his tour was going after just walking from a suburban house in dreary Orpington.

'It's great so far. It's all great. It sounds crazy, but what happened to us, the crash and everything, it turned out to be one of the best things could have happened to me, career-wise. I'm guessing not so much for you, huh?'

'Can I stay with you for a while?'

'With me? My life is real crazy right now, Luke. It's no place for a kid.'

'I can work. Help you out with something on the tour maybe.'

'Nope. Someone's gonna recognise you and will want to know why the fuck you're here. And your grandparents are gonna worry.'

'*Step*-grandparents.'

'Why don't you want to stay with them?'

'They're OK, I guess. It's just that since the mountain, everything just feels... wrong. Off, somehow. Nothing feels right. I don't feel right,' the boy muttered and went red.

The breakfasts arrived and they both ate in silence, which for both of them meant pushing the food around the plate and taking an occasional bite.

'I know what you mean,' Royce said eventually, licking his knife with his tongue. 'It's like the world seems too small somehow, that you're being crammed into it and slowly suffocating. Even me, with all the travel I been doing, I feel too big for the world. And I ain't sleeping.'

'That's exactly it, that's why I came to see you!' Luke said, a rush of excitement and relief flooding through his exhausted system, 'I *knew* you'd get it. Please, Royce. Please.

Can I stay with you? I'll tell social services and they'll arrange it. They don't really know what to do with me anyway.'

'If you sort it and one of them social people talks to Buddy then OK.'

'OK, I will, I'll sort it. Do you have a phone?'

Royce tossed Luke his phone and Luke dialled a number.

'You can remember your social service guy's number?'

'I'm good with numbers.'

The waiter came and cleared away the two virtually untouched breakfast plates as Luke talked excitedly into the handset.

LUKE

Royce stuck the hotel door keycard into the door and the LED light built into the handle blinked from red to green. He went in and threw the card on the side table with Luke right behind him. The room was the most magnificent hotel room Luke had ever seen. The floor area was probably larger than the entire house in Orpington. Three enormous and ornate bay windows, draped with intricate nets and red velvet curtains overlooked busy Piccadilly. There was a fully stocked bar in one corner. A 60 inch plasma television on the wall. The bed itself was on a raised dais and the size of a squash court.

The open doorway to the bathroom revealed a huge gold dreamscape of gilt basins, bathtubs with solid gold taps and in the centre, a hot tub that would easily accommodate six people.

Luke didn't notice any of it, due to the three naked sleeping women lying on the bed. Two of them were mostly under the sheets, but one was lying on top and snoring softly with one arm draped over the other girls. After staring for what seemed like minutes, Luke shifted his gaze to Royce who was grinning at him.

'See what I mean?' he laughed. 'No place for a kid.' He started digging through the pockets of a pair of jeans that had been discarded in the corner, while Luke kept stealing glances at the girls, one of whom was stirring.

'Here it is!' Royce announced and held up a tiny vial of white liquid with a tiny cork stopper. 'Recognise this? This is what saved our lives up there. This is what will save our lives again.'

Luke shook his head. 'What is it?' he whispered.

'You know.'

Royce uncorked the vial and tapped a tiny drop onto his tongue. Luke watched him, feeling more and more uneasy.

'Stick your tongue out,' Royce said.

Suddenly his heart was pounding.

'Sorry? No, thanks. I don't think I... I'm not really sure about-' he stammered.

'Just come on over here and do it, man. I swear it'll be worth it.'

Luke shook his head. 'No, thanks Royce, I-'

'Fair enough, kid. Up to you.'

Then one of the girls on the bed came padding over, naked and lithe, a small tattoo of a Robin on the swell of her left breast.

Luke had never given much thought to his own sexuality. Up to that point the idea of sex hadn't bothered him at all, he had never found anyone interesting enough to want to engage with on that intimate, human level. He had once tried masturbating to the memory of Jennifer touching herself in the shower, simply because he thought he should, but he had grown bored with it before he had finished. Since then he only masturbated when his male physiology forced him into it for reasons of expediency.

But the girl with the Robin tattoo about to snog Royce Brims was so perfectly assembled, so uninhibited and beautiful that for the first time he felt himself becoming aroused.

She wrapped her arms around Royce's neck and stuck her long tongue out at him suggestively. He tilted the tiny white vial and the liquid crept down the glass side and dripped like honey onto her searching tongue. She turned to Luke and now her arms were around him, her body pressed firmly against his. She was a head taller so had to lean down to kiss him. Luke's head tilted up to meet hers, his lips frozen with fear and his mind utterly blank. Her tongue snaked into his mouth and he felt something unlock in his mind. He felt the Kin on her tongue, felt it inside him again, that familiar opening of his conscious mind. He finally began responding to her kiss, seeking out the last remaining traces of the drop of Kin on her tongue.

But the feel of her breasts pressing against him and her nakedness so close to him no longer held any sexual attraction. He only wanted to keep kissing her until he knew he had taken from her all he could.

After a minute he knew they had finished. The girl leapt back with a scream, blood pouring down her lower lip. Royce had moved under the sheets with the other two girls.

'He bit me!' she screamed.

'Calm down. He didn't mean to, did you Luke?' Luke shook his head. 'It was his first time, give him a break. Come over here, I'll kiss it better. Luke, why don't you wait downstairs for me, I'll be out in a couple hours. We'll ride to the gig together.'

Luke said nothing and slipped out of the room. He went downstairs to the lobby and sat down in one of the huge red leather armchairs in the reading room. He had believed that Royce could help him and now he knew for sure it had been absolutely the best decision he could have made. He fell asleep in the chair.

JOSH

When Dandridge returned to the house with yet another Kin in tow, Josh was not entirely surprised.

'Where have you been? You look slightly more terrible than when I last saw you.'

Dandridge had two black eyes and a cut on his cheek covered with a thin strip of gauze and a split lip.

'I know, but actually I feel much better. Josh, this is Jean. She needs somewhere to stay for a little bit. She's been through a lot, I just rescued her from some very bad people.'

The usually distinctive blue markings on the alien's body had faded to a almost invisible pale blue. A couple had turned blotchy and smudged around the edges with no distinct lines or shape, especially on the face and neck area. There were white bandages strapped around its torso and legs. Jean did not say anything.

Dandridge told Josh everything, as he always did.

'Oh Jesus. Now they're being cut up for *food*? This whole thing is getting worse and worse. We are in real trouble here, Dandridge. The Shack is getting full, I've not seen this many Kin in one place since Day One. Other Shacks are far fuller than ours. We're building new temporary premises just in case. What are we going to do?'

'We're going to wait until we hear from Adler then we are going to re-group and work something out. Where is he?'

'Stalking the plane crash survivors.'

'How's Marion?'

'Under sedation somewhere in Argentina.'

'That's ridiculous. I'll go see her.'

'Is that wise, you both being fellow addicts? No offense.'

'None taken. I'm as prepared as I can be but if the withdrawal worsens again I'll take myself off the table. For now, we really need Marion. She's been the figurehead of human and Kin relations for too long. We have to have her expertise and reputation. People listen to her.'

'Even now? After the... you know? The debacle.'

'Even now. Maybe especially now, if we play it right. I'll call Adler and arrange a transport to BA to leave in the morning.'

'What about Jean?'

'She can have my old room, I'll take the sofa.'

Josh stared at Dandridge as he lead the silent, sick-looking Kin upstairs, wondering how many humans would so selflessly and without a second thought offer up their own bed for a Kin.

ADLER

For some reason completely beyond him social services had allowed Luke McDonald to stay with Royce Brims. On one hand Adler was furious. Luke was now within the influence of a user of Kin blood soon to be without his fix, in more danger now than on the mountain. Staying with his step-grandparents had been a far safer option for the mentally fragile boy. But on the other hand at least Luke and Royce were in the same place and he could keep an eye on them both.

Adler watched Royce's latest performance in London from the shadows at the back of the auditorium. It had been a spectacular success. Royce was on fire, his lyrics and stage banter smart, incisive and funny. He railed against the government for all the common issues that were gaining traction and favour across the country, all the hot button topics like the continued ban on the internet, discrimination against minority humans in favour of housing Kin, the rising costs of living with the alien race. He was self-deprecating and in tune with his audience, who lapped up every word and song. Adler didn't see him but he knew that Luke was watching from the wings somewhere.

So far he knew that his main risks were contained. Hennessy, Jennifer, Royce, his agent and the boy were under his surveillance. Dandridge was mid-air, on the way to pick Marion up from the disastrous autopsy. He was right, Adler knew he needed Marion.

The Kin blood supply had been stopped, in London at least, for now. Dandridge had inadvertently fired a warning shot across the bows of anyone else who fancied themselves an illegal trader of Kin juice.

Now he needed to work out what to do about the reproduction problem. Josh was working on a short-term solution to housing but more Kin were inevitably going to die, reproduce and replicate and potentially overrun the planet, replacing humans as the dominant species.

As Royce Brims was so eloquently preaching up in the spotlight, unrest was brewing. There was a general rumble of discontent at the fairness being offered to Kin over human, a larger and larger movement of people upset about the continued restriction on communication channels, wild theories about the now visibly rising number of Kin. Adler well knew how fast rumbles could turn into thunder, could turn into storms.

His phone vibrated in his pocket and he looked at it. It was a text from Demelza Freeman, the PM's personal secretary, asking him to get in touch. He slid the phone back into his pocket. More time. He needed more time.

BUDDY

'What do you mean? I don't understand?' Royce and Buddy were backstage. Royce was still sweating from the show, his eyes bright, his bare chest heaving, out of breath. His dancers and backing singers milled around laughing and cheering, on a high from the adrenaline of performing. Champagne corks popped, food was devoured, stories from the gig were traded.

'There's no more. The supplier has vanished, we've been cut off.'

'Why has the supplier vanished? Find another supplier.'

'There isn't one. Word is that someone is going proper medieval on anyone who deals. Sorry Roy, we're going to have to do without for a while.'

Royce stared at him in rising panic. The idea that he might be addicted to anything, of any sort, never really crossed his mind. He just wanted to maintain his momentum. Everything was going so *well*.

Buddy had managed many artists and singers and recognised exactly what they were both becoming. Although the prospect of having to do without the white blood made him extremely nervous, he was quietly relieved. However, his young charge and business partner was beyond furious, rapidly approaching incandescent with rage.

He stormed around the dressing room, kicking out all the dancers and band members, who turned from euphoric and excited to upset and confused in about five seconds. They filed out, grabbing bottles of champagne and fistfuls of food as they went until the only people left in the room were Royce, Buddy, Luke and one of the pretty groupies from earlier, until Royce kicked her out too. She left, casting resentful glances behind her.

Buddy had never seen Royce so agitated. Luke was sitting on a chair looking inscrutable. He couldn't tell what the boy might be feeling. Buddy himself was feeling OK.

His right hand was stuck in his pocket and he carefully fingered the last vial of Kin blood, rolling the tiny cylinder back and forth between his thumb and index finger.

He could survive without it but it just gave him that extra energy and clarity he needed to manage everything, not just Royce but also Blue Mountain Records and their two new signings, Henrietta 'Etta' Brazil and Spanny Munro, both of whom were starting to gain some real traction in the hip-hop community.

'What are you going to do about this, Buddy?' Royce was saying, over and over again, pacing up and down the large dressing room.

'Roy, calm down,' Buddy pleaded, but knew that it was the wrong thing to say. Royce was on a high from the gig and surfing the crest of his own ego.

'*You* fucking calm down. And don't call me Roy *ever again*. This was all your idea. All of it. If I was being managed by Mulcahy he would make damn sure I had everything I fucking needed. It's not too much to ask, is it?'

'Actually it is. You remember where the blood comes from, don't you? A fucking *Kin*, Royce. They don't give it up willingly, you know that right? It's fucking illegal and now somebody has clamped down on it and from what I hear nobody in their right mind is going to start supplying again.'

'Why?'

'Because everyone involved was executed with, oh what's the expression? *Extreme fucking prejudice.*'

'Executed? You're kidding me?'

'Nope. Most of the dealers had to be identified from dental records and even some of those aren't conclusive.'

'Jesus. What are we going to do? I really need it, Bud. I don't think I can cope with feeling normal again. Boring again.'

'I know Royce, but we're in this together - all of us, even the kid. We'll get through it together. We don't need it anymore, your talent is too great-'

'But what if it isn't? What if most of the momentum is only because the juice makes us feel like there's momentum?'

'It's no good thinking like that, Royce. Listen, if it helps I can book us all into a rehab facility for a few weeks and we can ride this out. You, me and the boy.'

'And what then? When we get out? The momentum is gone, all our progress is lost and we're back to square fucking one. Even Etta and Spanny will fuck off somewhere else.'

'Well, actually they're on contract so they can't. But if you insist, then we really have no choice but to keep going. Get our heads down, keep gigging, keep pushing Munro and Brazil-'

Royce was pacing up and down again. Luke was perched on a chair watching the argument with a mild curiosity. If he was feeling worried about the lack of Kin juice, he wasn't showing it.

Royce stopped pacing and stared at his agent, a spark of hope almost visibly flickering in his eyes. 'You know who might be able to help us?'

For a few seconds, Buddy didn't. His forehead creased as he thought who Royce might be talking about before it dawned.

'No Royce, it's a bad idea. A very bad idea. He's not completely happy with us at the moment. We need to let sleeping dogs lie, and I doubt very much that he can help anyway.'

'He can get anything.'

'*Almost* anything.'

'I'm going to see him now.'

'Now? You aren't going to the aftershow at China Blue?'

'This won't take long, I'll show my face afterwards. Call Tarik and get him to bring the car around.' Royce turned to Luke. 'You coming?'

Luke did not need to be asked twice. He followed without a word as Royce pulled on his stage costume military jacket and left the room, the door slamming shut behind them and leaving Buddy alone with the half-eaten food and unopened bottles of Cristal. For a second he watched them leave with no intention of going with them. He could happily spend the evening stuffing his face and getting drunk until the venue security threw him out.

Foregoing a regular life with a wife, girlfriend or family to pursue the career betterment of a series of occasionally talented wannabe stars for Henderson Mulcahy had been his own choice, and Buddy had reconciled himself to it long ago. It was exciting, lucrative and challenging. He had travelled the world staying in the best hotels, driven the fastest cars, slept with the most beautiful women and enjoyed being kept in the lap of luxury. The reason for his success was an unerring instinct for guiding his charges along the right path, making all their decisions for them, controlling their images and lives more carefully and intricately than a mother would control her child.

He knew that life in the limelight was a treacherous road with calamitous falls either side of a wrong decision. Despite his current status Royce was far from secure. Long ago, social media could rescue even the most down-and-out, disgraced artist from obscurity, but that safety net was long gone. These days once you were out, you were gone and only a few really, truly made it.

Up to now Buddy had the might of Henderson Mulcahy backing him up but in the wake of the publicity he and Royce had received when they were rescued from the mountain, the mogul had grudgingly stepped back and allowed them to go solo with their own label.

Now Royce was heading right back, looking for something that he couldn't provide but that Henderson probably could. With a sinking feeling in the pit of his stomach, Buddy followed.

MARION

She opened her eyes, the room swimming slowly into focus. It was too bright, she could only manage a squint. Someone was holding a straw to her parched lips and she sucked in the water gratefully. Some of it went down the wrong way and she coughed, hitching in a breath. The same someone propped her upright and patted her back to clear the airway. She started breathing normally and opened her eyes fully as they adjusted to the light. Dandridge stood next to her bed, holding her up with one hand and the cup of water in the other. She lifted her arms awkwardly and hugged him for minutes, sobbing silently onto his shoulder.

After a while he let her back down on the thin mattress and hit the button that raised it up into an almost-sitting position while she sipped more water and recovered her composure. Doctors and nurses checked her over and hovered nervously nearby.

'Well?' she said, her voice croaking slightly.

'Well what?'

'Where the fuck have you been?'

'Here and there,' Dandridge smiled at her. 'You've been in the wars.'

'I guess so. The crash-'

'I'm not talking about the crash.'

Marion sipped more water. 'Is it out there? Pictures? Video?'

'Pictures, eye-witness accounts.'

'I feel so ashamed. And yet. I... I don't know.'

'You can still feel it, can't you?'

'Yes,' she whispered, 'I want it so much.'

'Adler told me. He's stalking the other survivors now, making sure nothing else untoward happens.'

'Mike? How's Mike?'

'Mike is an alcoholic. Even if he wasn't prepared for it, he recognised the signs of some kind of withdrawal. He called his ex-wife and is currently living with her and her husband and fingers crossed, hopefully going to ride it out. As are we. Together.'

'Thank god. Wait, what do you mean *as are we*?'

Dandridge told her how he been affected by his relationship with Belle, and how he took the blood to avoid being beaten to death by illegal Kin flesh dealers.

She closed her eyes.

'This can only get a whole lot worse-' tears filled her eyes, '-and I might just have fucked it all up. Everything we worked to achieve. The last fifteen years of my life. How will they ever trust me now?'

'You didn't ask to be in that plane crash. You didn't ask to be traumatised by the event.'

'It wasn't just PTSD and you know it.'

'Sure, but that information will remain classified. Adler's got the PM breathing down his neck and Josh is up to his eyeballs at the Shack. Adler's a good man but fires are starting faster than he can put them out. This may well get out of hand and if it does it'll snowball really quickly. He needs help. He needs you.'

'No. Not anymore. Not after this. I don't think that-'

'I wouldn't have flown all the way out here on the most uncomfortable RAF transport plane in the entire service if we didn't believe that you are still vital to the continuing success of this integration. First contact. First communication. A survivor, directly in contact with the Kin, with knowledge inside and out of how they work. You most of all.'

'And you. You too.'

'Ah well,' Dandridge smiled, 'that's debatable, but I'll try and be there until they chuck me out.'

JOSH

The repercussions of the increase in Kin population were being felt. As predicted, the Kin death rate was increasing exponentially. There was a strange unsettled mood hanging over the whole country as the remit and content of the factual and conspiracy newspapers began to inch closer and closer together. All of them had dedicated 24-hour rolling news channels on television to support the print copies, with new opinions and articles every few minutes on the Kin and their visibly increasing numbers. There were now thousands of human witnesses to the Kin reproduction process as their nature compelled them to grieve and mate with every passing.

Two more had died the previous day, one from walking too close to a cliff edge in Ireland, and the other at Richard Dandridge's house. Jean, the Kin that he had rescued from the flesh dealers had been unable to recover and Josh had walked in to find the body pure white and completely still. He had no choice but to store the body in the medical facility back at the Shack for later disposal.

Over the next few days more and more Kin began appearing at the Shack and Josh saw reports of massive increases of Kin numbers at Shacks all over the world. Housing was becoming desperately short.

He still reported to the PM every day by phone, but one call summoned him for a face-to-face meeting. He caught a train to Paddington and walked the rest of the way. It took about an hour and he was shocked at how many Kin he saw on the streets, with few of them appearing to have a place to be or go.

The heavily armed police guards at the gates to Downing Street ushered him to a side door where he was bundled inside, the door closing quickly and firmly behind him. One of the PM's aides lead him through identically decorated corridors to the same long Cabinet Room from their previous meeting.

This time only half the Cabinet were present but at one end, sitting and nibbling biscuits, were Adler, Dandridge and Marion Crandall. They all embraced briefly before he took a seat next to the pale and slightly trembling Crandall. The PM walked in flanked by two MI5 agents who stopped at the door and closed it for him as he took a seat. He wasted no time on pleasantries.

'We need a solution, Adler. My own eyes are telling me that we have a serious problem. I am aware that two more Kin have died since we last spoke so we can make some rough estimates on numbers but it isn't enough. We need a plan of action right now or we stay in this room until we do.'

'Will there be enough biscuits?' asked Dandridge, biting into a Jammie Dodger. The PM looked at him coldly and the rest of the Cabinet shifted uncomfortably.

'Mr. Dandridge, this not a time for flippancy.'

'I'm not being flippant. I haven't had any lunch and I'm hungry. All there seems to be is biscuits and young Josh here will definitely want his share.'

'A biscuit shortage will soon be the least of our worries, Mr Dandridge. My Deputy PM was murdered. I believe it was because he spoke out against the Kin, who are now proving him right and threatening to take over this entire planet.'

'Biscuits should never be at the bottom of a priority list, sir. But you are wrong about the Kin. They aren't threatening anything. A result of their genetic code being re-wired by living on a different planet than the one on which they evolved over millennia has had unforeseen consequences. For sure, they are replicating at a dangerous rate but this is not their fault, or intention.'

'Which is threatening our way of life.'

'Our way of life isn't anything to brag about, Prime Minister. I can tell you categorically that they are as confused and upset by this as we are.'

'And you know this because you are, as I understand, in a relationship with one of them?'

'Not anymore. Belle left me, for my own good. Being so close to Kin can also have unintended consequences.'

'Which is precisely why we are in this pickle now. Adler, how is the 'adopt-a-Kin' scheme going?'

'Very well, sir,' Adler replied. 'The take up is much better than we expected, and we estimate that we can home about four million Kin.'

'Which isn't nearly enough.'

'No, sir. It helps, but it isn't a long-term solution.'

'So what else?'

There was silence around the table. Minister for Kin and Human Relations Nile Cody spoke up, in his strong Belfast accent.

'Lets recap here. As I see it, the problem is two-fold. Firstly, whenever a Kin dies it is replaced by millions more. Second, it appears that consumption of Kin blood or Kin flesh by humans is not only extremely addictive, but the effects can vary greatly from person to person and can even heal injury, or disease-'

'-we think that's the case,' interrupted Marion, 'but there's been no real way to tell so far.'

'Aren't these two problems mutually exclusive?' asked Josh, 'how does one affect the other?'

'We don't know yet,' said the PM. 'I hope they are-'

'-but you can't help but see the dark side of human nature, can you?' said Marion. 'You think if it emerges that the Kin are good to eat, or can heal disease, then more will start disappearing and we'll have a global emergency on our hands.'

'Please do correct me if I'm wrong Ms. Crandall, but haven't we *already* got a global emergency on our hands?'

'OK,' said Dandridge. 'Realistically, we have only three options. Lets start with the first, presumably unworkable option. We banish them all from earth. Let's list the reasons this wouldn't work. We don't have the technology to do it and theirs doesn't work anymore. But let's assume we can build ships. Would they go?'

'It's unlikely unless something drastic happens,' said Adler. 'When Marion and I first managed to open talks they were diplomatic, but once we had answered that first signal and they discovered that earth could support them, they would have fought us for the right to stay here. They had little left to lose.'

'Great,' cut in the PM, his previously flushed face now darkening even more with anger, 'now they are potentially hostile.'

'Let's not get ahead of ourselves Prime Minister, but lets assume for any number of reasons that banishing them isn't going to work. Our second option is to re-wire them at a genetic and societal level so they can begin recognising family, community and social groups again, to somehow re-boot their reproduction cycle back to what it was on their own planet.'

'You can't just re-wire a whole species, Dandridge. They aren't transistor radios for Christ's sake,' Josh said.

'But it's an excellent idea, in theory,' said the PM. 'Can it be done, realistically?'

'I don't know,' replied Adler. 'Dandridge texted me the idea a couple of days ago and I've made some initial approaches to both the top genetic science departments at Cambridge, York and Stanford Universities and informed local Kin Shack representatives. I've also put out some feelers to locate some thought leaders within the social anthropology field. I'll have a scope of what might be possible in a week or so. It's a complex subject so whatever happens I doubt that there will be an immediate solution. And by that I mean in the next ten years.'

The PM sighed. 'OK, Dandridge what's your third option?'

'Segregation.'

'Jesus fucking Christ.'

'I think we can all agree He can't help on this occasion. Segregation on a massive, global scale. We'll have to allocate an entire quarter of this planet to the Kin. Set boundaries, borders. They can do what they like with it but cannot stray outside their allotted space, except with a special visa or license, and vice versa.'

'Do you have any idea where?'

'Not really. Somewhere with a lot of open, unused space, maybe Australia or a part of Russia, although they don't like the cold so much.'

'Russia will never go for it,' murmured Adler.

'I concur,' said Dandridge. 'Look, I'm not saying it's going to be easy, and of course the parallels to our own relatively recent history leave a bad taste, but in this case we aren't segregating because of racial inequality but for safety and supervision of numbers. We are in a unique situation and we all need to pull together, as two co-dependent species, to make some fucking room.'

'Giving them their own space won't work in the long term,' said Josh. 'Eventually they'll have no choice but to widen their borders and by then their numbers could be catastrophic.'

'Yes, but it'll buy us time while the anthropologists anthropologise.'

There was a pause. The PM took a deep breath.

'OK. We move forward with both plans. I don't need to remind you that no previous uses of the expression 'time is of the essence' have ever been quite as appropriate as it is right now. Adler, you and Crandall lead the plan to find somewhere for them to live. Anywhere, although Australia sounds like it might work, it's big enough. It is imperative that human and Kin work collaboratively and species rights remain as equal as possible. I want to see a workable plan in three months. Use every asset we have at hand, staff, premises, whatever you need. Dandridge, pick up the societal study and run with it. And I mean, run.'

An aide hurried into the room and leaned down to whisper in the PM's ear. The girl looked distressed, shaking. Her message took thirty seconds to relay as the room sat silently and expectantly. When she left, he spoke to the group.

'It appears that there has been an incident at a penthouse apartment in Kensington late last night.'

'What kind of an incident?' asked Adler.

'A shooting, although we'll have more information soon. Three men are dead and one more Kin. It was at the penthouse of Henderson Mulcahy, who runs-'

'-Uzi Bitch Records,' Adler said, his blood turning to ice in his veins. 'Who's dead?'

'Mulcahy is dead and also an employee of his, Buddy Tucker. And Royce Brims.'

There was a cold heavy silence in the room for a few seconds as the news sank in. 'What about the boy? He was staying with Brims.'

'No sign of anyone else at the scene. If the boy was with Brims, he's gone.'

PART EIGHT

LUKE

Sitting in the back of a chauffeur-driven black Jaguar with Royce and Buddy, Luke couldn't quite believe how suddenly his life had taken a complete upswing. He was in Royce Brims' inner-inner circle, had just watched a fantastic gig from the wings and now he was on his way to meet Henderson Mulcahy. *The* Henderson Mulcahy. He wanted to pinch himself, but instead flexed his right bicep and felt the stinging burn of his most recent cut under the sleeve of his t-shirt.

The car drew up outside a modern office block somewhere near South Kensington tube station and Tarik the chauffeur opened the passenger door to let them out.

'I thought we were going to Henderson's house?' he asked as they stepped into the London night air.

Nobody answered him.

The three of them pushed their way one by one through the glass rotating doors into the huge reception area. Directly in front of them on the grey marble wall was a giant logo of UB Records. Two security guards sat facing each other at two marble reception desks at opposite ends of the wide space. Royce turned immediately to the guard on the right and approached the marble desk. The guard had a huge Apple Mac on the desk and muted whatever it was he had been watching, pulling white earbuds from his ears with a trace of annoyance.

'Yes?'

'Royce Brims and Buddy Tucker to see Henderson.'

'Is he expecting you boys?'

'Just tell him it's Royce and Buddy.'

'Yeah, you said that already. And who's that?' nodding to Luke.

'Just a friend.'

'Are you all the folks that were on that plane that crashed?' he asked curiously.

'Yes, that's us, but we're not here about that.'

'I'll call him, but if he doesn't want to see you then you have to leave the premises immediately or me and Andrew over there will remove you, with force if necessary. Do you understand me?'

'We get it, removal with force, yada, yada. Please just call him,' said Royce.

The guard, whose blue name tag sewn onto his uniform indicated his name was John Abbott, didn't pick up the large phone that looked like a switchboard on the desk, but took a mobile phone from his pocket and with a sideways flick of his thumb seemed to unlock and dial at the same time. He said nothing and just held it to his ear for a few moments before placing it back into his pocket.

'Go on up. I'll unlock the far lift only. Top button.'

Buddy's black shoes clicked, Royce's Nikes squeaked and Luke's Converse made no noise at all as the three of them made their way across the impossibly shiny floor towards the lift.

The doors opened as they approached and they rode up

in silence. The numbers illuminated one by one until they reached the highest number, the forty second floor. They walked out onto a narrow glass-walled corridor that seemed to lead only to a balcony with a fantastic view across London.

'Gentlemen.'

A breathtakingly beautiful woman was walking towards them. She was dressed in an extremely short, figure caressing silver cocktail dress with matching eight inch heels. The outfit perfectly emphasised the luxurious, perfectly smooth darkness of her skin, the toned muscles of her legs and every wonderful contour of her body. Her lips were the deepest red and her jet black hair abundant. It was nearly midnight, and she looked absolutely stunning.

'Hiya Buddy. It's nice to see you again. We aren't yet at the top, gents. Please follow me,' she announced to them.

They followed her along the corridor that seemed to be a ring around the entire diameter of the building with a floor to ceiling 360 degree view of London on one side and a featureless beige wall on the other. The spectacular view was rather wasted on the boys as Royce and Luke couldn't take their eyes off their guide and Buddy was too preoccupied to really notice either. She lead them to another elevator with beige doors set into the beige wall. The doors slid silently open and she stepped in. They followed obediently.

'I don't remember going this way last time,' observed Royce. 'The lift just took me straight up.'

'It's been a while since you've been here, Mr Brims?'

'I suppose. A couple years, maybe. I don't remember.' Actually, he remembered very clearly the last occasion Henderson had summoned him to the penthouse. He glanced at Buddy, but his agent and business partner seemed lost in his own thoughts.

'Mr Mulcahy remodelled the security. The main elevator is switched off at seven o' clock every evening. The only access is via the lift to the forty-second floor and then this secure lift to the forty-third and forty-fourth, where Henderson lives. Or the stairs, of course.'

The lift doors opened to the waiting area and the opaque glass wall that Royce recognised from his previous visits to Henderson.

'Please wait here,' she stepped backwards through the lift doors and they slid shut on her. They heard the motor whir softly and then they were alone.

They waited silently for about a minute until without warning the opaque glass instantly turned transparent, and they could see Henderson Mulcahy standing in the centre of a mostly empty space beckoning them inside. He wore a dazzlingly white Japanese sarong and Royce could see he had shaved his head since the last time he had seen him. He looked taller somehow, more imposing. Royce's heart began to beat faster. Buddy pushed the door open and approached him, his hand outstretched. Henderson shook it firmly, followed by Royce.

'And who's this?' he asked in his deep, rich-velvet voice, shaking Luke's hand and smiling, flashing his gold tooth. 'No, don't tell me. This is Luke McDonald, fifth survivor of the plane crash that tragically took the lives of so many of my employees.'

'Yes, sir,' Luke replied. He was awed, completely starstruck. Henderson Mulcahy was among the most famous men on the planet. Wealthy beyond imagining and powerful in ways most politicians could only fantasise. He exuded an aura of almost palpable wealth and fame and exclusivity and confidence.

His suite was plain, a thick white fluffy rug covering a black marble floor with matching black marble walls. There was no furniture at all, the sofa that Royce's mother had once sat on was gone.

Henderson clasped his hands behind him and appraised the three people now standing slightly awkwardly in a line before him. Royce still wore the leather trousers he had worn on stage which didn't have pockets. He didn't really know what to do with his hands. He wished there was a chair, at least.

'I heard your gig tonight was incredible, Royce. Well done, both of you. Y'all are becoming a force to be reckoned with, eh?'

Luke watched with interest as Royce shuffled on his feet, looking uncharacteristically uncomfortable, like a child about to be scolded.

'We just got lucky, Mr Mulcahy-' Buddy started.

'How long have I known you, Buddy? You aren't my employee any more. In this room, it's Henderson.'

'Henderson. We got a boost from the crash and cashed in. You know how it is. We meant no disrespect to you, we just wanted to try something for ourselves just like you did back in the day.'

'Jesus, Buddy. No *disrespect?* Who do you think I am, some common gangster? I never for a second believed you meant disrespect. I believe respect has to be earned, and you and Royce are doing a pretty damned good job.

You two are striking out on your own, I get that. No, I know exactly why you're here, you don't even have to ask. We'll get to it later, I promise. But I do have a question for you, and this goes for you too, Luke,' he smiled at the boy, who was dazzled by both his charm and gold tooth. 'A question you must answer before I can help you out with anything. And you must answer me absolutely honestly or you leave with nothing.' He looked across the room to the three of them. *'Capiche?'* he laughed.

'OK, Henderson.' said Royce uneasily. 'Cut to it, what's the question?'

'So what I really want to know, and please trust me when I say I have done my research, is *how the fuck did you get off that mountain alive?* And remember, the truth now.'

There was a stunned silence.

'We... we walked,' Buddy said, eventually.

'Nah. Not without help. Not possible. The distance, the climate, the terrain. Not even the papers believed it but luckily for you there weren't no other explanation. Only I think there is, and I want you to tell me what it is. I want to hear you say it.'

The three of them looked at each other, confused and panicked.

'There *is* no story, Henderson,' Royce said. 'It was hell, but we walked out of there.'

Henderson smiled. 'Boys, if you don't give me what I want, then I can't get you what you want. And I *know* what you want.'

'I'm really confused, Mr Mulcah-'

'Henderson.'

'-Henderson. I really don't know what you want to hear,' Buddy said.

'Yeah you do. I want to hear exactly how you managed to walk all those miles on nothing but peanuts and yellow snow.'

'But why?'

'I have my reasons.'

'I need to talk with Royce,' Buddy said and taking Royce's arm firmly he lead his client to the adjoining room, the door swishing shut behind them. Luke stood alone with Henderson.

'Y'all made a pact, right?' Henderson said, gold tooth flashing. 'Signed the official secrets act, summat like that?'

'Something like that,' replied Luke.

'How old are you?'

'Eighteen.'

'Boy, that's so plainly not true that it almost don't qualify as a lie. How old are you really?'

'Fourteen.'

'Fourteen, huh? A year younger than Royce when he first walked in that door. Luke, you may be young but I get the feeling that you do things your own way.'

Henderson lifted the short sleeve of Luke's T-shirt to his shoulder and stared at the criss-cross of cuts on his skinny upper arm, some healing, some still raw.

'I think this secret is poisoning you, boy,' he said gently. 'You need to heal yourself from the inside before you can heal on the outside.' His voice dropped lower, softer. 'You're special. I can tell. I can *always* tell. It's in those blue eyes. Not just intelligence, but something else, something... indefinable. Your physical self is thin, weak - but you have real strength in you.'

Luke was mesmerised. He desperately wanted Henderson to like him, to trust him.

'So why don't you start by telling me the story. How did you get off the mountain?'

Tears sprang to Luke's eyes. 'It wasn't my fault. I didn't want to, I really didn't. But they held me down and forced me to. I would rather have died up there.'

'That sounds bad. It's not good being forced to do something you don't want to do. I've never forced anyone to do anything, not ever.'

'I wanted to kill them. I hated them for it. I still do.'

'I bet.'

'I didn't want whatever had affected them to happen to me. But it saved my life, probably.'

'How did what affect them?'

Luke told him everything.

BUDDY

Royce was in a whispered, heated discussion with Buddy.

'We made a pact. And we know for sure that Government bloke is keeping tabs on us,' Buddy said.

'So what? I don't honestly think that telling Henderson what happened will make any real difference.'

'Are you fucking *kidding* me? He's one of the most recognisable and influential people on the planet. Royce, we need to tread very carefully here. It's highly likely that if this got out to the public we could be in very serious trouble. We can't say anything.'

'How's it going to get out? Henderson won't tell anyone, and if we want a chance of more then we need him.'

Buddy felt frustration with Royce rising and tried to keep his voice low and level.

'Royce, you don't know him like I do. He'll use the information to leverage us when he wants something. It might be tomorrow, next week or decades from now, but it'll happen.'

'We can cross that bridge when we get to it, Buddy. If we get to it.'

'You're talking like an addict, Royce. I'd rather try and help us both out of this mess than rely on Henders-'

'I'm not a fucking addict, I just need the extra punch that it gives me right now. We've got so much to do Bud, so much to achieve and this stuff makes it all possible, more so than any faith or any drug.'

'You have no idea how much like an addict that sounded,' Buddy sighed. He sank back into one of the extremely uncomfortable Phillipe Starck waiting room chairs. He pinched his nose with his thumb and index finger.

'I can't stop you Royce, but if you tell him then we need to seriously re-think our partnership as I'm not sure-'

'What the fuck is that?'

They stared through the clear glass to Henderson's office. A section of the black marble floor had slid apart like a trap door and a structure the size, shape and height of a boardroom table had risen upwards into the room. Except this glass-topped boardroom table had a Kin strapped down and on display under thick glass. The Kin was missing its left arm and most of the left leg.

Royce and Buddy burst back into the room just as Henderson released the glass table-top, which split down the centre and retracted down both lengths of the table.

'Oh, hi fellas. It's OK. My good friend Luke here told me everything. Your secret, such as it is, is safe with me.'

'Oh no, Luke-' Buddy started, but Henderson held his hand up. 'Relax, Tucker. Nothing you can do about it now anyway. The can is open and the worms are everywhere.' He laughed a again, a deep, rich bass rumble that would have rattled furniture if he'd had any. 'I am assuming this is what you came for.'

The Kin was strapped to the bizarre boardroom torture table by metal straps around the neck, torso and thighs as well as its one remaining ankle and wrist. Royce recognized it as the Kin that Henderson had shown such affection for on his first visit with his mother all those years ago. The blue tiger stripes were pale blue now and not the bright blue they had been before. It turned it's head towards Royce and spoke.

'Royce Brims,' it said from the blank face. 'I request that you immediately inform the police or local Shack leader of my imprisonment. I estimate that I have been restrained for at least two years.'

'Holy motherfucker,' Royce whispered.

'Oh god. Oh no. Henderson, what have you done?' Buddy looked close to tears. 'This, this isn't right.'

'No?' Henderson countered. 'And do you want to tell the Kin how you escaped the mountain? How your broken, frost-bit arm healed all by itself? You treated its kind like cattle, eating its flesh when it suited you. How is that different from the chicken or beef you eat every day?'

'I'm vegetarian, and that's just not true. It was already dead and we were in a life or death situation. We were going to eat a human being.'

'But you didn't. You chose the Kin and now you are here because you want more. And both you and I know you will taste it, I can see it in your eyes. All of you.'

'Mr Tucker?' the Kin said. 'Mr Tucker, I believe that my current incarceration and torture is a violation of the terms and conditions of the Human/Kin integration manifesto. Please report this infringement to the authorities and arrange my release.'

Buddy staggered backwards, his hand to his mouth and white as a sheet as the Kin's restrained head swivelled slowly around to look at him like a blank ventriloquist's puppet. Buddy ran for it. He made it to the door and pulled the chrome handle. It didn't budge, didn't even rattle on the metal hinges. Somehow, it was locked.

ROYCE

Despite its distress the Kin's voice was smooth and steady with no difference or variation in tone or pitch, exactly like all the others he had heard. He felt nothing as he listened to its attempts to get help.

Buddy had tried to get the hell out of there but Henderson had locked the door. As Buddy struggled, Henderson calmly pulled out a metal drawer set into the side of his magic torture table and removed a carving knife. Luke was standing right next to him and watched the mogul as he leaned over the Kin and placed the serrated edge of the blade into the stump of its left thigh about an inch above the last cut.

Luke flashed to a recent memory of himself pressing a kitchen knife against his own thigh, feeling the anticipation of the burning pain leading to the empty bliss on the other side.

He watched enthralled as Henderson drew the knife across the Kin's thigh and dug it deeper, carving downwards until a round white disk of meat peeled off the leg. The Kin had stopped talking and even though the face had no features to express visible emotion, Luke could sense the pain emanating from it. It was intoxicating.

But Buddy Tucker didn't seem to think so.

'Enough, Henderson. Please, please stop. Right now.'

But Henderson was holding the dripping, white meat in both palms and offering it outwards to Royce like an obscene communion wafer.

Royce didn't hesitate. He gripped Henderson's wrists with both hands and lifted the dinner-plate sized slice of meat towards him, lowering his face in submission and taking his first proper bite of Kin since the mountain. He pulled his head back, stretching and ripping the flesh as he sucked a chunk inside his mouth and chewed slowly, his body shuddering convulsively as he was flooded with the powerfully intense feelings he craved so much. White blood dribbled down his chin.

Henderson went next with slightly more decorum, his face screwed up in concentration as he chewed his mouthful but giving nothing away as to how the Kin made him feel. He swallowed and held his hand out to Luke.

'Don't do it, Luke,' Buddy moved towards the boy and put one hand on his shoulder. 'It's OK if Royce and Henderson want to do this, but I think it's best if-'

Henderson reached into another shallow metal drawer and took out a gun. It was a matte-grey, snub nosed Glock 19. He pointed it at Buddy in one, white stained hand.

'Take your hand off the boy, Buddy,' Henderson said, and the agent stumbled backwards, horrified. 'Let him make up his own mind.'

'There's no need for this, Henderson. Look at all you've achieved without the Kin. You don't need to-'

'I can do so much more now. I already have. I've been close to the Kin for three years and my influence is already so much greater than you can imagine.' He put the gun down on the side of the table and withdrew a small handheld device from a deep pocket in the front of his white Kimono.

'You know what this is?' he asked. Buddy shook his head.

The tall man typed something on the device and held it out to show Buddy. 'This, my friend, is power.'

Royce stepped forward and stared at the screen. 'Oh my god. Buddy, this is-'

'The future,' said Henderson, 'and the past.'

'The most illegal thing on the planet.'

'That and eating the flesh of our brethren,' Henderson said.

'How did you do this? How did it happen?'

Luke was now staring at the small device with a look of wonder on his face.

'It don't matter. It took a long time but I finally figured it out. The infrastructure was already there. All it took was the right people in the right places with the right incentives.'

'Henderson, I insist that you let me out of here before somebody gets-'

'Insist?' Henderson reached to the table for the gun. It was gone. The Kin held it in its remaining hand, the restraining strap still buckled around the wrist now ripped from the table.

'Kin, no.' said Henderson.

The alien pulled the trigger. The bullet entered Henderson's head at a slight angle, through his right eye-socket and ploughing an exit right through the back of his skull, pulling a large part of his brain along in its wake. Lumps of grey and red brain matter sprayed up the window directly behind him, the bullet pinging off the thick glass. The entire right side of his dazzlingly white Kimono was soaked in the gushing dark red blood before his body hit the black marble floor.

The Kin aimed the gun at Royce Brims, who backed away, raising his hands beseechingly towards the smoking black dot of the barrel now pointed in his direction.

Luke clapped his hands over his ears slightly too late to muffle the deafening report of the second shot. The bullet passed cleanly between Royce's outstretched hands and took him in the throat, the force of impact throwing him backwards to the hard black marble floor, the back of his head connecting with a sickening thud. He landed in a spreading pool of hot blood gushing from the shredded remains of his throat. He tried to scream, to say something or call for help but heard only a desperate gurgle.

Images flashed before him, his mother whom he hadn't called in over six months, he and his friends rapping down the high street, Kai, Carl and Brandon, none of whom he had thought about since the crash that had claimed their lives. Punching Thomas Mabbett in the face, his first act of outright rebellion, his first victorious rap-battle, his first major gig, the crash, all the groupies he had fucked and the drugs he had taken, it all flashed before him in an instant. And then it went dark and he was fifteen once more, scared, dumb and blinded by promises. All he could see in the darkness was Henderson Mulcahy, half his head missing, the blood-stained Kimono now in a pile at his feet. From the warm pool of his own blood he stared helplessly up at the huge naked, oiled and hard body standing over him and in his final few moments of clarity, Royce Brims knew for sure that he was dead.

LUKE

Henderson and Royce died within about ten seconds of each other, even before the slightly acrid gunpowder smell from the barrel of the gun reached his nostrils. He was too shocked to even move, horrified and mesmerised by the suddenness of what had just happened.

The Kin was now pointing the gun at Buddy, who dived beneath the huge table, his arms over his head, screaming and sobbing. The Kin switched the gun to Luke. He was not afraid. He didn't really think he was going to die.

The Kin spoke to him.

'Please release the rest of my restraints.'

Luke searched around on the table and found a small silver lever set in to the side of the table like the ball release on a pool table. He pulled it and heard something catch. The straps released and the Kin sat up slowly and spoke again.

'Mr Tucker, please stand up or I will shoot this boy.'

Buddy stood up very slowly, his arms still over his head, still sobbing with terror.

'Please, help me up,' the Kin addressed Luke, who was definitely more with it than the agent. He hoisted the Kin's only arm over his shoulder, helping it down from the table. It was much heavier than he had expected, too heavy for Luke on his own and the two of them stumbled to the marble floor, the Kin on its one remaining knee, unbalanced. It had to put its one hand down to support itself and dropped the gun, which fell at Luke's feet. Luke picked it up quickly and straightened up, leaving the Kin still on its knee.

'Please call the authorities,' it said again.

'Oh thank god,' said Buddy. 'Well done, Luke. Now let's get out of here. We need to go right now. Luke?'

Luke held the gun loosely by his side, vaguely aware that a balance of power had just shifted in his favour. He figured that somebody must have heard the shots, if not the security guards then the beautiful PA who had showed them up in the lift. Somebody must still be working in the building. Should he go to the police? What would happen to him then? He dimly realised he was staring blankly at the gun in his hand which, like the Kin, was also much heavier than he expected. It was like he was staring at it through the wrong end of a telescope.

'Luke?' Buddy approached the boy. 'Luke, please give me the gun. We need to get out of here and call the police.'

Buddy reached slowly towards him for the gun. Luke still hadn't moved, struggling to process and absorb what had just happened to his mentor and his mentor's mentor, and not quite sure what he should do next. Buddy placed his hand on the gun and gently tried to lift it out of his hand.

Later, Luke would tell himself it was an unconscious reflex, a tragic, unfortunate accident that his finger had already curled around the hair trigger as Buddy tried to prise the gun away from him. But he would never really be sure.

MIKE

He had been at Joy's house for a little over a week. He had worked hard to engage with her husband and children but struggled with prolonged periods of sociability. Mealtimes were impossible so he chose to eat alone in the spare room, more often than not just staring at the food with an even mixture of hunger and apathy. He felt hungry all the time, but food wasn't going to cut it.

The morning after the shootings he sat silently on the end of the bed after another night of troubled sleep. The daily papers thudded down onto Joy's doormat. The family took one global newspaper, two conspiracy papers, one pure gossip, one entertainment and one sport and all of them, including the sport, lead with the story dubbed the 'Uzi Bitch Massacre'. The conspiracy papers were filled with nothing else. Mike and the other survivors were back in the news. Nobody knew where Jennifer was but Luke had been photographed with Royce the day before the shootings, blurry photographs of him standing in the wings of Royce's gig blown up and stuck on every other page. His current whereabouts were unknown.

Marion was back working with the government after her breakdown and was hounded wherever she went. The few pictures of her meltdown that Adler hadn't managed to suppress were re-printed over and over again. So Mike figured it was only a matter of time before he was found too. Mike Hennessy, alcoholic, crash survivor, divorced, not been at his home address for more than a week, it wasn't a hard leap for them to track him down and they duly obliged.

Within a day of the shooting, Joy and Graham's house was under siege by reporters, the two young children absolutely delighted with the attention but their parents not so thrilled.

Mike stood by the first floor spare room window

watching the mob of reporters and lines of news vans from a tiny gap in the net curtains. He had never realised how noisy they were. Didn't they realise that this was a residential street? Joy came in and stood behind him, careful to stay out of their view.

'We can't have this, you know that right?' she said. 'The children-'

'I know. You don't have to explain. I'll be gone first thing in the morning if that's OK. One more night.'

'That's fine. Mike, I'm still here for you. We're still going to go to the meetings, OK?'

'I know. I just hope-'

'What?'

'I told you everything. The whole story. I wish I hadn't involved you in this.'

'Well, you did. What can they do?'

He was still standing at the window, and she put her arms around him, resting her head on his shoulder. The phone rang. She ignored it, but it kept on ringing.

'The machine should have cut in by now.'

'Unplug it.'

'I will.'

She left him alone to carry on staring out at the reporters. He saw a huge, black Cadillac SUV pull up on the other side of the street. The door opened and a figure climbed out. It was the Government man, Marion's friend, Adler. He was holding a phone to his ear and lowered it as the ringing in the house stopped. Adler was standing just behind the mob of reporters clustered around the front gate. Mike drew the net curtains back and the two men stared at each other. Camera flashes began to pop and the crowd noise became louder as they all started shouting questions up at him.

The Government man pointed and gave the single curled finger beckon that Mike remembered from school. He let the curtain drop back into place and turned away from the window. He took his coat and went downstairs. Joy was in the kitchen fiddling with the answering machine.

He opened the front door and stepped out quickly into the solid barrier of reporters in his way, who instantly surrounded him, blinding him with lightbulb flashes and noise.

'Mike! Mike! First Marion, now Royce and Buddy. How are you feeling?' an Australian reporter shouted in his ear. There were other questions, all enquiring after his sanity. He held his arms up over his face and refused to speak. As he squinted he spotted a gap and an arm outstretched towards him. Adler stepped through, took hold of Mike's arm and dragged him forcibly through the pack to his car.

He pulled open the passenger side door and shoved him inside, slamming it shut. For a few seconds Mike was alone in the leather scented, air conditioned vehicle and although the side windows were tinted almost black he felt a sharp pang of fear. Then the driver's door opened and Adler pushed his way in through the rabble. Without buckling up he floored the throttle pedal and the car surged forward, parting reporters like the red sea as he gathered speed, ignoring the seemingly suicidal photographers leaping in front of them to get a shot. Soon they were free of the throng and speeding towards the South Circular.

'Where are we going?' Mike asked.

'Somewhere safe.'

'Do you mean somewhere I'll never be found ever again? Given what I know about the Kin?'

'What do you know?'

'Not much. They are addictive, like a drug, like alcohol. Also, I think they might contain healing properties.'

'And how many people do you honestly think have gone around eating them?'

'Royce Brims, for one. Tucker. Mulcahy. Probably the boy too, although he's an odd one, that kid.'

'And so, given the news might already be out, what

would I gain by locking you up in some solitary cell somewhere?'

'I don't know.'

'You're not being locked up, Mike. We need you. I really don't know how far down the rabbit hole we've all fallen, but we need to keep going.'

'I'm not sure I'm going to be much help to anyone right now, and also I don't really know what you're talking about.'

'I get that a lot. Bear with me.'

The two of them fell silent as the car made its way slowly into Central London, along Whitehall and a left turn into a side street lined with beautiful white stone offices, left again down into an underground car park pausing only to allow solid metal shutters to roll upwards and allow the car inside. They drove forward into the darkness as the doors rattled down behind them.

MARION

She had always thought that being part of a secret defence group called COBRA would be cool, until she learnt that COBRA stood for 'Cabinet Office Briefing Room A', which was something of a let-down even before she had actually seen it. She discovered to her further chagrin that it was an underground boardroom, standard in every way with a long table, bare concrete walls and a huge TV screen at one end its only real distinguishing feature.

She took her seat at the table feeling decidedly claustrophobic. Mike sat opposite her. The two of them had hardly spoken since he had joined the re-settlement team, taking pains to avoid her even though they lived in the same living quarters at Whitehall. She didn't blame him, a lot of people avoided her these days.

Dandridge and the PM were late for the meeting but walked in together, looking for all the world like old friends, the PM saying something that made them both laugh as they took their seats.

'OK let's begin,' the PM said and the room settled.

Adler picked up a small remote control unit and switched the huge television on, adjusting the input to AV1. The black screen switched to a large image of Luke McDonald's face. The boy was looking at something just beneath the camera and receiving some muffled off-screen instructions before re-directing his gaze into the camera. His hair looked greasy and there was a line of pimples across his forehead.

'*Hi,*' he said, nervously and uncertainly. '*My name is Luke McDonald. I survived the plane crash PK8342 along with Royce Brims, Buddy Tucker, Marion Crandall, Mike Hennessy and my step-mother, Jennifer Jones-McDonald. Today is my birthday, I'm now fifteen years old.*'

'Pause this,' said the PM, and looked at Adler. 'How did we get this, and do we know who's behind the camera?'

'We were sent a copy last night on RedDisc and I don't know who he's talking to yet.'

'OK, carry on.'

Adler pressed play and the boy continued. '*I have a statement regarding the truth about the survivors of the plane crash PK8342-*' he stopped and glanced down from the camera, then back up again. '*The truth is that the survivors were forced into a form of cannibalism to survive. There was a Kin passenger on board the aircraft but it was killed during the... the crash. We... they... tore it apart and ate it for food before we walked down and got rescued.*'

There was a shocked silence in the meeting room as the assembled group watched the boy tear up. It sounded as if he was given more encouragement from behind the camera before he cleared his throat, wiped his eyes and continued. '*I didn't want to but they made me. They held me down and forced my mouth open with a piece of metal and forced it down my throat. They stuffed themselves and ate the whole thing. All of it, even the head. But the Kin, the flesh, it saved our lives. It made us all strong. Really strong, and we didn't feel the cold so bad and we could just walk down the mountain, easy. Mr. Tucker had a broken arm, really bad, it smelt awful, but it healed up. It sounds unreal, but it's true. By the time the doctors looked at it, it was almost back to normal. But something happened to Royce and Buddy and Henderson Mulcahy I think. And maybe to the lady, Marion Crandall. I think... I think they got addicted to it. Because it makes you feel strong and good, like a drug or something. I only got a small bit so I'm OK but I think Royce and Buddy and the others might have had too much and now they're going crazy. We need to control the Kin somehow because even though they've lived here as long as I can remember we still don't really know what they want. But I think they're bad somehow, like-*' he looked down underneath the camera again. '*-like one of those venus flytraps or something. They're going to draw us in and then trap us somehow, and I'm scared that what happened to my friends Royce and Buddy and my step-mother will happen to others. We need to do something. We need to stop them.*'

The film cut to black. Mike spoke in the shocked silence

that followed.

'Who filmed this? Who's he with?'

'We don't know, but there's a press release that came with the message. It's a transcript of the film plus a warning that there is more information that indicates a wider conspiracy about the Kin, but whoever wrote it doesn't specify what. It's a veiled threat, but its going to cause hysteria,' Adler replied. 'It seems that as well as holding a Kin captive, slowly torturing and consuming it for more than two years, Mr Mulcahy had also become involved in any number of off-the-radar initiatives.'

'Like what?' asked the PM, his former good humour long forgotten.

'Well, among other things it seems that he has assembled a team of collaborators from the United States, the UK and Korea who have somehow re-booted the internet, albeit in a far more restricted capacity than before the shutdown.'

'He re-booted the fucking *internet?*'

'Sort of. Its not very powerful and data speeds are slow, but it can only get faster, and bigger.'

'How?'

'He was a very rich and powerful man. Very little was beyond his reach. And now it seems that it's in the hands of whatever group has taken the boy, so who knows who else might have access.'

'The papers?'

'I doubt it, but soon probably.'

'Why did he want to get rid of the Kin so badly? He had one as a PA for god's sake.'

'Yes, the one that was found dead with the others. It seems likely that he had become addicted to it. I don't know what else he may have known, but if he had somehow found out about their reproduction cycle, which is possible I suppose, then he would have figured out that if they stay here, they could eventually overwhelm the human population.'

'Why could he not just come to us and share this?'

'Prime Minister, he was a megalomaniac and addicted to Kin flesh. From what I understand the meat probably accentuated his feelings of power, of indestructibility.'

'It's amazing what a bullet in the head can do to puncture that misapprehension,' murmured Dandridge. Adler ignored him and continued.

'It's possible that the meat made him feel like a god. He felt he could take over the world his way and he had the facilities and money to do it. There's one other thing too, but I'm not sure it's relevant.'

'What?'

Adler paused and drew in a breath. 'During the investigation into his death, the police have discovered images downloaded from the internet and saved locally before it was shut down, thousands of them. Indecent images of boys, including more than a few of Royce Brims back from when he was first signed up. Mulcahy, or someone with access to his encrypted offline data storage, was a paedophile. I have no idea how the Kin meat might have affected this particular predilection but it might possibly have had some influence on events.'

'Fucking hell. Let's keep that one to ourselves for the moment. Adler, how do we know about the internet?'

'I know people too, Prime Minister. I found a contact who has managed to hack into it. Which is both helpful and slightly unnerving given that if we can access it, others will figure it out too. There's plenty of old technology lying around. I used an old tablet computer as a food tray for years.'

'We need to combat this. Rebuke the message publicly. We also need to bring in Kin reps from the Shacks, as I have a feeling that after this they will have some questions of their own. This is starting to get out of hand, Adler.'

'I know, sir. We are doing all we can here. I'll reach out

and try to find out who made this video. We need to neutralise it, somehow. Mike and Marion?'

'Yes?' Marion asked nervously, having watched and listened in the last 20 minutes with growing unease.

'You're up.'

MIKE

'-and next to Marion Crandall on the sofa tonight is lawyer Mike Hennessy, a fellow survivor of the plane crash that claimed more than two hundred lives.'

'Hello, Evan.'

'It's a real honour to have you both here on *Newsnight*, but I must ask - why now, why have you chosen this moment to come forward and agree to a broadcast interview?'

'Well,' Marion replied, 'firstly, we were all - we *are* all - still traumatised by the crash and what happened to us. When you're involved in something so extreme, when you've been so close to death, something happens to you that changes how you fundamentally think and feel, so it takes time to process. I can't answer for Mike, but I simply wasn't ready. In fact I'm still not even sure I'm ready to talk about it.'

'We'll come back to the lasting effects of trauma later on in the programme, but Mike - what about you? What convinced you to come on here and talk to us about your experiences?'

Mike paused for an uncomfortably long time. Marion nudged him gently.

'Well, I think you know Evan, really. I think the audience knows too. I don't read the conspiracy papers myself but some weird stories have come out about how we survived the mountain and what happened to Royce Brims and the others.'

'So you are saying that there's a different story about how you survived the mountain contrary to the one from the press conference that was held at the time?'

'Yes,' said Marion, 'it was a very confusing and strange time. None of us remember much from the whole time we were up there to when we were found.'

'But you remember now?'

'Yes.'

'Before you tell us - I am sure you have seen or read the transcript of the video released by young Luke McDonald?'

'Of course.'

'And is your story concurrent with what he says? Did you force him to eat the flesh of a Kin?'

'If we hadn't, he'd be dead. It's as simple as that,' said Marion.

Mike cut in: 'Evan, you have to understand that we were just trying to survive. We weren't eating the flesh of a Kin specifically, we just ate what was available to us.'

'If the Kin hadn't been there, would you have eaten something else - a human, perhaps?'

'Yes,' Mike said. 'There were dead bodies everywhere. We would have eaten whatever we could.'

'But you chose the Kin.'

'Yes.'

'Why? For all you knew it could have been poisonous to humans.'

'So we would either have died of exposure or poison.'

'But history tells us that human flesh is not poisonous to eat. It seems that you made a rather large leap of faith.'

'We were freezing to death and starving. There was no leap of faith, just a judgment call made in a desperate situation.' Mike snapped.

'Luke McDonald's video claims that Mr Tucker's arm was badly broken in the crash and the flesh seemed to heal it. How did the flesh affect you specifically, Marion?'

'I had no serious injuries. I was lucky.'

'Yes, but in the aftermath of the whole experience? I am referring to the incident in Buenos Aires, when-'

'I know what you are referring to, Evan. Listen, what Luke said was right. Kin flesh affects humans but not in a good way. The effects apparently vary from person to person like any drug. And like any drug there's a comedown. So when I attended the post-mortem of the dead Kin in Buenos Aires, straight after the crash, it was a mistake. I have never been addicted to anything before so I did not recognise the symptoms. I was overwhelmed and lost control and I cannot apologise enough to the Kin community.'

'Are you still addicted?'

'I am in recovery, yes.'

'And you, Mike? You were an alcoholic, yes?'

'I *am* an alcoholic, Evan. I believe, like Marion, that the Kin flesh is somehow addictive, more so than alcohol even, but if any good came out of my alcoholism it's that I was able to seek the right help immediately.'

'Do you now believe that the Kin flesh is poisonous?'

'Yes, in the same way that alcohol or heroin or methamphetamine is a poison.'

'A poison that can potentially heal broken limbs.'

'Cocaine and heroin were used for centuries in the medical profession to mask pain, but once their addictive and detrimental properties were known and recognised use was prohibited.'

'Let's move on to the Kin themselves. Their representatives declined an offer to appear today. Why do you think that is, Marion?'

'I don't know. We are in very close communication with the Kin - we are being very transparent with them about what's happened and I think they trust us to move forward in an appropriate way.'

'Marion - you know them better than anyone, you were with the first contact team, came up with the integration manifesto and worked alongside the Kin setting up the first Shack. How do you think that Luke's video and your subsequent confession will affect relationships with them? They are, after all, an alien species - is there any way to know how they will react?'

'Well, they are hard to read, in terms of facial or vocal expression, and their own language is virtually impossible for human ears to register. So I can only go by recent historical experience, which is to say that they will be calm and understanding and work with us to devise a solution. Because – and this is important, Evan - none of us have a choice anymore. It's vital for us all to remember that we have only been sharing this planet for *fifteen years*. This is a micro-cosmically short amount of time, infinitesimally short. We are looking towards the far future, to millions and millions of years of co-habiting the same space, a timeline so huge that it is virtually impossible to comprehend. We cannot know what will happen when we are all dead and gone but it is vital that we begin laying the groundwork here and now, so that when future generations look back in history, and I'm talking our children's children to the power of a thousand or more, the mistakes we've made will pale besides the astounding positive steps and tolerance we have shown. I want history to judge us to have done our very best and tried to do the right thing for a lost, intelligent species who simply needed our help.'

'Inspiring words. Marion Crandall, Mike Hennessy, thank you both so much for coming along today. After the break, Russell Brand.'

AGNES

The small house was painted white and had a red tiled roof that was more often than not covered with snow. This rendered it virtually invisible in the small copse of woodland in which it squatted. It was remote, twenty miles from the nearest town, deep in the countryside and at the end of a long lane accessible only by 4x4s or cars fitted with appropriate snow chains on the tyres. *No chains, no chance* Agnes' father was fond of saying.

The annual snowfall would announce its impending arrival with plummeting temperatures and frozen puddles at least a week before it actually deigned to appear, and then once it had decided to show up would overstay its welcome by at least seven or eight months, like an unwanted houseguest.

For thousands of years the residents of Hargosand in Vastnorrland County had expected, planned for and dealt with the snow in day-to-day subconscious routines, a muscle memory passed down from generation to generation. Driving with tyre chains, brushing down driveways, the sound of the gritter lorry and the plough rumbling through the countryside every day was just normal life.

Agnes was eight years old, a pretty, pale girl with wide blue eyes and white-blonde hair that she liked to keep in a single straight plait. She loved to wear bright, flowery summer dresses on the few occasions she could without freezing and watching old Walt Disney cartoons like Dumbo and Bambi and The Jungle Book, which she had watched at least a hundred times. She liked to sing along with Baloo and *The Bare Necessities*.

She was almost entirely self sufficient, taught how to take care of herself by her parents since she was a baby barely able to steady herself on chubby legs. She knew how to go through all the kitchen cupboards before making a shopping list, how to cook basic meals, how to change a tyre, darn a dress or treat a cut. She also knew how to turn the water off at the mains if the pipes froze, how to change a fuse if the electricity went out (which it did, with monotonous regularity) and how important it was to dress for the conditions and plan everything in advance. She didn't go to school. There was a good school twenty miles away in the town but Agnes' parents had decided to home-school their daughter to the superior academic level that they believed she deserved. Her mother took her to local youth and sports clubs and encouraged her to interact with children her own age, but the children who attended all went to the same school and had already formed their own impenetrable cliques. Even though they were all quite nice to her, Agnes never felt like she really fitted in and would stand awkwardly on the sidelines or sometimes hide until her mother came to pick her up in her battered old green Saab.

That's not to say she didn't have any friends at all. There was always Theo, her best friend and constant companion. Theo didn't much like the cold weather so tended to stay indoors and cook strange foods for her that shouldn't go together, like eggs and spaghetti or herring and fruitcake. He helped her clean the house and made terrible puns in halting Swedish.

He sat next to Agnes during her lessons with her mother, at the end of the bathtub every evening and sang strange songs to her as she drifted off to sleep. The songs had no words or tunes but a mellifluous conflation of sounds and rhythm that never failed to send her off, to dream of strange mountains and oceans teeming with life so bizarre and wonderful that she could never find adequate words to describe them the next day.

Her parents were both doctors. Agnes believed that they were very important because one or the other would always be getting phone calls really late at night or early in the morning before breakfast and they would have to get dressed really quickly and give Agnes a quick cuddle before driving away in their respective old cars - the Saab for her mother and a dark blue Volvo estate for her father.

One time a helicopter had landed in the small garden behind the house. It was more of a clearing in the woods than a garden, with no boundaries or fences except the semi-circular tree-line. Her father had kissed her on her forehead before gathering up his briefcase under one arm and running to the waiting machine, his other arm crooked across his face as he ran underneath the rotor blades to the door. It lifted into the air, carrying her father away and clearing a perfectly circular area of the garden from snow. He didn't come home for four days.

She celebrated her eighth birthday in the small house and her party was attended by her mother, her father and Theo. She had cake and wore a new dress her mother had bought during a recent trip to Stockholm. It was yellow with purple flowers on it. Theo baked a weird cake and sang strange songs with no words and her parents had laughed and cheered as she had tried to join in. It was the last time Agnes could remember being happy.

Then her father came home one day and announced he had left his job at Stockholm General Hospital and would no longer need to stay there in the week, working all hours away from Agnes and her mother - and Theo of course, he said, smiling.

Her father started looking after them both, her and Theo. He taught her lessons instead of her mother and was much more patient at teaching and coaxing out the right answers from her. He took them both outside and taught them how to play football and hockey and golf, using a yellow ball so they wouldn't lose it in the snowdrifts.

During this time Agnes was happy, but with a low gnawing worried feeling in her tummy, like she had eaten bad herring, but worse. Her father was becoming visibly thinner and paler, his grey hair had started to thin and his teeth were yellow. He would run out of energy earlier every day.

He started to do fewer physical activities with her and Theo, concentrating on her schoolwork. Then gradually he stopped doing that too and could only listen to her reading out her essays and stories to him, which she loved because he would always cheer and laugh in the right places.

Lying in bed night after night, her light out and Theo sitting in a chair next to her bed, Agnes could hear her parents arguing, followed by one or both of them crying. During the arguments Theo would reach out and hold her hand.

One night she was woken by the noise of the helicopter overhead. It flew low over her house and she stumbled out of bed to her bedroom window, watching the machine set down in the garden, the split windscreen lit up in the darkness like the glowing eyes of a massive insect. This time two figures dressed in green overalls jumped down and came inside the house, carrying a stretcher between them. She ran downstairs in her pyjamas to see her father being carried out, a saline drip already plugged into his left arm and the rest of him under a red blanket. His eyes were half open and he smiled when he saw her. And then the kitchen back door was open and he had vanished into the dark and the cold. Her mother called out to him *'I'll see you tomorrow, I promise!'*

And then she hugged Agnes tightly and wept silent, hot tears that soaked through her nightgown.

In the morning Agnes was woken by the sound of the Saab's tyres scrunching through the ice down the long driveway to the road. She went downstairs in her pink pyjamas and warm furry slippers and found a note on the breakfast bar. Her mother would be gone for three days but the cupboards were full, the fridge and freezer well stocked. There was money in the porcelain jar shaped like *Bamse, the*

Worlds Strongest Bear. Their closest neighbour would check in on her twice a day.

'Well, Theo, we're on our own again,' she sighed.

She turned around, but her friend had vanished. She was alone.

PART NINE

JOSH

Fifteen years ago, once the double-whammy shock of the alien arrival and then the severing of the internet had sunk in, after the dark years of unrest, attempted revolution, anarchy, riots, protests and hubub, the human and Kin species had slowly begun to pull together and integrate, just as Marion and Adler had planned.

During that difficult time the economy, not only in the UK but around the world, had collapsed, and remained vulnerable. Once stable nations faced severe, unrepayable debt and unemployment figures reached catastrophic levels, more and more Kin taking up lower paid forms of labour and a huge chunk of the digital population left without any marketable skills.

Methods and forms of industry and communication, once thought artisan or retro in the first world, had been brought back into the mainstream and updated, streamlined and modernised, lead by poorer nations whose technology and infrastructure had not been so highly advanced when the Kin had landed.

Fifteen years on, the world operated on a much more level playing field than ever before, a feeling of planetary community prevailing where there was once complete fragmentation.

Now there was the spectre of a new, rebooted internet that the papers had dubbed a 'DarkNet,' a means to talk, commune, disseminate and broadcast information. After so long without it and with their situation once again so uncertain and volatile, Josh was worried and unnerved.

The world changed again one Wednesday evening. Josh arrived back at the cottage from the Shack and started to prepare his steamed broccoli and Thai fishcakes for one. He was looking forward to a bath and shaving his chest ready for Ezra's return. Ezra was on a night flight and would only arrive home in the early hours of Thursday morning. Morning sex was always the best.

At work, Josh had his hands full. It seemed like the Kin were everywhere. Every bed in the Shack was occupied, every nook and cranny of the temporary housing, even the old ship was filling up again. Adler had assigned him and all the other Shacks extra staff and budget, but Josh was well aware that all the budget in the world wasn't going to help if their numbers kept growing unchecked. They were working full time to house them, find them work, give them training, integrate them. Every Kin being processed through the Shacks was being issued an ID number and phototagged, noting each individual Kin's blue markings.

So far, they had all been receptive and open to the ID tagging scheme and it was cheaper than the tracking devices. They were making some progress, although Josh doubted that his team would get through them all. Classic recipe Kin were being allocated senior positions in the attempt to co-ordinate and integrate their new, now indigenous brethren. There were a very few still with active trackers. Josh desperately hoped for an anthropological answer to their problem, and soon. He didn't like the relocation idea at all.

Another problem they were starting to face was an increase in resistance to integration from some human quarters. Despite the positive Newsnight appearances of Crandall and Hennessy, since the Uzi Bitch Massacre and the broadcast of the video from the boy there were an increasing number of folk refusing to help the Kin.

He had no clue how volatile the situation actually was until he finished his lone meal that Wednesday evening and switched on the television. BBC News 24 was in his picture-in-picture on the top right of the screen as he scrolled down the list of channels, when the Breaking News ribbon and the excitable tones of the newscaster caught his attention.

He maximised the miniature screen and stared at the flickering images in front of him. At first he thought the reporter was standing in front of a hospital of some kind, but slowly realised it was the exterior of a Shack. No Shacks carried names or building numbers but as the camera pulled back he could see the towering black hulk of a Kin ship looming in the near distance. He could see ambulances parked haphazardly outside, dozens of newspaper and cameramen and hordes of public crowding around, including some Kin, all being kept back by police cordons.

A BBC Sweden reporter-on-scene was talking at the camera in perfect English.

'Outside the Shack in Gustavsberg, Sweden there is a large crowd forming, waiting for the Doctor to come out. She broadcast her operation live on the so-called 'DarkNet' but the results are as yet unknown as the connection was interrupted midway through her procedure. Quite a crowd has now gathered here, excited to know the outcome.'

Josh shuddered. *Excited to know the outcome.* The reporter didn't seem to understand the ramifications of his words. His phone rang.

'Dandridge?'

'It's me.'

'I know. Where are you?'

'I'm in Japan. The food here is amazing. You watching?'
Josh didn't need to ask to what he was referring to.'

'Yes, but I don't know what this Doctor is supposed to have done. Are they referring to Dr. Vikander? She's the Swedish Shack rep. And what are you doing in Japan?'

'Its a long story. Wait, they're showing more.'

Holding the phone to his ear they both went quiet as the reporter on screen cut to an image of a Doctor in surgical scrubs, in a medical facility identical to the one in the UK Shack. The red Breaking News ribbon now displayed the words 'WARNING. Disturbing Images.' Josh's heart sank, it was indeed Dr. Vikander, the head of one of two Swedish shacks and in his opinion a dedicated, intelligent woman. In the footage she was standing over an operating table. On the table lay an unconscious man, naked save for a green sheet folded neatly across his groin. He was rail thin, ribs standing out like a flesh coloured xylophone, his head mostly bald with a few grey wispy strands hanging on here and there. There was a dark lesion on his scalp. His head was held securely by a neck brace.

On a gurney next to him lay a Kin. It wasn't possible to tell if it was conscious or not but its markings were bright blue, so Josh knew it was at least alive.

The Doctor was talking to the camera in Swedish, but the news channel had helpfully added subtitles.

'The Kin displays no emotion and no real resistance,' he read as she talked. *'I have administered a massive dose of Midazolam, which I believe has had the desired effect. This doseage would keep a human being under sedation for around six hours and woozy for another three. Of course, due to the lack of adequate research into Kin physiology there is no way to measure the creature's responsiveness to the drug and so I must begin immediately and hope it is adequately sedated. We do know that Kin have no veins or blood flow as such. In order to withdraw its essence one needs to either remove a section and exert*

pressure on it like a sponge or make a deep incision and squeeze either side to encourage the travel of matter.'

There was an edit in the video, a hard cut by the news channel, the next shot showing blue-gloved hands covered in human blood. The man lying on the medical bed was now mainly covered with a blue cloth, a small hole in it exposing only the area around the removed lesion. There was a drip in his arm. The Doctor was lifting the Kin's arm up over his head and making an incision in its side. The flesh must have been tougher than she was expecting as she had to saw a little harder. She was still talking.

'The flesh is very leathery. The smell is pungent, but quite pleasant, quite sweet. Here we go.' She had removed a disk of flesh from the side of the Kin about the same size as the hole in the size of the man's head. She took the meat and placed it in the hole, pushing in the edges with her fingers like she was crimping pastry, before bandaging it over.

'Are you seeing this?' Dandridge asked on the other end of the phone.

'Yes,' Josh replied, dumbly.

'What the fuck is she doing?'

'Ssshh,' Josh said as the woman continued.

'Due to the progressed stage of the disease, my husband is no longer able to ingest any liquids or solids orally. I do not have time to extract enough blood from the Kin to create a drip mechanism into his veins. My hope is that direct contact of the Kin flesh directly against the tumour will trigger-' then the screen went dark, and it cut back to the newscaster.

'And that's where the video was cut off. The Doctor has barricaded herself and her husband into the medical facility here at the Shack and refuses to communicate with police. We are expecting a statement soon. This is Karl Winberg, BBC News from Gustavsberg.'

The image cut back to the studio where the news anchor briefly moved onto another story. Josh muted the channel.

'We are in big trouble,' he said.

'Only if the Kin flesh actually does anything.'

'We kind of know that it does, don't we? It protected the crash survivors, healed their injuries.'

'Yes, but they ingested it. That woman's poor husband only has it stuffed into his noggin.'

'Fuck.'

'Where's Perron?'

'I'm Perron now too, you know. He's on his return flight now. Back in the morning.'

'You want me to stay?'

'Yes please.'

They talked into the night as the rolling news kept rolling. There was no movement from the Shack in Sweden and at some point in the early morning Josh fell asleep.

He woke up on the sofa early the next morning with the phone still tucked behind his ear. He could hear gentle taps and breathing at the other end of the line.

'You still there?' he asked.

'Where else would I be? Just doing some work. You slept for a few hours, which is good. Big day today.'

'Didn't you?'

'Nope. I only sleep a few hours a week. I just don't seem to need it so much these days.'

'A few hours a *week*? That's not normal, Dandridge.'

'I know, but lots of things aren't particularly normal right now, and my sleeping habits are the least of them. I've been able to work across both the social problem from here and the relocation issue remotely. Trying to convince an entire nation and its inhabitants to agree to a plan to allow the Kin to completely take over their country is probably the least normal thing in my life. The Aussies have been great, but are a proud, stubborn bunch indeed. But you know what's even weirder? I reckon they might actually come around to the idea.'

'Dandridge, I've got to get to the Shack. And oh crap, I've got about twelve missed calls from Ez.'

'Off you go then. Call me if you need to, and Josh-'
'Yeah?'
'Excuse the cliché, but please be careful.'

Josh hit the red handset button and cut the call off. He climbed the stairs to get showered and changed for the day. Then his doorbell rang and he looked out of the hall window to see three or four news vans in the driveway, doors open, dozens of men with cameras and microphones clambering out.

MIKE

He knew that their relationship was doomed. He knew it even as he gripped her hair and pulled her head back with one hand and a handful of her left buttock with the other, squeezing so hard he left deep red marks on her skin, hearing her gasp in pain and then moan as he sucked her exposed neck, both of them covered in the sweat of intense physical exercise. He knew that they were using each other, trying to forget the pain of their condition and avoid facing up to their mutual withdrawal from the effects of the Kin flesh - but right now, he didn't really care.

They were in her quarters at Whitehall, in her narrow bunk in the middle of the afternoon, having sex for the third time that day. He felt her shudder as she climaxed, her legs drawn up tightly around his hips, her fingers finding their way to her clitoris and rubbing herself to prolong her pleasure. He ground himself into her towards the building crest of his own orgasm. He started to fuck her hard and fast, the familiar orgasmic pressure building in his balls. His rhythm increased to meet it but as he felt himself beginning to tip over the edge it danced away from him, hovering just out of his reach no matter how hard he fucked her. He pulled out and turned her over and she raised herself onto all fours to meet him. He entered her from behind and carried on fucking her, his hips pistoning back and forth as he desperately chased the come that he was owed.

Marion urged him on but now he could tell that she was only waiting for him to finish, so he pulled out again and lay down next to her on the bed. He was still hard and there was no indication that his erection was going away any time soon. His face was flushed as red as his penis, twitching against his belly like a twanging harp string.

'You can carry on, I don't mind.'

'No. We tried that already, I don't want to hurt you. I just don't understand what's going on. I've been unable to get it up before when I was drinking, but this. I'm hard, I'm horny, the sex is great, I just can't seem to... finish.'

'It's OK. You have no idea how many times I've had sex and not come. We've swapped roles, apparently.'

'Thanks a lot.'

'Mike, we're both in a really strange place emotionally and it's messing with our minds, that's all.'

'I know. I'm really sorry.'

'Don't be, I came twice.' Marion stood up and padded naked to her en-suite, closing the door behind her. Mike began to masturbate, closing his eyes and picturing them both on the mountain, covered with the white flesh as completely as two pieces of raw battered fish ready for the fryer. He had been so confident of his own prowess, able to have amazing sex even in a life-threatening situation and surrounded by strangers. He remembered what it felt like to fuck in the pool of the Kin flesh and he gasped, his legs drawing up, his left hand squeezing his balls and his body arching as he came across his stomach and chest.

Marion came out of the bathroom with toilet roll and cleaned him up. They lay together for a few minutes more.

'Come on,' she said. 'We've got an interview tonight on Channel 4 News. We have to get ready.'

Two hours later, they were in light makeup and sitting behind the newsreader's desk, holding hands.

'Marion, the two of you have done some real campaigning lately, are you afraid that the Kin situation is getting out of hand?' the older, greyer distinguished newsreader was asking.

Marion smiled brightly at him. 'Jon, the reason we have been on everyone's screens so much is two-fold. Firstly, to address the issue of Dr. Vikander's illegal video and also to reassure everyone that there is no so-called 'Kin' situation. We are all as keen to integrate and house the Kin as we ever were.'

'But you must have noticed that numbers of Kin are

visibly increasing. No Shack has yet released a statement with any population figures or where they might be housed or employed in the long term.'

'When it comes to work and housing the Shacks all operate within the framework of local government infrastructure. I am sure that each of them-'

'But they all report to you,' he interrupted, waving his pen at her.

'No, they report to Josh Perron, my successor at Shack One.'

'And Perron isn't saying anything either.'

'What would you *like* us to say, Jon?' Mike cut in. 'What assurances would you like?'

'I just want the truth, Mr Hennessy. We all do.'

'The truth about what? There has been no deception. Nothing has changed. The UK Government, which was at the forefront of negotiations between species, has been 100% transparent with regard to planning and integration. It was part of the manifesto. No secrets. To live peaceably we can't afford to keep anything hidden, or secret. We're all in this together - politician, plumber or student. Man woman and child. It is vital that human and Kin find a way to co-exist or one or both of us runs the risk of extinction.'

Mike had said too much and the newsroom seemed to have gone quieter than usual. 'Can you elaborate, Mr Hennessy?' the newscaster asked.

'What I mean is that yes, there's a lot of us sharing a small space that's only getting smaller. That's obvious to everyone. This means we have to put aside our own natural human inclination for personal empire building. It's not *our* house, *our* garden, *our* field, or *our* country any more. It must all be shared, and we need to begin thinking better and broader.'

'Perhaps, but now we should address the next issue, which is that the Kin contain some kind of natural, addictive ingredient that seems capable of curing human ailments.'

'No they don't.'

'No? Graham Vikander-'

'-still has inoperable brain cancer.'

'Smaller, more treatable. His life has potentially been extended by five years or more. You both survived a plane crash hundreds of miles from anywhere. Buddy Tucker's broken arm healed itself.'

'We don't know any of that for sure.'

'Apparently not, but I find it hard to believe that in all the time we have been here, we have not been able to conduct any tests-'

'Tests?' Marion interrupted. 'They aren't animals, Jon. We haven't bred their species for cattle. They are sentient beings and more intelligent than us. Do we have the technology to build vast ships and travel through space for decades? No, we don't. They don't want or deserve to be treated like animals. We may be the incumbent species but we aren't the dominant one any more. Like it or not, they are more than our equal and if we don't start showing them some kind of respect then-'

'-then what, Marion?' the newscaster asked gently. 'Then what?'

'I don't know. But they aren't just going to sit around politely and let us violate them for their supposed healing flesh.'

'No?'

'No. Would you?'

LUKE

Luke lay on his mattress in the basement watching the interview with Mike and Marion. Like a lot of basements there was a washing machine and a tumble dryer, but unlike a lot of basements there was also a full-size flight simulator, a boxing ring, a snooker table and a large bar recreated to look like a tiny seventies nightclub complete with a disco dance floor, glitterballs and full sound system. Five or six classic arcade machines were placed around the walls. There was a 70-inch plasma screen showing broadcast channels he had no idea even existed. Luke's mattress was pushed against a wall between one side of the flight simulator and an ancient video arcade machine garishly advertising a fully realised Q-Bert character painted on the side that bore no resemblance to the pixelated blob that was actually playable on the screen. The basement was massive, a gigantic space underneath a huge country mansion owned by the late Henderson Mulcahy.

A few seconds after Buddy Tucker had been shot, the PA had burst into the mysteriously now unlocked room. She was still in the silver dress and heels, still stunning. She had cast her wide liquid-brown eyes around the carnage before stopping at Luke and the injured Kin. The boy held a smoking gun and the Kin was knelt next to him. The agent was on the floor, groaning and holding his leaking belly. She had ignored both of them and taken the boy's hand, leading him to a hidden service elevator. She didn't say a single word as the lift car descended. The doors slid open to reveal a short concrete corridor before another set of security-locked double doors, which clicked open automatically as she approached them. She pushed through into an underground car park. The cars parked in a neat row along one wall obviously belonged to Henderson; a Lamborghini Aventador, a Pagani Zonda, an Aston Martin One-77, a Koeniggsegg, a McLaren 650 and more. Nella ignored all of these and ran towards an old, nondescript silver Honda SUV in one corner.

'Get in,' she demanded and Luke complied, slightly disappointed he wouldn't get to ride in one of the hypercars. Nella started the engine and pulled out of the car park, struggling for a second to release a device from her large silver Aspinal clutch bag, and entering a code on it when it finally came free. She placed it on the dashboard and drove into the Central London night.

They drove for hours. Luke fell asleep, his head resting against the glass, only waking up as she thrashed the Honda along some pitch-black country lanes. The snatches of countryside he could see as they sped past did not offer any clues as to their whereabouts. After another half an hour the girl swung the car off the road and up an unmade dirt track. The tyres slid and bounced in two deep, muddy ruts slightly too wide for the wheelbase.

As they jostled and bounced along Luke stared at the girl's breasts barely contained in the thin silver dress until she glared at him sharply and he looked back at the track, blushing. The track lead to an enormous house that to Luke looked ancient, red-brick and flint walls covered in ivy and weeds. The window frames were all sash windows that looked as if they had never been replaced or repaired.

'Nice house,' Luke remarked.

'It belonged to Henderson. We'll be staying here for a while, until we can regroup.'

'They'll find us. They'll have followed us all the way here. CCTV is everywhere.'

She picked up the black box from the dashboard. 'No they won't. This device blocks all camera signals. You are hidden, my friend. Nobody knows where you are. Let's go in so I can get changed and I'll make us tea. Then you can tell me what the fuck just happened and why half of Henderson's head is decorating the walls.' Her voice was low and soft, throaty with a low rasp.

'Who are you?' Luke asked as she opened the car door.

'I'm Nella Monroe, Henderson's PA,' she said and stepped out, slamming the door behind her. Luke followed.

Half an hour later she was dressed in a white velour tracksuit and the kettle was whistling. The tracksuit clung to her figure and her hair remained in a perfectly glossy, spherical afro. Luke was telling her exactly what had happened. 'And then, Buddy tried to grab the gun, and... it... it just went off. It's not my fault.'

Nella was quiet, pouring the hot water through a loose-leaf tea strainer into two mugs and adding milk. She handed him one.

'OK, Luke,' she said finally. 'Let's go and sit down. You have a shitload of talking to do.'

She sat very close to him on the same sofa. She smelled glorious, of sweat mixed with citrus fruit. Luke's head started to spin.

It was late again when he finished and dark outside the old house. Rather than the abbreviated version of events he had hurriedly told Henderson while Buddy and Royce were arguing in the next room, he told her everything; the crash, the days on the mountain, the Kin, the rescue, his life since coming home. Before he knew it he was telling her about the cutting, and when she showed real concern for him he even showed her the most recent cuts and his scars.

When he finished, she sized him up for a few seconds.

'OK, first things first, everyone needs to know about how you got off the mountain. We're supposed to live in a world with complete honesty and transparency, so let's get this out there. Who knows what else they're not telling us.'

'How?'

He still had the tablet device taken from Henderson. She reached across him and slid it out of his inside pocket.

'With this.'

So he had told the story once again, but this time into a small camera. Once he was done, Nella dragged and hauled a mattress from a spare room down the stairs into the massive basement.

'Better off you stay down here, just in case,' she explained. 'If anyone does come around I can lock the door and there's a passage out of here into the woods behind the house if we need it.'

'Where?' he asked, but she wouldn't show him and over the next few days he couldn't find it for love nor money.

After he had made the first video she had left him alone in the basement, the door at the top of the stairs clicking shut behind her. He examined the door thoroughly. It had a flat steel locking plate and no handle. He was locked in, a prisoner in the most extravagant prison in the world. There was a vending machine full of crisps and snacks and a water cooler and that was it. Luke felt a brief flash of anger, but was too tired to expend energy on extended emotional outbursts, so he set about settling himself in.

Nella didn't return for three days, during which time he witnessed himself becoming the biggest news story on the planet. He watched the video of himself across every single television channel for hour after hour, hearing his own story related back to him dozens of times and analysed for days, each word picked open and examined for any possible intended permutation or inflection. He was too young to remember life with the internet but now began to realise how powerful it could be.

After a while he had to stop watching television altogether, so sick of seeing and hearing his own face and voice.

Nella returned to him clutching a greasy bag with two bacon and fried egg sandwiches. She wore the same figure-hugging white velour tracksuit but now it was dirty and grey around the sleeves and cuffs. He grabbed the bag of food from her and began stuffing his face.

'Where did you get this? Aren't the police looking for you?' he asked her through a mouthful, spraying bread and bacon crumbs.

'I turned myself in once I left you. I'm so sorry it took so long. I have been interviewed for the last 36 hours straight, but there's no evidence I was at the scene. I told them I left after I showed you up to Henderson's office. I'm a suspect but so far there's nothing they can hold me on.'

'So why are you keeping me here?'

'Luke, we need you because you were there, right at the beginning. You are the most useful asset we have. You've seen first hand what the Kin does to people.'

'Have I? The beginning of what?'

'The beginning of a new era of enlightenment.'

He could feel himself starting to panic, even as he took the last mouthful of sandwich.

'Oh god, I'm not sure, Nella, this... I'm just a kid. I don't know what my being here can do to help anyone. I'm not an asset.'

'You can help more than you think, Luke. You're not just a kid anymore. People know who you are, what you went through. You're all over the news and people identify with you.'

'I'm really sorry, I think I have to go to the police. I didn't do anything wrong and I promise I won't say anything about you-'

'No, Luke. This is bigger than you, bigger than me, and bigger than Henderson. It's a tragedy what happened to him and to Royce but Henderson had a plan and I'm sticking to it.'

'He had a plan? For what? And it included me? Please, Nella, I've been here for nearly a week. I just want to go home-'

'Home? Where's your home, Luke? Where do you live exactly, except with me?' Nella Monroe reached around herself and pulled off her tracksuit top. She wasn't wearing a bra. She smelt of acrid sweat, a reminder she had just been released from police custody. Luke didn't care, he didn't smell any better. She took one of his trembling hands and placed his open palm against the dark brown nipple of one of her small, immaculate breasts. The entire centre of his universe suddenly compressed inwards to the feeling of his hand pressed against her. At that moment the Kin might never have existed.

With his palm still against her, she hooked her thumbs over the waistband of her dirty white tracksuit bottoms and slowly wriggled them down and over her hips before stepping demurely out of them. Still no underwear.

'It's time you showed me how much of a man you really are,' she said. She was ripe, sweaty and unwashed, but Luke didn't notice, his breath caught in his throat, his gaze welded to her perfect, trim body.

Afterwards, before his breathing had even returned to normal, Nella took the remote from the floor beside the mattress and flicked on the huge television. There was another breaking news item at a televised press conference just starting. Luke had begun to doze off as his breathing slowed but he opened his eyes and sat bolt upright. Seated at a long table facing the cameras were a number of people he recognised, including the Government guy Adler and Marion Crandall. Between them sat his step-mother.

JENNIFER

She dreamt about her mother's house where she had spent her childhood; a normal semi-detached suburban home like so many others. She was in her bedroom but it was crowded, filled with people she didn't recognise, strangers, densely packed, standing room only. She fought towards her bed, wanting only to sleep, but the crowd was too dense and it took her ages to push her way through them. She saw that the bed was dirty and unmade and more strangers were having sex on her quilt, the quilt her grandmother had made for her sixth birthday. One of the people having sex only had half a head and was oozing grey brain matter onto her pillow. The other was rotten and decomposing, strips of grey flesh hanging grotesquely from the skeletal frame. She gagged and tried to get out of the room but the people kept blocking her way and pushing her back towards the copulating corpses. Her stomach cramped and she threw up on the thin rug that covered the old lacquered floorboards, now covered in muddy, snowy footprints.

She stared at her vomit on the rug and it parted like it was a T-1000 but made of vomit and not liquid metal, or a tiny vomit-filled red-sea and she was Moses, revealing a design woven into the rug that she had never noticed before. It was a recurring motif among the intricate paisley vinescroll design and looked a lot like a face. A face she recognised - the face of her second husband James. For a second her heart filled to bursting with desperate loneliness, but loneliness that was somehow comforting, a loneliness that she could live with and cry with and sometimes curse at the top of her voice, loneliness that she never wanted to leave her. But the loneliness turned to hate as she realised that the face in the rug wasn't James at all, but the boy. And then it moved, all the faces on the rug, thousands of them, all staring at her and sticking their tongues out at her, intricately woven tongues in the finest pink silk. She screamed. The crowd had vanished and she was alone in her room at last, but now she only wanted to get out. She took long running steps to get off the rug, to avoid walking anywhere near the awful faces but no matter how fast she ran she couldn't reach the door. She was running in place, faster and faster, the rug coiling up behind her as she pushed it backwards with her feet, legs pistoning in place like Wily E Coyote just before he discovers he has run off the edge of the cliff. Soon the coiled rug was a towering wall and it collapsed downwards on top of her. Thousands of tiny pink silky tongues from thousands of faces of the leering boy started to lap at her from the folds of the crushingly heavy fabric. She let out another scream of horror and tried desperately to claw her way out of the rug prison.

She screamed and screamed and screamed and then her eyes opened and she was staring into the faces of two concerned doctors and a nurse, all gently trying to calm her down as she fought her way out of the madness. There was another man wearing a dark suit standing behind them. There was a drip in her arm, and straps around her ankles, wrists and chest.

A nurse gently tipped a plastic cup of water to her lips. She took a sip.

'Where am I? she croaked.

'Safe. A hospital, back in London.'

'Where's–' she stopped, a look of confusion passing across her face. '–where's Luke?'

Adler stepped forward.

'He's fine,' he said. 'You've been through a lot, we can talk properly in a while. Take your time.'

'The baby–'

'–is fine too. Let the Doctors look after you. Relax.'

Adler went to get a coffee from a machine while her vitals were taken and she slowly came round. When he returned some colour had started to return to her cheeks.

'You're Adler, right?'

'Right.'

'Why are you here? And more to the point, why am I?'

'You had a bit of a turn, Jenny.'

'Jennifer.'

'Jennifer then. A lot has happened and I need to fill you in. It's going to be a lot to handle all at once, for which I apologise, but I have no choice. We need your help.'

'My help? How long have I-'

'About four months or so.'

Jennifer closed her eyes and breathed out slowly, feeling and holding her new baby bump. 'Jesus. What happened to me?'

'You had a breakdown of some kind. To best protect your child and because you were still under the influence of the Kin flesh a decision was taken to keep you sedated. Nobody knows how long the Kin stays in your system, if indeed it ever leaves.'

'You know? About the Kin?'

'Yes, I do. Unfortunately so does everyone else. But the reason I'm here is because of Luke.'

A dark cloud passed briefly across her face at the mention of his name.

'Luke has been involved in a multiple homicide that has resulted in the deaths of Royce Brims, Buddy Tucker, Henderson Mulcahy and a Kin.'

Jennifer's face turned from grey to white and tears sprung to her eyes. Her hand covered her mouth as she fought them back. 'Is he OK?'

'We don't know. He's gone, vanished. We don't know where. We need you to help us prise him out of wherever he's hiding.'

'I don't understand. Where could he have gone? He's only a boy.'

'There is an increasingly large community of people who are trying to rid the world of Kin. Either rid them or use them somehow. It was spearheaded by Henderson Mulcahy, the now-deceased music mogul, and is gathering momentum. The individuals concerned are all over the world and can coordinate through a new, limited form of the internet that Mulcahy developed. We think that Luke is with some of them.'

'This is too much, Adler. I don't want to know any of this. I never want to see Luke again.'

'I know. My apologies.' Adler got up to leave, making to put on his jacket.

Jennifer sighed. 'Why do they want the Kin removed?'

Adler sat down again. 'It's hard to pin down any one reason. The combination of fewer jobs for humans, fewer housing options, lack of space, house prices forced up, a fluctuating economy and the fact that Kin numbers appear to be growing rapidly. There's a train of thought that wants us to kill them for food. There's some fundamentalism in there of course, folk who believe that they are representatives of the devil sent to destroy us, despite not a single Kin ever having said or done a bad thing to us. On the flip-side of that, there is also a cult that lives on a decommissioned oil-rig out in the North Sea who worship them as Gods.'

'What do you believe?'

It was Adler's turn to sigh, and he passed his hand across his face, suddenly feeling very tired.

'I feel like I've lived with them all my life, even though its only been the last fifteen years. My instinct tells me that no, they aren't the devil. They are what they appear to be, just a lost species trying to fit in and as confused and worried as we are, so I guess I side with the folk on the oil rig. It's just-'

'What?'

'We've had it our own way for so long. Things can't change overnight. We knew it, but hoped that some compromise could be reached. I don't think we're going to share the earth quite as willingly as I had perhaps hoped.'

Adler filled her in on the Kin mating instinct, how their numbers grew when one of them died. He told her about Marion and Mike's confession on TV, and about the plans to move the Kin to their own territory while they conducted the sociology study.

'How many people know about these plans?'

'A few people, not many.'

'So why are you telling me?'

'I need your help, and I figured you'd better have all the facts upfront.'

'So what do you want me to do?'

A day later, she walked out from a plain blue ante-room at Whitehall into a huge press hall and sat down behind a long table between Adler and Marion Crandall, staring at a bank of camera lenses so dense that they resembled the face of a giant cybernetic insect.

Above and behind the lenses was a large crowd of people. She could only really make out the first couple of rows, but they all looked simultaneously worried and excited, like a group of schoolchildren unexpectedly called to the Headmaster's office. Her name was printed on a small folded cardboard printout facing the photographers. Microphones pointed at her face. She sat silently until the low hum of voices went suddenly quiet. She looked around and saw that the Prime Minister and new Deputy Prime Minister, formerly the Minister for Kin and Human Relations Nile Cody, had just come out of the anteroom and taken the last two seats. She had not known they were going to be there, there was no name tag in front of their places. The PM began to talk, and suddenly, she was terrified. She placed her hand protectively over her pregnancy bump.

'I'm not going to beat around the bush as there's a lot to cover today and we don't have much time,' the PM began. 'I am here with the blessing of the world's governing body,

NATO and the United Nations. The President of the United States is holding a press conference simultaneously to go over the issues that are threatening to derail our world. What we are about to say has been discussed at length with the Royal Family, the US Congress and the United Nations. As you know, Prime Minister's Questions are televised every week and the issues discussed reported in the press the following day. For the last month or so, plans have been moving ahead with regard to our relationship with the Kin, but have been left off the agenda for PMQs as we needed to fully understand the facts and begin some extremely delicate negotiations without risk of being misunderstood or misreported. I am asking for your forgiveness for this - I know that we all promised complete transparency with regard to our new friends, but certain events have come to light and we needed to assimilate all the facts and reach a considered opinion before sharing our findings and decisions with you. Here today, we have Marion Crandall and Ernest Adler, first contactors and originators of the manifesto of Human and Kin relations. Also, we have Jennifer McDonald, also a crash survivor and step-mother to the missing boy who we believe to be involved in the murder of Henderson Mulcahy and others. Jennifer.'

The room went silent, and with a crashing feeling in the pit of her stomach and a sudden roaring in her ears, Jennifer realised that they were waiting for her to speak. She leaned forward towards the black sponge-y microphone cover.

'Hello,' she started nervously, the camera lenses staring at her. Her mind had filled with the image of herself as a younger woman, wearing a summer dress and sitting on the kerb outside her old flat, surrounded by a few suitcases of clothes and some supermarket boxes of her meagre belongings, waiting for the love of her life to pull up in his fancy car and whisk her away to her new life. Tears sprang to her eyes.

'Jennifer, are you OK to continue?' asked the Prime Minister. She nodded, using a handkerchief that Adler had given her earlier to wipe away the tears.

'I'm here only to ask Luke to get in touch with me. He's a good boy who's had a rough time and I want to make sure he's safe and well. Luke, you don't have to come home if you don't want to but just let me know you're OK, please. And if you don't want to then that's your choice, but please listen to what everyone is going to say today and consider again afterwards.'

She stopped talking, and a voice called out from a few rows back in the room, 'Ms McDonald, please could you tell us who-'

'No questions until the end please,' barked Adler, and the room went quiet, although Jennifer knew exactly what the reporter was going to ask. The paternity of her child would remain a secret, although she was a pretty terrible liar at the best of times, and this was not the best of times.

The Prime Minister was talking again, and in brief bulletpoints he told the world everything they knew to date about the Kin, the same facts Adler had told Jennifer the previous day. There had been rumours and wild speculation, but now it was out, and official. The room seemed almost sickly quiet as the implication of what the Prime Minister was saying hit home. He concluded by confirming that the rumours in the conspiracy papers about relocating the Kin lock stock and barrel to Australia were true and moving forward. Jennifer sensed the quiet turning in a heartbeat from sickly to stunned.

'Are you fucking *kidding* me?' shouted a voice from the middle of the room, a voice that sounded very Australian. 'What about the fucking *Australians*? Do they get a say?'

'Who is this?' asked the PM.

'Steven Hammersley, *the World Today*.'

'Ah, the *World Today*. How lovely to have you here,' said the PM with some sarcasm, 'it is good to know that the conspiracy rags are represented.'

'We're all here mate, all of us. We're the only ones asking the right questions lately. How far along is this plan to turn Australia back into a fucking penal colony?'

'Mr Hammersley, we have no intention of turning Australia into anything. The space is big enough to accommodate-'

'Bullshit, mate. *Bullshit.* You want rid of the problem.'

'Absolutely not, quite the opposite. In order for us to live equably we need to stop thinking in terms of us and them, not just human and Kin but English, Australian, Russian, Arab, French, every nationality together. For a viable global economy of course we need to retain borders, boundaries, trade. Local customs and laws should be practised of course, but in every other way have to start seeing things in a much wider scope. It's hard for everyone, including me, but we need to try. Or start trying.'

'They're going to over-run us eventually,' another voice from the crowd, sounding panicked.

'As I said, we're working to resolve the issue so their population is controlled and understood.'

'And if you can't?'

'We can.'

The room erupted in a cacophony of shouting voices and Jennifer sat terrified behind the desk. It took about ten minutes for the room to quiet down to a level where individual questions could be asked.

'Prime Minister, Jacqueline Worthy, *The Empirical*. What about the healing properties of the Kin? Is there any way to utilise the Kin to help sick and dying humans?'

'No,' Nile Cody cut in, 'the flesh is not proven to help anything and as we have seen can have fundamentally life altering side-effects. It's not an option.'

'It was an option for Dr. Vikander. Her husband is recovering,' Worthy said, to murmured agreements.

'Her husband is not recovering. He still has inoperable

brain cancer. Ms. Worthy - everyone - this is not a court for us to defend our decisions. We have made choices, hard choices, after more hours of debate and research than you can possibly comprehend. We have experts, specialists, survivors, think-tanks, you name it. We are going to make this happen and make it work. We are going to secure a future for all of us, human and Kin, and we'll do it properly and transparently. You owe the people to report this honestly, impartially and not to believe everything you hear or see on the DarkNet. There's a lot of white noise out there. Don't be fooled and don't be swayed. Everything we do is for the good of this planet, because if we fail-' Cody fell silent and so did the room.

'Thank you Deputy Prime Minister. Everyone, we'll reconvene another Press Conference in a month and we will update everyone on progress and developments.'

Jennifer felt herself sighing with relief that it was all over. But it wasn't of course, not really.

PART TEN

DANDRIDGE

Megan Sasha-Meyer, an English socio-cultural and ethno-anthropologist, picked Dandridge up at Japan's Narita airport and immediately disliked him. During the drive to her compound he came across as flippant and self absorbed to the point of narcissism, even rude. She was disappointed; she had hoped that the man who had made first contact with the Kin would be slightly more open and approachable.

Chichibu was a busy, industrious city surrounded by mountains and rivers. For the last fifteen years the towering and ever-present Kin ship had loomed over the inhabitants of the city from a landing site in Chichibu National Park. Megan had been living and working in Chichibu since graduating from Bath University with a doctorate in Ethnology with Social Psychology and Anthropology five years ago, immersing herself in the life and habits of a large group of Kin employed by the city to keep public gardens and shrines clean and attended. Most of the Kin from their ship had been employed by the city or surrounding areas in some capacity in return for decent accommodation and a small wage. It was the most successful Kin integration so far, widely copied by other countries. However, the numbers had been increasing and the city was unable to employ all the Kin, most of whom had moved away to other areas.

She had moved in with a small group of the Kin so she could include herself in their routines and engage with them more closely, studying the blue markings, comparing whorls and patterns, interviewing them to find out more about their home planet and lifestyle. They were all different, but certain similarities had started to become apparent to her.

There had been four Kin sharing with Megan Sasha-Meyer in the compound when Dandridge had been introduced to them. Now there were six.

During his first night as he lay dozing on the living room floor in a sleeping bag, he sensed movement through the thin walls and felt a change in the atmosphere of the small building. He recognised what was happening immediately, but he shut his eyes against the movement and worked to calm his heartbeat and suppress the fascination and desire that had started to trample through his nervous system. He heard heavier footsteps in the house and knew that Megan was watching the Kin reproduction process. If he hadn't seen and experienced it for himself he might have joined her. On the downside, this meant that another one of them had died, and the Kin population had just gone up by more than a few million.

He mulled over these things as he lay there, now fully awake. Then the thin door slid silently aside in the waxed wooden runner and Megan stood there in a dressing gown.

'Have you seen this before?' she whispered.

'Yes,' he answered, closing his eyes again. 'They're reproducing again. One of them must have died somewhere.'

She went away again but returned twenty minutes later, flushed with excitement. 'Are you awake?'

'No.'

'They've just made another two Kin. It was amazing, remarkable. They let me get up close. It was the most fascinating thing I've ever seen.'

'No shit.'

Megan dropped her dressing gown to the floor and slid naked into the sleeping bag beside Dandridge. 'How old are you?' she asked him.

'Hasn't anyone ever told you it's rude to ask an old man his age? What are you doing, Megan? You need to get out of here and go to bed.'

'Dandridge, I haven't had sex for three years but I want it now more than I ever have. You are *so* in luck. To be honest I don't really like you that much, but you are quite handsome, for an older guy.' She gripped his penis as it hardened in her hand.

'That's very nice of you to say Megan, but I'm gay. I don't want to have sex with you. Please stop.'

'You don't *feel* gay,' she said, squeezing him.

'How do you know what 'feeling' gay is? The fact you've made my penis sit up and take notice is irrelevant. I'm not kidding, I really am gay. I like cock. Almost as much as you, apparently.'

She let him go. 'Seriously?'

'Seriously. But Megan, I know what you are experiencing. I've felt it too. I *am* feeling it. The Kin have an affect on humans, some kind of pheromone released during their reproductive act. The Kin affects us all in different ways. You're an incredibly intelligent, independent, gorgeous woman, probably twenty-five at most and yet completely ready to jump into bed with me, a man twice your age who you met about three hours ago, a man you claim to not even like. Under any normal circumstances I'm the last man you'd break your three year sex-fast with.

What's that all about anyway?'

She flushed a deep red. 'I'm sorry, I'll go.' Tears sprang to her eyes.

'I didn't say you had to go. You can stay here with me.'

'Make your mind up. Do you want me or not?'

'Not. But I want you to stay. You look upset and I need to keep my mind occupied.'

'OK. Just for a bit.' She fell silent and within the confines of the sleeping bag shrank away and tried not to make physical contact with him.

Then they started to talk, and the more they talked, the more they both relaxed until she was snuggled up against him for extra warmth, coyness and inhibitions forgotten.

'We need to break the reproductive cycle but it's not easy to identify a common sociological trait within a species we barely understand,' she murmured into his shoulder. 'And now I feel so under pressure. The government guy didn't tell me anything when he called. I had no idea I was now part of a plan to save the world.'

'Adler is a man of economical vocabulary when it suits him. Still, he found you and as usual he's right. You are the man for the job. As it were.'

'I'm not so sure. It's not a quick fix.'

'The short term plan will have to go into effect first and we'll buy a decade or so. I reckon we can crack it, if we're left alone. I hope people believe we're doing all we can.'

They talked into the night snuggled up warm next to each other. Dandridge told her of his car crash on Day One and breaking his back, his affair with Belle, how he first realised how and when they reproduced.

'I wonder how this latest one died. Let's try and find out.' Megan wriggled out of the sleeping bag and ran naked to her room, returning with a small rectangular tablet. She had pulled on some blue silk pyjamas. She handed the tablet to him as she wriggled back down into the sleeping bag.

'Holy shit, where did you get this?' Dandridge asked.

'It's illegal. And where's the 'on' button?'

'God, you are old. This is Japan, you can get pretty much anything you want.

She booted it up and typed some characters on the screen. 'There's only a limited number of feeds at the moment and most are really basic, although more are appearing every day. The news feeds are where most videos are posted.' The black screen glowed with green writing and she scrolled down and selected one of the listings. The display was replaced by a plain white screen with a list of dates down one side, most recent first, with subjects and file sizes down the right side. There was a video uploaded at the top with some editorial beneath it. She hit the small 'play' icon underneath the video and it maximised across the small screen.

It was shaky handheld footage that looked as if it was taken from inside a bush, with lots of background rustling and whispering, although the actual video quality was good. It was night-time and the two figures featured in front of the camera were both shushing the cameraman. They were wearing balaclavas.

Dandridge picked up his phone and dialled Adler, but got only a busy tone.

On the screen, the men had burst into a suburban home, terrorising the young family inside and forcing them to their knees at shotgun-point. They were young average-looking parents with two young daughters neither older than five. Both the father and the mother placed themselves protectively between the intruders and their daughters as they sobbed and begged for mercy for their children. Dandridge reckoned from the accents among the shouting and confusion that they were somewhere in the United States.

Then one of the men and the cameraman ran up the stairs to the first floor. They kicked open a couple of doors revealing bedrooms filled with dolls and pink wallpaper and posters from 'Frozen' before the third door banged open to reveal a Kin lying on the bed. It sat up and seemed to look directly into the lens. The man in the frame already had his sawn-off shotgun raised and he didn't hesitate, shooting the Kin in the head with both barrels. The white head just seemed to explode upwards from the neck, covering the walls, the two intruders and the camera with white blood. The shot must have been deafening in the small room, both Dandridge and Sasha involuntarily jumping as they watched. Then the cameraman whooped loudly, the obscene exclamation caught clearly by the microphone. The gunman hoisted the dead, leaking body onto his shoulders, ragged flaps of white meat hanging down from the neck where the head should have been. The body dripped flesh down the back of his trousers as the camera followed him back down the stairs, the footage jiggling and bumping around in their haste.

The three of them returned to their pick up truck, police sirens clearly heard in the background. The footage went too blurry to see anything for a few seconds as the body was strapped like a buck to the bonnet of the truck. Then the footage jumped to a face in extreme close-up with only the eyes visible from behind the balaclava.

'*These fuckers taste better than chilli-dogs!*' he yelled into the camera. '*Better 'n anything I ever tasted before!*' The camera pulled jerkily back to reveal the Kin now in three pieces on a cement basement floor, lit by a single naked bulb. The torso only had one arm and leg still attached.

'*I feel fucking great. Fucking fantastic. This is for you, mama, you gonna get well soon, ya hear. You gonna get well!*' Then he lifted the lower part of the balaclava and took a huge bite of the flesh. Then it cut to black and the video ended.

'Oh shit,' said Megan. 'The first actual murder, that we know of. What now?'

'Well, I guess we aren't just working against the clock any more, Megan. The clock has already beaten us. Now we're in damage limitation.'

'I've never thought of anthropology as a pressurised work environment before. I don't really know what to do. That guy has access to the DarkNet. He's gonna feed the Kin to his sick mother and if it cures her then this will escalate for sure.'

'I agree. Adler will track him down, find out who his mother is and where's she's at and hopefully put a stop to it.'

'Hopefully. Sounds like he has his hands full.'

'He'll probably delegate to some poor bastard.'

MIKE

'Why you?' Joy asked, as he packed a bag and prepared to leave, not for the first time, her spare bedroom.

'I suppose he trusts me. I'm not doing anything useful right now and I'm a lawyer. Perhaps that still counts for something, at least for him if not for anyone else.'

'An English lawyer. What do you know about US law?'

'I've watched every episode of Ally McBeal. I know a bit. Besides, the UK made first contact and came up with the manifesto. In terms of Kin relations we have generally run things for the last fifteen years so the PM expects one of us to be there, in name anyway.'

'I wish it didn't have to be you. You're not ready.'

Mike said nothing, and carried on packing.

Five hours later he was sitting in an aircraft seat for the first time since the crash, sweating and gripping the arm-rest so hard his knuckles went white.

It wasn't all down to his new fear of flying. He was desperate for a drink, desperate for Kin meat, anything that would take his mind off what he was flying into. Joy was right of course, there was no way he was ready for this. The aircraft was a Government owned private jet so there were no stewardesses or in-flight entertainment. The only other occupants in the cabin were two men dressed in plain navy blue polo shirts and beige chinos sitting silently in the row in front of him.

He gritted his teeth and kept his eyes screwed shut until the flight touched down at Lubbock International Airport. It taxied to a halt and the Captain stuck his head out from the cockpit and announced their arrival. Mike opened his eyes and exhaled loudly. The two men were already standing and stared down at him.

'You ready to go, sir?' one of them asked.

'Not really. You fellas go ahead.'

'We'll wait for you, sir, if that's acceptable.'

Mike stood and unstrapped his small luggage bag from the seat next to him and the three of them disembarked in single file down the stairs into the hot Texas sunshine, where a black GMC Yukon and further air-conditioned comfort stood waiting for them on the tarmac.

They all clambered in and the driver steered the huge vehicle out of the airport and directly to Trust Point Memorial Hospital in Lubbock. Nobody talked and Mike didn't pay much attention to the flat countryside they passed through until the SUV pulled up underneath a hospital drop-off zone and cut its engine.

They all stepped out from the vehicle's cool interior into an almost solid wall of thick, oppressive heat and too-bright sunshine. Mike's two bodyguards were already wearing identical Ray-Ban Aviator shades. Mike covered his eyes with his palm and surveyed the area. The hospital sat alone in an open, arid, dusty plot surrounded by miles of flat land as far as the eye could see.

They were immediately welcomed by three uniformed officers from the Lubbock Police Department who had emerged from a parked patrol car when they saw the SUV arrive. There were two tough-looking, serious men in immaculate uniforms, and an equally tough-looking serious policewoman, bulging biceps stretching the very limits of the sleeve fabric. They were also all wearing Ray-Ban Aviators as well as an air of don't-fuck-with-me that Mike had no intention of putting to the test.

There were no pleasantries. All had been briefed, and they squeezed into a lift to the third floor, where a worried nurse showed Mike into Sandy Ray's room.

She was in her late sixties with frizzy grey hair and a leathery face, a face that was pale despite the wrinkles and weathering of someone who had spent most of her life outdoors. She was flexing her arms up and down for the doctors, and smiling.

'Mrs. Ray,' Mike said, 'my name is Mike Hennessy. I'm

from the British Foreign and Commonwealth Office. I need to talk to you.'

'The British what?'

'Foreign Office. Mrs Ray, I understand you have been in a coma for some years.'

'That's what they say. Four years. Hit by a Chevy in the parking lot at Wendy's. Never did like Wendy's that much, or Chevys come t'a think of it.'

'And you have recovered recently because your son committed a crime, a crime against the Kin species.'

'Buddy's a good boy, he wouldn't commit no crime against no-one.'

'Mrs Ray, Buddy has a long history of minor felonies dating back to when he was ten years old.'

Her bright eyes narrowed. 'What's your point?'

Mike knew he had to tread more carefully. 'I know this is a lot to take in, Mrs Ray. You've only been awake two days and what I am about to ask you to do is-'

'What? What you gonna ask me to do?'

'Buddy broke into an innocent family's home and threatened them at gunpoint before murdering a Kin. He did this to get you what he believed is the cure for your condition.'

'Ain't no cure for being hit on the head by a Chevy. I just woke up is all. Paid my dues. Time to wake up He said, so I did.'

'That is true, ma'am. It was your time.'

'Don't ma'am me, son.'

'My apologies. Mrs Ray, I need you to go on record, a sworn statement, on camera, that Buddy didn't use the Kin flesh on you for your recovery. That it was your time, that God woke you up and you would never condone the murder of Kin, even if was by your son.'

'I ain't saying anything 'bout Buddy.'

'Buddy is in Police custody. He faces the death penalty. If you do this thing for us then the charge will be commuted to life imprisonment.'

'He goes to jail if I don't say what you want me to say?'

'He's going to jail either way, but if you don't say what we want you to say then he will be handed the death penalty. It is unfortunate that he murdered the Kin in Texas, I suppose.'

'But killin' an alien ain't murder, is it? Ain't it like shootin' a buck, or a mongoose?'

'Kin and human are equals on this planet, Mrs Ray. We co-habit. I need you to know that it isn't just us asking that you co-operate.' Mike was handed a telephone handset. He passed it on to Sandy Ray who placed it against her weathered cheek. A minute later, nodding dumbly, she handed it back.

'The goddamn President of the United States wants me to turn in my own son.'

'No, Mrs Ray. He wants you to do the right thing. I know it's hard to understand - I struggle to get my head around it as well - but this will help the entire world significantly. Not just Texas, or the United States, but the whole world. You need to renounce your son's actions. Today.'

'Where's Buddy? I want to see him.'

'That's not possible. He's in Police custody in the Lubbock County-'

They heard shots being fired outside. Then more, louder, getting closer. Some screams. Then a crash from just outside the hospital room that sounded like a tray of medical equipment going over. The two British agents who had been standing just inside the room turned towards the closed door and crouched down protectively.

The door was kicked open, the opaque safety glass shattering in the frame.

'*Leave my mother alone.*' Buddy Ray stood in the doorway. He wore a torn, sleeveless denim shirt and had arms as thick as tree trunks corded with veins and muscles that positively dwarfed any of the three officers that had greeted Mike at the car. He had stubble that looked like it could abrase the skin from a rhino. His jacket was spattered with blood and one of his huge arms was smeared blood-red from shoulder to knuckle. He wore an orange baseball cap with *76* on it and carried a lethal looking, police-issue shotgun and two pistols tucked into his belt.

Two virtually identical men stood next to him, distinguishable only by the different gasoline logos on their baseball caps, *Sunoco* and *Exxon* respectively.

Mike stood up from the bedside.

'Mr. Ray?' he said it calmly, but he shook so much he was worried he'd look like he was having a seizure.

'Yup. Buddy Ray. Who the fuck are you?' His voice had a not entirely unexpected thick Texan accent, but it still took Mike a few moments to work out what he had just said.

'I knew a Buddy once,' Mike said, 'a nice man.'

'*Who the fuck are you?*' Buddy repeated.

'My name is Michael Hennessy. I am here with the British Foreign Office and the Lubbock Police Department. As you can see.'

'The British what?'

'Foreign Office. We deal with all human and Kin Integration issues and incidents. In your case, Kin homicide. The first case of it's type. Congratulations Mr Ray, you've made history.'

'Please co-operate, Mr Ray,' one of the agents said.

'Buddy!' Sandy Ray cried out.

'Get the fuck away from her,' he snarled.

He raised the shotgun towards Mike. One of the agents stepped protectively in front of Mike, and the other went for Buddy, knocking the gun from his blood-greasy grip. Buddy swung at him but the agent ducked and came up with a quick, vicious uppercut which connected with the Texan's jaw with a hideous crunch. Buddy cried out and staggered back but remained standing. He shook his head slightly but his eyes never lost focus. The agent was clearly used to this being the definitive blow, confused as to how his man was still upright.

'Careful,' Mike shouted, 'he's had Kin flesh.'

Buddy advanced and the agent started battering him with a flurry of punches that would have felled a man built from solid granite. Buddy kept coming like a huge redneck Terminator. He swung once and was blocked, twice, blocked, then three times, finally connecting with the gut of his much smaller opponent. The agent was lifted clear off his feet and thrown backwards into a medical cabinet with a crash. The glass doors shattered and the contents spilled out everywhere as blood sprayed from his mouth, choking and coughing blood, unable to catch a breath and clearly badly injured.

One of Buddy's two brothers had snatched up the fallen shotgun and now pointed it directly at the other Foreign office agent who stood with his hands by his sides, watching helplessly as his colleague was felled.

'*Buddy!*' cried out Sandy Ray. '*Whatcha doin'?*'

'Ma! I ain't going to jail, not now. None of us are. We gon' get out of here, right now. The cops can't stop us.'

Mike was standing next to the bed, hoping they would forget he was there, but Buddy Ray turned and took a step towards him. 'Buddy,' he said, 'I know what you are feeling, I've felt it too, but you need to stop this right now before it gets out of hand. Tell me what's happened to the pol-'

'-it's already out of hand, it's fucking out of this *fucking world!*' Buddy shouted and he and his brothers laughed. 'Come on Ma, let's go. Get your clothes.'

Sandy Ray was cowering under the thin pale blue hospital sheet in confusion and terror.

'I can't let you leave, Mrs Ray,' said the other British agent. 'Your President has asked and now I am asking you one more time. Stay here, do what we ask and let's all wait for the authorities to come and collect Buddy.'

Buddy's brother stepped around and whipped the butt of a pistol across the mans' temple. Something gave with a loud crack in his head and he dropped to the floor like a sack of potatoes, bleeding from his nose. 'Jesus,' he cried with delight. 'I don't know my own fucking strength! This is *unbelievable!*'

Buddy's arm glistened with blood, his eyes were too bright, he had a broad, mean smile on his face and Mike could see the crotch of his jeans tenting grotesquely with the heat and ardour of his violence. He took Mike by the neck and lifted him off his feet, squeezing slowly.

'I could kill you so easily,' he whispered. Stars were dancing in front of Mike's eyes and his vision began to blur. 'Just like the cops outside. Everyone dies so easily-' He squeezed harder, and Mike began to suffocate.

'No, Buddy!' cried Sandy Ray, hanging off the arm that was holding Mike up like she was dangling from a steel monkey bar. Her other sons dragged her off and outside the room. Buddy threw Mike aside like an empty sweet wrapper. He crumpled into the foetal position, gasping and coughing, clutching his bruised windpipe.

'Nobody can catch us,' Buddy said, and took off after his family.

Mike heard more shouting outside and knew that the Kin flesh burning inside the Ray brothers was amplifying their rage. They were over confident and under cautious, and now they had their unwitting mother with them. He heard more gunshots and hauled himself to his feet and staggered along the corridor and down the stairs, emerging in the reception area behind the automatic glass doors, which were now stuck open with the body of one of the Ray brothers, his Exxon cap lying a few feet away in a pool of blood and still containing the best part of the top of his head.

Mike skidded to a halt, staring at the body in shock. He

had got used to seeing dead bodies on the mountain but this was different - this man had been gunned down.

He was grabbed roughly around the shoulders and pulled down behind the protective cover of the front desk.

'Hello, whoever the fuck you are. You're coming with us,' Buddy said. He stood up, his huge beefy arm pressing agonisingly against the developing bruise on Mike's throat, a pistol pressed hard against his temple. Buddy's brother supported their mother as they shuffled in single file towards the door.

'*Leave us alone*,' Buddy shouted. '*We're walking out of h-*'

His head suddenly snapped backwards and a split-second later Mike heard the gunshot. The gun Buddy was holding dropped fractionally and went off, deafening Mike in his right ear, the bullet grazing the back of his neck. He was dragged down to the floor in a tangle of enormously heavy arms and legs. As he struggled to get out from under the huge dead body, he witnessed two figures dressed in black body armour, helmets and goggles advancing on them. There was nothing but ringing in his ears from the shot but could see they were firing their automatic weapons at a target behind him. One of them motioned for him to stay down as he stepped past.

Through the persistent ringing he could make out another sound, something high pitched and insistent. He staggered to his feet, nearly slipping over on the blood covering the floor, and saw Sandy Ray kneeling in the bloody remains of her three sons, screaming and screaming and screaming.

ADLER

He hit the red button on his handset and cut the call off. Hennessy had relayed the events. Two MI6 agents dead, three Lubbock Police officers and the three Ray brothers. Eight people, nine in total including the Kin they had butchered. Sandy Ray was now virtually catatonic and wasn't saying anything. His phone rang again. He answered and listened to Dandridge's report. He rang off, almost wordlessly.

'Can we carry on now, Adler?' asked the Prime Minister, sitting in front of him and waiting impatiently.'

'Of course, Prime Minister. That was Hennessy in Texas. I think we can assume that's now a dead end, the mother's not going to renounce anything although I think we might be able to spin it to our advantage. Dandridge is in Japan with the anthropologist and making progress. He sounded quite positive.'

'Was it the right decision, to send Richard Dandridge? Is he qualified?'

'Oh yes. Megan Sasha-Meyer is doing the heavy lifting, in an anthropological sense. The thing with Dandridge is that nobody likes him when they first meet him. I mean nobody. And then the more time you spend with him the more your initial impression changes imperceptibly, without you even noticing. He becomes the person that you always think of first, the person you never want to do anything without, the one you're disappointed about when he can't attend your birthday party, the guy you rearrange your family holidays to accommodate. All for reasons that are utterly beyond me. He's absolutely the best person for this. That and the fact he has fallen in love with a Kin. He has more of an incentive to make this work than anyone else.'

'He can't really love it, can he? Isn't it more of an addiction?'

'That's love, PM.'

'And Sasha-Meyer is OK with him?'

'So far.'

'So where are we now?'

'We've broken the negotiation deadlock with the Aussies. They have now agreed to the Kin relocation in principle and surprisingly few of the locals actually need to move that far away. Budgets are being shifted around to allow for the building of new housing, new facilities. Temporary camps are being set up while the unhoused are placed. It'll be a proper city when its done, and a lot of the Kin already incumbent in Australia have been employed to build it. We are starting the move itself with the largest populations in the US, UK, Italy, Germany, Spain, Sweden and Switzerland. Aircraft are being requisitioned from every viable commercial airline to assist and the same with cruise liner operators. The ships will go back and forth for a few years but they can hold thousands more Kin than the aircraft.'

'Oh my god. Will it be quick enough?'

'Hope so. The first few are already en-route.'

'Do we have a population estimate?'

'It's difficult to say, but we are monitoring each Kin moved so we might have a more definitive figure at some point. With current information, we estimate that there are now around sixty million Kin, give or take.'

'From an original eight million.'

'There is another thing, too.'

'What's that?'

'Human population is growing too. Much, much faster than statistics for the last twenty years have predicted. In virtually every country on the planet, human growth rates have risen dramatically.'

'You're kidding me.'

'I wouldn't kid you, PM.'

'Why?'

'Because I respect you too much.'

'No, why is human population increasing so fast?'

'I'm not sure. Even though in general things are more peaceful, less civil unrest in the usual Middle-East hotspots and reduced crime in inner cities, living standards and house prices have taken a hit, jobs are scarce and the economy remains more uncertain than a fat man on a surfboard. I think we've been treating the whole situation with a collective war mentality, pulling together, helping each other out. People have had to hunker down and get on with it, despite the hardships. And that means more sexy time. And of course there is, just possibly, another factor.'

'What's that?'

'It's only a theory that Dandridge posited recently, but when the Kin reproduce they release some kind of... I suppose it could be described as a pheromone of some sort which has an effect on humans like a form of high, similar to but not as intense as consuming their blood or flesh. It makes emotions run higher and natural urges more pronounced. Megan Sasha-Meyer practically threw herself at Dandridge after witnessing the Kin reproductive cycle and she was still firmly in the 'disliking him' phase.'

The Prime Minister placed his palms over his eyes. 'This is disastrous, Adler. It's going to place intolerable pressure on the earth.'

'Temporarily. We can still fix this. Get them re-housed in one place, and work on their peer groups and familial society which, granted, might take a generation or so, but we can fix it.'

'I wish I had your confidence.'

'It's not confidence, PM. I am working towards an achievable goal using all the facilities of the United Nations at my disposal. No confidence needed. We will get this sorted, or at the very least get the foundations down, and if we don't, then none of us will be around to kick ourselves anyway.'

JOSH

The first coaches had arrived at the Shack to take the Kin to the cruise ships that would transport them to their new life in Australia. There must have been at least three hundred coaches crawling along the lanes towards the Shack, packing the white bodies inside and driving off.

After two days of constant movement, noise and activity, Shack personnel checking each Kin into each coach, the number remaining was still formidable. The housing and accommodation blocks were still almost full. Two days of work had barely made a dent in the numbers. A flexible rota of coach transports had been established so whenever an empty ship docked at Plymouth or Dover exactly the right number of coaches turned up to ferry them out to their allocated transport. It was working rather well, Josh reckoned, if he did say so himself. Other Shacks were not so organised, but he had provided all of them with the transport templates and schedules so he could do no more.

He was sat at the breakfast bar eating a bowl of Shreddies when there was a soft knock at the dark grey door. He opened it to see a Kin standing on the stoop. It took him a moment to recognise the markings.

'Kin,' said Josh, 'come in.'

The first Kin came in and sat on the sofa.

'I haven't seen you for a long time.'

'I have been travelling for a short while. This planet is beautiful. I am looking forward to living in Australia. I have heard that there are many sites of interest.'

'Yes there are. You do know that the Kin are still free to travel anywhere, Australia is just a secure base for you all, right?'

'Of course. We are grateful for all that is being done for us.'

'Can I help you with anything, Kin?' Josh asked, feeling faintly troubled by his visitor.

'Where is Marion?'

'She's in London, working on the emigration plans.'

'Excellent news. She is most qualified to assist with the plans. She understands that we take full responsibility for what happened to our own planet, which is why we have willingly accepted all your plans and manifestos. We have limited choice and have accepted our fate.'

'I don't understand what you are-'

'Something has happened to us. We are many more now than originally. The more of us die, the more of us there are. I myself have reproduced four times already, which would never have happened on our own planet.'

'Really? Shame.'

'Indeed. Although you don't reproduce, Josh.'

'I can, I'm just wired slightly differently I suppose. It's hard to explain to a non-gendered species.'

'Ezra Perron.'

'Yes.'

'You share intimacy, but do not reproduce.'

'No.'

'You engage in sexual relations despite not being of opposite gender. I have read much about human history, human relationships. You are part of a minority group. A homosexual. Homosexual humans have been persecuted for their sexual attraction to same-gendered humans for hundreds of years, perhaps more. Your history books do not go very far back.'

'I guess not, but the situation is better now, there is much more tolerance-'

'In this country, perhaps. But elsewhere on this planet, homosexual activity between like-minded men and women is still classified as against the law.'

'I know. We're working on it, but some prejudices run deep. A lot of people still need to work out the black issue before they can even attempt the gay one. Football has been trying unsuccessfully for years. But the Kin arriving here has really helped us, you know? You've helped to take some prejudices and put them into context. Just knowing that humans aren't alone in the universe has somehow made us more tolerant of each other, regardless of colour or who we want to fuck.'

'Some Kin are being murdered for their flesh. Persecuted.' The voice coming from the plain white face was inflectionless and the same as every Kin, but to Josh it sounded sad and tired.

'I know. I'm really sorry, it's awful. We're trying to put a stop to it, you know that, right? You know we're going to stop it.'

'I do not think it is possible, Josh. I have spent the last years studying humankind. I believe that humans will always be drawn to the things that are most addictive, most destructive. It is not your fault, it is your nature.'

'Kin, we're going to solve this, I promise.'

'I believe you. I believe that humans will eventually come to accept us without persecution. But I also believe that the situation we are in is going to get worse before it gets better. Acceptance will take too long and many Kin will die for their flesh. Through our particular and unforeseen circumstances, we will grow in number and eventually be the dominant species on this planet.'

'Kin, it's out there that it isn't true. We have it on record that Kin flesh has no discernible-'

Josh was talking desperately, frantically. He didn't know why but he couldn't help thinking that for some reason everything that happened from this moment forward hinged on this conversation with the first Kin, from the very first ship that had crash-landed, the Kin that had met Dandridge and Marion and Captain James at the old airbase that was now the Shack.

'No. It won't stop. The man, the husband of Dr. Vikander, he is getting better. The other woman, Sandy Ray, has recovered from her coma.'

'He isn't better, not really. And Sandy Ray claims it was God, not Kin, that brought her out of her coma.'

'She also claims it was God that caused her three sons to be shot to death by the local police department. I believe her testimony is unreliable.'

'Kin, can we not synthesise your physiology somehow? Try and use whatever it is that people think you have-'

'Marion promised that the Kin would never be treated like animals, experimented on or dissected. We are in many ways physiologically and mentally superior to humans and so this would be unacceptable. But we have no wish to see the end of our new home or any of it's incumbent species. So the bodies of Kin are now being dissected and examined with the intention of creating synthetic flesh that might contain the purported healing properties, although I hope this will be unsuccessful.'

'Why do you not want it to work? It would help us all, wouldn't it?'

'If a synthetic form of our flesh is successfully grown, then it is possible that some or all earth diseases and injury can be treated, neutralising the natural selection process even further than your medical science has achieved thus far. Human population, as well as Kin, will increase dramatically. This planet cannot hope to sustain two species both increasing in number simultaneously. Richard Dandridge's efforts to re-start our societal patterns would seem to be our only option.'

'Kin, we're the first generation who has ever had to tackle this kind of problem and it will take more years, more generations, but we'll get there. We *will* get there I promise. There's bound to be bumps in the road.'

'We do not consider the murder of Kin for their flesh to be 'bumps in the road', although your sentiment is accurate and appreciated. We are also aware that there is a large section of human society who has grown to hate us, who do not want us here and who consider us poisonous and wish us to leave. Who are killing us intentionally, forcing your governments into rash and dangerous decisions. Acceptance may indeed come eventually but it will come too late. I just do not know for whom.'

'It won't come to that.'

'It has already come to that.'

The Kin stood up and went to the front door, unclicking the latch.

'I am returning to the Shack if you need me.' It closed the door, leaving Josh on the sofa with an untouched, soggy bowl of Shreddies and a feeling of dread as black as pitch in the pit of his stomach.

CAPTAIN DON COLLIER

He had been at sea all his working life. He started as a Midshipman in the Merchant Navy and over the next twenty years rose solidly through the ranks, plying his trade around the globe, loading and delivering as many types of cargo to as many remote ports and places as it's possible to visit.

After leaving the Navy he captained vessels for at least twenty different shipping lines over the years, but as he passed his sixtieth birthday he decided he deserved a more comfortable cabin and better food, so switched to captain cruise ships which came with a welcome long-term contract and a steady paycheck.

Although he missed the long vodka nights with his Russian counterparts and the Greek Captains whose doors were always open with friendship and coffee on the table, coffee so thick you could stand a dessert spoon up in it, he was getting older and his body needed a little more TLC.

When the Kin evacuation plan was announced and a demand for all cruise ship operators to designate at least two ships to the cause, he had volunteered immediately. He reckoned that this job, going back and forward to and from Australia with Kin would probably see out the rest of his career. Not many Sea Captains had the knowledge of job security to retirement age. He knew that his ship, the PV Countess Marianne, wasn't the largest in the fleet but it was a good, sturdy vessel, quite new with a capacity to transport eighteen hundred passengers at a time.

The first embarkation was perfect, orderly. Coaches of Kin turned up at Plymouth right on time and shuffled up the gangway, picking a cabin number from an official as they filed on, directed by the first mate and stewards as they stepped on deck. They departed Plymouth Harbour at exactly 20:32 local time. Captain Collier noted the time in his log and was handed the passenger manifest by his first mate. He checked it, signed it and it was filed accordingly. The ship was at capacity, but not overloaded.

A cup of coffee from the Costa outlet in the ship's main atrium was handed to him. Collier sat in his chair on the bridge, staring out of the bank of windows as the UK shrank behind them and the horizon stretched out in front. He blew the steam from his first latte of the trip.

Their route would take them through the Suez Canal to Singapore for a two day layover before the final stretch to Australia.

A fortnight later they traversed the Suez Canal at the head of a procession of about eight ships all loaded with Kin. Four were from the UK, the others from other places across Europe. The Kin lined the guardrails and silently watched the country go by. The silence had been eerie at first but the few he had spoken with seemed happy enough with the vessel and the voyage.

They were out of the Red Sea and into the Arabian Sea, halfway across the stretch of water to Singapore when three more Kin were killed in a single night in separate incidents just outside of Lubbock, Texas, eight thousand miles away. The three murders were all retaliatory attacks to the deaths of the three Ray brothers, and took place over the course of two brutal hours, the Kin dragged helplessly through the streets behind trucks, stabbed and cut and beaten until finally shredded by automatic weapons.

After the first Kin was killed, all Captain Collier knew was that his ship, designed to carry no more than one thousand eight hundred passengers, suddenly found itself coping with two thousand, seven hundred.

Collier acted fast as soon as he realised what was happening. He could see Kin reproducing everywhere he went, on decks, in the recreational areas, in every cabin. Unable to ignore the urge of their genetic makeup they coupled, squeezing and pushing together until a new Kin was formed from the bubbling, urgent mass of white flesh that appeared between them. The Captain and his crew started to experience amplified, almost overwhelming emotion. Wherever Collier strode he felt powerful and in control, a lifetime of experience backing him up. His decisions were fast and clear. He also felt things he thought he'd never feel again; love, loss and a longing to talk to his estranged wife and daughters. It was a sheer, physical act of will that he pushed his own feelings away and gave his orders. His first mate and helmsman were chattering excitedly on the bridge, giggling and laughing like schoolboys. The Captain physically slapped them both, hard, and forced them to take note.

He ordered the launch of the lifeboats. He had run drills and knew that all GPS was active, each lifeboat in good condition and stocked with supplies. The ship was low in the water and listing to port. The 'abandon ship' alarm was sounding. All non-essential human personnel were evacuated first, then the Kin, old and new, filing to the lifeboats in an orderly fashion. Three lifeboats launched successfully.

And then the second Kin was killed in Lubbock. Unable to resist the rules of their society, the Kin had no option but to begin the process again. The Captain and his crew ran around the ship, trying to force them apart, but it was no good. The Kin were completely fused together, utterly inseparable until the new Kin emerged from the conjoined flesh of their union. The Captain tried to throw some overboard, but realised that if they died he was no nearer to a solution. Back in the bridge he began to radio for help, for back-up. The nearest ship with any capacity was only fifty miles away, a container ship carrying an eighty percent load. It could take about a thousand bodies and immediately diverted course to steam towards the stricken cruise ship. It had received distress calls from two other Kin evacuation ships.

The Kin were once again nearly all engaged in their

reproductive cycle. The Captain ordered the evacuation of all human personnel, all of whom made it to lifeboats and launched a few minutes before the Kin cycle completed and two thousand seven hundred became four thousand one hundred and ten, give or take.

The ship creaked and groaned and began to list, the waves lapping at the lower handrails. The Captain ordered all Kin to evenly distribute throughout the ship, now sitting so low in the water he could have leaned over and trailed his hand in the sea. He was the only human now left on board. The engines were cut, power was off. The ship drifted almost silently as night fell, the Kin like ghosts on the decks.

The container vessel was still about twenty miles out when eight thousand miles away, the third Kin was killed, shot point blank in the face by a seventeen year old boy pointing an Ithaca 37 shotgun, an enraged and excited crowd urging him on before falling on the body, tearing it apart with tooth and nail.

EZRA

The best thing about a slight delay at LAX was the amazing array of different coffees available to the flight crews. He sat in a leather armchair and sipped a Peruvian blend espresso that trickled down his throat like perfectly bitter silk. Then he had another. Finally his chief flight attendant fetched him and they walked down the tubular airway to the door of the aircraft. He turned left into the cockpit, the flight attendant right into the cabin. He found his co-pilot Clemence Bernard already there, ticking off her list of pre-flight checks.

As they could fly over six hundred and fifty passengers at a time in a class-free cabin, their charter flight had been commandeered as part of the relocation effort. Ezra had been fairly pissed off until he found out he was being paid double time, including a layover in Australia before the return flight to London, where he would once again be employed flying more Kin to Australia at double time.

Flight checks complete and all Kin passengers belted-in he fired up the aircraft systems and they were towed away from the departure gate to the taxiway. Three minutes later they were in the air and over the Pacific.

Ezra and Clemence settled in for a quiet flight. The flight attendants had come in with more coffee, inferior to the LAX brew but perfectly fine, and reported that the Kin were pretty much entirely silent but seemed polite and happy. The attendants were very happy about the quiet flight ahead.

They were only a few miles beyond Santa Catalina Island when the three Kin were gunned down outside Lubbock, Texas. Ezra had no idea anything was amiss until one of the flight attendants, bright and sunny just a few moments ago, ran back into the cabin and informed them the Kin passengers were pretty much entirely locked together in an unbroken mass of white flesh. Ezra went back and took a look. They were rocking backwards and forwards, almost entirely fused together. The sight made Ezra think of a tube of toothpaste.

He got on the radio, signalling a Mayday and alerting LAX tower that he was turning around. But it was too late.

It was an eventuality that had never been considered, a vital piece of a much larger problem somehow lost in the planning.

The catastrophically overloaded aircraft went down about eight miles shy of the West Coast of the United States. It hit the water and flipped over, killing everyone on board.

PART ELEVEN

JENNIFER

'Please tell me where you are, Luke. I'm worried about you. You don't have to come home, I just want to know if you are safe.'

Even to her own ears she sounded desperate and unconvincing. She looked up at the faces above the camera. 'This isn't going to work,' she said. 'He's too popular, and I sound just awful. This is going to do more harm than good.'

A single camera lens was aimed at her as she tried to talk to her step-son, again. She had never quite managed it when they were face to face so she had no clue how to do it to camera.

Luke McDonald had now made nearly a dozen videos inciting and urging people to rise up against the Kin, and in each one he gained in confidence, speaking more plaintively, clearly and convincingly. In every video he refuted the Government's claims and explanations, showing tightly edited clips and interviews taken from the news and the DarkNet to make his point; persuasive, articulate arguments about the Kin 'uprising'. His videos were posted on the DarkNet, watched and discussed by everyone who had access, a community growing by the thousands each day as instructions how to re-activate old discarded tablets and computers became available.

He was growing up on camera, in height, stature and poise. Jennifer hardly recognised him now and dimly remembered that he turned fifteen some weeks ago. The spots on his face over the first few videos had cleared up and his hair that had looked lank and greasy now always looked washed and clean, combed back in a mock-eighties style that somehow suited him perfectly. He was young, handsome and compelling.

His broadcasts were disseminated, quoted and repeated by every news channel and paper, from the insanely popular conspiracy papers to the gossip papers, who commented mainly on what he was wearing, how good he looked, who was styling him, speculations on his star sign and if he had a girlfriend. He was a rock star.

Adler stepped around the camera and knelt in front of Jennifer.

'Jennifer, you need to try. Say whatever comes into your head. Just say it and we'll get it out there. Say whatever you think might get him to crawl out from wherever he is and come to you.'

'Can't you track him or something?'

'He's too well hidden. The signal is being disguised somehow. Tracking his broadcasts leads to a small Welsh mining village or a hotdog stall in Iowa.'

'Oh my god, I hate hotdogs. I still don't know what to say.'

'Try Jennifer. It's important. Do you want a break?'

'No I'll carry on, get this over with.'

Adler stepped back into the darkness behind the bright light above the camera lens. A make-up girl came and dabbed her glowing forehead. Then she too stepped back and Jennifer was once more alone in the spotlight.

'Luke-' Jennifer started to feel overwhelmingly tired. Then she felt the baby kick inside her and her feeling of weariness began to turn into something else.

'Luke. Listen to me. I'm your step-mother. We aren't related by blood but I've been looking after you since you were eight years old. You've had a tough time, I get it. Your parents were murdered, horribly. It was awful and no kid should ever have to go through it. You didn't have to see the body of your Dad, but I did. I loved him and knew every part of him, and even I hardly recognised his body.'

I get it, I do. I wasn't ready to be a mum to a spoiled eight year old kid and I wasn't very good at it. But you know something, Luke? Getting revenge for your shitty childhood is not an excuse to kickstart *the end of the goddamn world*. Fucking *grow up,* Luke. Take some responsibility for your actions for once. All these nutters on the fucking DarkNet have no idea what they're doing, they're just following you blindly.

But you, Luke. You're clever. You've proven that. You're a clever kid, but weird, always off in your own world, never opening up. Well, now is *not* the time to start fucking opening up. We are standing on the brink of disaster, a catastrophe the likes of which you can't even comprehend, and you're not helping. This is bigger than you, bigger than your shitty new haircut. I want the DarkNet to know what kind of a man you are - because you're not a boy anymore that's for sure - I want them to know everything. How you raped me on the plane before it crashed. How you were so desperate to lose your virginity you raped me in my seat, just as I thought we were getting along better. I presume you thought we were going to die so it didn't matter. Well, guess what? We aren't dead and although I *did* want to die, and nearly let myself die, I can't let it go. Not yet. And the reason I can't? I'm pregnant, Luke. I'm pregnant and it's yours. I never knew you had it in you, only being a fourteen year old sociopath, but there you go. I'm pregnant, and so I want you and all your acolytes on the Net to know too. You're a rapist and soon to be a father, to a child conceived to your step-mother by rape. So you thought your life was fucked up before? You don't know the half of it. I think it's time to put all your followers right, don't you?

Come on out Luke, I dare you. I double dare you. Come out, face up to your responsibilities. I won't press charges. I just want you to look me in the eye and tell me that you're sorry. And failing that, just stop acting like a spoiled, self-serving *cunt*.'

She stopped speaking, and the room stayed silent for a long while.

'Can we use any of that?' the cameraman eventually asked, to no-one in particular.

LUKE

Jennifer's message uploaded to the DarkNet unedited. He watched it with growing horror and disbelief. When it cut to black he flew into a rage. Nella tried to calm him down as he stormed around the basement kicking and smashing and punching everything in sight, fury and hate burning through his veins and destroying logic, reason and everything else in its path. Blood ran down his knuckles.

'I'm going to see her,' he shouted. 'If that's what she wants, fine. Then I'll pound her fucking face to a pulp and not stop until she's *unrecognisable*,' he screamed out loud.

'That's what she wants you to do, Luke. You'd be doing exactly what they-'

'I don't *fucking care*,' he screamed in her face, his eyes ablaze with fury. 'How dare she accuse me-'

'You have to calm down. We're so nearly there. Don't jeopardise the movement now. If you-'

'What fucking movement?' shouted Luke. 'It's just me, stuck in a fucking basement.'

Luke hadn't left the basement in nearly four months. Occasionally he wandered up to the main house but for the most part he was living in the basement of Henderson Mulcahy's run down country estate. Nella had offered to try and relocate him but the space had everything he needed; food, games, a running machine that he ran on for four hours a day while he watched television and the DarkNet - and of course Nella Monroe herself, her daily visits where she did not bring food or a camera or questions. The times she wore nothing underneath her white velour tracksuit or occasionally simply nothing at all, the staring, lustful gaze of her young charge as she slowly descended the basement steps drawing her towards him like a tractor beam.

'Then be proud of what you've accomplished Luke, all on your own and stuck here in a basement. It's working. The whole entire world is talking about you. It's incredible.

You're incredible. We'll soon be rid of the Kin completely, one way or another.'

'Why do you even want them gone anyway? Henderson's dead, he's gone forever. Why do you give a shit?'

His face was flushed, his mouth curled into a snarl.

'They're poisoning the world. Taking it over, piece by piece. The Kin have everything to gain and nothing to lose. Henderson knew it and was trying to stop it and I'm going to finish his work. *We're* going to finish his work. The moment you came off the mountain and did all those press conferences and interviews he singled you out, he knew all along that it was you that was going to help him. And you *are* magnificent, Luke. Whatever your stepmom says on the DarkNet makes no difference. You've already hooked them, they're already yours. I think that her video is only going to make them love you more.'

'Don't be fucking stupid, she just told them all I *raped* her, which is a lie.'

Nella draped her arms around him, lacing her fingers in his clean hair, pulling his face down to hers. She was sure he'd grown at least two inches since arriving in the basement.

'Don't tell me - tell them,' she whispered, and kissed him. He tried to pull away from her.

'I can't. They'll never-'

She didn't let him finish and kissed him more firmly, urgently.

She wore her usual immaculate white sweat suit. Luke reckoned she had a wardrobe full of identical items and picked a fresh one every day, throwing yesterdays in the bin. His hands were all over her, squeezing and pulling her against him. He slid his hands over her hips and under the elasticated waistband, pushing them down. She was shaved, smooth and perfumed. The top followed, her small round breasts in no need of support.

She pulled him to the mattress, their lips locked together. Luke's hands were all over her but by some alchemy that he could never entirely work out she managed to quickly and expertly strip him without him noticing. As soon as his boxer shorts were around his ankles and he kicked them clear, she straddled him and guided him inside her, keeping her lips pressed to his and her tongue in his mouth as she rode him. She could feel his ardour increase and his breathing quicken. They had been together many times in the last few months but despite her efforts longevity still wasn't one of his strong points.

She reached underneath his mattress and pulled out a long, sharp hunting knife. She took his wrist and pulled his arm up and over his head, holding his wrist as she rocked him back and forth. He twisted his head away from her kiss.

'No, not today,' he whispered, his voice ragged and scared, catching in his throat. *'Please.'*

'It's up to you my love,' she whispered, drawing the cold flat of the blade against the exposed underside of his forearm, pressing it against barely healed cuts and scabs already red and sore against the otherwise pale skin.

'I'll do the video OK? You don't need to. I'll say what they need me to say,' he moaned as the flat blade ran across his cuts.

'No, Luke,' her whispered voice barely audible in his ear. 'Say what *you* need to say. Do it for you and do it for me. You never let me down.' She turned the blade so the sharp edge was pressing against a fresh patch of white skin, her grip on his wrist tight and unyielding.

'*No!*' he shouted and bucked his hips against her, trying to throw her off him. His arm somehow stayed over his head, exactly where she pinned it, tight and unyielding. She pressed the blade down, the razor sharp edge opening the skin. Blood began to dribble down his arm and collect in his armpit, damping down the fresh new curls of his pubic hair.

Luke screamed loudly, tears streaming down his face as

Nella leisurely drew the blade across him, the blood now starting to flow freely over his arm and down his body, pooling onto the crisp white sheets of the mattress. He was dizzy with pain, his whole arm on fire, the feeling of warm blood leaking out of him almost too much to bear.

'Stop,' he sobbed. 'Please stop, please, please-' the sob turned to a pleading whisper as the blade finished it's aeons-long journey from one side of his arm to the other and Nella dropped the knife next to the mattress. His whole body was consumed with the burning pain. She kept hold of his arm, gushing with blood, her hips never breaking their insistent rhythm and holding him tightly inside her. As she fucked him, Luke struggled to separate the lust from the pain, the two feelings mutating together into an excruciating dark mass until the only option he had was try and let it all out.

Nella felt him tensing up, his movement under her more pronounced, his breathing ragged. She leaned down and clamped her mouth over the bloody, pulpy mess of his forearm, biting into the fresh cut. He screamed out again in genuine agony, trying to pull his arm away but not succeeding, unwilling to pull against her teeth buried in his arm. The pain blazed and blossomed so hot it was practically a third person in the room.

With his free hand he took her left breast and squeezed it hard, like he was trying to squeeze the juice from an unpeeled orange. She cried out in surprise.

The bitter tang of Luke's hot blood filled her mouth and she knew her face was smeared with it. Her breast throbbed and she gasped. Her own climax, her first with him, happened too quickly, a betrayal. An inexorable slide, a mysterious dark pit rushing towards her. She fought it, desperately pushing backwards and away, not knowing how deep the pit might be and frightened by it. But she was sliding too fast and her resistance was too late. Her body tensed against Luke's penis as the pit swallowed her up completely. Intense pleasure washed powerfully through her, overwhelming her senses. Her face was still buried in Luke's armpit as she ground herself against him, eking out every shudder and spasm before she could open her eyes and let the light back in.

It was a full thirty seconds before she came properly back to her senses. She was still on top of him, breathing hard, covered in sweat and blood. She hadn't felt him finish but she could feel his come inside her. Blood still flowed freely from his arm and he didn't seem able to speak. She rolled off him and ran naked and dripping through the house to fetch a first aid kit.

Luke lay silently on the bloody mattress until she returned, bathing his wound in a basin and expertly dressing it with savlon and a bandage. Deep teeth marks surrounded the cut which looked as if he had been attacked by a wild animal. He grimaced in pain as she tightened the bandage.

'No more,' he said finally. 'No more of this. It hurts too much. I hurt all the time.'

'You need the pain, Luke,' she said, concentrating on the bandage knot. 'You need it to see clearly and I need you to keep a clear head.'

'You *need* me? Is that what this is all about, really? You don't love me at all. You just need me for your plan.'

'I do love you, Luke. I love you very much, more than you know. I can't do what you do. You've become a hero to them, a survivor, someone who has been through emotional and physical pain and come out the other side. That's why your step-mother's video won't work. She's way too late.'

She glanced down at the bruises around her breasts. 'You're lucky you know, in a way. I know what Henderson would have done to you. I knew everything about him. You would have ended up doing the same thing, but it would have been with him, not me. The weird thing is, you'd probably have loved him more.'

'What do you mean?' Luke felt a cold shiver down his

spine as he thought of Henderson Mulcahy, lying dead in a pool of blood and brains.

'I mean that he would have fucked you and you would have recorded the video messages with him instead.'

'What the fuck? No way. I'm not... I would never-'

'You would, and you'd go back to him again and again, willingly. I saw it happen. Boys your age, sometimes younger. Blinded by his personality, visions of fame and wealth dancing in wide, innocent eyes. Even your hero Royce Brims. They'd do anything for him. Anything.'

Luke wasn't quite sure he was hearing her right. 'But I'm not... I mean, I wouldn't have-'

'Yes you would. You wouldn't even know you were being seduced until you were in his bed and happily sucking his cock like a Strawberry Mivvi.'

'Not a fucking chance. You knew about this?'

'He made a promise to me and he never broke it. And I'm not going to break my promise to him.'

'You loved him.'

'Love takes many forms. Yes, I loved him and our love ran deep, but I knew exactly what I was to him and he knew what he was to me.'

'You're fucked up. You and him both.'

'Maybe. Now let's make a video.'

'Now? I'm covered in blood, and so are you.'

'Let's just do it.'

She set the camera up, aimed at the bed where Luke sat naked in a spreading puddle of his own blood.

'You're crazy,' he said. 'You and Henderson. Fucking crazy.'

'We're all crazy, Luke. You, me and Henderson together. Now, let's make history.'

ADLER

When it was released, Jennifer's confessional video response to Luke's campaign had racked up the highest number of views on the nascent DarkNet up to that point. It created a storm in the traditional press and she went on hundreds of press interviews, asked hundreds of intrusive, personal and persistent questions. She tried her best to bat them away, simply and repeatedly asking for Luke to come home so they could talk.

Then the world was shaken as a series of events threatened to spiral out of control. Mike Hennessy was involved in the hospital shooting of Buddy Ray and his brothers at Lubbock and the whole state of Texas went crazy. Three Kin were slaughtered in the streets in broad daylight, crowds feasting on the bodies, overpowering local police and tearing through the town, angry, crazy, fast, strong and convinced of human superiority over the aliens. There was widespread violence, properties burned, shots fired and stores ransacked as well as many reported cases of public exposure, nudity and sexual activity, a town running amok.

Hours and hours of handheld footage of the carnage appeared on the DarkNet, broadcast and analysed over and over on the news. The United States Army arrived and the outraged town went to war.

Most citizens were armed and some were jacked up on the Kin meat. Gun battles in the streets of the city raged for an entire night before it was slowly brought under control. Twelve Lubbock citizens were killed in firefights, including a boy of twelve.

A curfew was imposed on Lubbock, and enforced across the whole state of Texas. The Army began to patrol the streets, granted full 'stop and search' permissions, setting up roadblocks at main junctions in an attempt to confiscate weapons. Lubbock was cut off from the rest of the state and the American media went crazy, literally thousands of reporters and vans turning up, desperate for more information. Neighbouring townsfolk began patrolling the Lubbock perimeter in force, heavily armed and riding in the backs of trucks. Local knowledge of back-roads and geography became valuable currency traded between locals and reporters, some making it through the perimeter before being caught and ejected by the Army.

Adler sat sipping coffee in his hotel room at the Hilton Hotel on Park Lane. A black tablet sat on a glass table in front of him constantly updating green text on a grey screen. It was still basic but as its influence grew, it's usability and speed increased exponentially. He had no choice but to watch the news unfolding along with everyone else, on the television news, in the papers and on the DarkNet. There was nothing he could do. The US Army was involved and diplomatic relations were becoming much harder to negotiate.

He and Marion were still working on the relocation plan. Since the disaster of the *Countess Marianne* where nearly three thousand Kin and the ship's Captain had perished, all transport ships were now restricted to a third passenger capacity and carried extra life-rafts. They had also lost four passenger aircraft with the deaths of fifteen humans and anther eight hundred Kin. Flying Kin to Australia was now banned.

Adler blamed himself for the tragedies, something he should have foreseen but had not taken into account. He had personally broken the news of Ezra Perron's death to his husband Josh, who had not taken it well.

So now the ships were taking way too long. It was faster to fly them but the risk was too great. Kin were not being moved quickly enough and they were now threatening to overwhelm the Shacks. The majority had nowhere to live or go and the Prime Minister had issued an order for all human families with spare rooms to offer them immediately to house at least two Kin until they could be evacuated.

A yellow warning triangle blinked onto the screen of his tablet, indicating a new update. Adler hit the link. It was a new video from the boy; it buffered for a good minute and a half before playing.

The boy was shirtless and framed from the top of his head down to the curve of his hipbones. Streaks and splotches of blood were smeared on his face and across his neck and body. His carefully combed hair was mussed and matted with blood and sweat and he looked frantic, his eyes wide and lambent, jacked up, and to Adler, slightly insane. A blood-soaked bandage was wrapped around his upper right arm in an unsuccessful attempt to stem blood from dripping down his arm to his fingertips.

Adler had wondered what his reaction to Jennifer's message might be and was not surprised that a counter video had been uploaded. He hit pause and made himself a fresh coffee before sitting down and steeling himself for the response. He resumed the image and on the screen, the feral looking boy began to talk.

When the video finished, Adler picked up his phone and ordered armed police protection for every Shack across the world and issued an alert to all Kin to lock themselves indoors and stay there until further notice.

DANDRIDGE

They sat together in their tranquil garden, a clear blue sky over them, mountains on either side. The original group of four Kin with whom Megan had shared an apartment now numbered thirty. They had created dorm rooms from bedrooms and extended a canvas roof across the garden to house more. Megan and Dandridge had moved to a nearby guest house and shared a room. The Kin pheromone so close to both of them had melted away their inhibitions and created an awareness and closeness of each other that suited their work and situation perfectly.

They had split their group of thirty Kin into four groups, each of them differentiated by similarities in their markings, roles, responsibilities and ages - in some cases only a few days. There were no original Kin in the group but each one had retained some vague dreamlike memory of the Kin from whom they were spawned and some could remember snatched images of their own homeworld despite never having been there. Megan split them up further according to information she gleaned from past memories and kept each group as separate as possible.

'You think this is working?' Dandridge asked one evening, watching the sun go down, first of all disappearing behind the Kin ship in the distance and then behind the mountains beyond.

'I don't know. I doubt we'll ever know in our lifetimes but I think we're making a solid start. We need to micro-analyse behavioural changes, thought processes, intimacy events, responses to verbal and practical tasks and group dynamics to differentiate them further. We need to break them down and separate them by as many variables as possible, to a granular level. We need more Kin, more time and more space.'

'Intimacy events?'

Megan laughed, her voice sounding out over the

darkening sky like a clear bell. Dandridge leaned over and kissed her gently on her cheek, as the tablet on the hemp rug next to her gave a slight ping and a yellow triangle appeared on the screen. She idly reached down and hit the triangle. The screen opened out to a video screen where after a few moments she saw the boy, covered in blood and looking more than a bit crazy. She picked up the device and held it out in front of her so Dandridge could see it too.

They watched the whole thing through twice. Then they ordered all the Kin indoors and locked the apartment down as tightly as they could. Dandridge gave his instructions and left them to it, making sure they dead-bolted the locks on the flimsy doors behind him.

He ran the half-mile to town and took a cab to the Shack twenty miles away inside Chichibu National Park. There was a line of police vehicles already snaking their way up the hill towards the main entrance, well-trained Prefectural Police Kidotai officers carrying riot gear, shields, batons and pistols forming a protective line around the black ship. An armoured car with a water cannon on its roof was already in place outside the front. The Shack leader walked among the officers nervously. He was called Aki Hirota and knew Dandridge well. They spoke briefly and Aki tried to usher Dandridge inside the building, but he refused. He had only come up to the Shack to check they were adequately prepared and he wanted to be back home with Megan and his Kin study group.

The time was nine o'clock in the evening and the video had been posted from somewhere in the UK shortly earlier, about midday given the time difference. They didn't have long.

His taxi had left so he borrowed Aki's bicycle and began to pedal hard back down the twisting road, feeling energised and exhilarated despite the coming storm. He could see virtually the whole road ahead of him, looping downwards in long coils towards the lights of the town twinkling peacefully in the distance. A few miles away he could see a line of cars, a snake of glinting metal creeping upwards towards him, a large pick-up truck filled with people at its head.

Dandridge gripped the rubberised handlebars of his borrowed Tsunoda bicycle and pedalled on. A couple of miles further down the twisting road he met the line of traffic coming the other way. There was music, shouting and catcalling, but he didn't stop. The crowd seemed mainly young with a few middle aged couples and a lot of girls joining in the shouting and chaos as well. Dandridge knew from Japanese television news that the girls, and a lot of the boys, adored Luke as fervently as if he was in a J-Pop boy-band, his videos inciting hysteria in his followers. He imagined the latest video might have sent them into hormonal meltdown.

Dandridge pedalled faster, the bike flying down the road past the endless line of brightly coloured cars making their way up to the Shack and the Kin ship. The police were in for a long night.

The cars were still turning onto the long road leading upwards when he cut the corner of the junction and bounced over a verge, skidding the bike in a sideways turn and pedalling towards their apartment. It took him another half an hour and he was hot and gasping for breath, but he had not stopped or slowed for an instant. He could see two cars parked outside the compound, a modified Nissan GTR and a Toyota GT86 in metallic orange with a double spoiler on the bootlid. He pedalled towards them, not slowing down, ramming the bike into the front of the Toyota and leaping cleanly from the bike onto the roof of the garish car, taking a step from the roof to the spoiler then a jump up to catch the top of the high wall that surrounded their yard.

He pulled himself up and over, splashing down on the other side into a river of white blood. He made his way through the house slowly. All the Kin were dead. Most had been beaten or cut open and all of them had chunks carved out of them. There was no sign of Megan. Upstairs, he found four Japanese youths in the larger bunkroom, three boys and a girl in their late teens or very early twenties. He recognised one of them, a pizza delivery boy he remembered over-tipping.

The youngest Japanese male had a sword of some description. The handle was ornate and the steel blade gleamed, probably an heirloom kept sharp by his father. The tip of the blade was buried in a Kin and he was twisting it cruelly. The Kin was making no sound but his hands were futilely trying to pull it out. The girl wore a new, oversized T-shirt with an image of Luke's bloody torso printed on it.

'That's enough,' Dandridge said and they all turned in surprise. 'You've done enough damage here. It's time you left. Right now.'

One of them drew a short, vicious looking billy club from his belt.

'He's leading you wrong,' Dandridge said, nodding at the girl's shirt. 'Please don't listen to him. You're causing irreparable damage.'

He could see white smears and splatters on their faces and hands. They were currently being overwhelmed by the sort of confidence, arrogance and anger that only Kin flesh could offer.

Dandridge held his hands up and backed away from them.

'Where's the girl?' he asked. One of them nodded towards the smaller bunkroom next door. He ran to the door and slid it open. Megan was on the floor surrounded by more dead and decapitated Kin. She was lying between two Kin bodies, a large red bump on the side of her head. She was unconscious and unresponsive, blood dribbling from her nose. Her pulse was weak and her pupils showed no response. Dandridge put her in the recovery position and called the emergency services. The phone rang and rang but was answered eventually. The operator spoke perfect English and took all the details calmly, promising help within three hours before hanging up. Megan's breathing was shallow. She had a head injury and three hours was too long.

Dandridge sat back on the polished wooden floor and stared at her for a few seconds. He reached over and tore white flesh from one of the Kin bodies next to him. He pressed it to her mouth, turning her head so it could dribble down her throat. She stirred, but did not wake up. Then he tore off more and squeezed the white juice into his own mouth. He recalled the dry sense of humour the alien had displayed when they had spoken just that morning, the generosity and interest it had shown in their work.

Dandridge quivered with the now familiar sensation that crept over him as the meat insinuated itself around his bones, weaving around his muscles and sinews, soaking into the very fabric of his soul. Sadness, frustration and anger formed before his eyes as living breathing entities, helping him to his feet and taking his hand, leading him from the room.

The four Japanese youths had finished tormenting the Kin in the other room. It was dead, it's throat slit open and white juice oozing sluggishly from the wound. Dandridge stood in the doorway and cleared his throat.

The one with the billy club came at him first, swinging wildly. Dandridge ducked the attack easily, bobbing down and then up again with a vicious right hook to the boy's jaw, which broke with sharp *crack*, teeth splintering in his mouth. The boy went down and received a final kick to the face, hearing his nose break with the same splintering noise, his newly rearranged features destined to be a permanent reminder of this day. He started sobbing, spitting blood and teeth.

The second and third came at Dandridge together, the

one just in front holding his father's sword out and up in front of him with no real idea how to use it. He chopped it downwards like a meat cleaver towards Dandridge's head, but he swayed back and it whistled down past him, the point an inch in front of his nose. At the lowest point of the wild downward swing Dandridge raised his leg high and stamped down on the blade, snatching the handle from it's owner's grasp and slamming it to the floor. He kicked it away.

The third man had launched a punch at his face, which connected and threw his head to the side, white stars briefly blossoming in his vision. He shook them away and launched his own offensive, managing to block a second punch to his gut and counterpunching once, twice, three times, each hook harder than the last, connecting hard, each one breaking something in his opponent's face who was driven backwards with each blow, unable to properly deflect and desperately trying to cover his head with his arms.

The swordsman, the youngest of the three and now with no sword to protect him, tried to attack at the same time, but Dandridge easily pushed aside his weaker punch and kicked him hard between the legs, causing the young man's world to split apart in white hot agony. He went down to join his friend, in too much pain to even scream or sob, only managing strangled gargling noises. The last boy standing was holding his head in his hands, tears streaming down his face, his eyes already blackening. He held his arms up in a gesture of surrender.

Then the girl jumped on Dandridge's back, pounding his head and trying to squeeze his throat, clawing at his face and neck. He spun around and threw her off. She crashed straight through the thin wall, her scream of shock as she was thrown abruptly cut off as she hit the ground in the next room and the air was knocked out of her. She crumpled to the ground, wheezing. The boy still with arms outstretched had dropped to his knees beseechingly.

Dandridge picked up the discarded sword.

'Mercy?' he asked. 'Really? Did you show *them* mercy?' indicating the dead Kin all around them and stepping towards the cowering boy, whose own t-shirt had an image of Sonny Chiba as the assassin *Golgo 13* on it.

'Please,' he whispered.

The girl had regained her feet and ran at Dandridge again with pure hate shining in her eyes.

He sidestepped her and used her own momentum to trip her down to the floor. Her brief distraction gave the boy some more courage and he lunged forward at Dandridge, but found only the point of the sword raised up towards him, his forward momentum impaling him on the blade, straight through Sonny Chiba's cool white suit. His eyes went wide in shock and terror and he made a gargling whimper as Dandridge withdrew the blade. He collapsed, writhing in agony and clutching his belly as his blood spurted onto the wooden floor.

'Don't worry,' Dandridge said, 'an ambulance is on the way. It'll be here in three hours.'

The girl knelt next to her mortally wounded friend, her own screams adding to the general din.

Dandridge held the sword towards her and she scrambled backwards away from it until she was pinned against the wall. This time the point was pressing against the image of Luke's head on her oversized t-shirt, his enraged face staring at Dandridge from between the girl's breasts.

'*He's bad news,*' Dandridge whispered. '*Don't trust a word he says.*'

He pushed the point of the blade through the image and didn't stop until it was wedged in the wall behind her.

JOSH

A line of riot police had linked arms and formed a virtually impenetrable human chain around the entrance to the Shack. It was dark and most of the Kin were engaged in their reproductive cycle, unable to resist the pull of their genetic heritage, merging themselves together to replace their lost numbers. One of the few Kin that resisted the pull of their genetics was the first Kin who stood next to Josh in the huge, airy glass reception of the Shack, both of them silently watching as a large, organised crowd shouted and pushed against the police barricade. Some carried placards urging the removal or control of Kin without delay, but in shorter, ruder phrases. Somebody lobbed a bottle of burning liquid right over the heads of the Police line and it smashed against the glass doors, erupting briefly in flames before sputtering out, leaving a black sooty mark on the glass. Josh leapt back in shock.

'Kin, you'd better go. Go and find somewhere safe.'

'I fear nowhere is safe, not any more.'

'Safer than here then, right in front of them. You're probably going to incite them more.'

'I will go downstairs to the medical facility. There may be casualties.'

'OK. Kin. I'm sorry.'

The Kin cocked its head and seemed to look directly at Josh, in that curious way most Kin had developed.

'It is not your fault, Josh. Humans have a word called 'fate' that we do not. Perhaps we were supposed to die on our own planet with all the others. Perhaps fate brought us here, and merely delayed the inevitable.'

'There is no fate but what we make, Kin,' Josh said, conscious that he was quoting from *Terminator 2* and hoping the Kin hadn't seen it. 'I do not believe you will die today, or tomorrow. We will get through this and move on.'

The Kin moved away down the corridor towards the

medical centre. The lifts had been disabled and as many Kin as possible were sheltering in the subterranean levels.

'I hope so,' it replied, 'because it didn't end so well for humanity in that film.'

It disappeared and the door swung shut with a soft click as more objects were thrown and the police surged forward, forcing the crowd back as far as they were able. The shouting intensified. The crowd sounded like it was getting bigger and more vociferous. Josh cursed the boy. His words had incited the entire country and now lives were at stake, not just Kin but human too.

The Shack was in Gloucestershire farming country and Josh wasn't entirely surprised to see two tractors approaching from the distance, parting the protesting crowd like Moses, if Moses drove two huge green, diesel-belching Massey-Fergusons. The police had two dark blue armoured cars lined up in a triangular formation at the front gates to prevent vehicular incursion, but in a face-off between them and the tractors, which had large, lethal-looking digging scoops, Josh wasn't sure which would come out on top. At best one would cancel out the other, which would leave a fairly uneven confrontation between the police and a crowd of thousands, some of whom had already killed and consumed Kin flesh.

The main glass wall of his and Marion's office afforded a view of the main entrance on one side and the interior of the Shack on the other. It was fully soundproofed so he could watch the crowd outside completely isolated from the noise and shouting, like a Bond villain relying on his army of henchmen as his lair was overrun.

It took nearly an hour and a half, a truly exceptional effort by the police, but the swelling, surging crowd eventually proved too large and too persistent to hold back. The tractors had neutralised the water-cannon and with a great roar of approval that Josh heard even through the solid windows of the office, some of the crowd broke through and sprinted towards the Shack. The glass double doors were not designed to withstand a prolonged attack and were forced apart almost immediately.

The first few to gain access sprinted in to the lobby and then stopped dead, perhaps wondering where to go, but as the trickle of people behind them became a flood they were pushed forwards towards the far end of the reception area, another glass wall with two much smaller locked glass doors leading outside onto what was once the parade ground between the three main buildings of RAF Wenham, now surrounded by the vast hulk of the Kin ship and the newer Shack buildings.

The relocation to Australia was ongoing, but the Kin ship was still almost fully occupied. Josh had told them to stay put until the violence calmed down. Alongside the base of the ship and just behind the older original buildings were the temporary accommodations, also jam full of Kin.

More and more people surged in and now the whole reception was full of shouting and screaming, hundreds of protesting people waving flags and anti-Kin placards, holding flares or burning effigies of Kin crudely made from white pillow cases and sheets. The reception was being trashed. More people pushed in and more were being forced up against the far double doors that weren't opening. A breakaway river of people had found the stairway door and were disappearing downwards towards the subterranean centre where most of the Shack science facilities were located.

But the stairway door was narrow and only a few people at a time could push through. The first few who had made it past the police line and into the Shack were now being crushed against the unyielding safety glass at the far end. Josh watched from his office as a heaving, churning crowd of people in brightly coloured waterproof outerwear helplessly washed up against the glass as more and more people were pushed into them from behind. The screams of protest were turning into screams for help.

With a growing horror Josh realised that the doors were the only thing protecting the Kin from the crowd. If he opened them to save the humans now suffocating under their own weight, there could be a massacre. Josh had diverted all control of the Shack's external and environmental security controls to his own desk. His finger hovered over the left button of his mouse, the pointer of which was positioned over the grey button marked *atrium doors* and *unlock*.

He hesitated.

ADLER

It was the boy, of course, in the end. His final blood-soaked and merciless rallying call against an oppressive, secretive government, the Kin themselves and of course, his stepmother. The people watching and re-watching his video for inspiration and guidance, more and more of them getting jacked up on Kin flesh, letting the pure meat soak into their bones and muscles and thoughts. They seemed to love Luke unconditionally.

Incited to a wild, panicked frenzy, the whole world was being upended. Kin were being slaughtered by the thousands. More reports than Adler could keep up with. More and more humans were getting hooked on the flesh, consuming it in huge quantities, feeling stronger, faster, healthier, cleverer, *better*.

There were too many deaths now for the Kin to keep increasing their number by such huge leaps, but the few that were clear to replicate were doing so, adding millions more every few hours and during the night when even the jacked-up humans had to sleep.

The Prime Minister, looking tired and desperate and frazzled, gave the order for a curfew. It was a desperate measure and he was well aware that martial law was not something modern civilisation was going to easily accept. And so it proved.

The curfew was reasonably well adhered to in suburbs and outskirts of towns, traditionally places where families tended to live and commute. Those who had been sharing with Kin kept them inside, kept them safe. Elsewhere attacks against the Kin and the police assigned to protect them increased. There were more violent anti-Kin demonstrations and riots in every city, with regular battles on the streets. Where access to automatic weapons was more commonplace the military were overwhelmed and outnumbered, still unwilling to shoot civilians despite the aggression.

Although the flesh affected people differently, in a fight the result was the same. The military were being beaten back as the very people they were sworn to protect kept on coming at them, full of hate and convinced of their own righteous course of action, blinded by the heat of conflict, a new feeling for most and utterly intoxicating; feeling stronger, healing faster, the flesh melting away fear. Some soldiers had started to ingest Kin flesh to level the playing field but they were still outnumbered and there were frequent reports of military personnel abandoning their posts to kill and eat more Kin to feed the desire of their own burgeoning addiction.

Adler read the reports as they came in and watched the footage as the world dissolved around him. He monitored and waited. He wasn't sure what he was waiting for and the Prime Minister had now stopped taking his calls, but he knew that one way or another something had to give. So he waited for a window of opportunity, a chance to try and step in to change what the world was becoming.

And then his phone rang and he answered it and listened, and the window opened, just a crack.

Twenty minutes after the call he was standing alongside an old Police-liveried Vauxhall Astra in the underground car park beneath Whitehall. He wore a Kevlar vest over his usual grey suit. His driver was fully decked in riot gear from head to toe, right up to the helmet and clear faceguard.

'You protected enough, Sergeant?' asked Adler, glancing at him up and down.

The Sergeant nodded.

'Can't be too careful, sir. Don't know if you've heard, but there's a bloody war going on out there. Are you sure we can't wait for the SWAT team?'

'They're busy. They'll follow on later.'

They climbed in and the car was buzzed out of the garage, driving up the ramp into the late afternoon sunshine. Almost immediately they could hear the sounds of shouting. Armed guards stood aside, aiming their SA80 assault rifles up and out, protecting the building as the car accelerated, clearing the gates quickly and accelerating away, the Sergeant swerving past groups of people walking in the middle of the road, waving placards and weapons - bats and pipes and sticks and other makeshift and lethal looking objects. They were cheering and chanting and threw debris at the car as it went past.

Their fastest route to his destination was straight through the West End. Wherever they went they observed people fighting; with the police, the army, with Kin or each other. Three times they had to back up and find a way around clashes between the authorities and the jacked-up populace.

They drove past the shattered remains of Kin. White bodies, parts of bodies, smears of white on the pavements, injured Kin crawling and staggering away from the violent hordes. A huge crowd had gathered outside the British Museum, holding aloft the bodies of Kin who had tried to seek refuge in the nooks and crannies within the ancient edifice.

Adler and his driver didn't stop. They kept on driving, sounding the siren when the crowds didn't get out of the way in time.

Turning onto the Euston Road they faced a huge crowd of people coming the other way, herding a group of Kin like cattle. The unresisting white and blue aliens were being poked and prodded by sharp sticks to keep them moving forwards. The police sergeant slowed the car.

'I'll find another way around, sir,' he said, and spun the wheel.

'Hold on. Stop a sec. You got a megaphone?' Adler opened the door and the policeman stamped on the brakes.

'Sir, I wouldn't advise this. There's too many of them. Let's just save the ones we can.'

Adler hesitated, his hand on the car door handle, watching the crowd. Then an object was thrown, a bottle, and it shattered over the bonnet and windscreen of the police car. He stepped out holding the megaphone. Even with his voice amplified he had to shout to make himself heard, but the crowd didn't seem to hear him and kept on coming towards them.

They were nearly at the police car, parked side on to them straddling the street. The Sergeant stood next to Adler, holding a semi-automatic.

'Put that away. We don't want to incite them.'

'Bit too late for that.'

Adler raised the megaphone. 'Please disperse and leave the Kin here. I repeat. Disperse immediately and leave the Kin here. Go home.'

The crowd kept coming, herding the Kin before them. Adler motioned for them to get into the car, but there were too many of them. They all ran forward and four managed to squeeze in, a dangerous game of musical chairs. The ones left out stood behind the car as the crowd met them and came to an awkward halt. The shouting was so loud Adler could barely hear the voice of the woman standing right at the front. She was in her mid-fifties, carrying a silver baseball bat that was smeared with white.

'Those Kin are ours. We're holding them.'

'For what?' Adler shouted back.

'For later!' she shouted and the crowd around her cheered and laughed.

'I can't let you take them,' Adler shouted back at her.

'You can't stop us. The Kin are taking over our country, taking over the whole *world*, don't you see? We need to kill them all. Don't be so *blind*.'

'That isn't true. We need to protect them.'

'Stand aside!' the woman shouted, raising her bat against Adler as the crowd surged forward. She was pushed into him and the two fell to the tarmac as hundreds of feet rushed around them, trampling them both. A large section of the crowd gathered and began shaking the police vehicle, rocking it violently on its wheels.

There was a loud gunshot and everyone leapt back as if the car had just electrocuted them. The Sergeant pulled Adler to his feet, briefly engaging the woman in a tug of war using Adler as the rope. She let go when the Sergeant kicked her in the face with his steel toe-capped boot. She fell back to the ground, spitting blood and expensive dental work from her ruined mouth.

Witnesses to the assault launched themselves in fury at the Sergeant who disappeared under a heaving mass of bodies. Adler heard gunshots and panicked shouts from under the struggling mass. By the time he had fought his way in to reach him, the Sergeant had killed at least two people and was covered in blood.

The crowd surrounded them both in a wide circle, waving their weapons, jeering and chanting. The policeman held his gun out, pointing at them in turn and keeping them back, but they seemed to sense that he wasn't willing to pull the trigger any more. The police car was overturned with an almighty crash, the windows exploding outwards. A man threw a lit Zippo and it caught fire in seconds.

As the smell of burning petrol and the intoxicating smell of incinerated Kin reached their nostrils, the crowd set upon them both.

MARION

She sat on her bunk at Whitehall as the curfew came into effect. The British Army and the police continued to patrol the streets of London but large crowds defied the official State of National Emergency and there were running skirmishes around the capital. Any Kin caught in the crossfire were beaten or hunted or mown down by vehicles. They had learned very quickly to stay out of sight but the sheer number of them on the streets made it hard to do.

Every single coach company nationally had been commandeered to ferry them out of harms way to all the major evacuation ports where a huge number of luxury cruise ships had been ordered to get them out of the country.

Australia still seemed a relatively safe place. All the Kin arriving and being birthed there were being protected by the majority of the population. Marion thought that they seemed rather proud that they would be the new custodians of the alien species.

She and Mike and their team had worked together to negotiate with Australian officials all over the country; councils and planners, contractors, surveyors, farmers, small holders and lawyers. They had bought, bartered and requisitioned three hundred million empty acres of farmland in the Northern Territory for the relocation. It was hot out there but preparation for a new Kin city had begun to take shape in the vast, dusty expanse. The Kin, averse to cold, seemed not to mind the heat and the area was ideal. The sparse local native population were being offered the chance to relocate anywhere - globally - or to live with the new species but to date remarkably few had taken up the offer.

For a while, Marion had dared to hope that it might actually work. She and Mike were fighting their personal demons together and the unexpected success they were having with their massive and unlikely plan to relocate an entire species was somehow helping them recover and normalise. But as they both sat on her narrow cot at nearly nine o'clock in the evening listening to sirens and gunshots on the streets outside, the two of them sat and wept and cuddled and talked and wept some more.

'The world is falling apart,' whispered Marion, 'and it's my fault.'

'It fell apart the moment they arrived,' replied Mike. 'Not that I remember it very well. And of course it isn't your fault.'

'I wonder where he is. Luke, I mean.'

'I don't care and it doesn't really matter, not now. The damage is done. All we can do is carry on with the plan.'

'But there's going to be so many more of them now,'

'They won't be able to replace all the dead. More than a few million more though, all the ones in safety.'

'So is that how we kill them? Slaughter them faster than they can reproduce? A war of attrition?'

'It's not a war.'

'No? Can you not hear the gunfire outside?'

'A war requires two armies. Currently, we're only fighting amongst ourselves.'

Somebody cleared their throat behind them. Both Mike and Marion leapt up like two guilty teenagers.

'Prime Minister. I didn't know you were there. Where's Greta?' Marion asked, referring to the PM's closest aide and general lackey.

'Sleeping, next door. She hasn't slept for three days. Marion, you know the Kin better than anyone. Do you know how they are reacting, as a whole, to this crisis?'

'I have no idea, Prime Minister. I've not been back to the Shack for months, since I got on that damn plane to Buenos Aires. Josh is there though, right?'

'Perron. Yes, he's under siege at the moment, like all the others.'

'Is he OK?'

'So far. The Army are sending reinforcements.'

'Where's Adler?'

'I don't know, he's not answering his phone.'

'Dandridge?'

'I'm not sure, although the region of Japan where he and the girl were studying has been hit pretty hard. The DarkNet is really popular over there, for some reason.'

'Easier accessibility, I suppose,' Mike said.

'Yes, but in general the Net has slowed to a crawl. There are too many videos being uploaded to the newsfeeds. Hundreds of hours. The available bandwidth is being clogged up. I've got a couple of people downloading everything for future identification of potential culprits.'

'Good.'

They stood for a few awkward seconds more, before the Prime Minister cleared his throat.

'Ah, Marion, the Australian PM wants to talk to you.'

'Oh, right, thank you sir.' She stood up, feeling slightly confused as to why the Prime Minister would wait so long to tell her that his counterpart in Australia was hanging on the line listening to the 'on hold' muzak. She kissed Mike on the lips before following the Prime Minister from the room. She followed him through the myriad complex of winding corridors in which it was all to easy to become hopelessly lost. She entered the empty communications office and sat down on her swivel chair. The Prime Minister sat on the edge of her desk. She glanced up at him.

'Sir? Do you need to be on the call? We can do this in the conference room on speaker if you'd prefer-'

'There is no call, Marion. My apologies for the deception. Something has happened, and I need your help.'

'What's that, sir?' she asked nervously.

The PM reached into the inside of his tailored suit jacket and withdrew a narrow plastic container about the size of a chocolate biscuit. He snapped it open, revealing a smear of white flesh inside it. Marion's heart seemed to leap in her chest.

'Sir,' she said, standing up and pushing the chair away, backing up. 'I don't understand.'

'That's OK, Marion,' he said, 'because for once since they arrived, I think I do. For the very first time since this whole fucking thing started, I understand everything. I know what I have to do.'

DANDRIDGE

Strapped securely into a narrow metal seat on an RAF Lockheed C-130 transport aircraft and illuminated by a single caged red lightbulb, Dandridge watched through one of the tiny windows opposite him at the pitch black sky, which seemed not to be moving at all. The world seemed so small when he considered that he could get from Japan to the UK in a little under twelve hours.

The plane had arrived to collect them as Japan was imploding into violence and chaos. It seemed that there were very few pro-Kin citizens in the country and nearly all of them were on the streets, defying the curfew and slaughtering as many Kin as they could find. Most of the Kin were locked in helpless procreation and easy targets. The few who weren't were cut down. The streets were awash with white flesh.

The Shacks had capitulated easily, the human aggressors driven relentlessly onward by the energy and clarity that the flesh had given them. It was still happening, unabated.

He was tired and sickened to his core. He was flying back to London but he wasn't sure to do what, the whole world was treading the same path and there was little he could do to stop it. A pattern of behaviour and violence was emerging that wouldn't easily be broken.

The rattle, shake and engine roar of the huge uninsulated aircraft was deafening and his metal seat too uncomfortable. Sleep was impossible. His phone vibrated in his pocket, the merest touch of a butterfly wing compared to the vibration all around him. He could only feel it because everything seemed a little too bright and too real since he had, for the second time in his life, ingested Kin flesh to fuel a retaliation.

It was a number he didn't recognise flashing on the small blue screen. He raised it to his ear not expecting to be able to hear a single thing, but the voice at the other end of the line cut clearly through the noise and roar of the aircraft.

'Richard.'

All their voices were identical and yet he recognised her immediately. All of a sudden she was all he could hear, her voice flooding through him like a freezing cold Mojito on a hot tropical evening.

'Where are you, Belle?' he said.

'Safe, for now. But it's time. Time for us to do something. We have acquiesced long enough.'

'I understand. Shall I come to you or will you come to me?'

'We shall meet in the middle. I have spoken with Ernest C. Adler and Michael Hennessy.'

'Before me?'

'Now is not the time for jealousy, Richard.'

'Fair point.'

'The British Army is clearing the first Shack of Kin and human corpses and should be finished in about twenty four hours. Thanks to the actions of Josh Perron far fewer Kin were killed there than at any other Shack.'

'Is that right? Good lad.'

'I assume that you have not had access to the news channels or the DarkNet recently or you might have been aware. His actions also resulted in the deaths of at least sixty humans. He is currently in custody for manslaughter and negligence.'

'Shit.'

'We shall meet in exactly 48 hours at the first Shack.'

'I'm across time-zones, what's the time now?'

'Eight o'clock in the morning. And Richard?'

'Yeah?'

'I have missed you.' The line went dead, but Dandridge held it to his ear for the next minute as the noise of the plane gradually seeped back into his consciousness. He didn't mind it any more.

PART TWELVE

NELLA

She started her career as a pub singer, touring backwater country pubs in Kent singing soul classics; *Midnight Train to Georgia, Rollin' in the Deep, I'm Every Woman*. Henderson Mulcahy was a moderately successful hip-hop artist who had just controversially fired his old label and started his own. His first signing was a rapper called Tanque Grrrl. Nella had auditioned as a backing singer for Tanque Grrrl (*'call me 'TG'*, the rapper informed her) in a small recording studio in London's Soho when Henderson had first noticed her. After her audition he called her mobile number before she had even made it down the couple of stone steps to the narrow pavement outside the studio. He instructed her to wait, then a few minutes later picked her up in a long black Mercedes, rolling the tinted window down and gesturing for her to get in.

Within a week he had overturned her life completely. He moved her in to his small suite inside Uzi Bitch Records, back then located above a hat shop in Camden. Her backing vocals graced all his record releases for the next eight years and she occasionally released her own, moderately successful, singles. When UBR took off and Henderson stopped recording to become a mogul full-time she stepped willingly into his PA's shoes, becoming his confidante and full time companion.

Compared with singing to indifferent chain pub audiences in Kent night after night she was living the dream. Each morning she woke up next to Henderson in his gigantic bed she would pinch herself for reassurance that it was still all real. Then she would relax again, but tried never to kid herself that it was going to last.

For some reason inexplicable to Nella, Henderson's favourite restaurant was one of the dirty and cheap all-you-can-eat for five pounds, pack 'em in tight, fill 'em up and get 'em out quick Chinese food joints in Soho. Such was his charisma, Henderson had somehow convinced his entire staff that this place served the best Chinese food in London. They didn't normally take reservations but one evening all of UBR took over his preferred branch of Mr. Wu. They were loud and enthusiastically tucking into the dry looking food as Nella was picking on a prawn cracker.

In that place, over his plate of spring rolls and shredded beef covered in a glowing orange sauce, Henderson told Nella that he wanted her to stay with him, in his room and in his bed, but their sexual relationship was over. He enjoyed her company, needed her warmth, loved her voice and respected her counsel but he no longer wanted her body. Blinded by her love she had agreed, convinced that once they were naked together again he would not be able to resist her.

That night she opened herself up to him, mentally and physically, but he didn't touch her. Not then, or ever again. They lived in every respect like a couple, both in public and private. There were no barriers or secrets between them but their physical relationship had ended.

Within a year she was running UBR and involved in the day to day decision making of all his affiliated businesses, as well as acting as his PA and chauffeur. She slept no more than four hours a night and never took a holiday, except with Henderson.

And then the Kin arrived and it all changed again. She was forced to share her responsibilities with a supremely intelligent alien being, which took some getting her head around. Henderson started to act more erratically, but not so much that anyone but her really noticed.

After a couple of years of rubbing along with the alien reasonably well Henderson sent her to run the New York offices of UBR for a month. On her return, the Kin was strapped into a hollow prison in the centre of the penthouse and being subjected to slow torture and gradual dismemberment.

She had screamed in horror, tried to free it, tried to run. But Henderson was fascinated by the Kin meat, permanently high on the euphoria it was generating inside him. He was already successful, ambitious, shrewd and manipulative, but on the goodness of the flesh he had become fixated on his own empire building and his own desires.

He insisted, and she, as always, capitulated to him. He fed her the meat and they shared in the bliss it gave them and they made love for the first time in years, right there on the floor next to the trapped creature. It was the most intensely passionate experience of her life, but never repeated.

There was no part of Henderson's life that was closed to her, not even the darker threads of his complicated psyche. She knew that his desire for young male company was a chink in his virtually impenetrable armour, an aspect of him that she could not fathom or reconcile. There was nothing she could do but to ignore it.

Not long after he began to ingest the Kin flesh and his

behaviour started to change, she invested her own money into a fledgling recording studio based in North London. She would retreat there whenever he interviewed prospective artists for the UBR label, all boys still in school with stars and fame in their eyes and minds. She found herself at her studio more and more often, writing songs or laying down tracks three or more times a week.

On her return to the penthouse the evidence left lying around and on storage devices became more and more explicit and disturbing. The Kin flesh was peeling away his layers, stripping his armour and making him incapable of suppressing any desire or idea he had ever harboured. He was as fully reliant on the flesh, both human and Kin, as a junkie to heroin, only there was no recourse to help or rehab without exposing his addictions to the world.

It seemed to Nella that the more boys he seduced the more he hated the Kin. When she raised it with him he shot her down, getting angry with her for the very first time.

By this time he had been working for a couple of years on a new information platform. He showed her the evidence he had gathered from hacking into completely unguarded local networks, Government and Shack records and databases. The number of Kin were rising, it was a recorded but unpublished fact. Rising fast. Their meat was addictive, encouraging humans to destroy and devour, and as soon as they did, more would take their place.

It seemed clear to Henderson. This was an invasion, an insidious parasitic invasion. He became determined to stop it, recruiting people around the world to help him, gradually gathering his own army ready for the right moment to strike.

Then the plane crash happened and the cogs of his plan started to turn. The death of Royce Brims, a promising young artist who had once been so easily seduced by promises of fame and fortune, turned her world around again, and she knew the time had come to fulfil

Henderson's plan.

At six in the morning four days after Luke's final incendiary message, and the world was on fire. She was already up, showered and dressed. She wore her favourite dress, a simple, shimmering silver Burberry number, fitted so closely that it seemed almost sheer. Her hair was up and out, almost perfectly spherical and glowing in the early morning sun. Her makeup was minimally applied, only underlining her beauty. Her lips were full and glistening red.

The outside alarm sounded along the stone wall that surrounded the house, but she wasn't surprised. She was actually more surprised it had taken them so long.

She went downstairs. A man stood in her living room. He wore a dark overcoat that had seen better days. It was covered in red and white blood and torn in a number of places. One of the sleeves hung on by a thread. He had cuts and bruises on his face, a black eye. His hands looked raw and pulpy, knuckles still bleeding.

'I can mend that sleeve, if you like,' Nella said softly as she descended the stairs.

'Where is he?' Adler asked.

'Who?'

'The boy. I know he's here. I want you to get him for me, right now.'

'He's here. But he's asleep. He sleeps quite late, you know how teenagers are.'

'Not really.'

'Well, come with me.'

She lead the man down the steps. Luke was fast asleep on top of his mattress soaked in blood that had now dried to a rusty brown colour. There was a fresh bandage around his upper right arm. The large television was on, set to rolling news.

They stood looking at him but he didn't stir.

'Is he a prisoner here?'

'Not at all. I have offered him a room in the main house,

but he prefers it here in the basement. You know how teenagers are- oh wait, you don't. Sorry.'

Luke showed no signs of waking up.

'What are you going to do with him?' she asked, looking down at his softly breathing form.

'I'm not willing to discuss it with you, Ms. Monroe. You are under arrest, by the way.'

'What are the charges?'

'Harbouring a minor and the suspected murder of Henderson Mulcahy, Royce Brims, Buddy Tucker and a Kin.'

'I didn't kill them.'

'You know what, Ms. Monroe? It doesn't really matter. You planned, participated and incited the possible genocide of an entire species. A species that only wanted a place to live, somewhere to stay.'

'They want more than that.'

'Possibly. I don't believe so and now perhaps we'll never know. But it wasn't your call to make, was it? Not yours. Not that sack-of-shit Mulcahy, and certainly not this boy. I had to kill four human beings to get to you today and one police officer died to save me, although he had every right to leave me there. I hold you personally responsible.'

Luke stirred and opened his eyes. He sat up, scrambled backwards and snatched up the sheet, quickly covering himself with it.

'Too late for modesty now, Luke,' Adler said. 'I think we've both seen everything, haven't we Ms. Monroe?'

'Come on, sweetheart,' Nella whispered to him, 'we have to go now.'

'Where?' Luke asked, his voice panicky, a world away from the smooth, confident, enigmatic speaker from the videos.

'I'm not sure the nice man is going to tell us.'

Nella opened a dresser and pulled out fresh underwear, still wrapped in the shop's cardboard packaging. She tore it off and threw him a pair. She found jeans and a fresh shirt in a trunk. As Luke hurriedly dressed himself, Adler saw the old and new cuts and scabs on his thighs and arms. The kid was a mess.

After he was dressed, Adler motioned him upstairs with a nod of his head. He went first, followed by Nella. Adler climbed up behind them. Luke opened the front door, squinting and holding his arm across his eyes against the first bright morning light he had seen for months. As soon as he stepped onto the cracked stone doorstep, he was grabbed by two black-clad SWAT police and taken to the ground in seconds, his legs kicked out from under him and his arms pinned behind his back. He screamed in shock. A medic in full Kevlar protective clothing stepped up and jammed a syringe into the side of his neck, pressing the plunger. Luke drew an agonised, hitching gasp as if gathering his breath for a massive scream of pain, but it never came. It only took a few seconds before his unconscious body was being carried to a dark blue unmarked van and placed inside, the doors slamming shut behind him.

'What are you going to do with him?' Nella asked. Adler ignored the question.

'I want to take a closer look at where he was staying, Ms. Monroe. Please show me.'

Nella Monroe lead Adler back down the steps to the basement. He put a bullet in the back of her head as she stepped off the final step. It parted the tight curls of her afro, blowing out her forehead and left eye. She fell forwards, almost dead before she even hit the concrete. Adler placed another bullet just underneath the first.

He went back up to the waiting vehicles and dialled out a signal to a radio operator five hundred miles away, who gave the standard issue 'thumbs up' sign to the drone operator sitting next to him. As Adler and the SWAT team bounced away from the remote building down the unmade, rutted track through the densely packed trees, the house went up in an enormous blue and yellow explosion behind them. Rubble rained down around the blue vans as they retreated, clonking and bouncing off the armoured plates. The entire house, ramshackle but historic and ancient and beautiful, collapsed in on itself, burning.

They kept going, and nobody looked back.

*

MIKE

Mike had always believed that the perceived differences between North and South London were entirely the figment of proud, territorial Londoners, but as he picked his way carefully through the unfamiliar streets he realised that he might as well be in a foreign country.

Before he had run out of the building to his secret rendezvous, Adler had telephoned him with an address and told him to meet him there. He had memorised the address and instructions and destroyed the paper. It was in a part of North West London with which he wasn't familiar at all.

He figured that the best way to get through the war zone of Central and North London was to just go alone and avoid the trouble spots, pretend to be a Kin-hater where necessary and merge into the marches. Any kind of police protection would only incite violence. It took him close to two hours from Whitehall but he reached the address without incident, an industrial estate near Stonebridge Park Tube Station.

It was close to curfew but there were large swathes of people and protestors still out and scouring the streets with baseball and cricket bats, golf clubs, hockey sticks and a variety of other blunt instruments designed for killing Kin. Mike wandered through the huge industrial estate for a few minutes until he found the nondescript, beige corrugated unit he was looking for. He made his way around to a back door, picking through shoulder-high weeds and derelict rusty equipment the purpose of which was long forgotten. The back fire door had once been bright red but had faded to pink and was peeling in rough, brittle flakes. As he approached, a Kin pushed it open and motioned him inside.

Mike stepped into a small, filthy kitchenette area. The white worktop had long since turned mottled brown. A battered kettle was still plugged in, but looked as if it hadn't heated any water for a long, long time. There were cupboards but no cupboard doors, the shelves empty of anything but mouse droppings. The Kin lead Mike from the kitchenette into the warehouse, which had metal steps leading to a galleried area overlooking the main unit and three smashed glass cubicle offices all in a row. One entire side was a closed metal shutter for loading and unloading.

The whole place, ground floor warehouse, gallery and offices, were filled with Kin.

'Mr. Hennessy,' the Kin said.

'Yes.'

'My name is Belle. Where is Mr. Adler?'

'He's got something else on. He'll be here soon, tonight I think. Did you say your name was *Belle?*'

'We need to get to the Shack as soon as possible. Why did Mr. Adler not send policemen?'

'There aren't any. I'm here to tell you to wait, to stay put and that Adler is on his way with SWAT. The plan is still green.'

'That is good to hear, Mr. Hennessy, although it was unnecessary for him to send a messenger.'

'I think he was afraid you'd run or change your mind.'

'We have nowhere to run. And that is why I called him.'

They were interrupted by hammering on the shutter, which made a loud crash in the large empty space, rippling like a wave with a metallic vibration. All the Kin turned toward the sound. They heard shouting from outside, a crowd.

'*We know you're in there!*' came one voice, louder than the rest, and the hammering on the door resumed.

Mike motioned to the Kin to stay, and he left the building through the pink fire door and headed round to the front. He turned the corner and was faced with a small crowd, twenty, maybe thirty men and women, all armed.

'Help you?' he called out.

The man at the front, who held a bat with a long, jagged nail pointing out of the top of it, stepped up. He wore a lime green SuperDry gilet over a dark brown hoodie and jeans. He was spattered with white Kin flesh.

'We saw you go in there. Who are you?'

'What do you want?' Mike countered.

'Is this yours?' indicating the unit.

'Why are you banging on these doors?' Mike deflected. 'Do they belong to you?'

'I own that one down the road over there. Plumbing supplies. I've not seen you about before.'

'So why are you banging on these doors? I don't need plumbing supplies.'

'There's Kin in there, I've seen them.'

'I doubt that. Move on. There's nobody here but me.'

'I want to see inside,' the man insisted, stepping towards Mike who took a step back.

'You're trespassing. I'm going to call the police,' he said.

'Fuck you, I'm going to look inside.'

'You're not. Move on, please.' But Mike was shouldered out of the way. Followed by most of the others the man went around the back to the faded red door. He took the handle and yanked it hard, pulling and pushing with some force. It didn't budge, not even a wobble. He gave up and stepped back. There was a misty spackled window next to the faded red door and he cupped his hands around his face, peering in.

'*There's Kin in here!*' he shouted. He stepped back, raised his bat and smashed the window. He made to climb in but Mike leapt forward and dragged him back. The man spun around, raised his bat and slammed the nail-end high into Mike's bicep. Mike screamed in pain as it went in and louder as it was yanked out, releasing a geyser of blood as it exited. He dropped to his knees, holding the puncture wound with his opposite hand, trying to stop the bleeding. His assailant had scrambled through the window and pulled open the fire door from the inside. The crowd poured in, and Mike could hear shouting from inside.

Somebody still had sense enough to stop and tear a sleeve from a t-shirt, wrapping it tightly around Mike's injured arm before running inside after the others. Mike felt light-headed, but staggered to his feet and inside the darkness of the unit.

'*Stop!*' he screamed, but his voice was lost in the cacophony of madness bouncing around the unit. He stepped into the darkness. The men were in a group, weapons outstretched, catcalling and whooping with delight, advancing slowly towards the Kin, who were all shrinking back along the far wall and squeezed up the metal steps onto the gallery. Mike started clawing at the people at the back of the group, desperate to get to the front and get between the humans and the Kin. One of the men at the back spun round to face him. He had a sheen of perspiration on his forehead and his eyes were moist. Mike wasn't sure if he was upset, happy or quite mad. Probably all three. There was a large, grotesque bulge in the crotch of his sweatpants he seemed unconcerned about concealing. He pushed Mike hard, who stumbled back, unbalanced by the injury in his shoulder. He went down, and the man kicked him in the stomach, hard. Once, twice, three times. The breath whoomphed out of him and he curled up into the foetal position.

'*That's enough, please.*'

The voice was distinctively the tones of a Kin, but it was raised, and there was something else in the tone, something the crowd had not heard before. It was Belle, standing at the railing of the gallery area and looking down at the advancing gang of humans.

'Please desist from any further violence towards us.'

'Or what?' the first man in his lime green gilet shouted. Mike's blood stained the nail that had been hammered through the bat.

'We have been waiting for the authorities, but I believe that they are not coming. If you persist, we will protect ourselves.'

'Protect yourselves? Do you know how many of your kind we've killed today? Hundreds. There's nothing you can do. You'll all be gone soon. Gone from this planet.'

'You are incorrect. This morning, we were four but now we are nearly forty. It seems we will always come back. We need to find a way to live, and not to fight.'

'You're fucking invading us. We're never gonna stop, not till every single one of you has fucked off back where you came from!'

'That is not possible. Where we came from has been destroyed.'

'So you say.'

'It is the truth.'

'I don't fucking care. I don't trust anything any of you say, not any more.'

Mike, now on his feet but doubled over, trying to hold in his bruised stomach and his punctured arm at the same time, spoke up.

'Don't believe what the boy said. I was there with him on the mountain. It's true what the Kin is saying. Please. Nobody need die here today.'

'There's only one thing gonna die here today-' the man started to say, before Belle took an easy vault over the railing of the gallery and dropped straight down to the dusty concrete floor beneath, landing directly in front of him. The startled man took a step back, raising his bat in defence. As fast as Mike had seen anything move, Belle snatched it out of his hands and spun it smoothly around in her palm until the bloodied nail end pointed away from her.

'I have learned,' she said, 'that sometimes there is no point arguing with humans.'

She lifted and swung, a short but perfect and powerful 45 degree swing. The nail made a soft 'chunk' as it entered the side of his neck. Belle pulled it out. The man stood speechless, making only a shocked, gurgling noise. Blood spurted from the wound and as he hitched a short cough, more blood sprayed onto the white figure in front of him, who was raising the bat for a second strike.

The second impact took the man in the temple, and he went down, the nail embedded to the hilt in his skull. Belle let the bat fall to the floor with him rather than pull it out. The figure on the floor twitched, gurgled and coughed blood, his eyes glazed over. Blood rolled and dripped off the lime green gilet onto the floor without really staining it. In his shock, Mike idly wondered if it had been waterproofed with something. Some men ran to his assistance but none seemed too keen to remove the nail from his head, or get too close.

There was shocked silence in the unit, until Belle said, 'I would advise you to call emergency services, but I understand that they are extremely busy today and I doubt they could get here in time to save this man.'

'You *killed* him,' one of the men crouching by the bleeding figure said, as the life oozed away onto the dirty floor of the industrial unit.

'I did. And now I would ask you to leave, before any more of you get hurt.'

'We're gonna fucking kill you.'

The kneeling man sprang up and launched himself at Belle, grabbing the alien around her waist and lifting her off her feet, bringing them both crashing down to the ground, where they wrestled, the guy punching Belle around her head. It was the starting pistol for the rest of the group who all attacked the closest Kin they could reach.

The melee was loud and chaotic, a dim blur of white and dark. Mike backed away into the kitchen. He watched as Belle got her thick white arm around her assailants neck and twisted. Mike heard the neck snap, the sound cutting through the rest of the noise like a twig snapping in an empty forest. The noise hurt him more than the nail in his arm. Belle was up on her feet and had taken hold of someone else from behind, twisting him away easily and stamping on his knee joint, hearing the scream before taking his head and twisting it nearly clean off his corpse. She moved onto the next one. The rest of the Kin weren't doing too badly either. They all seemed to have the measure of their human lynch-mob.

As the screams became louder, Mike had fallen to his knees in the kitchen, his forehead touching the soup-stained linoleum, his arms over his head. Then he heard engines. Loud engines. He looked up. The whole room was struggling, fighting, strangling, beating, punching. Then a noise, an ear piercing screech of metal on metal, and a chink of light as the old metal shutter began to lift. Gradually, activity stopped as the shutter rolled itself up higher and higher, revealing a pair of once-polished black brogues, a dark grey suit, the front tyres of a vehicle. A bumper, a dark khaki bonnet, and then Adler standing in front of it, holding a Russian Grach 433 pistol at his side. He was bruised and torn, his suit ruined, and he looked angry. He was flanked by four Marine Commandos. Every human and Kin in the industrial unit had stopped in the middle of what they were doing to stare at them.

'*Mike Hennessy*,' Adler called out.

'Here,' Mike called back, moving forward through the unit towards the light. He held his injured arm, which throbbed almost intolerably. Mike stepped over dead humans and dead Kin, red and white blood mingling on the floor, staining the grey concrete a shade of pink, a stain that would never be removed or scrubbed away, not until the units were torn down years later.

ADLER

'I shouldn't have sent you, I'm sorry.'

'No you shouldn't,' Mike replied, as a medic gave him a tetanus shot and bound his arm tightly. They were in the back of one of the three vans, Adler, Mike, Belle, the medic and the Commandos, sitting in two rows facing each other. 'I'm a fucking *lawyer*, Adler, not whatever the fuck you need me to be when it suits you.'

'I'm sorry. I just know I can trust you and the Kin trust you too.'

'How do you know? I'm an addict just like the rest of them.'

He cast an eye towards Belle, sitting silently opposite Adler, her front still spattered with the blood of the man she had impaled on his own lethal weapon. 'How do you know what I'm capable of?'

'I don't know. I don't know what any of us are capable of any more. I'm just trying to fix it.'

'Some things are unfixable.'

'I don't agree.'

'It's your job to not agree. It means nothing.'

The van drove through the broken, burning streets of London. Curfew was approaching and the City was quieting down, but there were still groups of people milling around, mostly now just drinking and laughing, excited, high on the flesh and thrilled to be breaking the law.

'What happens now? Even if you do manage to restore order. What happens then? They're all addicted, just like me. What happens then?'

'We'll work something out.'

'You're an arsehole, Adler, you know that?'

Adler did not reply. The convoy rumbled through London, past Wembley, Uxbridge and out into Buckinghamshire. The roads were practically deserted. Occasionally they saw a fire burning or vans full of people ignoring the curfew, driving in the other direction towards London, waving flags and makeshift weapons out of the windows in defiance of the Army convoy going the other way.

They drove for more than two and a half hours. Belle said nothing and both Adler and Mike dozed as much as they could. The Commandos all sat upright, none of them sleeping or saying anything.

The motorway gave way to A-roads, then country lanes. They drove past the gravel entrance to Dandridge's cottage in the woods although only Adler and Belle recognised it. And for miles and miles, almost as soon as they had turned off the main roads, they had been following a long white trail of Kin, thousands of them, all walking towards the Shack, towards the black spectre of their derelict spacecraft. They were lining both sides of the lanes, moving silently through the woods on either side of them. It was now full dark, and the white figures loomed in the headlights of the van at the front of the convoy, which slowed to a crawl to get past them. They turned onto the driveway of the Shack, but there were too many Kin. They were crowded on the wide round driveway and car park outside the main building, spilling over into the roads and fields surrounding the area. Armed police and soldiers stood guard at random intervals around the perimeter.

Adler dialled a number.

'Josh? We're outside but we can't get in. I knew we should have built a bigger car park.'

A few minutes later, Josh Perron clambered into the back of the van and squeezed up to one of the Commandos on the bench seat, who shuffled along awkwardly. Josh looked haggard. He had a cut over one eye with a strip of gauze across it, holding two jagged edges of skin together over a black eye. He looked tired and sick.

'Thanks for getting me out of prison,' he said to Adler.

'Hennessy here is a lawyer, if you need one,' Adler said.

He gave a nod to the driver, who revved the loud diesel engine and pulled out in a looping U-turn in the road, picking their way around crowds of Kin that were still turning up outside the facility, which itself didn't look too great. Most windows were smashed and covered with large X's of yellow tape. Police cordons criss-crossed the entrance.

'I'm a civil lawyer, Mr. Perron. Not a criminal lawyer, sorry,' he shook Josh's hand in greeting, 'but from what I understand you won't be needing one, whatever it is you did.'

'I murdered about sixty people.' Josh said, staring at Adler.

'No, you saved thousands of Kin lives,' he responded, and the van went quiet again, the stark silence between them louder than the engine.

The three vans retraced their route back down the darkened lane populated by streams of silent white figures walking the other way.

'What are they doing?' wondered Mike. 'Why are they congregating here?'

'I don't know,' shrugged Josh. 'They won't, or can't, tell me.'

They turned into the driveway of Dandridge's house and Josh hopped out to open the gate.

It wasn't a large driveway, but the first van turned slightly right, the other slightly left, parking almost exactly where Dandridge would have parked his blue MG, and the van at the rear did a smart three point turn and backed in, creating an almost enclosed triangle with the rear doors all facing inwards. The Commandos got out and began setting up camp in the space between them, taking orders from an identically clad Senior Officer that Mike hadn't even noticed up until now. They set up lights powered from one of the vehicle batteries, forming a well-lit camp in the driveway, where they somehow found cookers and water and began brewing tea.

Adler, Mike, Josh and Belle went to the house. The second van contained as many Kin from the industrial unit as could have been fitted into the back, about sixteen of them, and they filed away into the night, joining the throngs of Kin making their way to the Shack through the darkness.

The house was cold. Josh put the heating and the kettle on. As it came to the boil they heard another sound, the sound of rotors in the distance, an engine getting closer. A few seconds later the sound of the rotor blades was deafening in the small house, and a large white helicopter touched expertly down in the middle of the lawn, perfectly avoiding the close-set trees just a few feet either side of the spinning rotors.

The engine was cut and the rotors whooshed around and around for a couple of minutes with a diminishing whine before the door swung open. Marion Crandall stepped across the lawn to the back door, head down, one arm protecting her face from the residual downdraft. Josh let her in and closed the double-glazed patio doors, cutting the wind off completely just like the Everest commercial.

He was setting out another tea mug when the doorbell rang. Mike answered it. Jennifer stood on the step, very visibly pregnant, flanked by two Commandos with their guns raised.

'How did you get here?' Mike asked. 'Please put the guns down, she is clearly not a threat.'

He ushered her inside, and Josh got out another mug. He was running low.

'I hired a car,' she said. 'It's parked on the lane, I hope I'm not blocking anyone in.'

'How did you know-'

'Adler sent me the address. Is Luke here?' she called out.

Adler nodded to the two Commandos who took Jennifer to the back of a locked van and opened the doors. Light flooded the dark space and the figure inside shrank back into the darkness. A solid metal ring was welded into the chassis of the heavy van and a length of chain threaded through it. A pair of handcuffs looped and locked at either end of the chain. Two slim wrists were securely locked inside each silver bracelet.

One by one all the others gathered behind Jennifer as she stared at the boy silently. They stared at him with a mixture of disgust and curiosity as if he were a fascinating exhibit like a snake with two heads or an eight legged goat. Luke saw Jennifer, but spoke to Adler.

'Where's Nella?'

'She's dead.'

'I don't believe you. I'm not saying anything until I see her.'

'I think you've said quite enough already, don't you?' replied Jennifer. She turned her back on him and went into the house. Two of the Commandos slammed the van doors shut, plunging Luke back into the blackness.

Jennifer called out from the doorway. 'Er - there's a man in the kitchen.'

The Commandos spun on their heels towards the house, the Commanding Officer barking orders, and two of the soldiers entered the house with SA-80 rifles raised. In a few seconds the man was marched at gunpoint into the small camp, his fingers interlocked on the top of his head.

'Not sure how you're making tea,' Dandridge said. 'You're out of milk.'

JENNIFER

Josh had installed a second fridge in what used to be the garage and which was now a utility room, so it turned out they had plenty of milk. They all drank mug after mug of tea, as if the hot, comforting and quintessentially English drink could drown out what was happening around them.

They chatted and laughed, secure in the comfort of Dandridge's living room and feeling protected by their own small camp of Marine Commandos in the driveway.

Jennifer noticed that Dandridge, who she wasn't sure she liked at all, kept himself very separate from the Kin in the room. Jennifer sat at the end of the sofa and was forced to press up against Belle when Josh sat down at the other end. Her heart started to pound when the Kin's white leg pressed up against her, and the baby inside her kicked. She was starting to feel flushed and uncomfortably warm. Fortunately Marion Crandall noticed her discomfort and red face and moved her onto the armchair, kicking Dandridge out of it.

'Josh, where is the first Kin?' Marion asked. 'Is it alive?'

'I don't know. I haven't seen it since the attack.'

'I heard you rather saved the day over there,' Dandridge remarked.

'No, I did the opposite. I made a choice and I'm not sure it was the right one.'

'You picked a side,' Belle spoke up. The group fell silent for a few moments.

'Is that what this is now?' Mike said eventually. 'Sides? War?'

'No,' said Adler. 'Not war. Not quite yet. But sides will have to be drawn.'

'I watched this Kin murder at least three people earlier. Does that avenge all the Kin who have already been slaughtered or are they going to have to kill more of us to compensate? Because that sounds like a definition of war to me.'

'Sounds like you've picked a side already,' said Marion, her face flushing red with rising anger.

'No, he hasn't,' Adler spoke in a conciliatory tone, 'but he has seen some pretty unpleasant shit today and has a large hole in his arm to show for it.'

The dull throb from his wound had rather faded into the background for Mike, but at the mention of it the pain came flooding back.

'Jesus, Mike,' Marion rushed over to him. 'What the hell happened? We should change the dressing.' Marion grabbed him and marched him upstairs. They heard the bathroom door close and lock.

'Interesting,' said Dandridge. 'Do you think that Belle being here is affecting us a little bit?'

'Whenever I go near it, sorry *her*, I mean Belle-' Jennifer said, 'my baby kicks, really hard. In a good way, like it's happy. But then-' she blushed. 'I feel something else too. Something nice. Sorry. I'm over-sharing.'

'No, you're not,' Josh said gently. 'It's OK, go on.'

'When we were on the mountain we only ate the Kin to survive but - well, we all know what it does now. It made me feel so *capable*. Since both my husbands died I have pretty much lived like a hermit, really. For some reason, fate decided that I am to be alone, and that was fine by me. But the meat made me feel like I wanted to get out into the world and live again. And that I deserved to. It's faded away since I went crazy in hospital but with Belle right here I am starting to feel like... like it's all possible again. Like I could actually find love again. Even with this-' she indicated her baby-bump.

'It appears that my presence is making everybody uncomfortable. I will leave,' said Belle.

'No,' said Dandridge. 'you haven't done anything wrong. Let's go for a walk.' The two of them stood and went out to the garden, closing the patio door behind them.

'How did you find Luke?' Jennifer asked Adler to change the subject.

'We finally managed to trace the source of the video uploads to a house owned by a corporate subsidiary of Henderson Mulcahy. It took too long, I'm sorry.'

Jennifer shrugged. 'It's the Kin who should hate him, not me.'

'He raped you, Jennifer. You have more right to hate him than anyone,' said Josh.

'The Kin-'

'Forget the Kin. Luke's words have incited the masses, but he's not responsible for their actions. He might have loaded the gun, but he didn't pull the trigger. Everyone is responsible for their own actions. You are the only one he has directly hurt, and in the worst possible way. I don't suppose you've talked about it yet, have you?'

'I told the whole fucking world.'

'No, I mean talked about it to somebody, as opposed to announcing it in a video.'

Jennifer shook her head, tears running down her face.

'When this is over you can stay here, if you want. I'm on my own now, most of the time. Dandridge won't mind.'

'Thank you, Josh,' she said. 'I'll bear it in mind, for after whatever happens tomorrow.'

Josh's phone went off, the ringtone set to a tinny version of Royce Brim's number one hit 'MaKin It Up'. He went into the kitchen to take the call.

Adler and Jennifer sat alone in the living room, both cradling empty mugs of tea.

'He's nice.'

'Indeed. Jennifer, I don't want you to take this the wrong way and I am aware that this might be the effect of the Kin, although I'm hoping not, but I-' he paused, then laughed. 'Yes, its definitely the Kin talking. I'm really sorry. Perhaps the whole world is being taken over. Perhaps I have been wrong this whole time.'

'I don't know, I'm just a graphic designer. But I do know that even if the Kin *are* invading you did the right thing, the only thing. All this madness is just circumstantial. If the flesh wasn't so fucking addictive we wouldn't be in this situation. What did you want to say? Out with it.'

'I was going to offer you the same as Josh. A place to stay, to live. If you want. Somewhere safe for you and the baby. I have an apartment in Amsterdam. It's on the third floor, but there's a lift and the view across the canal is really pretty. No obligations, just a place.'

'Let's talk about it after tomorrow, OK?' she said to the Government man, who now stared awkwardly at the empty mug in his hands. Adler nodded, and coughed.

'It's definitely the Kin,' he said, and went to the kitchen to wash their mugs.

She was left alone in the living room and looked out at the vans in the driveway. She could hear the quiet conversation of the men outside the window, the occasional low laugh. The back window of Luke's van was tinted. She couldn't see in but imagined him in there, cuffed, cold and uncomfortable in the pitch blackness, unable to lie down or rest properly. Then she pulled the curtain across and Josh showed her to the spare room. She lay down and fell asleep almost instantly.

DANDRIDGE

He and Belle joined the throng heading towards the Shack. It was a trip he used to make a lot but usually behind the wheel of his MG. He felt a brief pang of regret about the car. The two of them were surrounded by thousands of Kin making their own way along the dark road. Helicopters constantly buzzed overhead.

'Things will change tomorrow,' Belle said. 'I am not sure we will see each other again.'

'What will change?'

'The Kin cannot stand back any longer and allow our unopposed slaughter to satisfy human cravings.'

'Cravings?'

'Addiction, whatever it is we make you feel. There is no such compatible feeling for Kin so it is quite hard to understand.'

'So, what? You're going to declare war?'

'Whatever it takes.'

'Can we have sex again?'

'No. The first time was a mistake, clearly.'

'And the second?'

'Another mistake.'

The two of them made it to the Shack. The Kin filled every surrounding field and road, a densely packed white mob of hundreds and thousands of Kin, like a gathering at an alien music festival. The crowd was so dense they couldn't get anywhere near the main building. Dandridge presumed that they filled the buildings and the vast hulk of the Kin ship itself as well.

A lot of Kin were coupled together, engaged in their reproductive process, but most were not.

'Why aren't all these Kin reproducing?' Dandridge wondered aloud. 'There must be Kin still being killed somewhere.'

'I do not know. Perhaps the cycle has been broken. In

which case the killing must definitely be stopped.'

'I wish Sasha was here, she might have some kind of insight.'

'Sasha?'

'She's the social anthropologist I was working with in Japan. Very clever lady.'

'Perhaps I should be jealous.'

Dandridge laughed.

'Where is she?'

'She's in an army hospital in Wales. She got injured before we could get pulled out. Are you *all* here?'

'Not even an eighth of us.'

'But how are you communicating? How did you all know to come here?'

'I do not know. We cannot read each others thoughts but in much the same way that our grief and reproduction processes are triggered we are in some ways empathetically in tune with each other.'

'Like cows.'

'I do not appreciate the analogy, given cows are bred to be killed and eaten on this planet.'

'Sorry. So the rest of you are on the way?'

'Some, not all.'

The light was slowly starting to come up. The sky was clear, it was cold. Dandridge realised that they had been walking for hours.

He heard another helicopter approaching and this time it flew low over their heads and on to the Shack, landing on the roof. The crowd of Kin surged forward, and Dandridge surged with them.

MIKE

They all climbed out of the helicopter onto the roof of the Shack. Josh lead Adler, Jennifer, Mike and Marion into the building via the narrow staircase that lead to the top floor service lift. It was out of service so they walked down four floors to the first floor and to Josh and Marion's office.

Josh took his seat behind the desk and put the news on the huge screen. The images flickering in front of them were all the same; war zones across the world - fighting, protesting, burning, killing. Only the different tourist landmarks in the background of each report distinguished them from one another.

Millions of Kin had been killed. Millions more were taking their place, but the rate of attrition was high. They were being killed as they reproduced, helpless. Killed as they stood doing nothing, killed as they went to a place of work. Killed as they were born. Dragged from their homes and slaughtered. And all the while the humans were getting hooked on the meat, the euphoria consuming them. Mike felt sick and ashamed.

Marion had also turned pale. The Shack felt strange to her, despite having spent the better part of the last fifteen years there. The cold glass walls pressed in on her.

'I don't belong here any more,' she announced to Mike and gave him a peck on the cheek. Then she just walked out, down the remaining two flights of stairs to join the throng of Kin crowding the reception. She moved among the crowd, familiar feelings coursing through her as she pushed through them and they pressed and squeezed against her.

Mike could only watch her from the office window as she made her way through the crowd of white alien creatures. They were too densely packed for her to get very far.

He had no idea what he was doing there, other than

circumstance and simply being in the wrong place at the wrong time. Without Marion at his side he felt superfluous, lost.

In the bathroom at Dandridge's house she had dressed his wound and then undressed the rest of him and they had sex on the shower mat. Fast, urgent, passionate. For the first time it felt fuelled by natural, normal human desire. He thought that he might love her but he didn't particularly want to mingle with the Kin. In the first few years of sobriety he had not so much as put a foot inside a pub or bar, and rarely stayed long at dinner parties for fear of temptation or slipping back into old ways. Somehow the feeling of being trapped together in dense crowd of Kin with no escape or way out felt equally as suffocating.

He wondered why the Kin around them at the Shack were not reproducing. He asked the question to Adler, who shrugged.

'Ask Dandridge, perhaps he has some wonderful insights,' he replied, slumping back into the corner of the small leather sofa that sat in the corner of the office.

'Don't you think it's important?' Mike pressed. 'These Kin aren't having to answer the usual call of their genetics, as I understand it, at least.'

'I don't know, Hennessy. Plenty of time to figure it out after today.'

'What do you mean?'

But Adler had gone silent, and refused to say anything else.

JOSH

Sitting at the desk seemed strange. He didn't know what to do, so he put on the news. It was a mistake, showing nothing but complete global carnage, so he quickly switched it off again. They waited in silence. After an hour they heard another helicopter approaching. It flew close to the building, and Josh recognised the official livery of the PM's personal transport.

About ten minutes later Niall Cody walked into the office flanked by three security men in dark suits and radio comms devices in ears. The new Deputy Prime Minister didn't waste time on pleasantries.

'Can you switch this on?' he asked, indicating the screen.

Josh switched it back on. The screen was now filled with an empty lectern in front of a red and blue curtain. A few seconds later, the Prime Minister of Great Britain and the President of the United States stepped up, side by side. The PM started speaking immediately.

'When the manifesto for integration with the Kin was first proposed to me it was written, to all intents and purposes, on a napkin, put together under intense scrutiny and general panic. It was the best, most concise and intelligent response to the arrival crisis I had seen. It made sense then and it makes sense now. The steps we took in such a short amount of time are remarkable. Regrettably, unforeseen circumstances have forced our hand. We do not believe now, nor will we ever believe, that the Kin species is purposefully invading our planet. However, we are now at risk. The Kin flesh is addictive and the side effects and withdrawal are dangerous. They are also reproducing exponentially. The more are killed, the more appear. I must emphasize that these issues have only recently come to light and were not apparent to us when the Kin arrived. And so we come to the events of the last few days.' The PM stopped speaking, and the President cleared his throat, his deeper baritone requiring him to lean slightly closer to the mic.

'As a species, we have a lot to answer for. As the dominant force on this planet for millennia we have slaughtered trillions of our own kind and hunted to extinction countless other species. But when the Kin arrived we found a common purpose, a reason to get along. At last we knew that we weren't alone in the cosmos. There hasn't been a serious territory or religious disturbance between any human faction for nearly fifteen years. Anywhere. Hard to believe but that is an unprecedented occurrence. We have a lot to thank the Kin for, but now thousands or millions of Kin are dead. Only Australia has honoured the agreement to give them safe haven, but this means that the Kin are now overrunning the Northern Territories in Australia, which covers over five hundred thousand square miles of terrain. The time has come where we have no choice but to draw a line in the sand.'

Like the worst comedy double act ever, the PM stepped back up to the mic.

'We must preserve our way of life, whatever we now perceive that to be. Every single human individual will pay some price for what we must do to ensure that humanity remains the dominant species on our planet. Every single one of us must bear some of the burden for what comes next. We must now fight to survive.'

There was a silence in the office as the words sunk in.

'Why weren't we briefed on this?' asked Josh. 'Surely the Shack leaders should have had some kind of-'

The others shushed him as the PM continued.

'As of the exact time and the exact date of this transmission, which is being broadcast on a loop on all channels globally for the next forty eight hours, as well as being released on the DarkNet, I can confirm that we are at war with the species known to us as the Kin. Our armies are being mobilised and no prisoners can be taken.'

'We anticipate some fightback at this stage,' cut in the US President again, who looked deathly pale against his usual tanned, leathery skin. 'Stay away from any and all Kin species, especially if they are in groups. It will be safer if all civilians remain calm and indoors. Do not harbour any Kin. This will be a punishable offence. Our forces will not be directing their bullets at humans, but do not, I repeat, do not attempt to join, interfere or influence the fight in any way. You have been warned. Human death by crossfire will be noted as accidental and no action will be taken. I repeat, stay away from the Kin.'

'We are out of options,' said the PM. 'By intent or accident, we are being overrun, and so it comes to this. May God have Mercy on our souls.'

The transmission cut to black, and in a few seconds began to loop. The shocked group listened to it again, and again, stunned.

'Did you know about this?' Josh asked Adler, who was still slumped on the sofa. He shrugged.

'I suspected. I was locked out of the last few meetings.'

'What about Marion?'

'I don't think so. She and the PM argued about something, but I don't know what.'

'And you didn't think to raise your suspicions? Even to me?' Mike shouted.

Before they could argue a sound was heard. It was soft at first, but getting louder. The sound of machinery, an engine, rotors. A helicopter. Three helicopters, appearing over the trees and advancing rapidly on the Shack, and the huge crowd of Kin below them.

'What the fuck!' Mike shouted. 'Adler, call them off. Right now!'

Adler reached for his phone, but Niall Cody and his three bodyguards raised Glock P99 semi-automatic pistols and pointed them at the group. Josh was stunned, staring incomprehensibly at the weapons.

'No guns in my office. Put them away, right now,' he said, a request that hit the room with a palpable sense of futility.

'Nobody say anything, nobody do anything. We're here to make sure you all stay right where you are, let the Army do what they have to do and don't get in the way.'

'No, Cody,' said Mike. 'This is lunacy. We need to try and stop this right now. Let me through.' He stepped forward and one of the guards lowered his gun and put one shot into Mike's right kneecap. The bullet shattered the bone like glass. Mike screamed in pain for the second time in two days and went over, his whole existence suddenly focused on the unbearable pain in his leg. By contrast, the hole in his arm had been a mild pinch.

Adler stood still, staring at Niall Cody while Josh and Jennifer leapt to Mike's assistance.

'Why don't you just send something remotely? Wipe them all out at the same time. This-' Adler indicated the three helicopter gunships hovering just above them outside the window. '-is barbaric.'

'Too many civilian residences and businesses in the area, but thanks to you other Shacks were conveniently chosen away from human habitation and can be dealt with much more efficiently,' replied the DPM.

'What happened to you, Cody? This is the wrong choice, and you know it.'

'There is no right or wrong choice, Adler. Not any more.'

'There's always a right choice, Cody. You're just too dumb to find it.'

DANDRIDGE

He and Belle had somehow made it into the Shack. As they approached Josh's office they could see the three armed guards with their backs to them. Dandridge heard a number of things one after the other; the PM on the screen saying the words 'Stay away from the Kin' and then he heard the helicopters outside. He saw Mike Hennessy step forward and say 'Let me through' before taking a bullet in his knee, a loud retort in such close, glass-walled quarters that it echoed around his eardrums for a good few seconds. Belle grabbed his arm and dragged him away. Together they ran up the stairs, up and around and up again four times to the roof. The official helicopter that had delivered Niall Cody sat silently.

Dandridge and Belle ran to the very edge of the flat roof. Three helicopters had arrived at the Shack, hovering over the white alien crowd beneath them but about level with the two figures on the roof. Dandridge recognised them as Agusta AW159 Wildcats in Royal Navy livery, equipped for air-to-surface warfare, large gun doors locked open on both sides, vicious Browning M2 machine guns pointing towards the ground on pintle mounted turrets.

'Oh fuck,' said Dandridge. 'They've gone and declared war.'

All the gunners opened fire simultaneously, probably responding to a green light radio message. The Kin beneath them didn't stand a chance, the white flesh and blood flying as the vast mass of bodies was viciously torn apart, the 850 rounds per minute of the Brownings cutting them down as efficiently as a scythe decapitates dry corn.

Belle took a few steps backwards and for a second Dandridge thought she was retreating back down the stairs. Then the alien took three, four, five long, powerful strides and launched herself off the edge of the building. The leap was ridiculously long and Dandridge, heart in his mouth, was sure that gravity would exert itself before the white and blue figure could reach the open hatch of the hovering helicopter. It nearly did. Belle reached the long, gun barrel by the tips of her fingers. As she took hold, her weight pulled it downwards so the handle and trigger were yanked out of the operators hands and it pointed straight down at the ground far below her. She managed to get two hands around it and haul herself up hand over hand until she had leverage to swing neatly inside.

The gunner was stunned into immobility and she pitched him out of the machine with ease. He tumbled screaming downwards until he jerked to a halt on his safety harness, dangling helplessly a few feet beneath the machine. She yanked the clasp and he fell once more, silent this time until the squelching thud of his arrival on the concrete below.

The second door gunner on the opposite side of the cabin swivelled around, half crouched and drawing his sidearm, but too slow. Belle kicked him hard in the gut and out he went. She yanked the clip that released his harness but didn't stop to watch him join his comrade. She took hold of the Browning and aimed it at the second helicopter, pulling the trigger. Bullets tore into the fuselage, ripping through the cabin and killing both door gunners, both of whom toppled from the machine to dangle dead and bleeding from their harness. The pilot pulled back and it began to rise rapidly into the air away from her. She tilted the gun upwards, and squeezed the trigger again, the tracers tearing through the underside of the cockpit, missing the pilot, but shredding the instrument panel into scrap metal. The machine juddered and whined and slid backwards out of the sky. It started to spin, tumbling end over end to the ground where it hit with a crash, followed by a bright explosion as the wreckage ignited.

The whole attack took just a few seconds, the pilot of Belle's helicopter realising too late what was happening. He jerked the stick hard over to the left to stop her from taking aim at the last machine still fully operational in the air. Belle lost her grip of the machine gun handle and tumbled over, sliding backwards across the metal floor and just managing to grab hold of the opposite turret mounting welded into the floor to stop herself from falling out.

She dangled over the edge. The pilot was waggling the machine sharply left and right but she hauled herself back in again. He unclipped himself from his seat and turned and stood, drawing his service pistol and aiming it at the alien coming towards him. He fired two shots that thudded into her white chest before she reached him, pulling the gun from his hand and flinging it behind her before taking him by the scruff of his flight suit and flinging him the same way. He collided against the far bulkhead of the helicopter's cabin with a sickening thud and crumpled to the floor. Belle took his seat and wrestled with the controls of the helicopter, which she had no clue how to use. It pitched abruptly to the right, the pilot tumbling silently out of the open hatch.

It began to spin and Belle had no idea how to control it, but found that when she took her hands and feet away from all the controls it righted itself and hovered in place on some kind of autopilot. She stared at the dizzying array of dials and controls and almost didn't notice the third helicopter drawing level, flying across her bows, the side door gunner taking aim at the white figure sitting in the cockpit, his compatriot just behind him.

Belle stared at the man in the green helmet, saw his eyes narrow and the black dot of the gun barrel pointed straight at her.

Then she heard a louder engine and her view was suddenly blocked by a blue and gold metal wall as the PM's official helicopter, a much larger, older and bulkier machine, floated downwards directly between the two attack helicopters. Belle could see Dandridge in the pilot's seat, gesticulating and shouting at someone. She noticed the discarded radio headset on the instrument panel in front of her and picked it up, placing it over her featureless head.

'*-enough*!' Dandridge was shouting.

'Sir, remove the vehicle from the line of fire,' the pilot was saying, very calmly. At the same instant, he pulled up and the gun now pointed down at Belle, directly across the top of the invisible, whirring rotor blades of Dandridge's bulky transport. Dandridge responded and increased his own altitude to match the gunship, blocking the view of the gunner.

'Sir, we *will* fire on you. The alien in that helicopter has just murdered six people.'

'And how many Kin have you killed today?' Dandridge countered, unnecessarily. He knew time was running out.

'Sir, we are going to open fire in five. Four. Three-'

'Do not fire,' Belle said, her voice calm and smooth, loud and clear on the headset speakers. 'Richard, take the Prime Minister's helicopter out of harm's way, please. It is going to be alright. I promise.'

She could see his face staring at her from the cockpit, shaking his head.

'No.'

'Do it now, Richard. For me.'

'No.'

'I insist, Richard. Do it now.'

She took the headset off and stepped back into the cabin, taking hold of one of the Brownings and swinging it round so it faced forwards, towards the cockpit.

When Dandridge complied and the large white helicopter lifted clear, for a split second the human gunner and Belle had clear views of each other, both pointing the two guns directly across the now-empty air between them. They opened fire at the same instant. The human was flung backwards against his harness as the bullets tore through him, his insides spattering the flight suit of the man standing behind him, the gun falling silent. Belle was practically cut in half by the strafing fire coming the other way, but her finger stayed firmly on the trigger and she angled it sideways, cutting a clean line of holes along the side of the fuselage until a bullet found its mark and the pilot's head snapped grotesquely sideways as he was hit, a spray of blood hitting the glass.

The second door gunner had stretched across his dead colleague and managed to get hold of the Browning's trigger and he emptied the gun into Belle, even as his pilot slumped forwards and they went down, angled towards the ground almost vertically. It hit the concrete with a *whoosh* of fire and heat.

Belle's own machine was critically wounded, also spinning out of control, lurching and pitching sideways towards the Shack. Dandridge watched numbly from his own pilot's seat as it collided with the glass building in a huge explosion before it crashed burning to the ground.

MARION

She watched the three helicopters above them, heard the machine guns, felt the silent panic among the Kin. They were being cut down around her and she ran with them towards the Shack, crouched over, arms over her head in a futile protective gesture. There were too many Kin and she couldn't fight through them all. To her left, a strafing line of fire chopped them up like meat, their blood spraying her more effectively than a fire hose. She slipped in the spilled flesh and went down, landing face first and breaking teeth but feeling the flesh reassuringly and temptingly close to her mouth. She shook off the feeling, appalled at herself, but bodies of Kin were falling over her, all around her. She felt one of the bodies on top of her jerk as it was struck by a bullet. It passed through the white body and hit her, entering her shoulder. She cried out, but didn't move, couldn't move. She wasn't aware of it, but she must have passed out, because when she came round the world was on fire.

JOSH

It was one of the armed guards who first realised that the stricken helicopter was going to hit the building.

'*Get down!*' he shouted, a split second before the explosion. Josh threw himself under his desk as his world briefly narrowed into a Venn diagram labelled *heat*, *noise* and *smoke*, converging in the middle marked *pain*. The heat of the explosion was so intense he was sure he going to burn alive, and it was so loud that later he found that blood had leaked out of his ears. The smell of burning oil and gasoline was acrid and his eyes watered so freely he struggled to keep them shut. All the huge windows shattered on impact, then as the machine fell to earth there was another explosion that shook the whole building and broke the few remaining windows that hadn't already shattered.

When the heat lessened he peeked out. His office was destroyed, completely open to the billowing black smoke that came roiling in. Adler was on top of Jennifer. He had pulled the sofa over them both like a long wigwam and they seemed intact. He could see Hennessy's body covered in glass but couldn't tell if he was alive.

Deputy Prime Minister Nile Cody was almost certainly not alive, lying on his back with a shard of glass protruding from his forehead and down through his collar bone to his shoulder. One of his eyes had been popped and Josh could see the clear viscera against the glass. He gagged. One of his armed security contingent, the one who had been closest to the window and shouted the warning, was also extremely dead. Josh could only really see independent parts of him.

Josh stood up unsteadily as Adler and Jennifer crawled out from under the upturned sofa.

'*Come on*,' shouted Adler, 'we need to get out of here, right now.'

'No,' coughed one of the two surviving security agents before doubling over and hacking up a huge ball of sooty phlegm onto the floor. 'We stay here until we get new orders,' he wheezed. He still held his gun.

'Your orders have just gone out of the window,' Josh said, feeling his own lungs filling up with dust and smoke. 'We have to get Jennifer out of here. She's pregnant.'

The agent looked indecisive for a second. He stood upright. 'No. We stay. I'm sor-'

And that was when he took a bullet in his chest, and went straight down onto the broken glass covering the floor. The Kevlar vest took the impact, leaving him numb and immobile.

Josh looked down to see Mike Hennessy, his knee an oozing, blackened crater, dazedly pointing the dead guard's Glock at the empty air where his target had just stood.

'No time to argue the point,' he wheezed.

Adler hoisted Mike over his shoulder, who cried out in pain.

'Stay conscious and keep hold of that thing, Hennessy,' he said, and gestured to the only security agent left standing. 'Coming? You'd better give your friend a hand.'

They all ran out of the office, hunched over to try and stay below the dense smoke still pouring into the building. Alarms rang constantly and the sprinklers had activated. They made it downstairs but there was a fire on the ground floor stairway, completely impenetrable and billowing black smoke. Jennifer began to cough.

'*Up, up, to the roof,*' shouted Adler. They reversed their steps, Adler carrying Mike, Josh helping Jennifer and the two security agents limping along behind them as they climbed slowly back up to the roof as they hacked and coughed the smoke from their lungs.

They reached the top and the door banged open under Adler's heavy foot, tumbling into the fresh air just as Dandridge was landing the PM's helicopter. He leaned out of the pilot's window and beckoned to them. They ran through the billowing dust raised by the *whoomphing* rotor blades.

Josh helped Jennifer into the sumptuous beige leather interior and Adler hauled Mike roughly onto the deep shagpile. They all scrambled in and Dandridge lifted off from the burning building. Adler made his way to the co-pilot's seat.

'We need to get to the Prime Minister, right now,' he said.

'No!' Jennifer half coughed, half shouted. 'Hospital first, then the PM.'

Josh was looking down. The Kin seemed to be streaming towards the opening on the side of their old derelict ship. 'What are they doing?' he asked, then saw the three Challenger 2 tanks, in a wide formation closing in on the crowd from across the fields. 'They can't do this!' he shouted.

Dandridge banked the chopper round towards them and buzzed them close. There were three tanks fanned out across the fields and closing in on the crowd. He flew out over the lane that lead to the Shack, still clogged with the white figures surging forward over the bodies of their fallen towards the vast black ship.

'Why are they going to the ship? They'll be trapped.' asked Josh.

'Harder to winkle out, perhaps they think they can stage a fightback,' said Adler.

'Or an easier target. After today the PM will launch whatever he can get his hands on at them, regardless of the human consequences,' Josh replied, staring down at the running crowd.

'Is one of you a pilot?' asked Dandridge to the two remaining security team.

'I am,' the agent Mike had shot replied as he shrugged off his Kevlar body armour.

'Good. Come and take over. Fly to the nearest hospital, probably Gloucester Royal, and drop off Hennessy. Then you take orders from Adler, and *only* Adler, do you fucking understand? He is the senior officer now and you do what he says. I don't give a flying fuck at a rolling doughnut what your orders were before this moment, d'you hear me?'

The man nodded and Dandridge relinquished the controls.

'Where are you going?' Adler asked.

'To help. Marion's down there somewhere.'

'You are not.'

'You're not *my* senior officer, Adler.'

He turned to the pilot. 'Set me down here, then get them the fuck out of here.'

The helicopter touched down between the approaching tanks and the crowd of Kin heading towards their ship. Dandridge hopped down, followed by Josh.

'*I'm coming with you,*' Josh shouted over the noise of the rotors. Dandridge didn't argue, just started running towards the three tanks. Josh followed him as the helicopter lifted off into the clear blue sky behind them, Jennifer and Adler staring out of the small window, watching them head straight towards the chaos.

MARION

As she struggled to her feet she was jostled and pushed and carried along by a tidal wave of Kin surging towards the dark ship that had dominated the skyline for so long. The wreckage of three helicopters were scattered across the gravel driveway and grounds of her Shack, one of them burning just a few feet from where she had fallen.

She was knocked back to the ground and started to panic as the Kin kept coming, running for their lives, trampling her as she tried and failed to regain her footing in the dense crowd.

A strong arm reached down and lifted her easily to her feet. She stared at the blank white face and double blue markings criss-crossing it's face and down it's smooth torso.

'You need to get away from here Marion,' the first Kin said. 'Far away. There are more Army arriving, in tanks and other vehicles. Their intention is to kill every Kin before we can reproduce. That means they can leave none of us alive. None. You will get hurt if you stay.'

Marion was stunned, uncomprehending, unbelieving. She stood with the help of the first Kin holding her up, unable to withstand the buffeting of white bodies swarming and pushing around her on her own.

'You're wrong,' she said.

'I am not wrong.'

'Where are you going?'

'To the ship.'

'The ship doesn't work, they'll just blow it up with you all inside it, like a can of baked beans on a bonfire.'

'I do not understand the metaphor but perhaps you can explain it to me later.'

The first Kin scooped her up and began to carry her against the flow of Kin towards the road. They both clearly heard a low booming noise and a split second later an explosion directly in front of them threw them down to the ground. Chunks of rubble, tarmac and Kin were blown skywards in a geyser of white flesh, crowds of Kin simply dissolved by the impact, earth and flesh splattering and crunching down around them like lethal rain. There was another boom, and another group of Kin went up, pieces of them littering the countryside for miles. The first Kin and Marion were soaked from head to toe in white flesh. They could hear the roaring, crunching sound of huge diesel engines.

'It's getting closer,' she said, 'come on.'

The first Kin pulled her to her feet, and then another brutal looking Challenger 2 tank rounded the corner into the wide entrance of the Shack. It was directly in front of them, rolling forward and unconcerned about the maimed and wounded Kin it crushed under the two giant tracks. The long turret pointed over their heads and went off again. They were both slammed to the ground once more from the shockwave of being so close to the explosion. Marion cried out in pain but the tank wasn't stopping. She staggered to her feet again and stood her ground as the metallic green behemoth filled her vision. She looked up and saw the tank commander peering out from a hatch in the top of the tank's turret. It ground to a clanking halt inches from her nose. She breathed out.

'*Marion Crandall*,' called out the tank commander. She stared at him numbly. 'We don't need to be any closer than this, ma'am. The targets are well within our range. I advise you to stand aside or risk further injury.'

'Fuck you, Brad Pitt,' she said, and placed herself directly in front of the long turret gun. The tank commander sighed. 'As you wish, ma'am.'

He hoisted himself out of the turret and jumped easily down, a practised move, and Marion heard jeering and catcalls from his crew as he stepped around and took her by the arm attached to a shoulder with a bullet wound. She screamed in pain.

'Please let go of her.' The first Kin stepped up behind the tank commander, who turned to face the alien.

'I must ask that you-'

'Please let go of her now. I will take her away for you.'

The rest of the crew had now emerged from the tank and were crouched or sat on the metal, sidearms drawn. The commander let go of Marion, and the first Kin took her uninjured arm, leading her to one side. Whilst he did this, a crowd of Kin swarmed silently around and over the back of the tank. The commander turned back to his crew and let out a shout as his second in command was pitched over the side to the gravel, his neck twisted and broken. The whole crew was overwhelmed by the Kin. Shots were fired, bones were snapped. He plucked his sidearm from his low slung, cowboy-style hip holster and aimed it at the first Kin who stepped protectively in front of Marion as the shot was fired. The bullet caught the Kin low in its side. It took two long steps forward and grabbed the gun, twisting it as it went off twice more, both shots passing through the white body before it yanked the gun from the commander's grip. The Kin whipped it round and caught him in his temple with the butt of the gun, dropping him like a stone. By the time he went down the whole crew lay dead on the gravel around the machine. Marion stared in shocked, numb horror.

The large group of white figures stood on the silenced tank and the first Kin addressed them directly. 'I believe there are other tanks. You must all come with me.' Then it turned to Marion.

'Please find shelter and medical attention, Marion. I have some business to attend to now.'

'No. You're hurt too. You've been shot.'

'I am fine. And if I am not, well then-' the alien trailed off.

'Kin-'

'You were true to your word, Marion, always. I will

never forget that.'

It took the small band of Kin and they ran towards the giant hulk of their ship and the three tanks approaching from the opposite direction. She watched until she lost sight of them in the crowd.

•

MIKE

He passed out briefly on the deep shagpile carpeted floor of the helicopter. It was comfier than many mattresses he had slept on. When he came to, Jennifer McDonald was clutching his hand and pain throbbed up and down his right leg from his destroyed knee. The pain was intense but he felt strangely calm, his mind clear.

'Where are we going? Where's Marion?'

'We're going to drop you off at the hospital, then we're going to see the Prime Minister and put a stop to this,' Jennifer replied. 'You'll be at the hospital soon, and all the pain relief they have will be at your disposal.'

'Where's Marion?'

'Somewhere back there.'

'Back there? You mean among the helicopters and genocide?' Mike raised his voice to shout to Adler sitting in the co-pilots seat up front.

'Adler, what the hell are you thinking? By the time we reach the PM it'll be too late. Go back, right now.'

'I can't, Hennessy. It'll be too late for a lot of Kin, but somebody has to try to talk some sense into him.'

'No, Adler. You weren't in the last few meetings, remember? The PM is done listening to you. We need to get to Marion, now.'

Adler twisted around in his seat and addressed the MI5 agent sitting next to Jennifer on the beige leather. 'What's your name, Agent?'

'Simons, sir.'

'Agent Simons, please ensure that these two don't cause any trouble.' He turned back round to face the front.

Simons looked at the two other passengers. A pregnant woman and a man with a severely fucked-up knee. Unfortunately, the pregnant woman was pointing a gun at him, which was a first in his career.

'Sir, I don't think I have much option in the matter.

They have the only gun.'

'Turn this fucking helicopter around right now, Adler,' Jennifer said.

Adler sighed. 'Fine. Agent, do as the lady says.'

Their pilot put the aircraft in a steep banking turn to head back the way they came towards the black alien skyscraper in the distance.

Within a few minutes they were up close. They flew over a tank that seemed to be stranded in the middle of the Shack's gravel driveway, and could see bodies scattered around it, human and Kin. Mainly Kin. A solitary figure sat on the concrete in the middle of the carnage.

'There she is,' shouted Mike, staring out of the window. 'Land here.'

They touched down and Agent Simons, the least injured or pregnant of them all, hopped down and helped her inside the helicopter. She was covered from head to toe in Kin flesh, human blood and dirt.

'There are more tanks over the fields. We have to help them,' she said.

They lifted off again and flew around the wide circumference of the great Kin ship.

'Over there,' Adler pointed to a large field on the opposite side of the Shack, where the tanks and a vast white sea of Kin had gathered.

'Get closer,' Adler instructed.

'What's going on?' asked Mike. 'Why aren't they firing? And what are the Kin doing?'

Then he and Adler and the pilot and Jennifer and Marion, all of whom were staring out of different windows at the crowd below them, realised that the barrels of the long turret mounted cannons were pointed directly at two humans standing right at the very front of the Kin army.

DANDRIDGE

As they ran towards the tanks he heard a boom and the first incoming shell, a high pitched whine turning almost instantly into a low growl as it passed over his and Josh's head and slammed into the crowds of Kin behind them. There was an explosion of intense light and fire and they threw themselves to the ground as clumps of earth and Kin fell around them. There were two more howls of incoming shells and more explosions.

'*Jesus Christ!* This is slaughter,' cried Josh, his ears ringing once again as they both got to their feet. The tanks were getting closer.

'We need to get closer, put ourselves between the tanks and the Kin.'

'You heard the PM. We'll get caught in the crossfire, classed as accidental deaths and that'll be that.'

'Do you know how many wars in the last fifteen years since the Kin arrived have required tank units?' asked Dandridge.

'No.'

'None. None at all. These guys are probably following the first affirmative action orders they've ever had. I think we need to put some trust in human nature.'

Another shell was fired and passed over them, and they went back down to the ground, arms over their heads and ears.

'Our current situation is not giving me much faith they'll listen,' Josh shouted as they were showered in debris once again.

'Well, let's find out.'

They began running towards the tank in the middle, arms waving desperately at them. They were close enough to make out the tank commander, only his upper body visible from the turret hatch. It stopped moving forward, and so did the other two. Josh looked over his shoulder as he ran, to see an army of Kin at his back. They were gathering Kin followers like a snowball rolling down a long hill.

They came to a halt, leaving a clear distance between them and the end of the long barrels, all three of which were now pointing directly at them. Josh held his arms up in a gesture of surrender.

'Put your arms down,' Dandridge said, so they held hands instead. He turned to face Josh. 'I'm sorry about Ezra, by the way. I never got a chance to say. I thought he was wonderful. I'm so sorry for your loss.'

Josh stared at him, tears running down his dirt streaked cheeks. They kissed briefly.

The tank commander in the central tank cleared his throat and spoke, his voice routed from the internal radio to a loudhailer.

'Please stand aside,' he said. 'Understand that we will fire on you. The Kin are in contravention of human rights Order Twelve-Zero-Three. Your presence here will be classed a threat and neutralised.'

'There is no threat here,' Dandridge called back, raising his voice so it carried clearly back to the Commander and crew of the tank. 'The Kin are not a threat and never have been. I am not aware of Human Rights Order Twelve-Zero-Three. Is it new?'

'It is a directive endorsed by the Government and the Secretary of Defence and is being initiated across the world as we speak. The eradication of Kin before they can replicate and overrun this planet.'

'And you say it's being carried out across the planet right now?'

'Correct, sir. I will ask you one more time, please stand aside.'

'You have killed Kin with your first assault. More have died today, millions more across the world probably. Why aren't they replicating, right now? That's how it works, isn't it?'

'I don't care, I have orders.'

'They aren't reproducing. All you are doing is destroying a species.'

'That is not our concern, sir. I am going to give you five more seconds and then you, and these Kin, are going up. *Five.*'

'This isn't fighting for freedom or a righteous cause, Commander. This is not a fair fight. This is genocide, sir. Pure and simple.'

'*Four.*'

'Even a highly trained, capable human like you doesn't follow orders blindly, kill senselessly, for no reason at all.'

'*Three.*'

'These Kin are not replicating, they pose no danger or threat to this planet.'

'*Two.*'

'Last chance Commander. You need to back off, do the right thing, give us some time to work this out.'

'*One.*'

ADLER

The PM's personal transport touched down in the field between the three tanks and the Kin army, Josh and Dandridge holding hands at its head. Adler ripped off his headset and jumped down. Josh was crying. Dandridge looked at Adler with a strange look on his face, pale and tense.

'I didn't hear you coming,' he said.

'Commander,' Adler shouted. *'Stand down.'*

'Sir, I must ask you to remove the helicopter or I will drive right *the fuck* over it.'

'He seems angry, what did you say to him?' Adler asked Dandridge.

'Nothing, but he was just about to blow us all to smithereens. That is one useful helicopter.'

The first Kin stepped up to Adler.

'I need to speak with the man in the tank,' it said.

Adler, Dandridge and the first Kin walked the short distance to the tank and spoke with the Tank Commander who had jumped to the ground. His crew sat impassively, watching.

'We need to resolve this in the next sixty seconds, sir,' he said to Adler, 'because my orders are crystal clear and I will not be responsible for extending this situation any longer. The more Kin live today, the more will live tomorrow, and we'll just have to do it all over again. None of us want that.'

'I will give you a guarantee, Commander,' said the first Kin. 'A promise, if you will accept one from me.'

'And what's that?'

'I need you to give us one hour. One hour only, and I promise you will not have to do this all over again tomorrow. We will be gone for good and will not be a bother any longer.'

It began to dawn on Dandridge and Adler at the same

time why the Kin had been streaming back to the ship.

'No,' they both said at the same time, but the first Kin ignored them and seemed to stare, in that way they had, at the tank Commander, who stared back. 'That's not possible. There's too many of you.'

'Perhaps. But in that case the time you will have to spend fighting us will be greatly reduced. Please Commander. One hour.'

'How do I know that you won't come back to earth and try to destroy us?'

'If we had wanted to do that, we would have done it in the first place. For what it is worth to you, I give my word. We will be gone. Forever. Most of us.'

Marion stepped forward and took the first Kin's hand. She was crying.

'I give you my word too,' she said.

Dandridge, already holding Josh's hand, took Marion's other hand. Adler stepped in, taking the first Kin's hand, and Jennifer's hand as she stepped in too, closing the circle around the confused tank commander.

'Jesus fucking Christ,' he muttered.

MIKE

From his awkward vantage point on the floor of the Prime Ministers helicopter he couldn't hear anything they said but could only watch them form their crazy circle around the tank guy. His crew was getting agitated at the manoeuvre, but it broke apart after a few seconds and he went to speak to the crews of each tank as the small civilian group huddled. The Kin army stood silently behind them like ghosts on a battlefield.

The tank commander returned to speak with them again. Then the whole crowd of Kin started to withdraw towards the ship, quickly and just as silently. They poured back towards it. Mike had never been this close to one before and could see that the actual base of the ship had probably settled hundreds of feet down into the soft earth. His knee hurt. Marion and Jennifer came back to him.

'You OK? There's more painkillers here if you need them,' Jennifer said.

'Can we go yet? I really think I need a hospital now.'

Marion kissed him gently.

'I'm sorry. If you can hold on, I think we need to stay just for a little bit longer.'

'Why?'

'To make sure those tanks don't start opening fire again.'

'My leg really hurts, Marion. If they can wrap it up faster, I would be truly grateful.'

After nearly an hour the army of Kin had almost all disappeared into their great ship, the last few lining the base in an orderly queue and heading quickly towards the forced entry point. The tanks sat silently, the long guns all now pointed at the ship, the crews in their positions and waiting as time slipped though the hourglass.

Mike was drifting in and out of consciousness, his periods of wakefulness filled with desperation for more drugs to ease the pain in his leg and grateful every time his mind slipped away into the blackness.

The ground beneath the wheels of the helicopter began to vibrate, almost imperceptibly, and Mike jerked awake from his fever dream.

'Uh, can we possibly get out of here now?' he called out.

The wheels of the Sea King shifted underneath him.

The others had felt the movement in the ground, and they started to run towards the helicopter. The pilot pulled a headset over his ears and started flicking switches and the rotors began a lazy, whining spin. The air around the Kin vessel had begun to shimmer slightly, like a mirage.

The engines in each of the three tanks fired up in great gusts of diesel to begin their retreat.

'Where's Dandridge?' Mike asked suddenly, looking around the dazed faces.

'Shit. Where is he? I can't see him,' Josh said, sounding slightly panicked before jumping down and running back towards the tanks. Mike saw him gesticulating and saw each crew in turn shake their heads. Josh ran behind each tank like a frantic child looking for a lost toy behind the sofa.

'What's he doing?' Mike said.

'He's looking for his friend. Wouldn't you?'

The rotors were nearly at full spin and the tremor beneath the wheels was getting stronger, distinct even underneath the helicopters usual engine shake. The joystick moved of its own accord in the pilot's hand.

'We have to go, right now,' he said.

'Close the door, we'll pick him up,' shouted Adler.

As the helicopter lifted off the air shimmered and warped, causing the machine to slide sideways through the air as the pilot fought the controls. They could see Josh running towards the Kin vessel as a dry heat and the strange mirage curled and twisted the air around them, spreading outwards from the base of the ship and up through the ground around them.

'We need to get out of here, now!' shouted the pilot.

'Not yet, set down over there,' Adler pointed to a place between Josh's frantically waving, running figure and the immense, intensely shimmering ship, now almost impossible to look at.

The helicopter easily overhauled him and set down hard where Adler had indicated, bumping and skidding across the grass as the pilot slammed the machine down. The impact jolted Mike's knee and he cried out in pain. He could feel himself passing out, only vaguely aware that the door was open and Marion and Adler had both left the helicopter.

For the next few seconds he swam in and out of consciousness, desperate to pass out and forget the pain in his leg but also unwilling to give in and miss what was happening. He was in a foggy, delirious state as he watched Marion and Adler drag Josh back to the helicopter, hauling him in fighting and screaming, as the agent at the controls dragged the sluggish and unresponsive machine into the air before the door latch had clicked shut.

The whole earth was now shaking, sending shockwaves through the air to the small aircraft now dangerously close to the gigantic spaceship. The metal body began to shudder and creak as the pilot fought the controls.

'*She's not responding*,' he shouted.

'*Try harder*,' shouted Marion, and the pilot wrestled the controls, lifting and accelerating as the massive Kin spaceship began to rise out of the earth into which it had settled, pulling half the countryside out from under it as it rose slowly and majestically upwards.

Finally the helicopter began to pull away, every window filled with an anxious face staring out in awe.

The Kin ship looked the same as when it had arrived. There were no holes, no rust, no decay. The Kin had healed it.

It cleared the surface of the earth behind them as the pilot flew the old Sea King as fast it could possibly go away from the shimmering atmosphere and vast cloud of earth and dust rapidly enveloping the entire countryside.

For a few heart-stopping seconds they were in complete blackness as the dense cloud overtook them before they finally burst clear.

The small group could clearly see it's engine shaped like a dazzlingly white spider, dwarfing the sky at first but shrinking as it gained speed and momentum, rising steadily higher and higher. They all craned their heads up to watch it for as long as they could before it dwindled to a tiny white speck and vanished.

EPILOGUE

FIVE YEARS LATER

AGNES

She was dressed simply, foregoing her preferred floral prints for plain black. Her uncle's hand rested protectively on her shoulder. It was a cold day and it was snowing, as usual. Her aunt had bought her an elegant black overcoat that was buttoned up around her chin. She had removed her hat and the snow settled on her shoulders and long blonde hair.

There were few people in attendance at her father's funeral. The priest, her aunt and uncle, her mother and her mother's prison guards. That was all. Everyone was dressed in black except her mother, who wore an old dark blue fur-lined parka over her canary yellow prison overalls.

Agnes kept her head down and did not look at her. She listened to the priest's words but did not really hear them. She did what she was told to do and threw a handful of brown earth over the plain wooden coffin, the surface of which already had a thin covering of snow. Everyone present took their turn, except for the police. Her mother tried to catch her eye as she stepped forward, but Agnes kept her head down, as her aunt had instructed.

When it was all over she held her uncle's hand as her aunt went over and talked to her mother. Agnes heard raised voices, hastily hushed, before the guards escorted her mother back to the black prison van standing at the side of the road opposite the cemetery. The engine shattered the reverent quiet as it was started and warmed up before driving loudly away, turning a corner and vanishing from her sight, if not her hearing.

She turned to look down at her father's grave one final time. She had loved him dearly but he hadn't been the same after her mother had been arrested. He had a haunted, lonely look in his eyes that never really went away in the days after.

The cemetery fell silent and the snow kept falling steadily, covering the graves in their white winter blanket. From the corner of her eye Agnes saw some movement and for a brief, fleeting second she saw Theo, standing among the snow covered gravestones, watching her in that way he had. Then she blinked a snowflake from her eyelash, and he was gone.

MIKE

He packed his briefing notes and books into a plain black leather briefcase, pushing a foil-wrapped sandwich out of the way to accommodate them. He snapped it shut and left the courtroom, ignoring the crying and hugging family in the spectators gallery, escaping before he could be included in their celebrations.

He hailed a cab which took him home to his flat on the high street that still overlooked gangs of loitering, bored kids and the old decrepit clock tower which had stood elegantly for two hundred years, long before the bright lights of Primark and KFC and TK Maxx had bathed it in their strip-light glow.

Mike sat in his armchair and opened his laptop. The internet was growing again and was almost back to where it had been before being shut off. It wasn't as fast as it used to be and there was a stricter element of site policing and governance that drove him mad, but he had to admit it was good to have it back.

He scrolled through his preferred news channels. A political scandal, fighting in the Middle East, a new character on a soap he didn't watch. There was no mention of any Kin.

As Mike languished in hospital and rehab in the days following the attack, the Kin had been systematically hunted down and slaughtered. Many rallied together, fought back. They were fast and strong and cunning and the human death toll was high, but in the end the Kin were simply overwhelmed by sheer numbers and firepower.

For the second time in his life Mike had ignored Kin-based history because he was fighting his own demons. He started to drink again and relied too heavily on the pain medication he had been given for his knee. After another year of letting more people down, he realised he couldn't fight it any more and tried to overdose. It failed, and he woke up in hospital. Somebody, Mike suspected it was Adler, transferred him to rehab and he had stayed.

He was nearly four years clean now and reasonably happy, successful and alone. His law practice was going well with four staff on the books.

He still walked with a pronounced limp but it was amazing how the surgeons had reconstructed his knee from plastic and silicone. It ached in the cold and every time it ached it reminded him of the mountain and the price that they had all paid.

His phone rang, a number he didn't recognise. It was Marion, to whom he had not spoken for nearly five years.

LUKE

The image of his boyhood face, bloodied and feral, had quickly become a banner for the Kin embarrassment, flashed on TV screens as part of the story every time a new group of Kin were flushed out and destroyed.

He had spent three years living under house arrest with Jennifer and the government guy, drugged to the gills on a variety of pacification meds that kept him subdued and malleable. He had completed school, made a public statement of apology and stayed hidden. The drugs were strong and he remembered very little of any of it.

When he turned eighteen he was weaned off the drugs and tried to blend in, get out more. He grew a beard, grew his hair long and plaited it into dreadlocks. But it was still his face, and although the features had hardened he was still recognisably Luke McDonald.

Now twenty, and although he didn't know it, Luke was a lookalike for his father at the same age, 6' 2', the same pale blue eyes, chiselled jaw and dimpled cheeks. He rejected university in favour of travelling and lived off the map, wandering the world with no specific destination or intent in mind. He moved across the earth like a wraith, coasting on his looks and infamy. He met thousands of people who still recognised him, made friends easily, enemies even more easily, got into fights, slept with dozens of women, got drunk and high, collected and dumped travelling companions quickly.

He kept the beard and dreadlocks, but gradually realised that being Luke McDonald wasn't actually a curse after all.

People responded to him. Wherever he went there was a reaction, a response to him, a dialogue, and whether it was positive or negative, he welcomed it. He stayed away from news, didn't want to hear about how the world was moving on without him in it, wasn't interested.

He was living on a beach on the west coast of Ireland, in

a small blue beach hut loaned to him by a local who had recognised him in a pub and offered him a place to stay. On his second night in the hut he had passed out drunk from the Guinness the friendly locals had bought for him. It was still fully dark when he woke with a start, his head giving him a throb to remind him he was going to have a hangover in the morning. He'd always been told that Guinness didn't give you a hangover. *Lying Irish bastards*, he thought as he sat up slowly.

The hard wooden floor of the hut was unyielding, and he needed a wee. He listened for the noise that had woken him and after a couple of minutes came to the conclusion he had imagined it. He got to his feet and stepped outside. The moon was full and the North Atlantic lapped gently onto the rocky shoreline. He stepped two paces away from the hut and pushed his trousers to his knees, releasing his urine without holding or aiming.

A white figure stepped silently up behind him and wrapped two long leathery arms around Luke's body, trapping his arms at his sides and lifting him clear from the ground, squeezing harder than a human would ever be able to manage. Luke was pissing all over himself and his assailant. In separate blinding flashes of agony, four of his ribs snapped in his chest one after the other. His breath had been forced from his body and he was unable to draw another to make a sound. All he could manage was a wheezy gurgle that didn't sound healthy even to his own ears. He struggled feebly, but the grip was inescapable and he couldn't move without blinding pain from his chest.

He wasn't scared, or even surprised. He just watched the sea lapping up against the shore as grey fringes in his vision leaked closer and closer towards the middle until all he could see was grey, and then white, and then nothing.

In the morning, the local who had offered him the beach hut came down and found Luke's dead body, trousers still around his ankles. He placed one foot against the body and rolled it into the sea.

ADLER

Jennifer and the baby had taken over his life. He had retired from active duty immediately after the evacuation. All the Kin ships had taken off within an hour of each other. Some had taken off barely half full, the UK ship the only one to escape at capacity. Running battles across the world, millions of Kin slaughtered as they tried to escape.

In the intervening years they had all been hunted down, a coordinated effort from dedicated military task forces globally. It had taken a long time and thousands more humans had perished in the war than predicted, but eventually the rate of attrition proved too great for the visitors.

The Kin evacuated to Australia were incinerated by napalm-based bomb attacks that left nothing alive for hundreds of thousands of miles. Five years later it was still a scorched earth. Every now and then a group of Kin were spotted somewhere and hunted down or a solitary Kin was discovered and killed, but no Kin had been found alive for the last six months. The internet was back up and intelligent satellite communications were nearly back to full capacity. Finding, tracking and killing things was as easy as it ever had been.

Adler wanted none of it. His life was nappies and playgrounds and that was how he liked it. He and Jennifer had looked after Luke during his house arrest for nearly three years before he had grown his hair and left, never to be heard from again. He was somebody else's problem now.

Adler and Jennifer were happy living in Amsterdam. Jennifer had a job at a large local ad agency designing product packaging and Adler was a stay-at-home dad. The baby, who they had named Stephen James, had replaced national security as the centre of Adler's world, and now Jennifer was expecting their own child.

Stephen was one month away from his fifth birthday.

The Goodness Within

He was a chatterbox in a hybrid of Dutch and English and had a mischievous sense of humour. Occasionally he would suddenly stop what he was doing or playing with and look at Adler askance, and in those moments the child looked a lot like Luke. Adler didn't care. He had never imagined that fatherhood could be so engrossing, fascinating and fulfilling.

The boy was happy and healthy. Very healthy. He had never been sick, not once in his life. Not a sniffle, not a cough. After a year of perfect health he and Jennifer had taken the child to a number of doctors and specialists, none of whom could do anything with a child who was a picture of health. They kept him close, kept him safe, and could only watch and wait. So far, the child seemed bulletproof.

Then Marion called him, the first time they had spoken since the helicopter five years ago.

MARION

She sat in her windowless office in the basement of the British Museum, the dim light cast from the overhead lightbulb supplemented by two glaring anglepoise lamps shining onto copies of ancient parchments spread across her desk.

'You are wearing glasses now,' said the first Kin, who sat opposite her. She nodded.

'You did not return to the Shack.'

'No. They're rehab units now. So many people were addicted and couldn't cope once the supply was shut off. The Shacks have been repurposed to help them. Good facilities. How did you find me? And how have you not been caught?'

'I found you through the internet. I stole a tablet from the backseat of a car. And as to how I have not been caught, luck I suppose.'

'Where have you been? Why didn't you leave with the others?'

'I could not leave. I fought alongside my brothers, my sons, but it was fruitless in the end, as it was bound to be. I have been living for the last year in Ireland. Very beautiful and some remote areas.'

'And now you are back. If they found you here, they would kill us both.'

'Would you prefer I left? I understand.'

'No,' Marion began to cry, tears she had not shed for a long time. 'I tried to- to help, you know- I couldn't stop them. I'm so sorry.'

'There is no need. Our species survives, somewhere.'

'But not here. We weren't good enough, were we?'

'No. But perhaps I think it was inevitable. The same might happen wherever we settled.'

The phone on Marion's desk rang and she answered it. She got up and left the room, returning after a few minutes with Mike Hennessy, who stopped short when he saw the Kin sitting primly in a wooden chair at Marion's desk.

'Why did you call me here?' he asked, his voice raised. 'Not a word for five years, Marion. *Five fucking years.*'

'We need your help,' she said.

'They'll kill us all, without any hesitation, if they find that thing here.'

'That thing? Is that how you thought of us, Mr. Hennessy?' asked the first Kin.

Mike paused, drew breath slowly. 'No, of course not. It's just a shock, is all.'

'Mike, the first Kin is the only one left now. We need to help him.'

'How?'

'We need to go to court to fight the Order Twelve Zero Three. He's my friend, we have to help him.'

'So long as more than one exists then this will never be over, you know that. They'll just keep coming back until we're back to square one billion, and then the shooting starts again.'

'That might not be true. Megan Sasha-Meyer has published a paper that says-'

'I've read Sasha-Meyer's paper.'

'Then you know we might stand a chance.'

A voice came from the doorway. 'Stand a chance at what, exactly?'

Adler stepped into the darkened room and seeing the Kin, his mind filled in the blanks.

'There is no precedent for this Marion,' said Mike. 'No fall-back option, no bargaining or plan B. Sasha's paper is good but not conclusive, and can never *be* conclusive. Not any more. They might just force us to reveal where the Kin is and kill us anyway.'

'I'm willing to take that risk. It's OK if you're not. We don't have to rush into this. It's safe enough here, and we have time to prepare.'

'Prepare?

'A case for his life. To save his life, the last Kin. The very last one. Please help us.'

'I'm a civil disputes lawyer, you know that right?'

'But you used to fight for Kin rights and everyone knows it. He trusts you and I trust you. You're the best man for this. But we do need help.'

She turned to Adler. 'Will you help us? One last fight?'

Adler shook the last Kin's hand. 'Let me make a few calls,' he said.

JOSH

Josh sat in Hut 3 eating Chinese food from the carton. It was past midnight and the food was cold, but he didn't mind. All the kit was up and running again, making the low thrum and occasional chirrup noises he hadn't realised he missed so much, monitoring transmissions around the world.

Outside the hut used to be an enormous crater where the Kin ship had stood. It had taken a few years, but it had slowly been filled in. A small civilian airfield had sprung up in its place, lots of small Cessnas and Piper Cherokees, a few small private jets occasionally. It was quiet. The Shack was in the distance, a gleaming glass and chrome rehab facility for humans addicted to Kin flesh, of which there were hundreds of thousands. He hadn't been inside for five years.

He still lived in Dandridge's house down the lane and somehow he was still getting paid to keep the Huts going as a transmission station. He had been quietly waiting for someone to shut him down for a number of years now.

It was a chilly night, and he was ready to leave. He had Sky+ the new series of *NCIS: New Orleans* and was looking forward to going home and binge watching it. He had a crush on Scott Bakula.

He stood up from the high-backed leather chair, his back cracking. He placed his hands to the old headphones with the worn sheepskin cushions around the earcups and started to pull them off, but stopped. He had caught something, very faintly. It was barely audible, behind some background hiss. He sat back down, twisting a few dials to cut out the background chatter. There it was again. He adjusted the dials, turning one volume up and another down, matching the frequency to mask the hiss as best he could and clarify the sound. He worked fast, it really was a chilly night and there was still no heating in the huts.

The hiss softened in his ears and the noise was now much clearer. It was a strange signal, a rhythmic pulse. *Wait, no-* it was a series of undulating pulses, interrupted by clicks and tonal differences repeating every twenty seconds or so. Josh's heart began to beat faster. He turned it up and listened to it for ten minutes. It was definitely repeating.

His heart ached as he remembered his lost friend, a man who had vanished five years ago and who had not been seen or heard from since, despite a concerted search effort. Josh placed his fingertips on the shiny, grooved black conical dial, listened to the sound one more time, then clicked it off.

He took off his headphones and left the hut, closing the door gently behind him.

ACKNOWLEDGMENTS

Many thanks to everyone who helped and encouraged me during the writing of this book, especially my parents Wendy and Mick and my wife, Soo Pitty-Rose.

My son Noah also encouraged me, in ways he couldn't possibly comprehend, but he *is* only five.

Thanks so much to Dan Anderson for the cover design.

And thanks of course to Soo, Lina La-Rotta, the estimable Bill Pragnell, Nicola Martin, Tarik Haksever and Peter Baxter for reading various versions of this book and giving me such excellent and honest feedback.

You all rule.

Printed in Great Britain
by Amazon